ON GOOD AUTHORITY

ON GOOD AUTHORITY

a novel of suspense

BRIANA UNA MCGUCKIN

This is a work of fiction. Names, characters, organizations, places, events, and incidents are either products of the author's imagination or are used fictitiously.

Published by Thomas & Mercer, Seattle

www.apub.com

ISBN-13: 9781662500909
ISBN-10: 1662500904

Cover design by Eileen Carey

Printed in the United States of America

For Kristen, and anyone else who was made to say "sorry" for taking up space.
Be sorry for nothing, sweetheart.

Author's Note

This book deals with some heavy themes, including sexual assault, domestic abuse, grief, death, infertility, and child loss. My intention in shedding light on these topics is good, but intention and impact are often very different things. You deserve to know this information going in, so you can judge the impact it may have upon you and make healthy decisions about the media with which you engage.

After

21 January 1867

Dear Friend—

I wasn't sure whether to address you by first name or last, after everything that has happened. Even this solution seems wrong—"friend" is too familiar, surely. A presumptuous claim to make on you. And yet it is woefully inadequate in describing your claim on me.

My mind drifts often to Valor Rise—to the crime I committed there. But it's not my actions that I'm ashamed of, and I don't blame myself. Or, I don't blame myself only. My so-called victim had power enough to take away nearly all my choices; it is not my fault the one choice left to me was fatal.

No, what bothers me about my conduct is that it tore me from you, after you dirtied your own hands to help me. When I imagine you, utterly alone, the guilt is terrible, more terrible than any jealousy. So tell me you found someone else who cares for you. Tell me she's as good as I meant to be—that she's better. I promise only to be happy for you.

And as I preach honesty, I suppose I should practice it: even though I am not guilty, I often find myself afraid. The tailoring shop is open, and there is no shortage of customers, all of whom seem pleased with my work. Yet I live as if every person were police and my wrongdoings were written right across my face. I stick myself with pins as often as whatever cloth I'm aiming for.

But don't pity me. I bear the anxiety well; I almost deserve it. You see, I have come to accept the truth I was running from, that first day I came to Valor Rise: the way some women long to be rescued, I have always longed to be captured.

Marian

Before

1

I set out to be a good servant, truly, the morning I left for Valor Rise.

Shut into the coach that would lead me off, I peered out at Parish Street Workhouse. It was strange: this dreary, gray fortress had been the container of eight years of my life, and yet its facade was unfamiliar to me. And now, to the optimistic rhythm of the horse's hooves on the cobbles, we passed easily out through the iron gates, my former prison erased line by line in London's morning fog.

The street was busy for such an early hour. Fruitmongers pushed carts, crying out their wares. Harried girls and boys, smaller even than I had been when I first arrived at the workhouse, wove past my carriage. They looked so fragile, unprotected under a menacing, leaden sky. They filed into a factory smoking thickly enough from its chimneys to have been on fire, and yet no one panicked. There was no disaster; this was but the usual state of things.

Turning, I tried to see the workhouse. I could not make it out anymore. I was free.

Mother was not. I felt an ache in my chest, pressure on my shoulders where she'd gripped me, saying her goodbyes. But I was grateful, still, to be going.

I sat straight-backed in the coach, and for the first four hours of the trip, I never even looked out the window. My life as a pauper was past, I rode steadily toward my future, and nothing in between concerned me. I kept my eyes on my lap, on my hands, which held sometimes too tightly to an envelope.

The stock was thin and queasy white, the ink already smudged, but the name addressed in Mrs. Martin's severe hand could not be diminished for me: *Mrs. Wythe Bornholdt.* My new mistress, to whom I would be lady's maid.

When the coach stopped to change horses, I folded Mrs. Martin's envelope and put it away in my drawstring coin purse, which was empty otherwise. I stepped out only to stretch my legs and find a lavatory, but the coachman pointed me beyond the posting house to an inn, and told me my meal was paid for by my new employers.

"A generous family," I said.

He shrugged. "You want the cow to milk, you feed it."

He turned away to unhitch his horse before I could decide what reply to make.

The inn was warmly fitted in honey-hued oak—with water lighter, and tea darker, than any I'd had in years, and more bits of beef in my broth than I'd probably had over all my meals at Parish Street put together—and yet, that remark of the coachman's stayed in my ear like an unpleasant flavor does upon the tongue.

We rode on into the evening, the sun sinking lower and lower until sunset forced its way directly into the coach, staining my hands. Twisting in my seat, I lowered my window and called up to the coachman: "How far have we to go?"

"We're on the estate already, in truth!" he shouted back. "Half an hour, I reckon, to get past the tenant farms."

"Tenant farms," I said, quietly and not to him. I sat forward and put my hand to my forehead, shading my eyes. Sure enough, there went a modest cottage—no more than two rooms—set back from the road, with rows and rows of turned soil just behind. Spots of new, bright green shone out of the dirt like faerie tracks.

To have traveled so far only to find myself someplace so familiar made me shudder. This land belonged to my new master. Just such a man as he had brought the law down on my family and put my mother and me in the workhouse.

I caught myself rounding my shoulders, curling in like burning paper, and sat tall again. The past didn't matter; the future was my concern. I was eighteen now. I had control of my life, and I would never let it be wrested from me.

"You can see the house now!"

The coachman pointed far ahead. Beside the tired eye of the sun, a grand house stood in silhouette, hoisted high above the heads of trees, whose thick oak arms seemed to tremble under the weight of it.

"Is it many stories?" I asked, over the tramping of hooves.

"Just three." After a pause, he added: "It's sat on a cliff."

I reddened. "Of course." Valor Rise.

The carriage bounded up a steep incline, along an uneven path through thick trees, and night fell fast. I felt by the lean of my body that we were turning as we went. We must have been coming around the cliff from the back. At any moment, lights from the windows of the house would peek out—seeing me, I imagined, like a living person, and judging me neither grand enough nor good enough to reside there. My stomach turned.

We rounded a wall of trees and slowed to a stop beside a cottage. I could see the hulking shape of the manor in the distance. There was not a single lamp lit by any window after all, yet I was not relieved; it seemed less to me like the house slept than that it waited, watching keenly—and seeing better in the dark than I, like an owl or a cat.

The coachman opened my door, helped me down from the high step, and bade me wait while he went into the cottage. He returned with a woman. She was dressed for bed, but had put on boots and held a lantern. "Evening," she said to me.

The coachman led his horses leftward, toward a high-roofed stable. I turned from its towering silhouette, feeling meeker than ever beneath it, to follow the cottage woman through the grass, toward the house.

"You'll be exhausted, I imagine," my guide was saying. "But the missus will want a word with you tonight, before the master returns."

My head came up. The way she whispered made me anxious. "Before the master returns?"

"She's scheduled your coming during some errand of his." The woman's voice was harder suddenly—frozen over. "So as she can tell you that your wages may come from the master, but you're the lady's maid and she's the lady—for whatever good that'll do her."

I frowned. "Are their orders often at odds? I'd hoped to serve well enough to please both of them."

The woman laughed and looked me over. "Indeed. Bit of a short skirt, yours."

Cheeks hot, I hunched, gripped the fabric around my knees, and tugged. "It's my mother's dress, the only dress I—"

"None of my business," the woman said. "Just not the first impression you want to make in this house, that's all."

I smoothed my skirt down. But my escort was getting too far ahead of me. I chased after.

The wide, hulking shape of the house grew more substantial as we approached, but its features were still mysterious to me. Instead of going to the front steps, the woman led me around the side, under a roof where a lamp was lit, and pulled the bell there.

The door opened, revealing a thin man with gray hair in a dark suit.

"There's the new maid, Ledford," the woman said, and before he could reply, she'd turned back around. "Good night."

If Ledford was surprised, he didn't show it. "I am the butler, miss," he said, and opened the door to let me pass.

I found myself in a large, silent room, where only the stairway out was lit. I followed Ledford there and up the steps to the main floor, where some lamps in the walls burned low. He motioned me into a room with a fireplace, armchairs, and bookshelves. "The lady of the house will be along shortly."

I stood by the fire to wait, to show that I welcomed close scrutiny in full light, and spread my hands before the fire. It seemed especially warm after such a chilly reception, and especially bright in such a dark house.

"That dress is scandalous," a woman's voice declared.

I turned, hunching to pull again at my hem, but I couldn't see who'd spoken: I'd been staring into the fire, and my vision was clouded with bleeding purple spots. I blinked until a shape stood out, drifting closer.

I made out a drawn, pale face, with a flat mouth and dark hair pulled tight into a bun. There was a green tint to her skin, set off terribly by the deep purple of her gown. Not the color I would have chosen for her, I thought first, and then second: no wonder the last lady's maid had been let go.

"I am Diana Bornholdt, mistress of Valor Rise," she declared. Her voice was hard. She held out her hand, but when I gave mine to clasp, she ignored it. "Do you have your matron's reference, to identify yourself?"

"Oh—yes, ma'am." I handed over Mrs. Martin's letter.

She opened the envelope and bent toward the firelight. Her eyes had fine wrinkles around them, yet she read the words before her faster than I could do.

From the way the cottage woman had spoken, almost mocking, I'd expected my mistress to be not quite meek, but a woman allowed to stay soft, surrounded as she was by only gentle society. But Mrs. Bornholdt's features were decisively drawn, as by an artist who knew his skill, and when she lifted her gaze it quite pinned me in my place.

"Marian Osley," she said.

I nodded. "Yes, ma'am."

"Your matron speaks highly, in all her letters, of your good character and work ethic under her roof."

I bowed my head. "That's very kind of—"

"And what did you do in London before the workhouse?" She pointed her finger, close to my eyes. "I will know if you are lying."

I held out my open palms to her—as if falsehoods were kept in fists. "I was a child when I was brought to Parish Street."

"How young a child?"

"Eleven—no, ten."

"Which is it?"

"Ten, ma'am."

"And your parents, what did they do?"

"They were farmers, ma'am."

"Farmers." She tipped her head back. "And how do good little farmers' children end up in workhouses?"

I took my hands back and twisted my fingers. "We had a few poor seasons in a row, and my father couldn't pay the taxes, ma'am. He went to debtors' prison, and my mother and I went to Parish Street."

"And how did you fill your time there? Were you left alone to run about and play as you pleased?"

I flinched. "No, I—I worked. My job, together with many of the other little girls, was to pick the oakum fibers out from between strands of rope, so it could be waterproofed and used on ships." The tips of my fingers itched as I spoke, and I saw the long workroom in my mind. There had been no table before us to rest our elbows on, so we'd teased out the threads from the lengths of rope in our laps, sat in a row on a hard wooden bench, plucking and pulling until a mess of dark fuzz covered the floor.

"But you have had other training?" Mrs. Bornholdt asked. "Mrs. Martin assures me you are a skilled seamstress."

"Yes. She trained me herself."

Mrs. Bornholdt raised her eyebrows. "Why would she do that?"

The question made the back of my neck warm. Not that I resented the disbelief. I'd often wondered whether I deserved such attention, myself. "I . . . showed an aptitude for the work, as I got older," I said. When Mrs. Bornholdt still looked disbelieving, I added: "She needed mending done on her own clothes. Her hands had begun to bother her, I think."

"Aha," my mistress said, but she was frowning. "Is that all you know, mending?"

"No. She gave me her own pattern books after that, ma'am."

"But you never made new clothes, only read about them?"

"I did make new clothes." I hesitated. "She gave me the clothes paupers came in with for fabric, after they'd been given uniforms."

So far, she'd had a new question for me as quickly as I could get out the answer to her last, but this seemed to make her think. At length, she asked, "And the other paupers did not mind, when it came time for them to leave the workhouse, that they had no clothes?"

I looked down. I had raised this very objection to Mrs. Martin, once. "Most do not know to mind, ma'am, as they do not ever leave," I said. "My own mother is there still. I'm very lucky to have this job, and I hope to pay her way out with my wages one day."

Mrs. Bornholdt watched me for a long moment. "You will excuse me for interrogating you. I asked your Mrs. Martin for someone well behaved. However, some of these institutions' good matrons," she said, putting peculiar emphasis on the adjective, "fall into telling half truths. Trying to help their charges, not thinking of how the lie might hurt somebody else."

I made myself take a breath. "Yes, ma'am, I understand. I come from a low place, but I can assure you that I mean to raise myself to meet your standards."

Mrs. Bornholdt searched my face. "Your mother's welfare is a worthy cause for your efforts," she said next. "The least you could do for the woman who has looked after you. But in a sense, I will be the woman looking after you now. Think of that in your service to me, before you think of wages."

"Yes, ma'am." I remembered, finally, to curtsy as Mrs. Martin had told me to. "I'll be dutiful as any daughter."

I thought this would please her, for I was only expanding on the theme she'd begun, but she scrunched her nose as she studied me.

"I will ring for the housekeeper," she said at last. "She will show you to your room, and bring your uniform. You may take it in, so that it looks neat on you."

I curtsied again. "Thank you, ma'am."

"But do not shorten the hem to suit your taste," she added, indicating my dress with a dismissive wave. "This is not a brothel."

I swallowed, feeling my cheeks go red. "Yes, ma'am."

◆ ◆ ◆

The housekeeper was called Mrs. Davies, and she was a chess piece of a person—pale but sturdy. Old as she was, she seemed to glide before me, parting the darkness with her candle as we went across the checkered floor of the main hall. The farther we got from Mrs. Bornholdt, the heavier my body seemed to be, until I had to let even the weight of my embarrassment about the dress go from my shoulders. I could not have kept moving otherwise.

Mrs. Davies took me through a door and up a dingy staircase, and we emerged into a corridor with walls the shade of bruises—heavy, purple ones that have hardly begun to heal. She unlocked a door and waved me in, the only flicker in her face owing to the inconsistent candle.

"This is your room." She lit a wood taper and took it to a round table in the center of the floor. She touched the flame to a candle there, which she gave to me.

Lifting it, I saw a chest of drawers on my right, made of dark wood, and on my left a bed, the mattress thick, made up with good covers—the only bed in the room, for I was to be the sole occupant. My lips slipped apart.

"It's usual I rise at four," Mrs. Davies said. "You're not needed until five, but tomorrow I'll get you up early and take you on my rounds, so you get to know the house."

"Yes, Mrs. Davies." I sat on the end of the bed. The mattress gave a little under my weight, and I was so surprised at its softness that I nearly dropped the candle.

"Those will do fine, but they're filthy," Mrs. Davies said, glaring at my shoes. "Set them out in the hall for the footman to take, and you'll find them fresh in the same place come morning."

I roused myself with a shake. "I can clean them—he needn't bother."

"It's his job to do it," she said. "I'll bring your uniform in the morning. Now. Have I told you everything?"

I looked around me, trying to think what else I wanted to know.

She waved her hands. "Everything will keep. Good night, Miss Osley."

"Good night, Mrs. Davies."

The door creaked shut behind her, and her footsteps faded, until the only sound was a soft, elongated *who*-ing at the window—as if the house itself were wondering about me. It made me think again about what the cottage woman had said, about my mistress making sure her husband would be away when I came. I felt strongly that I did not belong there: with a soft bed, in a room to myself, under a fine roof.

I had been summoned here, I reminded myself. But had that been done in secret?

The candlelight flickered, and seeing that my hand was shaking, I set the holder down beside the bed. There was a drawer there. I opened it to put my coin purse in, and found a few sheets of blank paper inside.

I put my hand to my heart and curled my fingers against the fabric of my dress—my mother's dress. *Write to me,* she'd said.

That morning, we'd stood together in the women's parlor at Parish Street, as we had done often, and yet we seemed to me to stand on different planes: I in the vivid color of the living, and she in the land of ghosts, faded as a mophead.

"I'm so happy for you," she'd said, taking my hands.

I wondered whether she saw herself in me, across time, from the night of my father's arrest all those years ago. I knew I was ill fitted to play my mother's part in the scene, for I was so much taller. The dress's waistline was too near my bust, the hem too high on my legs; these were the only problems I could not fix myself, not having more of the same fabric to hand.

If eight years at the workhouse had drawn me up, stretching me out so that I had to stoop to hold my mother, it had pulled her quite the other way—grabbed her by her very cheeks, it seemed, given the great pouches there. She had permanent worry lines across her forehead, etched in deep over time. Worry lines for Father, whose debt only increased in prison, and worry lines for me.

Now it was my turn to worry for her, I thought, turning down the bedclothes in my new room. Every week, Mother would incur expenses at Parish Street—for her washing, her tea, the use of her bed. But my salary was to be fifteen pounds for the coming year. I couldn't work miracles, but I could make some difference. And if I could release Mother from her debt and situate her somewhere near me, then maybe we could both work. Maybe we could free Father.

"I'll send you everything I make," I'd promised her that morning.

"Don't be foolish; you'll need money for yourself."

"I'm sure I'll be happy with whatever my master and mistress provide for me," I said, not adding that I was used to little. I never wanted her to think of my suffering again.

But her eyes were hard—determined. "I don't want your salary. I want to know you're happy."

"But, Mother—"

She squeezed my hands. "Write to me."

And then she'd let me go.

I released a shaky breath and began unbuttoning myself, starting at my collar. I worked my arms loose in the sleeves, and finally my mother's clothes, comfort and constriction both, fell away onto the floor.

I slipped myself between the bedcovers and shivered at their coolness. I would have to buy a nightgown. I would have to buy many things, now. And in the meantime, yes, I would have to write my mother. Until I did, she would know nothing of how I fared—how I lay in a nice bed, and not in a ditch someplace.

I blew out the candle. I drew the covers closer around me, felt my body, whole and healthy beneath them, and tears gathered in my eyes in a rush so strong it made my cheeks hurt. Not everyone I'd known at Parish Street lived to get free of it. But somehow I had. And though I felt small in the bed, unequal to the dark shapes of furniture in my room and the grand sprawl of this place, there was an insularity to the feeling, too—as if I were so tiny as to be missed entirely by whatever monsters lumbered by in the night.

In the morning there would be a whole new life to face, but for now I was hidden, swallowed up to the neck by a fabric more fluid than I had ever touched, on a mattress softer than any into which I'd been allowed to sink. The wind whipped itself into a higher passion, but its chill did not touch me.

Who, it said still, as it sneaked through at the edges of the window glass. *Who, who?*

2

"Up you get."

I opened my eyes on almost perfect darkness, and thought the shapes in the shadows were the cots of the other women in my ward. My feet remembered the cold of the floor in the morning, my stomach the congealing breakfast gruel, and both recoiled at the prospect of their immediate future. Then a curtain was drawn aside, and gray morning gave shape to Mrs. Davies, tying the sash. I sat up.

From the center table she brought a tray of toast and tea. In grateful, bleary silence, I ate, and watched her lay out my clothes. It struck me that, on the previous morning, there had been a different woman to be roused to work from what was now my bed. How quickly fortunes changed. I wondered if hers were better or worse.

"Dress, apron, stockings, cap," Mrs. Davies said, touching the garments as she spoke. "New underthings you'll need to get yourself. The last girl may have left some of hers in the drawers, if you need them."

"Oh," I said. "That's—"

"This black dress is for the morning, for cleaning the house in. You must keep it neat, though, as you serve the mistress her breakfast in it. Midday, you change into the white dress, so you're fit to be seen by the family or their guests. Got all that?"

I nodded. "Yes, Mrs. Davies."

She pointed to a corner where a cloth and pitcher sat on the rim of a wooden washstand. "Have a wash, get dressed. I'll wait for you." Then she stepped into the corridor, shutting my door behind her.

Not wanting to waste her time, I undressed as hastily as I ever had at the women's washbasins in Parish Street. I expected the water I poured to ache my hands and shock my face, but when I dipped my fingers in, I found it warm.

Clean, I dressed myself in the black uniform, and studied the white. I expected to see some stains, but there was nothing. The dress had even been pressed. I felt like a lady in a proper shop, receiving a garment nobody had worn before.

But I could take no comfort, for I had that feeling still that I would not be allowed to stay.

I rejoined Mrs. Davies in the corridor, and she took me to the bottommost floor—the kitchens, where I was struck at once by humid air and discordant smells: garlic and coffee. It was darker than abovestairs, for there were no windows; the kitchens relied on lamplight.

Much of the space of this central room was taken up by a wooden preparation table in the middle. Along the walls were two ovens, a range, many cabinets, and three sinks. The sinks had faucets; in fact, Mrs. Davies explained, there was plumbing up to the second floor, too, for the family bathrooms.

Off the main room were archways, and she told me which went where: to dry and wet larders, the butler's and footman's pantries, a servants' dining room, and Mrs. Davies's own office.

On a blank space of wall was a bell-board, each bell labeled underneath. "You're to answer the bells for Mrs. Bornholdt's apartment," she said. "And the bell for the lady's parlor will be meant for you, when company comes."

She took me all around the floor, which was populated by other people in black, who scrubbed the floor and the pots and pans—all too focused upon their work to even glance at us. Every clatter of dishes echoed off the stone floor anyway; if Mrs. Davies had tried to introduce me, we could hardly have had conversation. She gave their positions right in my ear as she pointed them out: "Kitchen maid—she helps the cook; scullery maid—she does the kitchen cleaning; and parlormaid, who tends to the shared rooms: library, drawing room, and the parlors, obviously."

I peeked into a thin, adjacent room at a man polishing silver.

"This is the footman's pantry, and that's the footman. He's to the master what you are to the mistress—and he did your shoes." She pointed at the other boy there, a child perhaps twelve years old, scrubbing filth from boots. "And that's—"

"The hall boy," I said.

Mrs. Davies turned her head toward me, her eyes narrowed. "I thought you never worked in a house before."

I touched my hand to my cheek. "I haven't. Only I had a . . . friend at the workhouse when we were young, who went away to be a hall boy." Heaven help me, I still sounded sad about it, six years later.

"Well, come along," Mrs. Davies was saying, as she turned from me. "Lots to see, yet."

I followed.

Mrs. Davies's morning business was supervisory; she made sure the parlormaid had set firewood in certain rooms, and that the footman had cleaned the oil lamps. Following along, I learned the lay of the ground floor, at the center of which were the main hall and the dining room. The library, ballroom, and morning parlor could be reached from the former; the drawing room and the afternoon parlor were off the latter.

As we made the rounds abovestairs, I saw again the faces I had seen below, only now the women were kneeling on hearths, making fires, and the man I'd seen polishing shoes was turning up the lamps. Everything was quiet here, as if the kitchens existed not just below us but on another plane of existence entirely—and more, as if we inhabitants of that otherworld were insubstantial, like the dead creeping along in the land of the living.

Once, Mrs. Davies and I passed through the foyer, where a grand staircase hugged the walls as it climbed, turning with every corner—a wide, squared spiral. But we kept to the dimly lit servants' stairwells, which ran up and down the whole house at the west and east ends, the steps creaky and the space thin.

On the second floor the lamps were low, and we treaded softly across the carpet. Mrs. Davies pointed out Mrs. Bornholdt's bedroom as we passed it. At the thought of our last meeting, my stomach twisted.

"Better look in on the study," Mrs. Davies said as she bent to unlock a heavy, black walnut door at the end of the hall. "The master mightn't come in here at all, on a travel day, but if I take comfort in that as fact, it'll surely turn to fiction." She used the same whispering tone as the cottage woman had done, speaking of the master the night before.

"Is it uncomfortable to have him home?" I asked, working to make my tone casual.

"Not a comment on him, just a comment on the work," she said. "Never vary your routine, however the family moves, unless it's their idea. Otherwise, whatever you think won't be wanted will suddenly be needed desperately." She fixed me with a sage look as she turned her key.

The room beyond had a close, rich smell: book leather and firewood. Following Mrs. Davies in, I saw that the walls were darkly paneled, with a grain that made me think of coarse fur, such as wolves have. To the left, a formidable desk stood before a wide, arched window that took up most of the wall on that side. To the right were two built-in bookcases with thinner windows between and beside them. An oxblood leather couch and chair sat together dead ahead, before a fireplace with a handsome mantel and, above that, an even handsomer portrait—of a man with wheat-yellow hair brushed to a high shine, and eyes of a ripe, well-tended green.

"Is that the master?" I asked.

"Aye, that's Mr. Bornholdt," Mrs. Davies said.

But he wasn't frightening at all. Why, here was a product of goodness: good family, good treatment, good food, good sleep. He fit here, in this house, like an emerald set into the center of a fine ring. And more, stranger though he was, his expression was familiar to me. Or, it gave me a familiar feeling. His eyes issued a challenge, and I felt inspired—eager, even—to meet it.

"Stare as long as you like," Mrs. Davies said. "Not impertinent when he's made of paint."

I started, tearing my eyes away, but she had already moved on to scrutinize the floor, hands on her hips.

"Maid's not been in to scent the rug." She glanced left and right. "Nor opened any of the windows, nor laid the firewood. It tempts disaster, but what do they care?" Shaking her head, she gestured that I should lead us out of the room.

In the kitchens below, Mrs. Davies lit the hulking black range and showed me how to open or close the vents to divert the heat to the three different grates. While the kettle was on its way to boiling, she set some slices of bread to toast.

"You!" she snapped.

I jumped, but it was to one of the maids she'd said it—a fair-haired girl who'd just arrived.

"Lucette Weekeley," the housekeeper went on, with an exaggerated bow. "Your Majesty, the master might have need to conduct business today, without thinking to inform you, important as you are, and his study's stuffed up as a cold!"

"It's not me what does the study!" the girl said. "The lady's maid does it after she brings Mrs. Bornholdt's breakfast tray. She took that job off me months ago!"

"Does the lady's maid decide who does what, or do I?"

"It was the master who—"

"Never mind that," Mrs. Davies said, with half a glance at me. "There's a new lady's maid, and how's she supposed to know to do your job for you?"

"I forgot about the study is all." Lucette's gaze caught bitterly on me as it drifted floorward.

"Forgot your job, right, which makes sense, as you haven't been doing it."

I offered Lucette a smile. "I don't mind."

"You don't want to start by doing favors," Mrs. Davies said, her voice stern.

I kept my eyes on Lucette. "If I can't manage, I'll tell you."

Mrs. Davies tutted but turned back to the range. Lucette, far from appreciating my intervention, looked me up and down as if I were filthy—so convincingly that I checked myself for spots. When I looked up again, she'd strode away into a pantry.

"You're never to make anything richer than bread for Mrs. Bornholdt in the morning," Mrs. Davies said, calling me back to the task at hand. "No breakfast meats. Doctor's orders."

I frowned. "Is she sick?"

"I did not say that," she said, pointing into my face, "and you won't, either, especially not to the missus herself, isn't that right?"

I nodded. "Of course, Mrs. Davies."

I followed her around the kitchen and pantry as she loaded the breakfast tray with toast, butter, jam, teapot, milk, and sugar, trying to remember it all for myself. When everything was arranged, she tucked a dustpan under my arm, and stuffed a brush, a matchbox, and a packet of tea into my apron pocket.

This last gave me pause.

"You scent the rug in the study with the loose tea," she said. "Sprinkle it on, then sweep it up."

"Oh. Yes, Mrs. Davies."

She handed me the tray of food. "But first, you give the lady of the house her breakfast, then you do Her Majesty's job." Casting her eyes to the ceiling, she shook her head so her cheeks wobbled. "Then go back to Mrs. Bornholdt to draw her bath and help her dress."

I nodded and turned to leave.

"Wait." She grabbed my shoulder, and I stumbled backward. "You've got to put Epsom salts in the bath. They're in a tall pot under her washstand. Two generous scoops, stirred into the tub while the water's hot."

"Yes, Mrs. Davies, thank you."

This time she let me go, and I hurried up the stairs. If I could only get it all done quickly enough, perhaps I wouldn't forget anything.

At Mrs. Bornholdt's door, the china on the breakfast tray chattered in my hands. I shifted my grip so I held the tray in one arm, and leaned the dustpan against the wall. Then I knocked.

"Who's there?" She sounded annoyed.

I cringed. "It's the maid with your breakfast, ma'am."

"Come in."

The room was dark, but there was a suggestion of blue in with the blackness, as if we were underwater. I could make out uneven, curving shapes of furniture, and farthest from me I saw the stiff shape of a woman, sitting up. "There you are," she said, in lieu of a greeting, her head turned pointedly toward the window. The sun was strong, but the curtains were closed; the only light was a glowing line of gold around their edges.

"Apologies, ma'am." I brought the breakfast tray across the room, avoiding all the shadow-shapes between us, and set it on her lap. Then I went to the curtains and threw them open.

The room's walls were light blue, with linens and upholstery to match. There were gold accents everywhere—in the medallion of the rug, the edging on the nightstand, the pattern of Mrs. Bornholdt's rumpled duvet. By the fireplace was a chair with a footstool; the cushions of both were the same powdery, eggshell blue, with gold buttons embedded in them. I was so uplifted for a moment, with the sun warm on my back, that I smiled.

But Mrs. Bornholdt's gaze was cold. Perhaps she couldn't help it; still pale and green-tinged at her cheeks, she looked half-frozen. Which of course she would be, as I hadn't lit her fire yet. I turned my back, bending at the hearth and finding the matchbox in my apron.

The match wouldn't light. Perhaps the trick was different than with Mrs. Martin's matchbox? But that was silly; it had to be a bad match. I tried another, struck too hard, and snapped it—loudly—in two.

"Is there a problem?" Mrs. Bornholdt asked.

"No, ma'am." Hands shaking, I struck a third match, but I was so surprised at my success that I dropped it. I looked down to see a small, black burn in the beautiful robin's-egg rug. I put my hand to my mouth. "Oh, Lord help me."

"Indeed."

I shuddered to hear my mistress so close, doused by icy dread, and turned to find Mrs. Bornholdt standing a few feet off in her nightgown.

"I'm so sorry, Mrs. Born—"

"If I ring for someone to light this fire, will you be able to draw my bath in half an hour?" she asked, her voice cold and flat. "Or will you break the tub?"

I shrank from her, and swallowed. "I can do it. I'll be careful."

"See that you are," she said. "You are dismissed."

3

I trembled, alone in the hallway. I did not belong here, and soon, I was sure, I would be sent back to Parish Street.

But that reminded me: I may have stood on finer carpet than I did there, but in another sense the spaces were the same, and I had been here before: Mrs. Martin had found my character wanting, and been cold, too. She was mean and it had been uncomfortable, of course it had, but she'd also pushed me to grow into somebody better. I could grow again.

I relaxed my shoulders, and took up the dustpan and brush like sword and shield. I remembered my way to the master's study, let myself in, and shut the door behind me. Here was an opportunity to do a useful task with no watchful eyes or interruption. I would go into the room intimidated but come back out serene—once again but a clear, calm pool at my surface, so my mistress could see down to the bottom of me.

Mr. Bornholdt's portrait judged me on my entrance, and this time I treated his likeness as I would have done his person: I curtsied and did not meet his eye. I did one other thing, too. I blushed.

I threw open the windows first, and because a breeze tugged on the curtains, I went to tie them back. Reaching out for the fabric, I suddenly felt that I was my mother. Not my mother in the workhouse—there were no curtains on the windows at Parish Street—but before all that. Right before. The night of the arrest, when I was but ten.

She'd had a candle in her hand. The glow of it gilded her, and she smiled at me as she freed the window curtains from their sashes, tugging them closed against the night. I had been trying not to fall asleep at the table, because then I would be sent to bed. My arms were heavy from an afternoon spent polishing the copper—a chore that had coated me in brick dust, necessitating a rare evening wash. I sat in my nightclothes, wet hair slicked to my scalp, near enough to the hearth to be warmed through.

My father had just settled in his corner chair, and when she came to the window nearest him, she touched his shoulder.

"Bloody pheasants," he'd said, rubbing his temples. "Always at the wheat—and I can't do anything about them. The livelihood of those birds is better protected than ours."

"We'll manage," my mother answered, the words wax-soft and rosy, like the lip salve she made us wear all winter. "We'll all of us pull together, as we do."

He lifted his gaze, and his brow smoothed. "If the crop is as resistant to attack as your mood is, we may indeed." This made Mother laugh, and he leaned forward to watch her cross the room. "How am I so changed by a word from you? And always for the better?"

I picked my head up off the prop of my hand. "That's Mother's magic."

Father twisted in his seat to study me. "Magic? Really?"

I pointed. "See how she shines?" Most adults I'd ever met would insist on being serious, but there was some chance my father would pretend with me, if he was not too tired from his work.

"Now you mention it, Marian," he said, furrowing his brows, "she is an unearthly beauty tonight."

"She's setting the boundaries of a spell around us, with her candle," I said, rising from my seat and crossing to Father.

He smirked—but not as if he thought my idea was silly. In fact, the smirk was not directed at me at all, but given over my head. I turned to see its intended target: my mother. She was a short woman, but she'd drawn herself up as tall as she could, dropping her shoulders and raising her chin, leaning on one hip so its curve was clear under her skirt. She raised her candle like a toasting cup, and extended her free arm toward us, her fingers clutching some invisible thing. I grinned.

"Is she bewitching me?" Father asked, hushed, as if Mother were a hare he didn't want to startle.

I rolled my eyes. "No, Father. She's protecting us, of course, so we're safe—so long as we stay in her good graces."

"Well, that should be easy. I'd not displease your mother for anything."

I lifted my chin. "Nor me. Not even if she did bewitch you."

Chuckling, Father scooped me up into his lap. "That's lucky for her. But see here—how did you know she was doing a spell and I didn't?" He peered hard at me. "Is she training you up as her apprentice?"

"Oh, it's Marian who teaches me my magic." Mother bowed to me, twirling her hand as she did it. "Not the other way round."

High praise, his, and so I had been grinning like a fool when the knock came. The policeman's knock, as it turned out to be. And what a change, after that, in everything—all Mother's prepossession turned to furtiveness, grabbing me like luggage and bolting for the back door.

All for naught. After the arrest, Father and I were never to be reunited again. I remembered the look my mother had given him, outside the police wagon, as if he were already gone—as if he were a painting of himself, her husband, whom she missed very much. And when she and I were reunited that evening in the workhouse, when she opened her arms to me, she was in a Parish Street Workhouse uniform.

Footsteps in the corridor brought me back to Valor Rise. Some servant working, as I should have been. I wiped my eyes and sent a silent wish out the window, over the treetops in the village beyond the cliff, that my parents—separated from each other even as I was separated from them—should feel my love. Then I took the tea Mrs. Davies had put in my apron pocket and walked backward about the rug, sprinkling it before me like chicken feed.

Shaking out the last of the tea, I realized I hadn't asked Mrs. Davies how long to leave it before sweeping. I decided I'd build the fire first. I bent down to the woodpile in a corner, took some logs into my arms, and carried them to the hearth.

I heard the study door swing open behind me. "I wondered if I would find you here," a man said, and I knew from the richness of his tone that he must be the master.

At once I crouched, as Mrs. Martin had told me to do if any member of the family ever found me upstairs—*so they may pretend you're not there*—hugging the firewood to me. There was a long, torturous silence, and then the door clicked shut. I let out my breath.

But no: his footsteps approached, soft and heavy on the carpet. I tensed.

"Hope evidently springs eternal," he murmured. "Yours and mine."

I took a steadying breath, wondering at the tone of his voice—like a hunter, stalking. Then his hand closed on my shoulder, and in my mind there was a flash of a different master: the master of the workhouse, drawing back his fist. Cringing, I said, "I'm sorry, sir!"

The man withdrew his hand as if I'd bitten it. I opened one eye to find both of his wide, as if he were as startled as I was.

I leaned away, for it was him—the man in the portrait with ripe green eyes, his face so close that I could see all the different pinks in his lips, and smell the darkly sweet cologne he wore. Mr. Bornholdt.

"Well, now I am sorry, too," he said, in a new voice—gentler, as if I were some baby animal he'd nearly stepped on. He straightened up and brushed down the front of his coat. "I do not know you, do I? What are you doing here?"

I averted my eyes. "I was cleaning your study, sir. I was made to understand this is the time it's done. Please excuse me for my presence—I am so sorry."

"The offense being already committed, let us make the best of it," he said, and he sounded kind—forgiving. "Stand up. Turn toward me."

I put the wood on the hearth and rose, but I did not lift my gaze.

"Who are you?"

"Marian Osley, sir." I curtsied. "The new lady's maid."

As soon as I said them, the words stirred the air between us, thickening it, making it harder to breathe.

"I was not aware we were getting a new lady's maid," the master said.

I swallowed. So it was true: I was a secret.

"How long ago was it that you saw the position posted?" he asked, and I felt that his civility thinly cloaked some more substantial feeling underneath.

Quietly, I said, "It was in the paper in January, sir."

"Some months, then."

I bit my lip. The running of the household must have been a point of contention between husband and wife. Mrs. Bornholdt was trying to take control over the hiring and firing of the servants, without consulting her husband at all.

I watched the master's shoes turn from me, peeking as soon as it was safe. He wore a black suit that squared his shoulders, and displeasure radiated from him. He drifted farther from me, to the front of his desk, and placed his hands flat atop the blotter, leaning down as if in deep thought. The only sound in the room was that of his fingers quickly, almost manically, drumming.

He would fire me out of spite, now—not because I'd displeased him at all, but just to prove a point to his wife about whose house it was—and I'd be back in the workhouse. Or worse.

Unless I were to prove myself just as good as the old maid.

"Should I light a fire, sir?" I asked, brightly as I dared.

"Yes." The word was short, and soft, and he did not even look at me, but it was still a yes. I hurried to the hearth and knelt. I arranged the wood into a better shape and fumbled for the matchbox in my apron.

My hands shook, so I forced myself to move them deliberately. This wouldn't be like Mrs. Bornholdt's fire if I didn't let it be. I was not going to be dismissed because of other people's problems. I was going to take control.

Fingers steady, I struck the match, which flared at once. I touched the tip to the kindling at the center of the pile, then shook the match out, smiling.

"Your arms are thin as tapers."

I started, my eyes darting toward the master. He was leaning back against the desk now, facing me, his hands loosely clasping the edge and his long legs crossed at the ankles. He'd been watching me—and he was scowling. "Were you starving on the street when my dear, charitable wife found you?"

"No, sir." I drew my gaze back to the fire and worked to keep my voice from trembling. "I come from a workhouse in London."

"Ah, that explains it." His tone was amused, mocking—his anger still sharp just beneath, and getting rougher as he went on: "Broth and crusts. One of those institutions where they cannot be bothered to fill your stomach, so instead they fill your head with God and tell you to be satisfied."

I had been bristling, but as the sense of the words broke through the chill, the air around me seemed to thaw. I stole another look at him. I'd never heard anyone say such things—except myself, many years ago, before Mrs. Martin had set me right. Perhaps he was testing me.

But then—to his shoes, and quite sincerely—he said, "I cannot imagine ever learning to live happily with hunger."

I twisted toward him where I knelt. Perhaps he would be sympathetic to me—perhaps he wouldn't dismiss me after all. I said: "I never did learn it myself, sir."

He raised his head. "Oh?" And sure enough, there was some real interest in the question.

But his scrutiny made me self-conscious, so I looked into the fire, where the logs were catching. "I was an unhappy child at the workhouse, sir—and a disobedient one, I fear. I rebelled against my poor fortune. I did things I'm not at all proud of."

"Ah," he said, low and damning—a judgment. "A rebel. You must be as surprised to find yourself in service here as I am."

Dread overtook the excitement of the moment before. "Oh, but, sir," I said, "that was my youth. I know my good fortune all the better for how bad it used to be. This position is precious to me, and I want to be worthy of it. I endeavor only to be obedient, and as good as she who came before me—if you'll only give me a chance."

All the while I rambled, his eyebrows crept upward, and now he tipped his head back, appraising me in silence. I held his gaze, keeping my eyes wide open, willing him to see my sincerity in them.

He uncrossed his ankles and pushed lightly off from the desk edge. His coming near made me anxious. I turned my face away.

"Do you like my horse?" he asked.

I had to look, to see where he was pointing.

He gestured to an iron statuette beside the clock: a rearing horse and, standing before the animal, a man pulling hard upon its lead. "You were assuring me of your goodness," he said. "But, you know, when I buy a horse, I cannot take the self-interested salesman's word about its health."

I licked my lips. "No, sir, I suppose not."

"So, let us do an inspection, and I will determine for myself how fit you are for the position." He put his hands behind his back, walking a half circle around me as he looked me up and down. "Stand."

I did.

"And turn."

I did, and was conscious again of the closeness of him—his mouth, his musk.

He stepped around to the front of me, took my chin in hand, and turned my face by it. "Lady's maids are looked upon by guests, you know. They should not be pale." He shook his head and sighed. "They do you paupers a disservice, those pious workhouse people. They say a virtuous woman is a woman of beauty, and yet do not feed her body so that her skin may glow."

My eyes darted across his severe and shining mouth, his nose, the fine bone of his cheek. I swallowed, and the sound seemed loud with my throat offered out to him as it was. Any moment he would declare me unfit, and dismiss me. He had his reason already, from his wife—now it was just a matter of when he would tire of drawing out the blow.

It was then I realized my cap was slipping—with a dreadful chill, down my scalp I felt it go, helped by the extreme backward tilt of my head. I reached up to fix it, but instead of cloth, my fingers found the master's own hand. Mortified, I drew back, for surely I was filthy from the woodpile. I watched my cap fall to the floor between us, my face burning.

"Poor thing," Mr. Bornholdt said, clucking his tongue. He touched my hair, strands of which fell around my face. I heard two pins drop on the rug. "This is exactly what I mean. So dull. Just a few full stomachs would make it shine."

I frowned. "Yes, sir."

He dropped his hand and stepped closer, so I could feel his legs against my skirt, and bent close to my ear. "Would you like a full stomach now?"

I licked my lips, uncertain. "Sir?"

"I mean to say, I can take much better care of you than any workhouse."

My breath rushed out, and gratitude ran so strongly through me that I might well have actually bounced on my heels. “Oh, sir. That’s very kind. Thank you.”

“Kind,” he said, and patted my cheek. “Yes. I take a personal interest in the well-being of you working-class girls. I think Mrs. Bornholdt fears I get attached.”

He laughed quietly, and I thought I was meant to laugh as well, so I made myself.

“Some of the servants do misconstrue my attentions, filthy-minded as they are,” he said, and sighed. “But you understand. You would not give your mistress the impression that I dote improperly upon you. You would not punish me for my soft heart, my kindness—that is, if you are so good now as you say.”

“Yes, sir.” I bit my lip, thinking of the improper way I’d stared at his portrait, the blush I’d felt when I curtsied before it. “I mean—no, sir, I wouldn’t. I understand.”

“Hmm,” he said, considering me. “Do you know the surest way to tell a good horse from a bad one?”

“No, sir.”

“You check the teeth,” he said. “I wonder if it is the same with women as with horses.”

He smiled at me, as if we were sharing a joke, and I felt the corners of my own lips curl. Then he dropped the expression entirely, and said: “Open your mouth.”

The control beneath the command turned my stomach exactly as a key is turned in a lock; a door in my mind swung open, the room beyond too dark to make out what memory lay beyond, and over some emotional threshold I went, full of the uneasy exhilaration of free fall. Half dreaming, I did it. I opened my mouth.

“Good girl.” He gripped my face again, and leaned left and right, making a show of studying my teeth. “Yes, I think you are just as good as you say you are.”

Thinking we were finished, I tried to close my mouth. But still he clasped my chin, keeping my lips apart. He moved behind me and slipped the fingers of his free hand between my lips.

I took a step backward, but I bumped into him, and froze.

"Oh, you are obedient," he said. He touched my tongue, holding it down like a book page he didn't want to flutter over. He tasted of tobacco. I turned my head and found his face. Our eyes met.

Green. Not brown, as I'd for some reason been expecting—green. The deep green of grasping, choking vines, and the sight of them made my whole body cold. There was no humor in them—no kindness or care at all.

Mr. Bornholdt's fingers forced their way farther into my mouth, until I gagged. I tried to draw backward, to breathe, but met with the master's chest. He did not give way, but cradled me all the closer.

"Lift your skirt."

His other hand was in my hair, pulling at my scalp, pulling so hard my head bent back. My knees buckled, but I didn't fall. I was trapped against him.

"Lift your skirt, I said."

I tried to shake my head, but I couldn't move, and tears sprang to my eyes. I gripped his arm, trying to pull his fingers from between my lips so I could speak, but he knocked me off-balance, only to catch me up again—off my feet, into his grip. He dropped me over the arm of the oxblood chair.

"Please—" I said, the word blown out of me on impact with the furniture.

"Much better," he said, and I wondered—as if from someplace far above me—whether he honestly mistook my meaning. He turned my skirt up, as somewhere to my left a log snapped in the fire.

"No," I managed to get out. Pushing off the couch, I was able to roll onto my back, and when the master reached for my legs, I kicked, catching him in the face with my shoe.

His hand flew to cradle his cheek, his eyes wide upon me—shocked, and hungry still.

"Sir," I stammered, "you're married."

He laughed at that.

Mr. Bornholdt grabbed for my legs again, but I swung them away, taking to my feet. I scampered to the other side of the room, level with the door, out of his reach, hesitating. If I left without being dismissed—

"Stay right there," he murmured, and now he did seem a hunter, stalking toward me. "And not another word."

I ran.

After

29 January 1867

Dear Friend—

You're right—I didn't premeditate what I did. But I don't credit any virtue of mine for that. I was too afraid to see what happened at Valor Rise as anyone's fault but my own.

I could blame Mrs. Davies for putting that idea in my head. Funny how fully some women throw their weight behind the warped realities of men. But I didn't know, then, how complicit she was.

Anyway, such ideas as hers never would have taken hold if I hadn't had things I was guilty for, coming into my position.

You know, for all you say in your letter, about how you don't blame me, about how you are better off now than you were, in all your pages, you neglected to tell me the thing I wanted to know: whether you were sitting alone, brooding, or if you have a new companion.

You don't imagine that I'll murder her, do you?

Marian

Before

4

Halfway down the servants' stairs, I stumbled, twisting my wrist as I caught myself on the banister. The kitchens were loud still. Kettles whistled, pots hissed, and the general, industrious clatter echoed against the stone walls and floor. I descended into the noise but glanced over my shoulder as I went, and crashed into something hard.

"Marian!"

Mrs. Davies slopped stock from a deep-bellied pot over both of us.

I reached for her wrists. "Oh, Mrs. Davies!"

But she drew the pot to her chest. "Now you see me!"

"Please, you must hide me."

"Hide you?" Her eyes were wide. Then her expression sagged. "Is this about the burn you put in the mistress's rug?"

"No—Mrs. Davies, Mr. Bornholdt will be down here any moment—please!" I tried to push past her on the stairs, but she moved more deliberately in front of me.

"What did you ruin now?" she asked. "Something in his study?"

I gave up trying to move her, balling my fists at my sides and straightening up. "I didn't do anything—he did!"

She raised her eyebrows. Then something came clear in her face, and she started shouting. "Lord, you young girls! And there's me thinking I didn't have to tell you to behave yourself! I suppose I'll have to go and finish the study, will I?"

"Mrs. Davies—"

But she rolled her eyes and turned her back, storming to the bottom of the stairs with the big pot.

I chased her across the kitchen. Servants sat at the broad center table, every hand busy chopping or rolling or mixing. But as I rushed by, I saw Lucette, the maid who should have done the study, raise her head.

"Mrs. Davies—he attacked me." Hissing over her shoulder, I said, "I kicked him—I'm in danger—"

"You're not in danger." She didn't even spare me a glance, only kept on toward the black and looming range, where the rush of steam was loudest and oil crackled in pans.

No one else was near, so I said, more freely, "You didn't see his face—"

"I don't doubt he's angry," she said. "But, I tell you, he won't follow you down here. He wouldn't dirty his shoes."

She set the stockpot down on a grate, opened one of the range's flues so the heat flowed underneath, and turned to face me. Instead of offering me any consolation, she grabbed my soiled skirt, dragging me by it to the nearest iron sink.

I eyed the staircase. "I'm sure he's after me."

But she just scrubbed furiously at my dress. "Mrs. Bornholdt will be wanting her bath."

I gasped. "Mrs. Bornholdt—oh, poor Mrs. Bornholdt! I have to tell her."

"Tell her what?"

"About her husband!"

"Why would you do that?" she asked, flapping my skirt as if there were any hope of drying it out—as if that were the important thing.

I ripped the fabric from her hands. "She deserves to know what her husband's like!"

Mrs. Davies raised her brows. "I daresay she's got an inkling."

"Well, I hadn't!" I threw up my arms. "If I hadn't kicked him, I don't know what he would have done. It isn't right!"

"Fine. It isn't right. And?"

I gestured toward the stairs. "Mrs. Bornholdt can put a stop to it!"

"Aye, and she will." She put a finger to her mouth. "Only I wonder: Which of the two of you do you think she can live without?"

I frowned. "What do you mean?"

"I mean he is her husband, Marian, and you are a maid," she said, her voice brusque. "If you bring this problem to Mrs. Bornholdt to solve, you will find yourself back where you started."

"But . . ."

She turned. I drifted after her, back to the range. There was a platter on the cabinet beside it, with eggs and fish. As I watched, she cracked the eggs into a skillet and laid out strips of fish to smoke.

"But what do I do?" I asked, behind her.

"Go forward as if nothing happened."

I twisted my fingers. "I can't be alone with him."

"So don't be." She adjusted the fry pan. "Make it your business to know where he is and to be elsewhere yourself."

"And if he makes my whereabouts his business, and finds me?"

"Excuse yourself," she said.

"And if I can't?"

She shrugged. "Knock something over. Make a sound to send others running."

I put my hands to the sides of my head. "But that would lose me my job—being clumsy, costing money!"

"Not so fast as telling Mrs. Bornholdt that her husband has his eye on you."

"So now I can't assure my safety, my future, no matter what I do?"

"You never could." She wasn't brusque anymore. Only knowing. "No one can."

I let my hands slide off my face and held them loosely near my heart. I didn't know what to say, and I blinked about me—at Mrs. Davies's back, and then at the staircase. The master had not come down, after all. As if nothing had happened.

My heart no longer pounded. In fact, all of a sudden I felt so heavy and tired I could have lain down and slept.

"Here," Mrs. Davies was saying. "Have a drink of water."

I took the glass she held, and sipped. But the touch of liquid on my tongue revived the taste of tobacco in my mouth. I barely managed to swallow it before I gagged.

"What sort of woman does he think I am?" I wondered, mostly to myself.

"Have you been with a man before?"

My head snapped in Mrs. Davies's direction. "Of course not!"

"Just a question—one never knows." Some of her former sharpness had returned. "The last lady's maid had earned money with men."

I set my glass down. "The last lady's maid."

Mrs. Davies was back to fussing with the food on the range. "Seemed like Mr. Bornholdt gave her something she was missing since she'd got here."

I wet my lip. "You mean . . . you mean she enjoyed it."

"Why not?" she asked—not in a tone that approved, but one that remembered how I'd looked and looked at the master's portrait.

"Well." I drew myself up. "He's married, for one. And he can't have loved her."

"Neither thing stops him, though, does it?" She moved along the counter, reaching for dishes.

"But she's a woman."

Mrs. Davies snorted.

"What?" I asked, bristling. "Women aren't so lustful as that."

"I've minded a lot of maids. If anything, women are the lustier sex of the two."

I scrunched my nose. "That's not so."

"Science bears me out," she said, with the calm that comes from certainty. "The want of a woman is natural to men, lives inside them from the first. We know this. But a woman's desire sleeps until a man awakens it. Once he does, that desire flares up. It's been locked away so long that it burns stronger and brighter than his does."

"Awakens it?" I shook my head, wondrous. "How?"

Her shoulders rose, tightly bunched. "Oh, you know. He touches her. Gets close enough that his body speaks to hers."

My lips parted. "What does it say?"

"I suppose it . . . asks a question."

"Or gives an order?" My voice was small, distant to my own ears.

"If you like," she said, waving a warding hand. "Now, if that man is her husband, she can count on him to contain her passion, to feed it steadily, so it doesn't consume her—so she doesn't ruin her reputation. But woe betide the woman awakened out of wedlock. That's how you get girls like the last lady's maid, throwin' themselves at every man what comes near."

My own hand on my cheek felt like a stranger's.

"You're still upset." Mrs. Davies sighed. "Do you need me to go abovestairs with you?"

I clutched her shoulder. "Do they know?"

The wrinkles around her eyes deepened. "Who? Know what?"

"Men. Do they know when a woman is . . . awake?"

She scowled. "Well, sure, the women advertise it, don't they? If not by the way they dress, then by a look or a word."

I licked my lips. "Could a woman show she's awake by accident?"

She looked hard into my face. "What is the matter with you? You're paler than you were when you came down here."

"Would the man know, even if she wasn't trying—"

"How would I know? Do I look like a man?" She gave my shoulder a shove. "Stop stalling, Marian. The sooner you go upstairs, the sooner you come back down."

◆ ◆ ◆

I went up the servants' stairs and through to the second-floor hallway in a daze. My footsteps on the carpet were slow, muted.

Was it my fault, what had almost occurred?

Mrs. Davies's phrase, *woman awakened out of wedlock*, echoed in my head, reminding me of the night when . . . But we'd been playing, and that was years ago. I'd been but a child. We'd both been children.

I was surprised to find myself at Mrs. Bornholdt's door, surprised to have reached it already. I knocked and, when she bade me, entered. I saw her fireplace first; someone had been in to light it competently.

"Where have you been?" Mrs. Bornholdt asked. She stood in front of her bed, her arms crossed, taking me in from head to toe. "Climbing down the cliffside?"

I looked down at my dress, which had a large damp spot from Mrs. Davies's scrubbing.

"And where is your cap?"

I touched my hair, and I was chilled to find strands of it hanging all about my face. I'd forgotten some of the pins were out—perhaps because I hadn't been the ones to pull them. Even as I moved my hand to brush my hair behind one ear, I felt as if I were trespassing. But it was my body. The care of it was mine. I was responsible for what it did, where it traveled.

"Your cap?" Mrs. Bornholdt asked again.

I felt naked—as if not just my cap but all my clothes sat piled in Mr. Bornholdt's study.

"It . . . must have fallen off," I said. "Apologies, ma'am."

She studied me. Then, halting her thoughts with a hand: "Never mind. I do not care—it grows too late for caring. Come."

I followed her through the open door of her dressing room, which had in it a chest of drawers, an armoire, a vanity table, and a chair—all in the same blue she liked. There was a fire lit in this room as well.

She led me straight on to the bathroom at the opposite end—a small space, compared to her other rooms, with a white tile floor, wood cabinets, a porcelain sink, and a clawfoot tub on a marble plinth.

"You will boil water for my bath," she said. "I would like to start my day sometime before noon, for goodness' sake. Mr. Bornholdt is coming home today."

I felt my face flare. "Is that so, ma'am?"

"According to his letter." She moved to the far side of the room to peer out a skinny window. "His intention was to ride overnight in his carriage and arrive this morning."

I drew nearer, but when she looked at me, I shifted my gaze to the window. It looked out on the cliff side of the house, high above the treetops and village roofs. Even from as far back as I stood, the view made me light-headed. Part of me felt I was about to fall from this great height.

"Ahem." Mrs. Bornholdt looked pointedly at the tub.

"Yes, ma'am." I jerked into motion. There was a copper kettle atop the cabinet nearest the sink, which had taps. I'd never used one before, but sure enough, when I turned the knob, cold water came gushing out. When the kettle was full, I traipsed back into the dressing room with it, set it on the grate, and returned to the bathroom. The clawfoot tub had a tap as well, fed by a pipe that stuck up at the side of it. I left the valve open, running water, until the kettle whistled. Then I tightened the knob and ran back to the fireplace.

"My salts are there," Mrs. Bornholdt said when I returned. She pointed at a lidded pot on a cabinet. Its porcelain was overgrown with painted flowers, red and yellow blooms climbing the handles and petals flying across its rounded belly.

It was a sweet, hopeful piece, especially given that its purpose was to contain medicine. Perhaps there was a gentler woman beneath Mrs. Bornholdt's ailment—a thought that only increased my guilt. I'd pretended I didn't know her husband was home.

I added the salts, stirring them into the bath with my arm, determined not to mind the scalding I got, adding into the mix a prayer that she would get well.

"There you are, ma'am," I said when I was done, and got to my feet.

She sighed. "At long last. Wait for me in the dressing room."

I nodded and left her, closing the bathroom door behind me. Her morning dress was already laid out. It was a ruddy shade of lilac. I pursed my lips.

Had the last lady's maid set out this dress, before being dismissed? Even if she hadn't, she must have committed the criminal act of sewing it for Mrs. Bornholdt. Not that the dress was bad in itself. In fact, testing the seams, I found it well made—nothing loose or uneven. But it was wrong for the mistress's skin tone and would show her at a great disadvantage. Did the maid not know color theory?

Or had she done it on purpose?

My stomach turned. I looked toward the bathroom door, listening to the innocent, tumbling sound of drops of water falling from my mistress's hands, back into the tub.

I hadn't said anything, as Mrs. Davies had instructed. But who was she to say what was right? And now, with Mrs. Bornholdt none the wiser about my morning, in doing nothing I had done something. I'd kept a secret, a secret I shared with Mr. Bornholdt.

I told myself I didn't want this intimacy with him—that I was silent out of self-preservation, that this was different from selfishness. But wasn't that exactly what a selfish woman would say, so she could sleep at night? Perhaps the last lady's maid had told herself the very same.

I approached the ornate mirror above Mrs. Bornholdt's vanity, listening to the bathwater slosh and trickle beyond the door, and studied myself. My cheeks had gone pale. I pinched them to re-create the rush of heat I remembered from the study. I looked deep into my own eyes, trying to see something damning in their depths, searching for the black mark that must have caught Mr. Bornholdt's attention. But it was like looking into a witch's glass; perhaps there was some signal there, but not being a witch myself, I had not the powers to interpret it.

I did notice, mouthing approximations of all the things I had said to Mr. Bornholdt, that there was no way to hold my lips that did not seem suggestive. I could draw the corners tight in awkward apology, raise them in meek gratitude, or force them down with dread, but nothing could turn my mouth from what it was: soft, pliable, not quite pink—a private part of myself, stuck right on my face.

The knob turned on the bathroom door, and I spun away from the vanity. The cinch of Mrs. Bornholdt's robe showed how slim she was—too slim, I thought—but the warm water had at last brought some color to her cheeks.

I helped her first into slitted pantaloons, then into her corset.

"Put my hair up," she said, seating herself at her vanity.

I approached, my hands timid.

She gestured to a china box. "Pins are here."

"Yes, ma'am." I darted out my hand to take some as my mind raced. Mrs. Martin hadn't warned me about this. The only hairstyle I could remember was my mother's, before we were put away in the workhouse—I would watch her pin it some mornings. Three pins, I thought it must have been.

I could manage that.

I made a simple knot of Mrs. Bornholdt's hair, and fixed it in place. I'd meant for it to sit high on the back of her head, but as I watched, it sank under its own weight, to her nape.

She met my gaze in the mirror. "You will find a book in your room, belonging to the last maid," she said, "on doing the hair and face."

I nodded fervently. "I will read it tonight, ma'am, I promise."

"See that you do. Tomorrow is another day—and, for your sake, it should be a very different one."

"Yes, ma'am." I bowed my head, dropping a small curtsy. When I looked again, Mrs. Bornholdt's reflection still studied my own. It took all my willpower not to shrink from her, for I had the unnerving—if irrational—idea that she could see her husband's fingers probing my lips apart.

"How quickly could you fashion me a dress?" she asked.

My stomach clenched. "What sort of dress, ma'am?"

"Something gay, for a picnic with my cousin." But there was no joy in her tone—only doubt, or judgment. "She and her husband are coming out this way to stay with her parents two months from now."

My shoulders relaxed. "I should be happy to make it in that time, ma'am." Yes, it was another test—but it was one I knew how to meet.

"Then I should be happy to receive it."

I told myself I invented the threat I heard in this sentence—just my overactive imagination, agitated by a guilty conscience.

For the rest of the day I determined not to think of Mr. Bornholdt, of what had happened, or what I might have done to cause it, which was easy enough while I had work to do: preparing and serving Mrs. Bornholdt's meals, and seeing her put properly to bed. Even at the servants' dinner belowstairs, I was preoccupied, nervous to stick out as I ate among the other servants, afraid my workhouse manners would offend somehow.

I needn't have worried: as soon as food touched my tongue, I remembered what the master had said about proper diet being good for the hair, and pushed my plate away.

By the time I returned to my own room, I was exhausted, and grateful to lie down. But I could not sleep, for the wind was loud at my window. It seemed to say something other than *who* now—something like *whoa. Woe.*

Woe betide the woman awakened out of wedlock.

And with these words an image came: a boy's eyes, the color of worn brown brick, with bright flecks like the rust on wrought iron. An abandoned boy like an abandoned manor, that was how I'd thought of him when we were at the workhouse together. Neglected, but not ruined—his facade all the more imposing for its faults.

I sat up in my bed, lit a candle, and dressed again in some old slip of the last maid's. Then I dipped a pen in ink and put the point to paper. *Dear Mother,* I began. *Do you remember Valentine Hobbs?*

I stared at the sentence and worried my lip. Then I crossed it out, scratching until the words were fully obscured. It would do no good to ask Mother about Valentine. She could not know whether a young boy had shaken me out of a child's sleep too soon, because she was ignorant of the details. That I had kept her so at the time was enough to tell me what I suspected already: What we'd done as children was wrong. Valentine had changed me.

If I confided what had happened with Mr. Bornholdt, on the other hand, Mother might have been able to tell me whether I had done wrong. But then, regardless of who was at fault, the master or me, the facts of the matter would have ruined my mother's perfect picture of my life here and disturbed what little peace she got from letting me go away from her.

I could not look to her for help with this, any part of it. What was done was done. I would have to look after myself and take care that nothing like what had happened that day would happen again, as Mrs. Davies had said. And I would have to set aside my wages, if I could, in case something did happen.

I bent to the page again and wrote:

> Dear Mother,
>
> I am all settled at Valor Rise. I write to you from my very own room. The bedding is warm and the food is hearty, and you needn't worry at all about me.
>
> I am sorry to say I cannot share my wages yet. You were right to think I would have need of the money, for there's underclothes to buy, and I'll need my own stationery when this runs out. Soon, I promise I will send some money along.
>
> With all my love,
>
> Marian

It was the truth, just with an omission.

Over the next fortnight, I kept my hands busy and my head down. I learned to identify Mr. Bornholdt by his shoes, fleeing when I saw them come, and I tried to forget his face. I gave the cleaning of the master's study back over to Lucette. Yet no matter how little I saw of Mr. Bornholdt, he seemed always to be looming in the back of my mind. And meanwhile, Mrs. Bornholdt grew no warmer toward me. I lit her fires without incident, but every time I knelt before her hearth, I saw the black mark I had made on her rug.

At night I read the book Mrs. Bornholdt had mentioned. By day I sat in Mrs. Davies's office, sewing at a dress form by the fire, while the housekeeper was busy making supervisory rounds. I ate little at the servants' mealtimes, too anxious to sit long. By the second Sunday I'd been paid, and I went with the other servants on a trip into the village, to buy myself stockings and nightclothes.

And in that time, I got a letter back from Mother. Her reply was short and written sloppily, as if she were in a great hurry, but her sentiments were warm. She wrote that she'd meant what she'd said: She didn't want my money. She wanted only to hear of my happiness. She was keeping well, she said.

It was marvelous that, even though I'd lied to her about how I fared, I never thought she was lying when she told me the same about herself.

5

The morning I got the awful message from Mrs. Martin, I had been worried only about the dress. It was the day of the picnic with Mrs. Bornholdt's cousin, and I still had not presented her with the garment she had requested.

I might well have given it to her a week earlier, if not for my always finding new flaws to fix. She had asked me for a simple thing on the surface, but the tailor's truth was this: the plainer the design, the more impeccable the craftsmanship had to be, for there was nothing flashy for the stitching to hide behind.

If I could only get it absolutely right, I felt certain she would warm to me, and lift the oppressive gloom I had carried in my breast ever since the day I'd met her husband. It would prove to her—and to me—that I was a good servant, that I was on her side.

My hands trembled as I measured out her medication that morning. Her ailment was still a mystery to me, but the tonic for it I knew very well by then. The smell of it came up sharp, like a rap across my face.

I stirred the Epsom salts into her bath as usual, and when she was settled in the tub, I left her quarters. I hurried down the hall, took the servants' stairs all the way to the bottom of the house, and crossed the busy kitchen to Mrs. Davies's office.

The finished product was neatly folded on my chair, and I mastered the urge to shift it onto the form again for one last look. In my nervous state, I would never be satisfied. It was Mrs. Bornholdt's satisfaction that mattered anyway. If only I'd handed the dress over more quickly, there might have been time to fix anything that was not to her liking. As it was, she would have to suffer with it, and so would I.

Upon my reentry into the dressing room, she rose from her vanity—but when she saw the dress in my arms, she gasped. "Green?"

"Yes, ma'am," I said, startled by the sharpness of her voice.

"You have seen there is no green at all in my wardrobe, have you not?"

"Yes, ma'am, I—"

"And did you not think there was a reason?"

I cringed. "I thought you'd never tried it, ma'am."

"The year of my debut, my mother took me to a seamstress in London," she said, drawing herself up, "who told me I must never wear green. It is all wrong for my complexion. I should wear purple, or else warm tones such as orange or red."

I bit my tongue and tried to think what to say. I had no doubt that in the year of her debut, Mrs. Bornholdt had glowed golden. Her seamstress would have been right, at the time, to warn her against cool colors, for they would have robbed her of her riches. Purple, as gold's direct complement, would have been the only exception; indeed, it would have been the ideal. But somewhere along the way, she had gotten sick, and everything in her look had changed—except her wardrobe.

What I'd learned from Mrs. Martin was this: when a true shade of some color is in evidence in what one wears, it takes the suggestion of that same shade away from the skin because, by comparison, the true color of the accoutrement is more real. Opposing the shade only makes it more offensive; we must adopt some aspect of that natural feature we dislike in order to erase it. So I'd ordered a bright sage-green fabric—saturated enough to steal the sick tinge from Mrs. Bornholdt's cheek, but not so rich as to draw undue attention to her paleness.

I took a deep breath. "It is only a bit green. You might—"

But her features grew harder the more I spoke, as if I were devolving before her eyes from a human being to a bug that might need crushing.

I reached out. "If you don't like to try it on, ma'am, I'll take it away at once."

But she drew it back toward her. "One of you sewing women is much mistaken in her trade, and I would like to know which one of you it is. If it is you, Marian, you will learn better with some proof."

"Yes, ma'am."

"I will try it on to teach you only, and then you will dress me in something else."

"Yes, ma'am."

I helped Mrs. Bornholdt into the dress and did the lacing at the back, my fingers trembling. She examined herself in the glass of her vanity. Our eyes met in the mirror.

A knock at the bedroom door.

"Mrs. Bornholdt, ma'am?" It was Ledford. "Mrs. Malahide has arrived."

Mrs. Bornholdt shut her eyes and sighed. "Show her into the parlor," she called.

"Yes, madam."

We waited, both of us standing still, for the butler's footsteps to pass on. When some seconds had gone by and Mrs. Bornholdt still had not spoken, I offered: "Shall I help you back out of it, ma'am?"

"There is no time," she snapped, still addressing me in the mirror. "You will accompany me to the parlor, Marian, so I may tell my cousin why I am wearing this—certainly not because it was any idea of mine."

"Yes, ma'am." My gaze fell, to the jars on her vanity. Like all her trinkets, these were overgrown with lovely painted flowers. The lid of the one with her face powder had a golden cherub on it, blowing a kiss. Under the circumstances, it seemed to me a mocking gesture—as if the cherub, intimating my imminent dismissal from Valor Rise, were sending me smugly off.

I followed Mrs. Bornholdt out of her apartment, wordlessly parting from her in the hall so as to take the servants' stairs. We met again outside the parlor, where Mrs. Bornholdt lowered her shoulders and took a resigned sniff before opening the door.

"Diana!" cried the cousin within, getting to her feet. She was a brunette in a berry-red dress. "Goodness, what has happened to you?"

Mrs. Bornholdt allowed herself to be embraced. "It is the dress," she said. "A new dress, only . . . a bright idea of my new lady's maid."

"You are not on some new medication?" The cousin stepped back to take Mrs. Bornholdt in. "Or again with—"

"No," Mrs. Bornholdt said, loudly. "Not at all."

The cousin's smile was full of triumph. "So time alone has done it! Time and the right remedy."

"What? What are you talking about?" Mrs. Bornholdt shifted her scowl from me to her cousin.

"You are looking ever so much better!" she said. "I never could have said it when you were so poorly, but now that you are hardier, I must confess how worried I was. You were green last I saw you."

"Green?" Brow furrowed, Mrs. Bornholdt lifted a hand to touch her cheek, narrowing her eyes at the sleeve of the dress. "Green. Was I?"

"Oh, forgive me." The cousin's excitement gave way at last to a more sober, careful attitude. "I do not say it to make you self-conscious. It does not matter. It is behind you!"

"You must know better than I. I see myself every day, and so I would not notice any change . . ." Mrs. Bornholdt looked around. "Marian, did you . . ."

I stepped closer. "Yes, ma'am?"

"Did you . . ." She squinted at me as if my face were new to her. "Did you prepare a picnic basket?"

"Yes, ma'am. Shall I fetch it for you?"

Her eyes searched mine. Then she nodded. "Do that."

I curtsied and backed out of the room. Some minutes later, I sent a delighted Mrs. Bornholdt and her cousin off together with their basket. I went to a window facing the grounds to watch them cross the grounds. I was still standing there, basking in my victory, grinning in the sunlight, when someone said my name.

I jumped.

"I'm sorry," Ledford said.

I stepped away. "No, there are a thousand things I should be doing."

"I wasn't coming to scold you." He held out his hand. "There is a letter for you."

I wondered, if Ledford was not angry, why his face should be so dark. I supposed later that the postboy must have told him it was urgent; he was of advanced age and must have known, as I would come to learn, that urgent news was usually unpleasant.

The first time I read the letter through, I could not understand it. But it was a short thing, comprised of simple words. The second time through, I read aloud in a whisper to myself, the butler having gone away: "Your mother is sick. Come quickly to say goodbye."

I put the letter down and stared at it. I contemplated not the words but the fact of the paper, sitting on the windowsill in front of me. A moment before, it had not been there. The butler had brought it in to me, placed it in my hand, and now—here it was.

I, too, had been placed in this house, in this room. I had come from elsewhere. From London. And to London from the country. And to the country from her. From Mother.

I turned away from the window, touching my fingers to my face. I couldn't have said it then, but I was feeling for lines, for pulls in the fabric of my features.

I was young and well. *In bloom*—that's what they said of youthfulness. But what of my roots, buried lower down, out of sight and in the dirt?

I turned again, peering out the window. There was no sign of Mrs. Bornholdt or her visiting cousin. I could have run across the grounds to find them—but that would take time. And I knew the exact whereabouts of an even higher authority.

I rushed upstairs, outrunning my misgivings, stopping only when I reached the study door. I knocked, but the door was so thick and my hand so timid that I hardly made a sound. There was nothing from within. I knocked again, harder, and flushed at the rudeness of the noise.

"Yes?" Mr. Bornholdt's voice was even, a neutral tone, meaning nobody any harm and carrying no threat. I took a deep breath before I turned the doorknob and slipped inside.

He sat between his portrait and me, looking up from whatever work he did at his impressive desk. There was no fire lit in the grate—indeed, there were none lit in the whole house today—and the blue of the sky in his window promised that soon it would be summer. The room was airy, inviting, but I hesitated on the threshold.

"Ah, Marian." He waved me forward. "You may come in. But shut the door."

I frowned. But to protest would have taken time I did not have. I did as I was told.

"I'm sorry to interrupt you, sir." I crossed the carpet to him. "I would not have intruded but for something important."

"Yes." He folded his hands on his blotter, and lifted his head. "You stay far out of my way."

I set my gaze low, on his papers. "A good servant is seldom seen. Mrs. Davies reminds me often."

"That is so, when you have a face like Mrs. Davies's."

I felt myself go red, and my eyes darted up to his. A smile was spreading across his mouth, and I resented both of us—him for making the joke, and me for reacting to it.

I clenched my fists below the desktop. "Sir, I beg that you might give me leave."

"Some business that cannot wait until Sunday?" He leaned back in his chair, running his finger along his bottom lip. "I shall have to know what it is."

"Yes, sir." I clasped my hands behind my back—as if by adopting the pose for recitation, I might get some personal distance from the words I had to say. "I've gotten a letter from the workhouse. My mother is dying—"

But the last word cut me, and feeling bled into my face.

Mr. Bornholdt rose from his chair, came around the desk, and pulled me to his chest. "You are all right," he whispered, his lips in my hair, but he was wrong—every part of me revolted at the awful pressure of his body, the hardness of him. My stomach churned, threatening, and I thought I would be sick.

"Sir." I pressed my palm between us. "May I go?"

"Is that in question?" he asked me. "Do you think me a monster?"

I opened my mouth, then shut it.

"You shall take my coach." As he spoke, he crossed the study with long, purposeful strides. "You go to your room and pack your things. Wait for the footman. I will send him for your case."

He opened the door. He held it for me.

"Sir." I stood frozen in the middle of his room, while he hovered at the door—waiting to let me pass. My memories did not match up with this man.

"No time to waste," he said.

I took a breath and held it as I passed him. But he did not grab me.

Beyond the doorway, I looked back at him, wondering. Such noble features in a face filled with concern. Perhaps it had been a moment of madness that overtook him in his study, weeks before. Perhaps the only malicious entity, between the two of us, was me.

"You look guilty," he said. And then: "You are still thinking of that kick you gave me."

His hand came up to touch my cheek. My heart quickened, and a rush of feeling to my legs encouraged me to flee.

"I have quite forgotten it." He caressed my skin with his thumb, as if to show me where I'd struck him. "Sensitive there, is it not?"

"Yes, sir," I said, my gaze falling to his shoes.

"Would you be better able to accept my help if I allowed you to apologize?" Not waiting for my answer, he bowed forward and proffered the cheek I'd struck. No longer bruised, it was perfect and proud, as in his portrait. "I shall take a kiss just there," he said, touching the spot.

Time was flying, so I rose on tiptoe and put my mouth to his cheek.

At once his hand went to the back of my head, holding me in place. He pressed me against the arch of the doorway, and the wood dug into my back. His head turned, and our lips grazed. His mouth caught on mine, his lips pressing. I tried to move away. I couldn't. He pushed with his tongue, and my mouth gave way around it like melted wax beneath a stamp. The seal made, he drew back, holding my cheeks as in a vise.

"There," he said. "You are absolved."

It was awful, as a thinking, feeling being, to have one's obvious discomfort blatantly ignored by another. It made my bones ache, as if the very air in that room pressed me toward the floor. But this was not the battlefield on which I had been called to fight, and I made myself remember: the letter, my mother. London.

"Thank you, sir."

"When you return, I hope we will be less cool with one another," he said. "I can be kinder to you. Can you be kinder to me?"

"Yes, sir."

It was a long moment before he let me go.

I took a tentative step, not knowing whether my legs were fit for walking on. Then I was running down the corridor, but I could still feel his hands on my face, his mouth over mine.

"Oh, and Marian?" he called.

I froze, cringing. "Sir?"

"Godspeed."

6

For the length of the ride, I sat ready to leap to my feet, clutching the coin purse I'd tied at my throat, a case borrowed from Mrs. Davies beside me. I leaned forward in the coach, as if this would move me faster into the future. I did not mind the bumps in the road. Indeed, I wished the driver would be bolder. I could take it. I dreaded not making it in time.

I kept thinking of Mother in her uniform, alone—trapped in the workhouse, cold and ill—and pretending in her letters that she was fine. It was the same false strength she'd shown the morning after we'd been brought to Parish Street, when I was a child.

"I don't want to be apart again," I'd said, when the matron called that it was time to go to work.

"You're still in my good graces, aren't you?" she'd asked me. She'd hugged me, as if I were a precious thing. And when I nodded, she pulled back from our embrace. She gripped my shoulders, and with a warm ferocity, like fire has, she said: "Then my spell still holds—remember? Never you fear. You might not see me, love, but I will be with you."

But who was with her now, when she needed someone? I should have stayed.

"Wait for me, Mother," I murmured, my breath fogging the window of the coach.

It was dark when we stopped outside the workhouse, and I was in the street before the coachman could come down from his own perch to help. He called to me as I climbed the steps, but I never slowed. To return here was like diving into an icy river: I had to do it quickly or I could not do it at all.

A man took me past the iron gates, just like when I was a child, through a doorway dark and sour-smelling as an open mouth. This was the room where prospective inmates were held prior to admission. It was even smaller than I remembered, but just as damp and chill, and we were packed so close together that the cheap, shoddy fabric the paupers wore rubbed against my arms anytime they made a move.

It was maddening to have to wait there for the matron when I knew my way. Mother and I had been ripped from one another, once, in this room. She'd been swallowed up in a current going one way, with the other women, and I'd been pulled in another, by a woman in a black wool dress: Mrs. Martin.

I had wanted to shout out to my mother, then, and I wanted the same thing now. But she couldn't know how close I was, and so I was not close enough. I would not be calm until she could see me, and I her.

"God, you were fast."

I looked around to find the matron rushing toward me, as if out of the past. I rose before she reached me, and she turned to lead me out. Across the cobbles, into the main building, up a staircase, and down a long hallway. Only at the door to the women's sick ward did she stop. "Prepare yourself," she said.

I smoothed my expression, straightened my back. "I'm ready."

Grim faced, she turned the handle. The smell hit me at once: urine, stale and acidic, with something else underneath—something that made me think of being a child, smelling the roses my father liked to bring my mother on her birthday. I had always disliked their scent, had tried to explain to my mother that, even at first bloom, I could smell that they were dying. Beneath roses' perfume, light and dewy at some times and velvet-thick at others, there was always some part of the earth in them that stank—quietly, waiting its turn. It was at the back of the smell, but sooner or later I knew it would come forward, consuming the flower.

And there in the ward, I smelled people, the part of the earth in them—their sweat and the musk of their skin—like the roses, decomposing. It was indecent: human society gathered together, dressed down. The underneath of them all, stripped bare of everything hearty and strong. How had my nose missed this note of decay, as present in people as in flowers? How had I ever taken comfort in an embrace as if it were any more permanent?

I waded into the thick stew of smells, squinting in the dark. The candles burned low and were set sparsely apart, leaving most bedsides in deep shadow. The bed against the bit of wall nearest me was the only one I could make out clearly, and the woman in it must have been sick for a long time. She was thinner than I knew a person could be. I went by her as quickly as I could.

"Marian," the matron said, standing by the thin woman's bed. "She's here."

"No," I breathed, hurrying back. I looked for my mother in the woman's face, so gaunt and gray. I didn't recognize her until she opened her eyes. There was love in them.

"Marian?" she asked, in a voice wrung dry—a brittle, hollow shell of the sound in my memory. "Did you say Marian?"

I got on my knees and found her hand. "Mother, I didn't know you."

She turned her head, tried but couldn't lift it. "Oh." She laughed. "I didn't know you, either." The laugh turned into a cough, which made her cry. The tears ran down her face and I wiped them.

"You're all right," she said with some wonder.

"Of course I'm all right. But you—Mother, you didn't tell me."

Her eyes dropped from mine, as if she were a child. "I didn't want to worry you."

"But I should have worried!" I squeezed her hand tight, and when this was not enough to vent my feelings, I brought her knuckles to my lips. "How long has it been like this?"

"Almost a month," Mrs. Martin said, beside me.

I turned my head. "You might've let on."

"It was important to her that I should not." Her tone was even, though she drew a step back. "The doctor told us it was irreversible, but she said you wouldn't believe it. That you would pay to buy more time when there was none."

I hid my face from both of them, holding my head as if it ached me. There was nothing I could do to stop the tears that came, but I was determined to shed them silently.

"Water?" Mother asked, after a time. "Is there water?"

I looked up. Mrs. Martin had gone. But there was a pitcher and glass on the table beside the bed. I poured some for her and helped her to drink. The working of her throat worsened her cough, so I had her sit up and lean forward. I rubbed her back and found the fabric of her gown—for it was a nightshirt, and not a uniform—was stuck with sweat to her skin. I could feel every bump in her spine.

"Does Father know you're unwell?" I asked, the words coming as they occurred to me.

Mother shook her head. And there was something smaller hidden within the gesture. She winced, as if the question gave her pain.

I went cold. But I waited, concentrating on the course of my palm over her back. I counted each completed circle, giving her five in which to speak.

"He's gone," she said.

I stopped rubbing.

I opened my mouth to ask her to repeat it—to ask how, and why. But her back was bent, and when I leaned to look at her face, I saw how hard her eyes were shut, as if she were afraid to be struck—or as if she already had been, and still suffered greatly from the blow.

I took a deep breath and held it. When I let it go, I told myself, I would let go of Father.

And, oh God, it was more awful for how easy it was to do. Time had disappeared so much of him already.

I wiped my eyes and recommenced the massage. "You've been alone."

Mother sniffed. "So have you."

And all at once I had a feeling that, because she was my mother, I had no secrets from her—and Mr. Bornholdt was between us. Mr. Bornholdt and his claustrophobic kiss.

"Saw your Valentine."

I jerked to attention. "What?"

"Valentine," she said, enunciating. "The lad. I saw him yesterday."

I put my hand to my mouth, the corners of which dragged down. I forced myself to speak calmly. "That was many years ago, Mother. Valentine's a man now; he's not here anymore."

"He is," she said, raising her voice, startling me. "He came down from the attic. He asked after you to the matron."

"Mother—"

"He had flowers. Purple hyacinths, he had. Good enough to eat." She reached out and clutched my hand, and her grip was shocking in its strength. "But you mustn't, Marian. Don't eat them. He was insistent upon that."

I bit my lip. But I held her close to me, saying nothing. It didn't matter if she was going mad. The important thing was that she was here, and so was I. We were together.

Mother put her chin over my shoulder. "Will you go off with him? Once I'm gone?"

"Don't talk so, Mother." I patted her back. "You're not rushing off anywhere."

"But when I go." There was an anxious note in her voice—thin, and close to breaking, and again I thought she was like a child. "He's waiting for you, Marian. Marian?"

"I heard you, Mother," I said, too sharp—and I took hold of her hands, to take the sting away. I let out my breath slowly. To soothe her, I stroked her knuckles with my thumbs. "But don't leave yet; he can wait."

She leaned back into the bed, and her eyes were clear. "I need to rest, Marian. But he'll take care of you."

"Yes, rest." And when still she lay watchful on her pillow, I leaned over to kiss her cheek. It was cool, like something warmed only from the outside—a stone in weak sun. "Close your eyes, Mother. It's all right."

"Will you stay with me?" she asked.

"Yes, of course," I said, and patted her hand. "I'm here."

"And when I go, you'll have Valentine." She shut her eyes. Her face relaxed. She couldn't know how little comfort her vision brought me, indeed how discomfiting it was. But that was my fault, because I had never told her what I'd felt, what we did—Valentine and me, alone. She never even knew we'd met until after he was already gone.

◆ ◆ ◆

Valentine and I had been abducted to Parish Street on the very same night.

Separated from Mother, I was brought with all the other children across the wet compound and into the main building. In a line, we went one by one before a man who asked our names and put them down in his book. Then we were marched by Mrs. Martin down a drafty corridor, toward the smell of damp. When I turned into the room she indicated for us, I stepped in murky water that lingered around my feet.

It was a bathing room, relentlessly gray: the walls, the floor, the shallow tub—even the women at the head of the line were in uniforms of gray. With gray buckets they doused a little girl who stood naked and shivering in the tub, each splash echoing off the floor tile. I averted my eyes, mortified for her.

"I live in Sultan Street, Camberwell!" a boy cried, his voice high but hard, like the metal tongue of a bell clanging. His tangled hair was brassy, and there was a brickish hardness to his eyes—even down to the tint of them. He was no less a stranger than all the other children, but I felt a kinship with him. On his person I saw evidence of all the tortures I had lately suffered. He was in a red-striped nightshirt, with a twisted collar, so he must have been brought from his bed. The rash of filth across his cheeks suggested he'd fallen in the road as he'd fled with his parents. Or else a policeman had pushed him.

"The row house with a chipped blue door," he said. "I'm innocent, an' I demand to be taken home directly!"

But the women at the front of the line weren't listening. They were workhouse inmates, in those uniforms that would become so familiar to me—Property Of Parish Street Workhouse at the front, Stop, Thief! at the back, in case any pauper ever decided to abscond in clothes that didn't belong to them.

"I'm innocent!" the boy cried again, for none of the washing-women had even glanced his way. "It's my parents what did wrong, an' I demand to be taken to Sultan Street, Camberwell!"

Mrs. Martin stalked to the end of the line and bent low to look at him. "If you don't behave yourself," she said, her lips hardly moving, "you'll not see your mother at all tomorrow."

"Good!" was his red-faced reply. "I don' want to see her! I hate her!"

I cringed. The woman reared back, nostrils flared, and called for a Mr. Martin. Then a man came, slow and menacing as a storybook giant, his dark head bent—the man who had taken Mother. He delivered a hard, impersonal blow to the boy's head. That made the boy cry, but the crying he did silently. He let himself be put into the tub.

I would not see him again that night, for the girls were separated from the boys. We were taken to an attic where, under a deeply slanted roof, others already slept. They lay right on the floor, on gathered piles of straw, with only their hands for pillows. Their patched-up blankets made them look like calico cats, each one curled up beside her own chamber pot instead of a hearth. My body did not recognize my pile of straw as a bed. I whimpered into my balled hands, hating the hardness of the floor and the chill of the draft.

The next morning, Mrs. Martin led us downstairs to a dining hall for breakfast. I scanned half a dozen long tables for Mother, but she wasn't there. In fact, there were no adults in this room—only the boys, scattered along the benches. Our line of girls went between the tables, and when it came my turn at the top of the room, a woman in uniform thrust a tin into my hands. There was something bready in it, covered in brown sludge and smelling of smoke.

Suet pudding. I would become very familiar with it.

I spotted the boy from Sultan Street, Camberwell. He was on the end of his bench, and he had an empty place across from him. His head was bent, like he was sad or lonely. I glanced right. Mrs. Martin stood atop a box to make her taller, watchful of all the tables. But, looking out again, I saw girls who'd gone before me sitting near boys, and she'd not interfered with them. I slid onto the bench opposite him.

I worried he'd mind my being there—one of the neighbor boys back home hadn't wanted to be seen talking to a girl, at first—but this boy didn't even notice me. He only went on scraping the sides of his tin with his spoon, evidently trying to gather together enough gravy to make a mouthful. I considered making a start on my own breakfast, but another sniff made me push it aside.

"How's your head?" I asked.

He jumped, his eyes flying to mine. Then his free hand touched his hair—not where he'd been struck, but at the nape, like a man who has been sweating at his work. "Oh, still attached."

"But I'm sure it smarts," I said.

He shrugged. "Sometimes. Other times it dafts."

I squinted, and the corners of his mouth twitched. I had to repeat his words to myself in my head—then I laughed. I had not expected him to be funny.

"But really," he said, forcing his lips into a flat line, "I shouldn' have yelled at the matron yesterday. That was wrong."

"Anyone would have been upset," I assured him. "We all were; you only showed it."

He shrugged again, but there was a lightness to his shoulders that seemed friendly.

"I'm Marian Osley," I said.

"Valentine Hobbs," he replied, as if he were glad to give me his name—not like the neighbor boy at all.

I leaned forward. "I can't believe that man hit you. When we see our mothers, you should tell yours."

I had expected he would be happy to hear me take his side. Instead, his whole face set into something harder, like cement drying all in a moment. "I'll not tell her anything," he said. "I'm not speaking to her."

I tilted my head. "Why?"

"Because she's a terrible person."

I drew back. "That's not nice to say about your mother."

He snorted, regarding his empty suet tin. "Maybe not, but it's true. True o' my father, too. An' your parents."

I scowled. "You don't know that."

He looked up. "They're here, aren't they, our mothers? An' our fathers are in prison. What for, do you think?"

"My mother says it's a mistake," I said. "The landlord's just angry, and when he calms down, Father will make him see that we don't deserve to be punished, and we'll get to come home."

"An' you believe that?"

My eyes flew to his. "She wasn't lying."

"I s'pose that's possible," he said. "Maybe bein' here isn't a surprise to you. Maybe they told you all about whatever they were doin' wrong. But mine didn' tell me. An' that makes them liars, as well as criminals."

"Adults do keep things back from children," I said. "They know the things we aren't meant to know yet. That doesn't make them liars."

He tilted his head, considering me. "You're a good child, I s'pose?"

He'd said the words so sneeringly, I braced for a fight. "Yes."

But he said: "Me too—or I try. And when I do wrong—by accident, or in a fit—I know it, an' I run off to hide. An' last night, my parents ran from the law the same way I've run from them."

In my mind's eye I saw my mother, after the knock of the policeman. Her wide-eyed stillness. She had, indeed, run away. She'd taken me with her.

Valentine lifted his chin, sagely, as if he could read my mind. "I thought I was bein' trained toward goodness, not away from it. Didn' you?"

"But . . . I *am* a good child, really."

He raised his brows. "So says thieves. Or whatever your parents are. My father is a thief. He even hit the shopkeep who tried to stop him stealin'."

I licked my lips. "Just because they—I mean, *if* they did wrong, if they were bad, it doesn't mean *I'm* bad."

"It might, though," he said somberly. "As it's from them you got the measure of righ' an' wrong, how would you know?"

I flinched from this idea, and studied my untouched tin of suet. The smoke smell had gone, and so—to relieve the pressure to talk—I stuck my spoon in, dredged up a trembling, gravy-coated something, and shoved it in my mouth. It was cold and wriggled like a jelly, but it seemed to have been seasoned with soot. I gagged, my wide eyes finding Valentine in my panic.

"Swallow," he said, gesturing for calm with his open hand. "Just swallow, quick."

Against the urging of my mind and throat, I did. “God!” I got out, hurling the word at him.

“You have to eat it quickly,” he said. “Like I did.”

I stared, eyes watering. “I thought you must’ve been enjoying it.”

“Never.” His lips twisted. “I’m just used to it.”

Poor thing, I wanted to say, but that felt silly; no matter how hard his old life had been, his new life was exactly as awful as mine. I employed what tact I possessed to probe him further. I learned he was eleven—a year older than I—and that he had no siblings, either. But he was from the city, not the country. His father did dock work, before, and his mother had been in a factory. Between her long hours and his sneaking off to drink, Valentine hardly saw them, he said.

At first I wondered at how easily he could say the words—as if they didn’t hurt, as if he didn’t care for his parents at all. But the silence afterward seemed to wear on him, his spirit seeping from his face, leaving his features slack.

I joined my hands upon the table. “How do we tell what goodness is?” I asked. “If it’s not our parents?”

The question roused him, as I’d hoped. Blinking, he said, “Look to the people they were runnin’ from, I think.”

I narrowed my eyes. “The men who put me in their wagon to come here, you mean. Who dragged my mother by the neck, like a dog.”

“The policemen who upheld the law,” he said, spacing out the words. “Yes.”

I crossed my arms. “Even if you’re right, they’re not here.”

“No,” he agreed. “But they wouldn’ have left us in the care o’ bad people, would they? If the police are on the side of right, then the master of the workhouse must be good. They mean to make us attend church here, you know. My parents never took me to church.”

I frowned. I had gone to my grandfather’s funeral, but it was too far to walk to church regularly, and we needed the daylight hours to work in. “My father says God is everywhere—in the rain and the air and the earth," I offered. "He says the Greeks knew that, even if the English forgot; he told me how the priestess at Delphi breathed the steam coming up from between the rocks and spoke in God's voice."

Valentine rolled his eyes.

"But the master can't be good," I cried, smacking the table. "He hit you!"

Valentine's gaze dropped. "I deserved to be hit. I was disturbin' the peace. Behavin' like the spawn of a scoundrel—which I am. I've got to be better now. Act better. Speak better."

I leaned forward, trying to catch his eye. "Did the master call you that? 'Spawn of a scoundrel'?"

He nodded, still staring at the tabletop.

I brought my hand up, but I wasn't brave enough to touch him. "Well. Suppose he said that just to make you believe it. It costs him nothing to lie, you know, because he doesn't love you."

Valentine raised his eyebrows.

"I think it's the other way," he said. "The people who don' love you are the ones who tell you the truth."

◆ ◆ ◆

The words seemed to float across the years to me, sitting in the sick ward beside my mother. I'd been so certain Valentine was wrong at the time, but he'd been right: I'd kept so many things from Mother, and she'd kept her illness from me.

When I was sure she slept, I left her. I stood, uncertain, outside the ward—I didn't know how long—with nowhere to go, and nothing to do but fiddle with the money in my coin purse.

The echo of the matron's steps preceded her. She rounded the corner and saw me. "Gone to sleep?" Her hand was cupped around the flame of her candle, so the breeze she created as she moved did not snuff it out.

"Yes." My mouth was dry.

"Come on. I've made a room up for you."

I followed in her wake, though I knew the way myself. I didn't want her to see my face when I asked, quick, before I couldn't: "Mrs. Martin, do you remember a boy called Valentine Hobbs?"

"The scoundrel named for a saint," she said, immediately. "Did his best to corrupt you, he did."

Through a sudden shortness of breath, and a pressure in my ears, I made myself laugh. "That's the one. Has he . . . been back here?"

"No," she said, blandly. "Haven't seen him since he was hired out."

"Oh. Only, my mother said . . ."

But I couldn't bear to finish, and Mrs. Martin didn't prompt me to.

I expected her to take me to the women's ward, where I'd lived the latter part of my time at Parish Street, but she led me upstairs, where there were individual cells. She unlocked one, and I found it made up like a bedroom for one person.

I turned, surprised, a thank-you on my lips, but Mrs. Martin spoke before I could. "Get what rest you can," she said, setting the candle on a bedside table. "You'll need strength in the coming days."

I did not know how to answer this. She nodded as if she understood my silence, withdrew, and shut me in.

But I lay awake instead of sleeping, thinking of Mother. Mother smiling, Mother casting that pretend spell for my father and me. When had she begun to die? The night of the arrest, of coming here?

You're still in my good graces, aren't you?

Then my spell still holds . . . Never you fear.

All her prepossession, her light and her life, her power—reduced to nearly nothing. A flicker, like that of the candle hardly lighting this dingy room.

If there ever had been a spell, it was broken. And maybe I had broken it, and she just never knew. She had no idea I'd stopped believing in her magic and put my faith in Valentine instead.

7

The boys were kept on opposite ends of the workhouse for lessons and work, under the master's eye. But one dinnertime some three weeks after our first meeting, I happened to pass right by the bench where Valentine sat. He tried to smile at me, but it only made him look sick, as if he were holding back bile.

I set my tin of meat pie down, and slid onto the seat across from him. "What's wrong?"

"Had to see my mother today."

I frowned. "What? I didn't." All the other oakum pickers were young girls like me, and we'd all been at work this afternoon. It seemed terribly unfair that we should have been left out.

"It was only me that went," he said. "I guess the matron thought I'd be upset. Pitch another fit." He sneered and cast his eyes to the ceiling—and it was like last time, when he had made a joke of his own feelings. He was so determined to see badness in himself that he seemed to miss it in his surroundings. I felt protective of him again.

I poked my meat pie with a fork. "What did she have to tell you, your mother?"

"My father had his case heard," he muttered, tracing a whorl in the table. "They've put him away for two years. For injurin' the shop owner."

I studied him in silence, for what I wanted to say—that I was sorry, that it was awful—I thought he would not like. I settled on stating simple fact. "You won't see him for some time, then."

He shook my words off like a touch. "It doesn't matter. I don't want to be his son anymore. I don't care if I never see him again."

I hesitated. I could see his method, teaching himself to dislike the thing that was denied him, but I could not have done it. Misrepresenting my father to myself, forgetting him with all the rest of the world—I was sure he would have felt it, wherever he was, as a physical pain.

Like a bad spell.

And, anyway, what else of value did I have in this miserable place, other than my memories? Thinking to give Valentine some piece of his past as a talisman, I asked: "Wasn't your father good at all?"

Valentine scowled. "I've told you he wasn't."

"I know he stole. But was he a good father to you?"

"It doesn't matter if he was. He isn't now."

I gripped the table edge. "How can you say that? He isn't here."

"Exactly." He stabbed the crust of his meat pie, and then he did it again. "I might as well be the master's son, not his."

I shook my head. "The way you talk, you might as well be a police officer's son."

I smiled, to coax him to smile back, but his shoulders stayed humped, his eyes dull. Maybe he didn't believe in the idea.

Maybe I could help.

I leaned my body far over into his field of vision, putting my cheek in my hand and my elbow on the table. "Well, you'd better look sharp," I said, drawing my brows together.

He tilted his head. "Why?"

I glanced behind me, measuring the distance between my seat and the dining hall doors, which were propped open. There was one table in between, which would afford me some cover. If I made it into the corridor, there probably wouldn't be anyone to catch us. It wasn't a long distance. I could do it. But would it be worth it? I considered my dinner. Even if Valentine didn't give chase, the idea of not eating was less a sacrifice than a reprieve.

"Because I'm the spawn of a scoundrel," I said, turning back to him. "And I've got to be brought to justice by somebody before I escape."

His eyes were keen now, curious—but I looked past him at Mrs. Martin, standing on her box. She cast her gaze as a wide net over the sea of heads, staring from one end of the hall to the other. When her face turned far enough that I could see her profile, I slipped under the table, pivoted, and crawled out from under the bench.

Crouched low to rotten floorboards, I made my way down the table, taking care that my shoes clattered less than the metal spoons and dishes in use around me. And as dangerous as it was to laugh, I couldn't help it—for neither the matron nor any of the children eating were roused by my odd behavior. Slowing, I looked over my shoulder, fully expecting to see Valentine still in his seat, staring after me as if I were silly.

But he was following me.

My stomach jumped, and I tripped over my own feet, but I stayed upright and kept what lead I had. Ducking low, I darted out of the dining hall, certain I would be stopped. But no one hailed me, and my feet took me toward the oakum-picking room. When the door was in sight, I felt sure it would be locked, but it gave when I turned the handle. I slipped inside, keeping to the wedge of light I'd let in.

"Got you now," Valentine said—and daring to raise his voice a modicum: "Stop right there!"

I reached the end of the room and turned. "Who's going to make me?"

"Officer Hobbs," he declared, with weight. He stood in the light of the corridor, so all I could see as he approached was a dark shadow in the shape of him.

I went to meet him halfway, taking my time. I needed to figure out what to say next.

"Oh, you're police, are you?" I asked. "And how do I know you're not some ruffian who means me harm, just pretending?"

He stopped, and I heard him swallow. I looked left and right, as if for a way out, to give him a moment to think—but still he seemed lost.

"You have a badge, I expect," I prompted.

"Of course I do," he said, vehemently. I couldn't help but smile, and a smile sneaked out onto his face, too—then he stuffed it away. "But I don't need to show it to you. I give the orders an' you take them."

I raised my chin. "That's if you're really what you say you are."

"I am," he said. "Look at my uniform."

I pretended to appraise him, leaning right and left, though I could see nothing but his silhouette. Still, my attention made him stand straighter and hold his head differently. It wasn't hard to imagine him in brass buttons and sharp-creased trousers.

"You do look the part," I said. "But suppose you stole that uniform."

He stood still a moment, then strode over to the workbench—very near to where I'd sat earlier. He picked up a length of rope and turned back to me. "Look. This is official police rope."

I put my hands on my hips. "You might have stolen that, too. Perhaps you used some of it on the officer who is now missing his uniform, so he can't tell on you."

Valentine tugged his shirt, so all the wrinkles disappeared. "I'm not a thief like you!"

"Oh." I crossed my arms, feigning offense. "I'm a thief, am I?"

"Yes! I have . . . testimony," he said, plucking the word from somewhere. "Testimony from a shopkeeper who says you stole from him, an' he's all bloodied up besides!"

So this wasn't just any arrest. This was what he'd heard said to his parents, or something like it. I bit my lip. Perhaps the game had been a bad idea.

But Valentine turned his head, so the light from the hall fell across the hill of his cheek, and I saw the side of his mouth curl. "You're a criminal," he said. "An' you deserve to be locked away forever."

I stepped back as he advanced. "But . . . but maybe I don't deserve it."

"Oh yeah? So you didn' commit a crime?"

"I did, but—"

"Aha! That's all I needed to hear." He snatched at my hands. "Now keep still so as I can bind you, you . . . scoundrel."

"Wait." I wriggled in his grip as he pulled my hands behind me. "You only know I did wrong. You don't know why!"

"It doesn' matter why."

"What if—what if I stole for love?"

The rope, which had begun to twist about my wrists, stilled. "What do you mean?"

I licked my lips. "What if I had a child to feed, and . . . not enough money to live on?"

The rope moved again, winding up the widening wishbone of my arms. "You need a job then, don' you?"

"Suppose I had one, and didn't make enough at it," I said, thinking of my father—of the pheasants at the wheat. I stared into the darkness, Valentine's grip on my wrists the only thing grounding me. "Is a person bad if they were trying to be good and failed?"

"You weren't tryin' to be good," he spat, the rope winding tight behind me. "You used him, that child what you claim to care for. Had him stand in the street outside that shop, an' told him to shout if anyone was comin'. In case someone tried to snatch him, you said, but it was you who'd be snatched—you!"

I cringed.

"You made a criminal out o' him, too," he said, in his own voice—which was strangled, as if the rope were around his neck instead of my arms.

I blinked into the darkness, which seemed to shift before my eyes, like blood pooling. I had been so sure I was right about my own parents; I'd never stopped to think he might have been right about his, too. "I'm sorry," I said.

"Sure you are, now you're caught," he said, gruffly. "Does that fix it? You want me to just forget what you've done? Hang the law an' let you go?"

"No," I said, and I did not have to fake my humility. "I deserve to serve my sentence."

The rope slackened just a little.

"And my son, he—he's strong, and wise," I added. "I misled him, and—and maybe he'll be better off."

I was trying to tell him he'd been right, but Valentine didn't rejoice. He held still behind me—as if he weren't even breathing. Looking over my shoulder, I saw his fallen features, and I realized: certain as he'd been, a part of him had hoped he was wrong.

"But," I declared, raising my voice, "if he can be a better person, maybe so can I. I can change, and earn my way out of here. I will do that! I swear I will."

His expression was still dark, and I thought I'd made another mistake. Then he smirked. "Time will out," he said. "For now, you're comin' with me."

He pulled me by the ropes, and as I tried to turn, I stumbled.

But I didn't fall. He caught me by the arm. With his other hand, he tugged the gathered rope again, drawing me up straight against his body, and I felt sturdier than if I had been standing on my own two feet.

We'd repeated our game over and over that year, whenever the matron's attention was divided. The performance itself, from my criminal's flight, to Valentine's apprehension and punishment of me, took only a quarter of an hour. But just as actors rehearse their plays for months, so were we always refining our scene. We listened to the words the adults around us used, tucking colorful phrases away for later. We mimicked poses—the master's bearing in his case, my mother's in mine—and critiqued each other, advising this or that change. I learned to hold skirts I did not have when I ran, and to use my sweeping arms to direct my feelings, gathering them up or spreading them around as the situation required. Valentine made a mask of his face, with eyes that looked scathingly down and a mouth that never smiled, which he could put over his real feelings in an instant.

Even his accent changed, his consonants coming clear and sharp—but that wasn't so much to do with our rehearsals as his education. The girls learned dictation and knitting only, whereas when he was not mending uniforms in the tailoring office, he took lessons with the boys in history, geography, arithmetic, and grammar.

Nature chimed in, too, making him taller and leaving me short.

Every time Valentine used words I didn't know, or when he had to bend down a bit to speak to me, I feared he would soon forget me in favor of older friends; yet week after week, he sought me out, to play a part that he could have recited for himself by heart. Apparently, I didn't need to be improved by either education or nature. He wanted me exactly as I was.

I never imagined that, one day when I was twelve, I would want something different from him.

The game began as usual. I bolted from the dining hall at breakfast, and Valentine crept after. The door to the women's work-yard stood open, as it sometimes did on nice mornings—the matron's doing, perhaps in the hopes that a fresh breeze would carry off some of the stink of the place.

In the echo of the empty corridor, I could hear Valentine's shoes slapping against the floor behind me. I glanced over my shoulder, eyes wide, but this was performance. The real purpose of my look was selfish, for I liked to see him this way—singularly absorbed in the chase.

Valentine had grown into something grander than he'd been. His torso had taken on a new, angular shape, and his legs were longer. His hair was not brass, but tarnished gold—and the hard brown of his eyes not like dull row-house brick anymore, but bright rust on a tall, forbidding gate.

I fled, and Valentine followed with his hands in fists. His brows were drawn close, his eyes glinting with the promise that I would be caught. My legs weakened under me as if to surrender at once to his will, but I managed one last burst of speed, through the door and into the daylight beyond.

The women's work-yard was walled in on all sides. This day happened to be a washing day, which meant the ladies of the workhouse had been outside before breakfast, scrubbing uniforms. Gray trousers, shirts, and stockings hung on lines, which were strung between four sickly trees—all of them planted in the center of the yard, so no weight-bearing branch could reach the walls. I ran between the clothes so as not to be seen from the master's lookout, a window smack in the middle of the second floor.

Whichever path I took around the washbasins, Valentine followed, getting closer with each second, until I could count how many I had left before he caught me. The thought made liquid of my legs again. A bird sang from a tree beyond the workhouse walls, and Valentine grabbed me by my wrist. His hand was firm and warm. He dragged me back to him, and a nervous chuckle escaped me.

"See this as a laughing matter, do you?" he demanded. He made his voice deep, like a man's, though he spoke only in a whisper. We knew how sound could carry when we didn't want it to. "You're all the same, you ruffians, no sense of wrongdoing at all."

"I laugh when I'm afraid, Officer," I said, with false coquetry but real breathlessness. "Your grabbing me like this is a terrible shock."

He narrowed his eyes. "A shock? Is it? What were you running from, if not me?"

I cast my gaze toward his ankles. "I was running from you."

"And what did you think I'd do when I'd got you?" He reeled me in closer. "Give you a kiss?"

I drew back from him. "No good man grabs a lady."

He stepped closer. "And no lady runs from the law. You're a thief. And a thief makes a bad parent. You've endangered your children with your irresponsible ways. You had no right to do that."

Our noses were nearly touching, and I could smell the sweat and the sun in his clothes. It wasn't like the smell of the girls, all together in the attic. I had the urge to lean in. But a thief would have done no such thing.

"You've broken the law," he said, his eyes locked on mine. "And lawbreakers must be punished."

He dragged me down the aisle created by the hanging clothes. He held my wrists tightly together, for he knew how hard I would fight to get away—and I did fight to get away, for I knew how tightly he would hold my wrists. If I doubted for a moment his ability to keep me there, I would have been docile as a dog.

He led me to the only washing bucket still steaming and, with a yank, brought me to my knees before it. Pebbles pressed into my shins, so I was aware of my legs—the shape of them, and that they were mine. That my life here was real, and not a dream.

Valentine thrust my hands over the steam and held them there.

I scrunched my eyes shut against pain that wasn't there. In fact, I liked the humid breath of the water. It dulled the chill edge of the air, and my muscles relaxed even as Valentine's fingers found stronger purchase on my wrist. In that moment of silence, sitting still and posed, I felt not like a lowly pauper but like the priestess at the center of some ancient rite. Like the oracle at Delphi. And Valentine's grasp was not hostile at all, but supportive of—even subservient to—my purpose.

"How does that feel?" he asked.

I threw my head back, pretending agony. "It hurts!"

"Imagine the hurt of having you for a mother," he spat, "and take what you've earned."

He let me writhe and toss my head a few seconds before his next line. "Why would you do this to your children?" he demanded, boring into me with hurt and angry eyes. "How could you?"

"It was for love!" I cried.

"Sure it was." But the doubt in his voice was different from the doubt in his eyes; the former was hard, the latter soft. "I've never heard that one before."

"But it was! I did it for the children!"

Valentine shook me by the wrists. "Get to the point before I lose my patience."

I twisted in his grasp, appealing with my eyes. "Yes, all right, I did wrong. But my children would have starved if I hadn't stolen for them, don't you see? Providence forced my hand."

"Yes, I see all right." Again there was a disparity between the cruel satisfaction in his voice and the sweet relief in his face. "Unfortunately, it's still your hand that did the crime, whatever the reason."

He marched me over to another bucket, one that did not steam, and pushed my shoulders down so I went again to my knees.

Our eyes met for a moment. His brows went up, and I nodded once.

He plunged my hands into the water. It was lukewarm, but I shuddered as if I were being burned, turning wide eyes to his.

"This is what you get," he said, speaking through his teeth. "You ruined their lives, and this is what you get."

His breath tickled my ear, and it was as if some part of me were being nudged awake. Stirring. I swallowed, wanting to follow the feeling. But Valentine was pulling me to my feet.

"I'm going to lock you up," he announced.

We were near a tree that punctuated the clothesline, and he backed me up against the trunk, holding my arms above my head. We were close again, and it was like being in the steam of the wash bucket. I drank the air down. He held me firm, and when I closed my eyes, I felt steady. It was not like being trapped, but like having a place in the world. I belonged here—with Valentine.

I opened my eyes to find us face-to-face, inches apart, his arms still raised, his hands holding mine. His shoulders rose and fell with his heavy breath—as if he'd been running. He blinked at me, and I blinked back, my eyelids slow and sleepy.

I wished something I'd never wished before.

Valentine licked his lips. "Marian?"

"You little scoundrels!"

Valentine released me so suddenly I had to grab the trunk behind me to keep from falling forward.

"Get over here this instant!" Mrs. Martin shouted, jabbing her finger at the ground. "Marian Osley, your knees are filthy. And as for you, boy, you're on the wrong side of the house entirely. The master may never feed you again when I tell him. How are you ever to better your situation if you are always at your worst?"

I hurried to her, hoping my eagerness to obey would lessen her anger, but as soon as I was within reach, she yanked me to her by the arm.

"Oi!" Valentine said, too loud, and rough-voiced as he used to be. "We were only playing!"

"Playing, yes," the matron said, "on the edge of evil."

She was shunting us apart, but Valentine turned round at this. "We're not evil!"

"That's what evil people say in their ignorance," Mrs. Martin replied, scowling. "I know what you were up to better than you do. Now get going, to your own side."

On the threshold of the main building, she shooed him to the right, and he went, though he looked back to check on me. I shrugged, which hurt the shoulder Mrs. Martin had grabbed. But I ignored it. I cared only that Valentine cared.

"And keep away from this girl!" Mrs. Martin called, as he turned the corner.

I rolled my eyes and let her march me away. She had seen two urchins playing and wanted to discipline them. She didn't know Valentine had all the discipline he needed inside him. She didn't understand: the game was about goodness.

She took me to the oakum-picking room. "Don't let me catch you out of place again," she said. She slammed the door when she left.

I sat in a space between two other girls, who seemed too intent on picking to say anything to me. I didn't mind. I was thinking about the wish I'd had.

I wasn't sure what I had wanted; the longing hadn't come in words. It had been as if the warmth in my stomach had recognized a similar heat in Valentine, and my muscles stretched to reach it. It was like the yearning to go home.

At once, I conjured up my parents' farmhouse: the sweet smell of the woodstove; the certainty in Mother's eyes as she posed to cast her spell; the welcome weight of my father's arms, holding on to me.

The length of rope I picked, and my hands holding it, went blurry. I squeezed my eyes shut and made another, different wish. I didn't know if I would ever see my father again, and I saw my mother for only an hour at a time. But I wanted to see Valentine every day for the rest of my life.

8

I woke up in my second-floor room, confused—first, to see the bare walls of the workhouse, and then second, since I was here, to not have shrunken down into my child-body to suit the surroundings. The same feeling of heavy sadness I used to carry here pressed upon me, shot through with some vague hope of seeing a friendly face. Then I remembered fully: the sick ward, the dying-rose smell, and Mother raving about Valentine and purple hyacinths.

In yesterday's wrinkled clothing, my mother's dress, I burst from my cell. I didn't know my way from where Mrs. Martin had taken me in the dark, but I was sure there would be inmates about to ask. I came to the end of the hall just as Mrs. Martin rounded the corner.

"Good, you're up," she said, with neither a flinch nor a gasp as I nearly crashed into her. "Come down and eat."

"No," I said. "I want to see Mother at once."

"If you go to the sick ward, you will miss the breakfast hour, and there will be nothing left for you."

"I don't need to eat, Mrs. Martin. I can—"

"What nonsense—imagine if your mother heard you talking that way. Nobody ever cured anybody else by starving, and if your mother could be healed by such means, she'd refuse the treatment. She wouldn't approve of you neglecting yourself on her account." Mrs. Martin took my arm, and I let her.

I thought we'd pass the hall in which the child paupers ate, and move on to the women's room. Instead, Mrs. Martin turned in.

"Surely I don't belong in here with the children," I said, planting my feet in the doorway so that the matron lurched, stuck.

"You don't belong with the women, either, do you?" she said, indicating my dress. "You'll be an anomaly wherever you sit, and at least in here I can keep an eye on you. See that you eat instead of sneaking off to the sick ward."

I sighed, and went forward. The long tables and benches were smaller than I remembered. The children who sat eating seemed especially little. Had I been so skinny and fragile as they were? Had Valentine?

I set my sights on the line for the lady with the ladle, who stood over a big stewpot on a table, front and center. But Mrs. Martin turned me about as we drew level with an empty bit of bench on a table end. "Sit," she snapped, and marched on without me, around the line.

I lowered myself onto the seat. On my immediate left, a little blonde girl stared, horrified, at me—a giantess in a free woman's clothes who'd chosen to settle beside her. No doubt she thought me some new deputy of Mrs. Martin's, and now on top of enduring the terrible breakfast fare, she felt she had to be on her best behavior. I gave her what I hoped was an apologetic sort of look, but she only averted her eyes, shoving her spoon into her mouth.

"Here," Mrs. Martin said, putting a dish of thin broth in front of me. I did not even have time to thank her, for she headed straight back to her box of old, to stand tall and watch over all her charges. I took small, wincing sips and watched her do those same slow half-circle turns she used to do. The humor in it came through my fog of worry: after all the changes I had undergone, in situation and in age, I found myself following my matron's old orders. I was, now, just as closely watched as I had been after she'd caught me playing with Valentine.

"Sit, Osley," she'd said from atop her box at suppertime, pointing to the nearest empty place at a table. Her eyes followed me the whole distance, and her look was so severe I dared not glance around.

I had already decided I would communicate nothing of my realization to Valentine—about wanting him to be my family—because my feelings might have changed the game, and the game was what kept us close. At first, it had been easy to keep my secret, for the matron kept me from seeing Valentine at all. She told me where to sit at breakfast, and at dinner, and never left me alone anymore.

But she had to sleep, and three weeks into our separation, Valentine took matters into his own hands.

Startled awake at midnight, I'd shot up under my thin sheet and would have cried out, but Valentine's hand clapped firm over my mouth. I relaxed against the warmth of his palm.

"You sleep like a bear," he said.

A shiver ran up my spine at the tickle of his breath.

"Sorry," he said. "I did begin gently."

I peered about, blinking. The dark had a hallowed blueness in it, as almost-morning light filtered in through the recessed attic windows. All around the floor were the shapes of the other girls, apparently sleeping, unaware anything unusual was happening. Valentine beckoned me to follow him, curling a finger and pointing toward the open hatch and staircase beyond.

If I had been fully awake, I should have been shocked by his sneaking into the sleeping den of some seventy other girls, like a wolf among sheep. I should have feared stepping into someone's chamber pot, at least, let alone being caught out of bed and punished.

But I was half-asleep still, and I imagined I could touch nothing and disturb no one, like a ghost. I floated in the wake of the boy I haunted, down the stairs. I imagined he had come to the attic in a trance, drawn there by my presence—which must have been intensifying every day we'd been apart. I could see him in my mind's eye, at mealtimes, eating alone, thinking of me. Just as I'd thought of him.

There was a lamp still lit in a wall bracket at the bottom of the stairs, and as Valentine passed underneath, I saw the top of his head: filthy, but precious anyway, like pirate's gold. I followed him deeper into the house, to a side door by the kitchens. He opened it with a key he must have stolen, and let me pass through first. I recognized the men's yard, which I'd seen from the attic windows. It had a stable sat within its walls, and a high gate to the road.

Outside, we could relax, and laugh. I shot out in front of him, feeling free in the moonlight. He chased me about the yard, as he always did, but for the moment he was not a police officer come to catch me. There was no law out here; we had left it all inside.

He tagged me and reversed direction, and for a change, I chased him. He ran backward, watching my approach, speeding up whenever I got too close and only sometimes looking over his shoulder to see that he wouldn't run into anything. I cackled at the look on his face when he realized I could be fast like he was. It reminded me of another look, last time, playing by the wash buckets, when he had almost said . . . I did not know what.

"Wait." I skidded to a stop. "You were asking me something."

He slowed. "I was not."

"You were, last time, before the matron came. What were you going to say?"

He stopped. "I'm not sure."

"You were holding me against the tree." I raised my arms to demonstrate, one wrist over the other. That had been the moment I'd wanted him to . . . to be my family. And now he wouldn't look at me.

Maybe he had wished for the same thing. Maybe he was afraid to tell me. I reached out to touch him.

He stepped backward. "It must've been part of the game."

I shook my head. "You used my name. You called me Marian."

“Hm.” He seemed to puzzle over it. But he clasped his hands so composedly behind his back. He wasn’t thinking, only performing the part of a man who thought.

I put my hands on my hips. “Are you keeping something from me?”

To this he had no answer. He didn’t even glance up from the ground. But since he didn’t say anything else or run, it seemed to me he was waiting—wanting me to do or say something more.

After a moment’s consideration, I put one foot exactly, carefully, in front of the other. “Strolling the streets of London at midnight, refusing to answer an officer’s direct question—it doesn’t look good, I can tell you.”

“Oh no, you don’t.” He sounded breathless.

“Don’t tell me what I don’t do. I’m the law,” I said, before I could stop myself—and I felt a thrill of power. I tipped back my head. “Why don’t you tell me what you’re doing?”

“Not until I see a badge.”

I stopped. I couldn’t tell if his anger was real.

“No badge?” The question stretched, like the smirk spreading across his face. He took a step toward me.

So the anger was false. But I’d lost my moment, and his eyes were so dark. There was that warm, weak feeling again, in my thighs. Invisible hands wrung my stomach like a rag, and some of my life’s blood seemed to run out of it.

“It just so happens I am an actual officer, and this is my beat.” He mimed taking his own badge from a coat he didn’t have, flashing it to satisfy me. Then he grabbed me by the scruff of my uniform and turned me around. “I’m arresting you for impersonating an officer.”

I thrashed, as I often did for the theater of it, but this time my frustration was not entirely invented. I had been so glad Valentine had woken me, but his evasiveness soured it all. He was keeping something from me.

He pulled me into the stable, straw rustling beneath our feet. It was a small building, with a dirt floor and hay bales piled against the back wall. On the left was a table cluttered with gloves, ropes, and oddly shaped tools, and on the right was a single stall. The resident horse was missing.

"The master's away," I said.

"I am the master," Valentine replied, and pushed me forward, shutting the half door of the stall after me with a decisive click.

Turning, I watched him rummage through the tools on the table. He tipped his head back, studying the tack hung from hooks in the wall: reins, harnesses—all too fitted to a horse's shape to be of any use in restraining me, I thought. But there was a riding crop, too, hanging by its handle. That would be like a whip, and good for a prop. A shiver ran up my back.

I put my hands atop the half door, saw the latch to open it, and pretended I could not. My insides squeezed again—like needing to relieve myself.

"Put out your hands," Valentine said, facing me.

I obeyed, turning my head away as if I couldn't bear to watch. My eyes darted to the wall, but the crop still hung there. Instead of relief, I felt disappointed.

"You pretend a life that isn't yours," he was saying. "You must not like the skin you're in. Let me take care of that for you."

He flipped my hand over and pressed coarse bristles into the flesh of my palm. So he'd taken a horse brush. It stung, but pleasant thrills followed in the path of every bristle going back and forth. I stood still, holding my breath—afraid to make a sound, lest the torture end.

Valentine switched from strokes to circles. The pricking sensation grew so strong my hand jerked back without my say-so, but he pressed warm fingers gently down upon my wrist, holding me still. His eyes flicked up to mine, and when I met his gaze, something thawed between us.

He turned my hand in his, and worked the brush up and down the side of it. I never knew how ticklish the edge of a hand could be. I laughed.

"You think this is funny?" Valentine asked.

He laid my hand flat again, palm down this time, and brushed side to side across the tops of my fingers. Bit by bit, he moved the brush up, over my knuckles. I wasn't in pain, and I wasn't laughing anymore. I was hypnotized, the brush shushing me, soothing me.

The brush crossed into the territory of my arm, and every hair stood up, not only where it touched me but all the way to my elbow, like the people in a church rising at the command of the priest. Yes—it felt like the funeral service I had attended for my grandfather: sacred and a bit scary. The edge between life as I knew it and some dark, unknown part of human existence was blurring. Something beckoned, begged from deep in my belly to be considered.

I whimpered, in want of I knew not what, and Valentine relented at once, tipping my chin up with his fingers so our eyes met. I shook my head to show him it was nothing, I was fine—though I didn't know if that was true. I just didn't want him to stop.

"Your skin is raw now," he informed me.

I curled my fingers into my palms, imagining the sting and the redness, and showed him wide, vulnerable eyes. I wasn't acting anymore. I wanted him to see what he'd made me feel, and to do something about it.

He brought his brows together, studying me. "It didn't make a difference, did it?" he asked. "You're bad all the way down."

I bit my lips shut.

He narrowed his eyes. "You disagree? Let's hear that old sob story, then. Tell me about your poor children, and how much you care."

His leer brought him closer, so close we could've kissed, but I felt a distance still between us. He had been about to say something the last time we were like this. He was keeping a secret from me.

I turned my face away. "I don't care about my children."

"What?" His hand shot out, and he jostled my shoulder. "What did you say?"

I jerked out of his grasp, holding my head high. "I didn't consider them at all. It was for myself I did it, for the better life I wanted—all the lovely things in the shop windows I'd never owned!"

He stared, wide-eyed—a real, Valentine expression.

I raised my brows at him, but he turned away, and took the few steps he needed to reach the table.

"If that's how you want it, fine." I heard the brush hit the table, heard him moving bottles around. "A real punishment. Oil. I just need to boil it up."

He faced me again, so I could watch him pour something thick and slow into his palm. His policeman's mask was up again. He set the bottle down, rubbed his hands together. The bright, brisk smell of lemon struck my nose. It must've been oil for the horse's coat.

He lunged forward to the stall, and with finality clapped a hand over mine. I forgot to be angry with him. His touch was warm, and as welcome to me as if I had been freezing, and I clenched my teeth only in performance, against the burn he meant for me to imagine.

He flipped my hand over in his, and slapped his other hand down over my open palm. I cried out at the escalation of my character's torture—quietly, in a strangled way.

He squeezed my hand between both of his own, spreading my fingers as he laced his through. I made a sound—the sort of exhalation brought on by a stubbed toe, but quieter and less unhappy.

"Well?" he asked me, his voice soft and low. "Are you sorry now?"

His face was close to mine, and he held my hand so dearly. If this were a garden gate in a fairy tale, or if we had been neighbors instead of inmates . . .

I swallowed against a sudden constriction in my throat. "Yes. I'm miserable and sorry."

"Good. Then I'll lock you away forever." But he did not immediately release my hand. He raised it in his, holding my gaze. I thought he might kiss it. But the moment passed. Gently he untangled our fingers and lifted his top hand. He opened the stall door, holding it for me.

"Better wipe that." He gave me a rag from the table. "It's getting to be dawn. We should get back."

"Valentine?"

He looked over his shoulder to show he'd heard me, but said nothing. His gaze returned to the sky beyond the stable door.

Without his eyes pinning me down, I could be brave. "Do you feel strange lately?" I asked. "Afraid?"

"Afraid? Of you?" he asked, as if it were absurd. But then he looked my way again, and his face changed—his eyes wide and his mouth flat. He came back into the stable, closer to me. "Are you afraid of me?"

"No," I said, fast. "But . . . it feels like something's happening, or about to happen. Like before a thunderstorm."

"Oh." His throat worked in the gray-blue light. He looked away. "Well. Maybe it's going to rain."

I didn't believe that he believed it.

He made as if to step away from me, but drew his foot back. "We can't stay here. But if you're still scared tomorrow, tell me then."

Perhaps he had seen something of what I'd wanted in my eyes after all, and sensed the danger I was in when we were together. But it was too late. My descent into immorality had already begun, and would gather momentum with or without him.

9

The children were standing up around me. I stood up, too, taller than all of them. At last, it was time to see my mother, and I was glad to leave the past behind me.

The master had come into the room, and Mrs. Martin on her box bent to hear whatever message he brought. After he was done, she nodded and came to me, marching briskly, as before. I followed her, away from the tumult of children as they all went to work. Down one corridor, then another, until there was only the sound of our footsteps. When Mrs. Martin turned into a stairwell, I asked, "Aren't we going to the sick ward now?"

"Not quite yet," she replied.

"I don't want to delay another moment, Mrs. Martin."

"You'll not get through the door without my key," she said.

I stood irresolute at the bottom of the stairs, watching her trudge up and away from me. Finally, I followed.

I was surprised—the door she unlocked led into the room in which I'd passed the night. I knew it, with some shame, by the sorry state in which I'd left the sheets. "Mrs. Martin, what . . . ?"

She waved me in, her lips tight.

I advanced, and she shut the door. "Sit," she said, in the same tone as at breakfast.

I lowered myself onto the end of the bed. “Mrs. Martin, my mother—”

“Is gone, Marian,” she said. “I’m sorry.”

I blinked at her. “Gone where?”

She sighed. “Wherever it is her soul belongs, I suppose.”

My mouth fell open, but I had no words to say, and I left off breathing.

“She’s dead, Marian. Again, I’m sorry.”

I shook my head. “You kept me from her.” Just like being a child, over again, even in this. Just like with Valentine. “You kept me, and I didn’t get to say goodbye.”

“It wouldn’t have made any difference, Mar—”

“It would have made a difference to me!” I cried, rising from the bed. “You think just because she’s mad, just because she doesn’t speak sense, that nothing she could say would matter to me? I wonder whether other people have ever made such decisions for you, Mrs. Martin, about your family!”

“Marian, calm down this instant.”

“How dare you! Mr. Martin had to come and whisper it into your ear that she’d gone, didn’t he? But I could have told you, Mrs. Martin. I could’ve told you this morning, if you’d let me! But no, you give the orders; you get your way in matters that don’t even concern you—”

“She was dead an hour after you left her last night, Marian!”

I recoiled from the volume of her voice and then was overcome with cold shame. “No,” I said. “You’re lying.”

“I looked in on her after I settled you here, and she was gone.”

“She was sleeping—”

“Her eyes were open, and I’ll tell you I don’t appreciate any of this judgment, about my lack of basic sense or morals. I have done this job a long time, Marian, with care and goodwill besides. I thought I’d gotten through to you. I thought we got all this petulance out of your system.

Maybe you're regressing in your grief, and I'll not hold it against you, but neither will I stand here and humor you in the throes of a tantrum."

"But you pretended she lived," I said to the floor.

"I did no such thing. I said your mother would be appalled if you didn't eat, and that is true. You'll not have an appetite a long time after this, Marian—grieving people don't. She would want you to have had breakfast, and I made sure you did. You're welcome."

I cringed at the slam of the door, and the perfect silence of standing in that room alone brought scalding shame pouring down, from the top of my head over my temples and to my throat, which burned.

So I was not the only one comparing my old self with the new, and seeing little change.

I found Mrs. Martin in her day office, the door ajar. She did not look up from her ledger when I knocked.

"I'm sorry, Mrs. Martin," I said. "You were right, I was throwing a tantrum. I'm calmer now, and used to the idea that she—she's gone."

"What Mr. Martin came to tell me at breakfast," she said, licking her thumb to turn a page, "was that all her possessions, from her bedside drawer, had been gathered and dropped off for you." She pointed, still not raising her gaze, to a pile on the edge of her desk.

I drew near. I saw my name at the bottom of a page, in my own hand. *Write to me,* Mother had said, and kept my letters close. Letters I had filled with lies her dearest—her only—property. I could not bear to gather them for myself. They were worthless, insincere things. She'd deserved so much better.

"What happens now?" I asked.

Mrs. Martin didn't look up.

To bear this, I went to her only window. It showed me the women's and girls' yards, from a high vantage, so it was like I'd never seen them before. But then, this morning, I felt as if I'd never been anywhere before. Nothing was familiar. The world seemed to have tipped upside down, and I was in danger every moment of falling into the sky.

"She goes over to the cemetery 'cross the street," Mrs. Martin said at last.

I turned. "Do I settle with you, about what her stone says?"

"She doesn't get a stone."

"What do you mean?"

She shook her head, though still she did not raise her gaze. "No one gets a stone. You'd need a pillar, for all the names of them that go in the one grave."

In my mind, I saw my mother tossed onto a heap of people, she and they all thin enough to snap apart on collision. I felt every bump of her rolling down on top of them, heard the crack of her neck, smelled the earth where she stopped, facedown. Without my father, without a name, without a place I could come and speak to her.

"No," I breathed. "She must have a stone. And her own grave. Like any loved person."

"Then she won't be buried by the workhouse," the matron said mildly. "You'll have to pay for her to go to some other cemetery."

I untied my purse from around my neck and emptied it on the desk, sending pence skittering across her papers. "There," I declared, and felt justified, after all, in keeping my wages.

The matron's eyes jumped from coin to coin. At last, she looked up. "This is barely enough for the bed you took last night." When I scowled, she added: "I charge the rate you'd pay at any doss-house."

I watched her take most of my money, and put the pitiful remainder in my palm.

"Will you wait?" I asked. "If I send for money. Will you wait 'til I get an answer?"

She shrugged. "You have a few days, likely. We don't bury them until we've got enough, and we were there on Sunday."

I winced.

Mrs. Martin set me a place on the opposite side of her desk: pen, ink, paper. "Be quick. I'll get your message off this morning."

I did not allow myself to think about those things that should have stayed my hand. I thought only of the woman who had given life to me, the woman to whom I had given back next to nothing, and I wrote:

> Dear Sir,
> Thank you for the use of your coach getting to London. If not for your quick kindness, I would have been too late. Mother died this morning. I must ask another favor. If you would pay for a proper funeral, I will forgo my wages to make up the sum, whatever would be right. Please reply as soon as you can. I cannot bear seeing her put into a communal pit.
> Marian

◆ ◆ ◆

I spent the intervening time in the bed Mrs. Martin had made up for me, either sleeping or crying. I did not eat, and she did not try to make me. Mr. Bornholdt's reply came two days later. The matron brought it and, saying nothing about my sitting up in my sheets in the middle of an afternoon, left me to open it in privacy.

I studied my name written out in Mr. Bornholdt's hand. In what mood had he formed the letters of it? He might have cursed my greed and presumption, his pen a stabbing sword. I could imagine him denying me, knowing it would cut me deeply. But that was not the worst I could imagine.

I broke the seal. The letter was as kind as I'd feared.

> Dear Miss Osley,
> I leave off lengthy condolences to give you other words, out of which you will get more practical use. Of course your mother cannot be buried in an unmarked

grave. She will be paid the respect she deserves for having borne and raised such a good, virtuous child. You must see about everything for the funeral service and burial. Show the note enclosed to the undertakers, which instructs them to send me the balance. Go and buy mourning clothes. Refer the tailor's shop to the same enclosed note, and I will settle things.

Enclosed also is the fare with which you will hire a coach to return you to Valor Rise, but that is a concern for later. Meantime, you must remove yourself from that pitiful workhouse and find some hotel at which to stay until the funeral takes place. I do not condone risking your health among the sick and poor. I will pay the cost of any clean, expensive place gladly, but no such balance from Parish Street, so I warn you: do not ignore this direction out of some misguided attempt to lessen your cost to me.

My purse is open to you—so long as you are in my keeping, whatever you may need, I shall be happy to provide.

—W. Bornholdt

His signature was languid—lazily so, as if to show how little bother it was to write, to give, and to promise so open-endedly to give yet more in the future.

I let the paper fall onto the sheet, clutched my head, and cried, and only after the fit had passed did I worry what damage my tears might have done.

But the ink was undisturbed. Mr. Bornholdt's signature sat unblemished, an unflappable witness to my two griefs—the one for the fate of my mother, and the other for me.

10

Mrs. Martin recommended the Crows' Court Hotel to me, half an hour's walk away. The man at the front desk narrowed his eyes as I crossed the glossy threshold, rising as if he meant to chase me out. That was awful, but handing him the note from Mr. Bornholdt was worse—seeing his face change under the sway of a man who was miles away, entirely at his service.

I found my room mean in all its niceties—the pink walls too gay, the sheets and pillow on my bed too kind to be sincere. The maids brought fresh forget-me-nots to my room every morning, in a skinny vase by my window, and I resented the flowers' audacity to bloom. Even if their own lives had been snipped short at the stem, I was jealous on my mother's behalf—for though they died, at least they got to do it in fresh air and sunshine.

The man at the hotel desk recommended a tailor and a funeral parlor. With the power of Mr. Bornholdt's signature, I was fitted for two mourning dresses—one of wool, for every day, and one of matte silk, for the funeral. I wore the wool one to the funeral parlor, and brought Mr. Bornholdt's magic note with me to make arrangements. I settled so many matters—I must have—and yet I felt afterward as if I had been moved through all of it by others, each person passing me on to the next, all of them knowing better than I what was to be done.

At the end of the day, the vanity mirror in my room showed me to be as pale as Mrs. Bornholdt. It was only that I was wearing black, of course: black made white look whiter. Simple color theory. That much I could understand—that much, and little else.

◆ ◆ ◆

The morning of my mother's funeral, London did the decent thing, letting loose a torrent of commiserating rain. One of the hired mourners offered me a spare umbrella, but when I saw that only these employees of the funeral parlor walked with me behind the hearse, I closed it. I was drenched in a moment, the weight of the dress I'd bought seeming to double. I welcomed the added work it took to keep walking.

I turned my face toward the sky, and the rain fell along my mouth and down my chin. Were these my mother's tears? If so, they were cold, and falling so hard that they stung.

I bowed my head, and the rain poured down my neck, down my spine. I shivered as if I were being shaken in someone else's aggravation. If it was Mother, she was bitterly unhappy. At least in that I was not alone.

Wind pushed at my back, pressing my wet clothes into my skin. It reminded me of the force of Bornholdt's mouth, but where he had been all smothering heat, this was frigid, merciless chill. I gave myself easily over to my tears, for there was no one walking beside me to see.

The hearse reached the cemetery, and the ground beneath my feet changed from hard stone to squashy, sucking soil. As I stood by, my mother's coffin was lowered into the earth, the rain tapping relentlessly upon the wood as if her spirit were determined to rouse her body from its rest.

She had not been done living. Perhaps that was whence her anger came.

The mourners began to sing. The sound was rich, powerful, but the wind bore the verse cruelly away. I did not even know the hymn to join in, and this thought brought on a fresh wave of piteous tears.

The gravedigger pitched one shovelful of earth into the grave but no more. He would return later to fill the hole when the dirt was not so heavy with rain. Still, I stood beside the grave long after the mourners had gone.

"I'm sorry, Mother," I whispered, sniffing and shaking. "I'm sorry I couldn't do more to help you."

The wind pushed against my back again, hard, and I had a vision of myself falling into the grave and being unable to get out. I took a step back from the hole and, despite the mud, got down on my knees. I gave myself over to guilt—and not only for leaving Mother at Parish Street.

I'd done her wrong when I was a child, too.

The day after Valentine and I had sneaked out to play in the stables, I was convinced that Mrs. Martin knew, somehow, what we'd done. The whole time she'd led the girls in morning prayers, her eyes kept returning to mine. She would read from her Bible and then read from my face, as if comparing God's expectation of me with the reality. She seemed to know I'd fallen short.

Hands together, saying by rote what was required, I racked my brain. How could she have known Valentine and I had been out of bed? I supposed, if the master had come back already from his trip, the horse brush might have looked out of place to him. Or perhaps he knew the level of the oil for the horse's coat and had seen some missing. But even if it was clear someone had been in the stable, there was nothing to prove the someone had been me.

All the same, after the lesson, Mrs. Martin made straight for me. "Come," she said. "We're going to see your mother."

My stomach dropped. This was the wrong time. Visits between parents and children were conducted at the hour between work and supper. The only exception I knew of was the time Valentine learned of his father's prison sentence.

My mother sat alone, waiting on her bed, which was at the end of a row of six. The morning sun came through the windows, but it was a cold light that made everything pale—the floor, the bedsheets, and Mother herself. Thrown by the wide-open feel of the room, certain something out of the ordinary was about to occur, I stood still on the threshold.

"Go," the matron said. "I'll be back to collect you in a while."

She pushed me forward, then backed out. The door clicked shut, and my mother's eyes met mine. We listened together to the grind of a key turning.

"She's locking us in?"

My mother shook her head. "She's locking others out. Giving us some privacy."

"Why?" I rushed closer. "What's wrong?"

"Nothing here," she replied. "Everything's nice and calm."

These words, designed to soothe me, did exactly the opposite.

"Are you sick?" I asked, for she was pale and her eyes were solemn. "Is something wrong with Father?"

"No, no." She patted the bed. "I wanted to talk to you alone, and the matron granted that request."

I narrowed my eyes. "Why would she do that?"

"To be kind."

Of course, I knew by then that nothing in the workhouse was kind. It held open its arms to London's poor, but its embrace was uncomfortably close, so as to discourage the destitute from sheltering in it. The thinking was that charity should consist of only what was needed to survive—food, clothes, and room—all of the poorest quality; otherwise, the working classes might decide to put their feet up and their hands out, too. As if anyone would choose to need help, as if begging were amusing instead of shameful. Not a moment of my life had been playful since I'd passed through the workhouse doors, except the ones I'd stolen back with Valentine.

But seeing Mother always reminded me of how safe I used to feel in her presence. Her cheeks were dirty, like she'd patted her face with road dust in place of powder. But her eyes still shone like river water winking back sunlight, and I wanted to believe her.

"We always talk about how it used to be," she said. "Don't we?"

I let my shoulders sag and looked away. The only happiness she had to share was in the same tired memories—my picking flowers for the breakfast table or helping to make stock for stews. We passed our recollections back and forth like a ball, until they were filthy with the dirt of the workhouse. Each time Mother brought them out, I liked to touch them less.

I sat on her bed, as she wanted me to.

"But time is passing, whether I like it or not," she said. "A year is nothing for a grown woman. But you're changing so much."

I shrugged, looking at our hands together. Mine didn't have lines everywhere like hers.

"You never told me you had made a friend here," she said softly. "I had to learn about you playing together from Mrs. Martin."

I caught my breath. So this was about the stables.

"I'm sorry," I blurted. "We were bored, and I was half-asleep—but it's not his fault. He's frustrated, I think, and scared, and we're only trying to . . ."

But I didn't know how to put it, the comfort of the thing.

Mother was watching me.

"Please don't be angry with me," I said. "We won't go out at night again."

Mother's look turned sharp. "What's this about being out at night?"

She hadn't known that, then.

"Marian. When did you go out?"

I frowned at the floor. "Last night."

"With this boy, Valentine?"

"Only to the stable." I peeked up to find her eyes wide with alarm. "To look in at the horse, but it wasn't there."

"In the middle of the night?"

"Yes." I picked at her bedsheet. It sounded ridiculous.

She was silent. Then she sighed. "Can't you sleep?"

I hesitated, glancing up at her.

She crossed her arms. "Valentine woke you."

I was such a terrible friend. I kept giving him away.

"Can't Valentine sleep?" When I still said nothing, she gave my shoulder a shake and pressed me up against her side. Using herself as a brace, she straightened my curled back. "Did he tell you he couldn't sleep?"

I couldn't think of a lie, and how could I tell her there was no good reason for what we'd done?

"No?" she prodded.

I shook my head.

Mother brushed my hair back from my forehead, trying to see my face. "He was probably trying to be a man about it. But he's only a boy yet, isn't he? Poor lamb."

I frowned. Even if Valentine were having trouble sleeping, this was too soft. I lifted my mother's hand and looked around at her.

"Valentine got bad news some weeks ago, Marian." Now my mother looked like the one in trouble, picking at her clothes, not meeting my eyes. "It's not nice. I don't like to tell you, but . . . your friend's father has been hanged."

I stood up. "For thievery?"

"For murder."

"Murder?" I said—and then, as if my mother herself had charged him: "He only injured that shopkeeper!"

"So you know that much." She sighed. "The shopkeeper died from his injuries, and the jury decided it was Mr. Hobbs's fault."

I scrunched my nose. "That's not fair. That's not right!"

"It's done, Marian."

I turned my face toward the floor. I didn't care about Valentine's father. But Valentine cared, whatever he said. I worried about him then, as I should have been worrying for weeks—if only I'd known. It stung that he hadn't told me.

"Mrs. Hobbs died in a matter of hours," Mother said.

I blinked. "They hanged her, too?"

"No. She died in her sleep."

I sank onto the bed. "Of what?"

"They don't know. The doctor told her something that eased her mind. So she could let go."

I stared into my mother's face. Her gaze was significant, giving the words "let go" new weight, and they hit me fully.

Valentine had nobody at all, except for me.

I had to find him as soon as I could and swear he would never be alone. If that meant the world would try to take him from me, it could try. I would be nobler than his father and tougher than his mother. I would fight and not let him go. No master or matron was going to stop me seeing him.

And there was something else: Mother had admitted I was tied up in Valentine's affairs. Perhaps I wouldn't have to fight alone to keep him in my life. I looked to her with hope—but her face was all sorrow still.

"The matron told me you and Valentine sneak off every chance you get to play," she said.

"I'm sorry," I said, reddening. "I'm lonely."

"No." To my horror, I felt tears drop onto my head as she hugged me close. She kissed my hair and said, "No, I'm sorry. I wish I had something to give you, Marian. I'd give you your friend. I wish I could."

"What's the matter?" I asked, my voice muffled by her bosom.

She took a deep breath, rocking back with me in her arms. "The doctor knew of a family in need of a hall boy. He promised Valentine's mother that he would see her son situated there."

I pushed away from her, searching her face.

"The matron thought it best that I tell you." Her brows warped, as if her forehead were heavy.

"Valentine's going away?" I jumped down, ready to run off to find him. "When?"

She clasped her hands and bowed her head, closing her eyes as if in prayer. "He's already gone, my love. He was taken to the manor house this morning."

I pushed my mother's hands apart and ran to the door. The handle would only turn to a point. I pounded on the wood panels, but no one came to let me out. It occurred to me that this had been the point of locking us in. Mrs. Martin had expected me to react this way.

"Doesn't anyone care about me?" I shouted.

"I care about you," my mother said.

I turned slowly to look at her. There was kindness in the openness of her eyes—kindness, love, and sorrow—and suddenly all the bile in my stomach came up.

"I hate this place!" I said. "What did I ever do to belong here but be born to the wrong sort of people?"

She shrank from me, and in a small voice she said: "I know it's not fair."

"It's *not* fair." By agreeing, she hacked at the dam that had cracked in me, hastening the flood of my emotions. "I eat slop and sleep on the floor. I prick my fingers raw dressed in a smock a stranger must have died in."

She did not drop her eyes from me, and I could see hers were sad. I was glad for a moment to have affected someone—to have some presence again, some power.

"You might try to make a new friend," my mother suggested, watching me as I wiped my eyes.

I didn't tell her how Valentine had made my breath short and upset my stomach, how it was awful and wonderful at once. I couldn't. For though I didn't quite know what the feelings meant, I understood that their unfamiliarity must have meant they were not normal, not allowed.

Otherwise, surely someone would have warned me about them.

If I were mad, or evil, I didn't want my mother to know, and hate me.

But if she knew anything at all anymore, surely she knew what I had done with Valentine. What I did, even after he was gone. That I was bad even without his influence.

I clasped my hands before Mother's grave and gazed up at the gray and tired-looking sky. "I never should have complained to you of my unhappiness when I was a child," I said. "I was blessed to have you there to complain to. You were more than I deserved. I wasn't half as good a child as you thought me. And I don't know what I expected you to have done. You had no more power than I did to fix it."

I wiped my eyes with my sleeve. Again the wind roared behind me, and the air whistled in my stinging ears, shouting a new idea: if Mother knew how I fared in this moment—if death did lift a person to omnipresence—then surely she knew everything I had not told her. Not just about Valentine, but about Bornholdt, too.

I shuddered where I knelt. “Mother? Perhaps you have some power, in heaven, that you did not have before, and you could help me—help me resist my own destruction. Every decision I make seems to draw it closer. I am all but bought by Bornholdt, and if it is my fault, Mother, it is not my wish. Please help me. Please.”

There was no answer but the thunder’s rolling laugh, the joke being that I was all alone and talking to myself.

11

The next morning, having soaked and muddied my funeral dress, I changed into the wool to travel in. I hired a coachman to take me back to Valor Rise, explaining that I would leave from Parish Street. I wanted to see Mrs. Martin again, before I left the city. She met me at the workhouse gates with a basket.

"Here's a sandwich," she said, handing it over. "Maybe you'll want it."

I bowed my head as I took it. "Mrs. Martin, I wanted to say again that I'm sorry—"

"I don't want your apologies," she said, but not gruffly, only as if she were tired.

"Then . . ." I paused, considering her. "Then thank you. For being kind."

"I'm not kind," she said, as if it were an insult. "The workhouse shelters and reforms people—I simply perform my function within it."

I tilted my head, waiting.

After a moment, her eyes found mine. "Don't you lose ground again, Marian Osley. I didn't stay up all those nights improving you for nothing." Then she stepped back.

She did not stay to watch me away, but turned at once to go inside. I could not even catch her expression.

I sighed, stepped up into the coach, and sat.

The coachman loosed a noise from his throat, waking the two horses to their purpose.

I curled my knees close to my chest. I didn't care ever to arrive at the house, where Mr. Bornholdt waited, salivating.

Too soon, we passed through the farms on the Bornholdt estate. As we neared the top of the cliff, I roused myself. Arriving in the dead of night as I had when I'd been hired—and leaving again in such a hurry for London—I'd never gotten a proper look at the house. In the golden glow of afternoon, it seemed confectionary—its outer walls honey-hued, with dark-toffee slating for its roof. If only it were full of cake instead of people, I thought, I might have been happy to see it.

But in reality, of course, there was a tempted master inside, to whom I owed a debt. And a mistress who did not know yet quite why she disliked me, but might find out at any moment. Not anywhere in all the many floors of Valor Rise did I have friends to vouch for me—and if someone did argue my virtue, that would make them liars, and unvirtuous themselves.

If only I had any other prospects, I should have saved my mistress the trouble of dismissing me in disgrace, and left right then.

The coach rounded the stone service road to the side of the house, where the servants' entrance was—but the coach stopped prematurely. I poked my head out. A great tree, snapped off from its trunk, lay nearly longways in the road.

I pushed the coach door open and stepped down, spotting two men. They wore thick wool coats, and they stared down at the tree, shaking their heads and mumbling to one another.

"What happened?" I called out as I approached them.

The men peered at me. I supposed I was breaking etiquette—addressing them so bluntly, like a man, and being curious right out loud—and I envied them for their capacity to take offense. They still believed in men's rules.

But my mother had died. There were no rules.

"Lightning strike," one of the men said.

I gazed along the length of the tree, the end of which passed close by the corner of the house. It was a wonder it hadn't hit the roof. How could so thick a thing as that stand up in the sky?

I looked around at the living trees. What trust it took, for people to live beside such giants—but then again, their branches groped so earnestly toward the heavens. None of them wanted anything to do with us on the ground, if they could help it.

◆ ◆ ◆

I had looked forward to getting inside, to losing myself within the usual bustle of the kitchen. I wanted to be surrounded by activity and life rather than death. But the cacophony belowstairs was even more intense than I'd anticipated—several people shouting over the constant hiss of steam. I waded into the chaos just as the scullery maid threw a pan, apparently at nothing in particular. The gong-like ring of it reverberated in my head.

The housekeeper darted past me.

"Mrs. Davies?" I called.

"Don't bother me!" She hurried on toward the range, where a large pot was boiling over.

The cook was at the middle table, plating food. "Something is burning!" he said, his eyes intent upon the table he bent over.

I gazed around, trying to understand the cause of the commotion. Ledford was bolting up the stairs, a silver waiter overloaded with dishes in his hands. What I could see of his face was red and shiny as a burn. Every hand at the center table was busy.

I spotted Lucette at the drawers that held the silver. She had a cloth in one hand, with which she fastidiously rubbed the serving spoon in the other.

I crossed to her. "What's going on?"

"Dinner," she said, not looking up.

"Well, I see that. But why is everyone so . . ." I swept my arm, indicating the chaos.

Lucette sighed. "It's a dinner *party*, and we're shorthanded because o' the tree fallin' on the footman yesterday."

I whipped round. "The footman died?"

She rolled her eyes. "Did I say that? No, he broke his leg."

"How? What—"

"He needed to get the food for the dinner from the grocer's wagon," she said, as if she were repeating information I should've known already. "The tree fell on the wagon, whacked him down, crushin' all the food besides—an' we didn' get the new food 'til today, an' ever since we've been dizzy as wheels on a hill, tryin' to get it all made right. Meanwhile, the footman's comfy cozy in his sickbed, with his wife an' children, while we suffer the master's temper." She cast the serving spoon down on the counter, as if she blamed it, before picking up another to polish.

"The poor footman." My hand crept up to touch the coin purse at my throat. "What'll they do for money?"

"That's his problem. Some of us have to work to earn our keep." She glanced at me, then, her mouth twisted. "Least that's the world I live in."

I frowned. "What's that supposed to mean?"

"It means the footman isn' here to do what a footman does, an' so he don' get a footman's salary—just like if the lady's maid isn' here to make her mistress a party dress, she shouldn' get a lady's maid's salary."

I drew back. "I was at my mother's—"

"Oh, we know," she said. "You're an exception. Because the master likes givin' you what you want, don' he?"

My mouth fell open.

The cook came over with another silver waiter, this one laden with sauces in tureens and vegetable sides on plates. He left this on the cabinet beside Lucette's silver, and went away again.

She stuck a serving spoon in each sauce. "By all means, keep doin' nothin'. But get out of my way so I can work. I make my money on my feet, not off 'em."

"So do I, Lucette." I meant to be firm, but I shook with shame and rage in equal parts, and the words had come out shivering.

She picked up the waiter. "Right."

I blocked her path. "Let me take that up to them."

She raised her brows.

"Really," I said, lifting my chin. "Let me help."

"Fine. I don' care." She lowered the waiter onto my flat palm. Rolling her eyes again, she turned back to the silverware drawers—but I made my back straight and walked as briskly as I could without spilling, in case she looked to see how seriously I took the job.

Abovestairs, all was surprisingly calm, with only gentle sounds—clinking glasses, silver touching china, a lady laughing—coming from the dining room. I headed in their direction, down the wide hall.

"Where do you think you're going?" Ledford snapped, approaching from the direction of my destination. He must have been on his way back to retrieve my platter.

"Helping," I said, smiling as I weaved around him.

"Wait—"

I passed through the swinging door to the dining room.

The room was long, to accommodate a rectangular table at its center that could have sat sixteen. In the middle of the right-side wall was a fireplace, which was lit, and on the left were sliding pocket doors that led to Mr. Bornholdt's drawing room.

I came out behind the head of the table. Mr. Bornholdt's back was to me. Mrs. Bornholdt was at the other end, engaged for the moment in conversation. Sitting at the middle of the table were eight people: four men and four women. Including the hosts, that made for a dinner party of ten—a punishing service even for a household staff in perfect order. The majority of the guests seemed in good humor, however, laughing and chatting with their neighbors. The only sullen guest was the man directly to Mr. Bornholdt's right, who was entirely gray of hair, with all his frown lines permanently furrowing his forehead.

"Osley," Ledford hissed, having come back through the door to my side, "maids aren't to be seen at the dinner table!"

I got a full-body chill, and froze in place, as embarrassed as if I were naked. I turned to flee, offering out the silver waiter to Ledford, but—

"What the devil is this?" the elderly man asked.

All the faces formerly in conversation turned toward me. For a moment, the only sound came from the merrily crackling fireplace. I thought of Lucette belowstairs, polishing silver. How she'd raised her eyebrows at me.

"For goodness' sake!" This was Mr. Bornholdt, stiffly twisted in his seat, and I had to amend my assessment of the party—for he, too, like the elderly man, bore signs of prolonged strain. Eyes wide, and looking upon me as if I were a louse, he asked: "What are you doing here? You are not even in your uniform."

I looked down at myself, mortified. I had forgotten.

"What Mr. Bornholdt means to say, I think," Mrs. Bornholdt called into the quiet, from down the other end of the table, "is that you must be tired from your journey."

I was startled by the gentleness with which she spoke, but when I checked her face, I saw she wore an expression to match. She was smiling, not in mockery but in that small, concerned way mothers have.

"Forgive her," she said, to the wider party. "My maid is in mourning. No doubt she is befuddled, and did not mean any disrespect." Her eyes returned to mine; still, there was only sweetness in them—was it because she was in company?

"I'm sorry." I curtsied with one hand on my skirt. "I only wanted to help."

"Get out," Mr. Bornholdt said, through clenched teeth. He had shut his eyes as if he did not even care to look at me.

"What Mr. Bornholdt means," Mrs. Bornholdt said, again, "is that you must want to rest."

I stared, marveling at her stubborn kindness. And as my panic was replaced with curiosity, I found my feet sturdy in their shoes. "Actually, ma'am, I felt better with a job to do."

"Oh, let her help," one of the gentlemen said. "You could use it tonight."

"Hear, hear." This was the woman across from him, and I realized I knew her. She was Mrs. Bornholdt's cousin, Mrs. Malahide. The gentleman, who must have been her husband, raised his glass to me, and so did most everyone else. I looked to Mr. Bornholdt.

"Fine," he said stiffly. "Just get on with it."

The elderly man to Mr. Bornholdt's immediate right sighed as he sat back, studying Mr. Bornholdt, waiting to catch the master's eye. But Mr. Bornholdt never glanced his way; indeed, the master seemed determined not to notice the man.

"Marian," Ledford said, so close that I jumped, "as you're set upon this course of rebellion, do what you came to do." While the conversation moved on around us, he had me bring the silver waiter to a dark-walnut sideboard. He took some of the sauces, and I took the green beans and turnips, and we went to opposite ends of the table to serve.

Novelty that I was at the table, the guests could not perfectly ignore me as they should have done. When I served them, each of the ladies would go on talking but also smile in a small, fond way. Mr. Malahide, who'd toasted me earlier, thanked me aloud, and I was so flustered by this that I attempted a curtsy with my hands full and nearly showered his lap with green beans.

"I'm so sorry, sir," I sputtered.

"Nonsense," he replied. "Nothing happened, did it?"

So it was that I approached the elderly man feeling relaxed and easy. As I served him, however, he said to Mr. Bornholdt, at a volume for the whole party to hear, "What nonsense, Wythe. You should have called the dinner off."

"I did not want to disappoint you, Father," Mr. Bornholdt replied, in a restrained murmur. "I know you so look forward to your visits."

"Less so when I find you are staging comedy plays in my house."

His house? My eyes went straight to Mr. Bornholdt's. Yet the answering outrage I expected didn't come. Mr. Bornholdt's anger seemed to be trapped in his head. His eyes, wild and bulging, reminded me of the statuette in his study—the rearing iron horse pulling against its reins.

"It is all very funny," Mrs. Bornholdt broke in. She did it gently. It seemed to me the words were meant to touch her husband in particular, as if she were putting a soft hand on his clenched fist. Then she laughed—a real laugh, not loud or showy. "It was admittedly a bit silly to carry on with entertaining people, being shorthanded."

Mr. Bornholdt lifted his head as if it were on a hinge and regarded his wife with half a smile. The anger was not gone from his eyes, only touched with wonderment—a mad gleam. "Silly?" he said. "Yes. I suppose I was silly."

He gestured toward the center of the table, at a silver flower bowl made to look like an elaborate fountain. "But I can afford to be silly, when you are so clever, Diana. Look here, everyone—the servants are so overburdened belowstairs that they did not even put blooms on the table. But it is no matter at all, really. My wife chose this piece for all the embossed vines, flowering—so the belly of the bowl looks full of life even though it is perfectly barren."

Mr. Bornholdt speared a piece of meat with his fork, put it in his mouth, and smiled down at his wife, as if they shared a joke. But she did not seem amused. In fact, it looked to me like she was fending off a frown—the sort forced upon the face by a coming bout of tears.

"Marian," the butler whispered, and with a wave, he made clear that I was to help take away the empty plates. I flitted about the table after him.

"You really ought to have told us you were in a spot of trouble, Wythe," said Mr. Malahide, speaking across the people between Mr. Bornholdt and himself. "I would have brought along my own man to help."

"And take him away from worthy work at home, Christopher?" Mr. Bornholdt shook his head as if the idea were absurd.

"He has less to do as time goes by," Mr. Malahide replied, "what with the younger fellow picking up his duties . . ."

My waiter laden with dirty plates, I followed Ledford out of the dining room. I braced for an immediate telling-off as soon as he could speak freely to me, but he was entirely about his business, opening the door to the stairwell in silence. To my surprise, Mrs. Davies stood at the top of the stairs, waiting with empty hands to receive our burdens. She went away more quickly than I thought her capable of going, and was back to us with new dishes—all manner of cheeses—in moments. The softer ones, in shallow bowls with spreading spoons beside them, went to me.

As we returned to the table, Mrs. Bornholdt was speaking, in—or so it seemed to me—a forced attempt at joviality. "Six years?" she said. "And a hall boy all that time? He must have been young when you hired him."

"Yes," Mr. Malahide replied, "and he is too clever for that job. Has been for some time. If I can see that, so can he."

"So we would be doing you a favor, taking him on loan, as you put it?"

He waved a generous hand. "Keep him, if you wish. I like my footman, and I have no need of a second one."

"We do not need to steal the help from the houses of our friends, Diana, dear," Mr. Bornholdt said, speaking straight through a smile.

She tilted her head, coquettish. "It is not stealing when it is their suggestion, darling."

"Really, Wythe," Mr. Malahide said, over the rumble of Mr. Bornholdt's next protest, "he has grown too tall not to be in livery; he would be striking in that cocoa shade you have your men wear."

"Oh, think," Mrs. Bornholdt said, "a handsome manservant for you to go with my lovely maid."

"Let me send my coachman back for him," Mr. Malahide suggested. "He will return long before we finish in the drawing room. It is no trouble at all to us—is it, Elena?—and your lives will be easier."

I came around to Mr. Bornholdt himself and bent down to serve him.

"Of course," Mrs. Malahide said. "And it is only for the present. If you do not like him, once your footman is mended, we can see our Saint Valentine situated someplace else, so it is no bother to you."

The waiter wobbled on my open palm. I caught it.

"Well!" Mrs. Bornholdt said. "There is a name one hardly hears anymore."

"Yes, it must be a family one," Elena said. "Valentine Hobbs, he is called."

I made a grab for the rim of the waiter as it tipped again, but the dishes I carried fell and turned over. The thin bleu cheese ran toward the table's edge—toward Mr. Bornholdt.

"Damn it!" he shouted, throwing his weight behind him, sliding back in his chair.

The table went silent again. I could hear the spill, dripping.

"You clumsy cow!" he said to me.

Mrs. Bornholdt threw her napkin onto the table. "Wythe!"

Then there was the harsh sound of a chair pushed back at the other end of the table. "If you are incensed," Mr. Bornholdt's father said, "it is by your own design. That girl never should have been serving at a dinner table, and this particular dinner never should have been. You make a mockery of yourself, and punish a woman for your folly, just as you always have."

Mr. Bornholdt sat frozen, eyes cast down, and yet his face was red, swelling again with anger. I saw his Adam's apple jump as he swallowed, and this seemed to let the feeling down his throat. Evenly, he said, "Yes, sir."

Beside me, the butler cleared his throat. He was holding out a cloth to me. Trembling, I fell to my knees and busied myself in cleaning up the mess.

"So it is settled," Mr. Malahide said, somewhere above, and he even gave a brave chuckle. "We shall send for Hobbs this moment."

I heard Mr. Bornholdt sigh. "Very well."

"And we are grateful," Mrs. Bornholdt added pointedly. "Thank you, Christopher—and Elena—for your generosity. Some people in this world seek opportunities to wound with their power, but you use yours in quite the opposite manner."

"Oh, anytime. Wythe, might we send your butler as a messenger out to the stables?"

"Yes," he said. "He can escort Marian from the table as well."

"I'm sorry, sir," I began, my lips prickly numb.

"You have done enough this evening," Mr. Bornholdt said, through his teeth. "You are dismissed."

"Yes, sir."

I got to my feet. They were shaking.

The butler had been careful in closing the door directly off the dining room, but he slammed the one to the servants' stairs behind us. The sound echoed in my head, underscored the name on which I fixated.

"Why have you gone pale? It can't have been any worse than you expected," Ledford grumbled. When I began to follow him down, he added, "You're not coming to the stables. Go to your room."

I froze, but could not immediately bring myself to turn around.

He sighed, stopped walking, and regarded me more fully. "I'm sorry," he said. "I'm sure you are disoriented about how to carry on. I was, when my father died. My best advice is to take it one task at a time. Go upstairs. Clean up. Change. Attend to the mistress. Then you sleep. You worry about the morning when the morning comes." At the end of this speech, he smiled, as if he were bestowing a gift upon me.

I turned away. I had not been thinking of my mother. Now that I did think of her, though, my terror increased. She had predicted this very thing, the last time we'd spoken. And only in her ignorance had she thought it would be comforting.

I took the stairs one at a time at first, and I felt I was testing the strength of the steps out of hell. Any moment they would give, my foot falling through, and I would tumble down into a pit of fire, where I belonged. Valentine was coming.

Despite Mr. Bornholdt's best efforts to stop it, Valentine *was* coming.

And was that longing in my breast, despite what I knew about all that business now, how wrong we'd been to play those games? It was no fantasy, it was real—and so was the danger. Valentine wasn't even here yet, and he was already proving I had not changed. That Mrs. Davies was right about me, that I had put ideas in Mr. Bornholdt's head.

The master, to whom I already owed something, was now furious with me.

12

I changed into my black uniform, then spent the evening before Mrs. Davies's fire, staring into the flames. The housekeeper didn't ask me where my head was, because of course she thought she knew, just as the butler had thought he'd known. But I didn't think of Mother. I was too busy listening for sounds I probably could not have heard—a horse's approaching whinny, a coach's slowing wheels on the service road, the door swinging in to the kitchens.

Instead of any of these, what I got was the shrill summons of my mistress's bell, near to midnight. The waiting had grown to be so exhausting, I was relieved to go. Mrs. Davies, too, seemed to relax a bit. I suspected I was fraying her nerves as I moved constantly about, accomplishing little.

Mrs. Bornholdt smiled as I slipped into her room. "Marian." She was still in her dinner dress—green, but not the green I'd made her. She must have ordered it in the time I'd been gone. The thought shook me somewhat from my thoughts.

"I should've been here to help you prepare," I said, curtsying. "I apologize, ma'am."

"Nonsense," Mrs. Bornholdt replied. The scoff in the word was real, vehement. Her eyes were serious, yet warm as they'd been at dinner. "You were doing your duty as a daughter. That is no less important than your duties here."

"I appreciate your understanding, ma'am," I said—and I did. But as I moved forward to help her to undress, I wondered where it came from. There was no audience anymore; she could say whatever she liked to me. Yet she still had not hardened into the woman she had been before I left for London.

Perhaps it was because I grieved my mother, and her sympathies were aroused—knowing I had nobody. The thought certainly pricked at the corners of my eyes. But I could not break down crying in her dressing room.

Mrs. Bornholdt's dress fell to the floor around her, and I helped her step out of it.

The silence between us seemed breakable, so I asked: "Did all the guests go home, ma'am?" If I hadn't heard anybody leaving, I wouldn't be able to hear anybody coming, either.

"No, no." She rolled her naked shoulders. "The men are in the drawing room still, but I told the ladies to carry on with dessert alone. Ledford is serving. It is a lot of activity for me, I am afraid. You understand."

"Yes, ma'am," I said, though I did not. She'd still not told me what ailed her.

Mrs. Bornholdt lifted her arms, and I eased a cream cotton nightgown over her head. Perhaps her pain was more manageable today, and that made her friendlier.

"You look troubled, Marian," she said. "I do not suppose you can be comforted fully, but I hope you know that you are a good daughter. Your mother was blessed to have such a child as you."

My ears grew hot. "Thank you, ma'am."

She had no idea how terrible I was. I had only tricked her, like I'd tricked Mrs. Martin after Valentine was taken from the workhouse. I had blushed at Mr. Bornholdt's portrait. I had given him the idea to touch me.

To hide my burning face more than anything else, I bent to pick up the clothing my mistress had shed, gathering it into a bundle under my arm. I was on the point of rising when Mrs. Bornholdt touched my shoulder.

"I know the value of a daughter." She bent down, so our heads nearly touched. "The depth of grief, one for the other, must match the depth of love."

I searched her face, uncertain as to where this was going.

"I was a mother, for a moment," she said then. "In the eighth month my daughter came, and died soon after."

I didn't know what to say. I wanted terribly to look away from her, but a stronger feeling stopped me.

"I'm sorry," I said. The words felt pathetic to me, but they seemed to ease the strain of her mouth, her forehead.

"We try and try, since." She gestured toward her bedroom. "I do exactly as the doctor said to do. I hardly tax myself at all. I take the salt baths. I drink that wretched medicine."

She puckered her face, and even having been away for a week, I could conjure the putrid, nauseous smell of it for myself. But then, she wasn't sick. Her greenness, her weakness, was but a side effect of a treatment that was meant to help her. I didn't know how nervous I had been about it until I felt my worry lifting.

"But my body cares not for the plotting of my mind or the fervent wishing of my heart," she was saying. "Perhaps God gave me a chance, and since I failed, he will not give me another. After all, life is precious. Why waste it?"

"I hope God is not so harsh a judge as that," I blurted. "You didn't do anything wrong. If anything, you were the wronged one."

"That's very nearly blasphemous," Mrs. Bornholdt said, but she was smiling. "I do try to show him that I mean to do better, next time."

She gestured at the surface of her vanity, where sat all her boxes for her face powders and her hairpins and so on. There was the cherub blowing the kiss, and on everything, flowering vines, blooming roses—growing things. Just the same as the pot that held her Epsom salts. The same as the flower bowl that had been upon that evening's dining table.

The belly of the bowl looks full of life even though it is perfectly barren.

"Mrs. Bornholdt," I gasped.

"What?" she asked, searching me as if I might be wounded, but it was her, she who had been attacked. She had looked like she was fighting tears this evening.

"How he hurt you," I said. "In front of your family, who do not even know to scold him for it."

The skin between her brows pinched. "Who?"

"Mr. Bornholdt, at dinner—"

Her eyes widened. Then she waved it all away. "Oh, oh, no. Wythe is only frustrated, and not at me—not really. I understand it. I am frustrated, too, Marian. It is my body we are angry with, together. Together. I am the one who tells him my body is a stranger to me." She leaned back so she was tall in her chair. "But I bear it as best I can. I make things pretty for us both despite the darkness of it. He sees that. He sees my strength in it. That is what he was saying."

I frowned at her.

"What he tries to say," she amended. "But I am weak inside. As weak of heart as I am of womb, I suppose, and sometimes it does sting. But I cannot let him see. It would be but another disappointment to him."

I wondered at her expression. There was real anxiety in it, as if she were not mistress of a grand house—as if she were a servant herself.

"Please do not make me regret my confidence in you, Marian," she said, drawing her shoulders down, composing herself over again. "Why, I was only trying to console you, not looking for any consolation myself. Do not let this conversation leave this room, and especially do not report it to my husband. He has done no wrong. I wrong him, much as I do not mean to. He deserves children. But blaming him for how the situation cuts me—that would be a choice, and that is not what I want."

"Yes, Mrs. Bornholdt. I understand. I won't say a word, of course."

Her eyes were shrewd. "But you are still thinking of it."

"No, ma'am." I cast around, my eyes landing on her laundry. That gave me an idea. "Actually, I'm thinking about your corsets. Bone and metal stays aren't good for babies. I'd like to take them out of yours and make new stays out of jean instead."

She put a hand to her cheek and smiled.

◆ ◆ ◆

I stepped out into the hall with a bundle of washing under one arm and a few corsets under the other, and as Mrs. Bornholdt said goodbye, I smiled sincerely enough at her. I had a mission, a path forward to pleasing her again, to proving myself loyal, and to being of real, good use. I turned with spirit to be on my way and to begin my adjustments to her clothes at once.

But each step I took down the corridor was slower than the last, my eyes lingering on the dark-plum paint on the walls. It still looked like bruising to me, the severity only slightly relieved by the lanterns bracketed here and there. I drifted to the middle of the way, so that I walked apart from either wall, but even still I felt connected to some great pain of the house—as if I added to its grief just by being there. But if the house was hurting, it did so in silence; my light feet on the carpet were the only sounds, with no answering complaints from the boards beneath. Even so, my brief moment of elation felt to me like a brightly colored kerchief kept on for a funeral, and I stowed it ashamedly away.

Of course, it was I who had recently been beside a new grave. The wash of guilt at this thought, at having forgotten Mother even for a moment, made me stop.

My elation was, indeed, too bright a thing—not for the house but for me. If Mother's ghost were here within these walls, watching me . . . I grimaced to consider my own conduct. I deserved the punishment that Valentine's coming would be for me.

My heart quickened.

There was still a part of me that missed him. That had learned nothing from what damage had already been done by him. That did not care that to see him was dangerous to me, and only wondered when he would arrive.

I stormed the rest of the way to my room.

At my door, I set down the bundle of washing so I could take off my shoes, leaving them beside the jamb. They were crusted with dry cemetery mud and would need a polishing.

Inside, my traveling clothes and uniform pieces were everywhere—on the bed, on the floor, draped over the table. But I could not think of setting my room to rights. I shifted Mrs. Bornholdt's laundry pile just within, closed my door, and went to the window.

It was raining again. I could hear the shushing of it, like an admonishing parent. I thought of the other footman, home with a broken leg because he'd been unloading the grocer's coach at the wrong time. The roads were dark. They were slippery and narrow even in the best of times. A blustering wind could snuff a coach lantern as easily as a tired breath blows out a candle.

If Valentine hadn't arrived yet, he might never.

Would that have been better for me? The question conjured the image of him crying, after he was struck by the workhouse master, and brought with it a rush of feeling that burned my own eyes. I didn't wish him harm. But did he have to come here?

As I stood at the window, a bar of mellow gold stretched out across the lawn below. A procession of shadows came down through it, and distantly I could hear the rumble of men conversing. I was too high up and insulated to get the words, but the sound was merry, if rushed.

If they were going home, surely the Malahide coach had returned. And the party would not have been so jovial if the promising new footman had met doom on his journey—always assuming they had some sympathy in them for the lower classes. And Mr. Malahide had said Valentine's coming wouldn't take longer than their visit.

All I had to do was go down, and probably I would see him. My heart might burst, or break.

And what if he didn't remember me?

It had been six years at least since he'd gone away without a word. And he'd never written—even though he must've known I'd been miserable. He knew how pitifully I lived. And all that time, he'd been in a room like this one, and never thought of me.

I shook my head. I would not go down to see him when he arrived. He could find out I was here and come running to me if he liked. And if he didn't, well, that wouldn't be a surprise at all. Six years was a long time for a man, when I knew Mr. Bornholdt could strategically forget about his wife in a matter of hours.

And as to that—as to my being a woman awakened, as Mrs. Davies called it? That trouble had started with Valentine. I had been at his mercy when we were children. That was the way of the game, as he'd known very well. But he'd never used his power to hurt me deliberately—until then. Of course he had been powerless to stay, when the adults around him had found a new situation for him, but at least he could have told me. He could have warned me. He could have shared his pain with me. I could have borne some of it for him.

He could have told me the last game was goodbye.

Yet it hadn't seemed to worry him. If he had any idea what he'd done, any guilt at all, he'd had six years to make his apologies—six long years in which a letter sent to Parish Street would have reached me.

I forced myself away from the window and found the big silver scissors Mrs. Davies had given me to keep in my room. If I gave my hands work to do, they would stop their indulgent shaking.

I would see him in the morning—and I would worry about the morning when the morning came, as Ledford had suggested.

I set a chair between the table at the center of my room and the door. I listened to the house going deeply quiet, and meanwhile snipped holes in the bottom of one of Mrs. Bornholdt's corsets. I felt for the thin steel stay embedded in the tiny fabric tunnel, then worked it forward, toward me, with my fingers. It took its time, but by and by it came.

I set the first stay on the table and got to work on the rest. I had one left when I thought I heard footsteps in the hallway. The footman coming 'round for shoes to polish. The new footman, an old friend. A stranger to me now, or perhaps more like an enemy.

I hummed to cover the sound of his approach, snipping the last opening I needed with my scissors. His footsteps grew louder, and I pressed my lips together, my thumbs working the corset like rubbing a lucky penny.

The footsteps stopped at my door.

I stood up, the corset falling out of my lap, and stared as if I could will myself to see through the wood—to watch him bending down.

He was not my enemy. He was my friend—my friend, come back across time and miles, to stand inches away. A thousand things might have happened to him. He might have died, or been put away. Instead, he was alive. He was right here.

On tiptoe, I drew close enough to put my hand on the handle, and he didn't know my hand was there—didn't know I held my breath, straining to hear his.

But there was only silence.

Then the footsteps again, loud at first, so close. But they were fading.

I felt small again. It was as if I'd just burst out of Mother's embrace and rushed up to the door of the women's ward, meaning to search for someone already out of my reach. The door had been locked to me, then.

But this door was not. I was a grown woman. This door was mine to open at will.

I turned the handle and stuck my head out. My shoes were gone. The hallway was empty. Setting my jaw, I did what I had not had the power to do six years before. I gave chase.

13

I could hear him.

By the time I gained the stairwell, he was already out of view, but the echo of his footsteps came to me from below. I longed to peek down over the banisters to see the top of his head, but I kept to the outside walls and stayed two full sets of steps above him. Then I heard the door to the kitchen stairs swing shut.

I rushed to close the distance, but turned the doorknob as if it were the dial to a safe and I a thief, listening to the inner workings of the lock.

I pulled the door barely open and peeked through the gap.

There, by the light of candles all bracketed along the wall, was the gilt hair I remembered, but neater, with all the tarnish scrubbed from the bronze. He was tall and svelte in his brown coattails, and I marveled at how lively his steps were. He was new to the house, as I'd been new, and yet he showed none of the trepidation I'd had upon arrival. He took the remaining stairs as if he weighed little, as if nothing at all burdened his mind. But then, perhaps nothing did.

My shoes were in his hand, a fact I felt in my stomach.

Lucette came into view and, seeing the shoes, rolled her eyes. "What a fiasco."

"Sorry?" some man said, and when I realized it had to have been him, I had that feeling again, that feeling that the world had tipped upside down since Mother's death. A stranger's voice, coming from my old friend's mouth. What did that mouth look like now? He had not yet turned his face in the direction of the door.

"Don't you know why you're here?" Lucette was asking him.

"The Bornholdt family is in need of a footman," he replied.

I strained my ears, sifting through the sound he made for some hint of his younger self. His consonants were clear, his vowels gentle and soft. But instead of doubting this was Valentine, the change made me more sure it had to be him. His was not a servant's usual accent, rough and half-schooled. This man had studied the speech of the family for whom he'd last worked, just the same as the boy I knew had studied the workhouse master for our game.

"Mr. Malahide had one man more in his house than he needed," he said next, and his tone betrayed a dislike for the maid, or at least for her attempt to make him feel ignorant. "So I was sent where I was wanted."

"Well, yes, but don't you wonder why?" Lucette said. "Not every day a family friend gives a servant as a dinner gift."

Here she stopped to look him over. I drew my brows together, scowling.

Valentine turned, so I could see one dark eye, a fine cheekbone, the sharp edge of his nose. "Excuse me, I must brush these."

"Well, that's why I was saying." Lucette reached out, as if to forestall him physically.

But when he turned his eyes on hers, she stopped her hand midair, and it fell between them like a swatted fly.

"It was her, the owner of the feet what fill the dirty shoes," she said. "Came back from traipsing around London and burst in on a fancy dinner as if she was royalty. Dumped cheese on the master, she did."

"Oh, shurrup you!" Mrs. Davies stamped into view. "I've got a throbbing headache, and you're not helping it."

Lucette reared back as she turned. "Take it up with Osley! She caused it, not me."

"She has been through something," Mrs. Davies snapped. "Do you want to go through something, too? I could see to that."

"Osley?" Valentine asked, between them.

These syllables reached me warm—I felt them in my cheeks—and meanwhile both women, the one in her spring and the other in her winter, turned to Valentine like flowers to the sun. I had to hold the doorknob, or else I would have fallen through the door, drawing all attention at precisely the moment I felt completely naked.

"Is there an Osley here?" Valentine asked.

Lucette and Mrs. Davies looked at each other, both wearing the same startled expression. I wrapped my fingers tighter around the door handle, ready. But I made myself wait. The part of me that was pleased to be remembered was a small one, and not the wisest part besides.

"Would it be Marian Osley?" he tried.

"It would," I said, but my chest was tight, and the words came quietly, only loud enough for me to hear. I went on wobbly knees through the door, and held the handrail tight. Louder, I said, "It would."

He took a step back, staring up at me.

I grinned. He remembered me. For all I had misunderstood, he had been my friend. I had not imagined it.

Afraid to fall, I watched my feet as I descended. When I finally looked up at the bottom of the stairs, everyone was staring at me: the bratty maid, the brassy housekeeper, and—yes—the boy I'd known. I could see him in this man's eyes, in the curve of his mouth; I found him there, hiding—coming out by degrees to see whether it was really me.

Lucette put her weight on one hip, her body curved, a disbelieving question mark. "You know him?"

"I've never met this man before," I said, taking in his stronger chin and brow, the deeper set of his eyes.

"Seems like you have," Lucette said, her voice low.

I could not divide my attention to answer her further, for I was busy fighting the sudden urge—now that he looked so favorably upon me—to rush into Valentine's arms.

Mrs. Davies cleared her throat. I looked around to find her studying me in some seriousness. "Go along, Lucette," she said. "Let Mr. Hobbs get to his shoe shining, and let Marian . . . Well, let Marian alone, for goodness' sake."

"Yes, Mrs. Davies," Lucette murmured, and she stalked away toward a pile of dishes that needed washing, her skirt swaying not unprettily. I glanced at Valentine, to see whether he noticed her—but his eyes were on me. Intently so.

"I'm going to bed," Mrs. Davies said next—clearly a suggestion that I do the same.

"Yes," I said. "It's been a long day."

"Good night, Mr. Hobbs. The butler will wake you early to show you more thoroughly around." She looked between us again. "My door is thin, and my sleep thinner—I'll hear the lightest tap, if you should need something."

Valentine tore his gaze from me, touching his hand to the back of his neck. "Yes—thank you, ma'am. Good night, Mrs. Davies." He watched her head to the office, staring at the door long after it had shut.

His lips were bigger than they had been, redder. Or perhaps my memory was faded. But his hair was tended, different as a garden from wilderness; the back of it he kept short, but it was long on top, overflowing his forehead.

And just as the tarnish was gone from his hair, the rust in his eyes had given way to something livelier—like a cinnamon stick. But the look in his eyes—judging by the one I could see, anyway—was no different for the intervening years: sturdy, certain. I wondered: If I mattered to him as he mattered to me, then what did he make of that game we had played as children? Did the wild urchin live on inside the man? Or had the man been looking out of the urchin even all those years ago?

The phrase *woman awakened* came to mind and echoed there, each repetition more frantic than the one before. I should have taken my leave, now that we were alone. Yet I stood still. I waited.

Mr. Malahide had been right: the velvet chocolate jacket Valentine wore was complementary to him—lending him warmth. I wondered whether it would be strange of me to say that to him. Or perhaps it was stranger, and more revealing, that I worried over saying such a thing, and it would be more natural to say it than not. But as the seconds passed, the silence between us grew strangest of all. Panicking, I said: "Livery suits you."

"Does it?" He looked down at himself, plucking at the front of his vest, demonstrating how much extra fabric there was. "The fit's all wrong. It belonged to the last footman, of course—the real footman."

I waved a hand. "But that's easy to fix. I wonder if they'll let me take it in or send it out to a tailor."

"Oh, I can modify it myself, so long as—" He looked up. "You?"

"I'm good at it." I stood straighter. "I'm the lady's maid."

He crossed his arms, leaning back to take me in afresh. "The lady's maid."

He looked . . . proud. Or I thought he did.

Then his brows went up. "Did the lady of the house ask you to dump the cheese on her husband?"

"No," I said, and my first instinct was to shrink into myself. But Valentine was smirking, and I added: "That was all my idea."

He laughed. I laughed. Then silence, falling soft and sweet as snow—but seen from an inside window, out of the chill.

"I almost expect Mrs. Martin to yell at us," he admitted, looking around for her.

I looked, too, but really I was searching for something to say. Something about the past that wasn't about the game. That wasn't about his going away, or how lonely I had been. But there was something of one or both in every thought I had, and the silence was stretching, until finally I had to speak or else excuse myself.

"You didn't tell me your mother had died," I said. It sounded more accusatory than I'd meant it to be, and I drew my shoulders taut, already admonishing myself. That had been years ago, too many years to be answered for.

But he said, "I didn't know how." So fast, as if he'd been waiting for this attack.

In my guilt, I blurted, "My mother died, too."

"What?" he asked, sharp and strained. "When?"

"Just now," I said. "A week? Two?"

My shoes hit the floor with a soft slap, and Valentine's arms came up, his head turned to fit my shoulder. But it was as if he came up against a wall, and he could not break through to me. He pressed his lips tight together, and clasped his hands behind his back. "I'm sorry, Marian."

I balled my hands at my sides, trying to cover the fact that I had been ready to receive him into my arms. "So am I, for you."

"Well," he said, "that was a long time ago."

"You don't feel it anymore?"

"Not in the same way," he said, reaching—but only for the words, not for me. "Not so deeply as I did."

"Oh." I looked away. As awful as the pain of my grief was, I thought that not feeling it would have been worse. As if my mother hadn't mattered. Or as if she would matter less, someday, because I'd left her behind.

"I'm so glad you got out," he said. "It's wonderful to see you again."

"Like a dream," I said, raising my gaze. For a moment his face flickered in the candlelight, and the actual Valentine before me transformed into the Valentine I'd once seen in my sleep—in a dream, after he was gone. *Woman awakened,* I thought, and tasted the tobacco of Mr. Bornholdt's fingers on my tongue.

I stepped back. "I should go up to bed."

Valentine stepped back a pace as well. "Yes. You go on." He bent to pick up my shoes. "We can talk more tomorrow."

It was nearly what he'd said at dawn in the stables—as different as everything was. I wondered if he recognized it. Perhaps he'd be gone again in the morning. Perhaps that would be best.

I shook myself. "Good night, Valentine."

"Good night, Marian."

I went up the stairs, not feeling my stockinged feet, looking back twice before I'd reached the top to confirm that Valentine was still there. And all the time he stood still, watching me go, his expression clouding—as if he grew less certain I was real the farther I drifted away. But I waved my hand in final farewell, and his smile flared back into full life.

Grinning, too, I slipped through the door at the top. I turned tightly to take the next flight upward—and smacked hard into Mr. Bornholdt.

"I have been waiting," he hissed, as if we'd had an appointment I'd forgotten. But he didn't seem to care about any apology I might make; before I'd even gotten my head around his being there, he had my wrist clutched in his hand and was dragging me up the stairs behind him. The fruity, stale smell of a cigar wafted back to me—and, underneath, fumes of wine so strong he might have doused himself in it. On the second landing, he put his open palm between my shoulders and shoved, so I fell through the door onto the hall.

"You know where my study is." Then, as if I'd hesitated: "You find me when you need me there, do you not?" I rushed to the great walnut door; whatever vague danger there was in going, it was not the certain doom of resisting. I fumbled in my apron for my copy of the needed key. It went home and turned just before Mr. Bornholdt had hobbled within arm's reach of me. I threw the door open and stepped to the side.

"There you are, sir. Is there anything else I can do for you?"

"I thought you would never ask. Get in there, you."

I recoiled. "Sir—"

"Now."

He slammed the door so hard it seemed to shake the house. I thought surely it would wake someone—Mrs. Bornholdt, or Mrs. Davies.

The master strode across the room toward me, making me back away from him. His golden hair was loose and wild, and his eyes sparkled in the lamplight. "That business at dinner—is that how you repay your master?" He tried on a frown, but it seemed he couldn't keep it on his face. He shook his head and sneered. "I empty my purse to put your mother to rest, and you make a farce of my family home. You make me wear the food I pay for when you should be feeding it to me on your filthy knees."

He hadn't gotten any of it on him. But I could not say this.

"Do you know what your problem is, Marian?" he asked. "There is no give to you."

He reached out then for my hand—quicker than he should have been in his inebriation, much quicker than I in my shock—and shook me by it. I had to get closer to him if I did not want him to break my arm. "Loosen up, woman—you statue!"

"Sir, please—"

"Do not beg me for anything." He cast off my hands, as if I had been the one tugging him. "Look here. You are an ungrateful little thing. After what I have done for you, I expected you to take me seriously. To be wise enough not to trifle with me. But you are not wise, are you?"

"I'm—"

"I have thought and thought about what to do with you." He took two uneven, toy-soldier steps to his desk, executed a sloppy about-face, and sat on the edge. "My wife says I should go easy on you. Because you miss your mother. But do you know what I think?"

"What's that, sir?" I inched backward.

But he leaned forward, as if he were sharing a secret. "I think what you need is a man, Marian. Someone willing to slap the insubordination out of you."

My lips opened, for my instinct was to argue. But the image of a riding crop hanging on a stable wall came unbidden to my mind, and with it the damning way I'd coveted it. I cringed as I curtsied. "Yes, sir."

"Eager, are you?" He licked his lips. "You would like to be struck?"

"If your will is that I should be, sir," I said, as steadily as I could manage, as hot guilt and shame flooded my face.

"But there are many ways my will might be satisfied," he said, with a slow-spreading smile. "Indeed, I am not naturally so violent of mind. That is your fault. But in a better mood, I might will all sorts of pleasant things. Might you like to help me attain those instead?"

I had to fight not to physically recoil from the idea. My mind, my heart, and yes—my body, too—said no, ferociously. I was not bad all the way down. But faces were resilient, hardy things. I would be no less virtuous, if he hit me. And the blood that rushed to my cheek would settle and flow again, as if it had never happened. I took a deep breath, set my jaw, and said, "I would rather you hit me, sir."

"You fool," he growled. "I am telling you I do not have to hit you. I do not want to hit you. What I want is so simple and sweet that anyone else, anyone else I condescended to take it from, would happily give it to me."

And before I could stop myself, I said: "Like your wife, sir?"

He slapped me.

I touched my cheek—not because it stung but because it didn't. The feeling came back with the heat of my palm, and I turned wide, wet eyes upon Mr. Bornholdt. His hands came crashing down again, this time on my shoulders, so heavily my knees buckled. He dragged me by my uniform until our faces were so close his breath blew across my lips. "Oh yes, she does. Happily and often. But my wife is a fragile thing, as I think you may have noticed, and if I am not careful, I am apt to break her. I do not want to break her, Marian, but I also do not always want to be careful."

He pressed his lips to mine, and I couldn't get away. My weight was pitched forward, toward him, my feet too far behind me, and his grip was firm. I broke away long enough to get my breath before he was kissing me again. They were quick, pecking, stabbing kisses. "You got the slap you asked for," he said, his mouth against mine. "Did you like it?"

I tried to find purchase for my feet, but all I managed was to rumple the rug, which bunched, slack, behind my heels. "Sir, please—please let me go."

"Let you go? Would you not like your job any longer?"

His hands ran down my arms.

"Yes, but—"

"Then what you want is to stay on," he murmured, his arms snaking around my torso. "What you want is for me to be your master. Yet you look down on me."

I squirmed, trying to get control, or distance. "I'm not, I don't, I—"

"It is I who should be looking down on you, and I should not have to stand up to do it when standing up is not my prerogative." He shoved me away. "Kneel."

I staggered back. "Yes, sir." I shook as I obeyed.

"Good. Now." He uncrossed his legs. "Come here. Do not get up; crawl. Put your head right here. Against your master's knee."

This instruction, too, I followed. The scratch of his trousers against my temple made me shudder. "Yes, sir."

"What a difference we have made in a moment. You have remembered that you told me you would be good and take my orders."

I glanced up, to see what danger might be coming. His fingers touched my hair, and he studied the strands as if they were pearls he meant to purchase. I shut my eyes.

"You do not like to look upon me?" His voice was soft, dangerous.

"I'm tired, sir," I told him, and—though I fought it—a traitorous tear slipped from beneath one of my eyelids and rolled down the cheek that did not lean against him.

"Oh," he sighed. His large, hot, hateful thumb came down directly upon the tear, and it did not feel as if he were wiping it away; it felt like he was rubbing it in. "Poor Marian. You must feel so ill-used, with this mean old man keeping you awake. A monster—is that not what you thought me, when your mother died?"

"No, sir," I stammered. "You used that word, I—"

"This monster, Marian, put a roof over your head," he said, softly. "He gave you your own room with a comfortable bed. He sees that you are fed well, that you have clothes to wear. You come to him crying for money, having already kicked him—literally kicked him—for his past kindness, and yet he gives you everything you ask for."

"Yes, sir." Agreeing made more tears come, so many that the way for his thumb was slick. He went on stroking, working the wetness into my skin.

"And what have you given him in return?" he asked.

"Nothing." A sob escaped me, and his hand moved to my mouth.

"Oh, no crying," he tutted. "It will only get more uncomfortable for you if you continue to resist. Come here and we will set it right."

He was dragging me up again, through his open legs, this time by my collar. I trembled and panted as I cried, but I couldn't communicate anything to my body anymore. I rose toward his face with all the inevitability of falling down a hole. He was the center of the earth, and his pull was gravity's.

Somewhere in the background of my mind, I heard a keening—one slow, thin whine. I thought the sound must have come from me. Then Mr. Bornholdt threw me backward onto the floor.

Instinctively, I drew my knees toward my chest and rolled to the side, expecting he would launch himself upon me from the desk. The weight of him never came, however, and when I opened my eyes, I was looking at the study door. It was open, and a blurry figure stood in it.

I blinked. It was Valentine.

14

"Did you not knock at your last job?" Mr. Bornholdt's tone was light, bemused.

Valentine made a quick bow. "I—I'm sorry, sir. I was going round to the lamps, and I saw light under the door. I was certain you'd gone to bed."

"If you were so certain, what am I doing here?"

Valentine bowed again. "I was mistaken, sir. I'm sorry."

Mr. Bornholdt laughed. "No matter, no matter. Your old master was not plagued with insomnia, I suppose. I should take your good advice and see myself to bed this minute." Looking down at me for the first time since the interruption, he frowned. "Goodness, girl, get up. It is bad enough you make a fool of yourself in front of me, but what will your new colleague think of you?"

Standing, he offered his hand down to me, but I used my feet to push myself backward.

"As you like it," he said, watching me rise.

I hurried toward Valentine, my eyes trained strictly on the floor and landing, inevitably, on his feet in the doorway.

"Please excuse me." My voice cracked.

The feet moved mercifully to let me pass.

When I reached my room and lit a candle for myself, it seemed wrong that everything was exactly as I had left it. So much had happened in between. But the corsets lay across the table, except the one that I'd dropped on the floor. I found my scissors with my foot and picked them up.

I was too anxious to sleep. The better to keep from thinking, I went to work at once on a second corset. My hands trembled, slowing me down, but still the metal stays fell one by one to the floor. Some of them slid out of the circumference of my candle's light, and I let them go. That I might forget their presence and step on them come morning seemed just.

It had really happened, was happening, between Mr. Bornholdt and me. There was a witness—Valentine, who could judge better than most how far I'd fallen. Meanwhile, there I was, methodically stripping the steel supports from the effects of my mistress. And she was letting me, because I'd told her it would do her good, and that was not a lie. But weakening her defenses did me good as well, and at that dark hour I could not see what goodness I deserved.

I had thought I could choose to move forward from what Mr. Bornholdt did. But I could not make anyone else choose to move forward from it with me. And without that latter power, I did not really have the former one at all.

◆ ◆ ◆

My shoes were waiting outside my door in the morning, as shiny as if they'd never been walked in—as if the day before had never happened. But it had.

I passed Valentine in the kitchen, on my way to the range to make my mistress's breakfast. He was heading to the footman's pantry, where anything that should be shined was kept along with the stock of cleaning supplies and so on. He must have taken in his uniform himself already; he looked svelte.

"Good morning," I made myself say.

He didn't reply, or look at me, or even slow down.

I frowned.

But I remembered my first full morning at Valor Rise: there had been little room in my mind to examine anything but my own performance, for everything I did and said I'd put under a mental microscope, fussing and tutting even as—outside my head—I tried to do better, speak better. So I resolved to think little of his preoccupation, though really it was all I thought of while I worked the range.

I passed Valentine again while I was bringing up the breakfast, some twenty minutes later. He was taking apart one of the lamps in the servants' stairwell to clean it. I had Mrs. Bornholdt's tray in my hands, and he stepped in toward the wall so I could pass. I smiled at him, but he only stared. There was no little boy deep down in his eyes anymore. The brunt of his contempt was worse than the slap Mr. Bornholdt had given me.

I could not meet Mrs. Bornholdt's eyes when I wished her a good morning, but she didn't seem to notice. She was still unwell from the exertion of the dinner party. That I was grateful for her distraction was my fourth or fifth strike against myself—I was losing count of the things for which I felt ashamed.

The Epsom-salt jar in Mrs. Bornholdt's room was almost empty. I drew her bath, then excused myself to refill the jar when she was ready to get into the water. When I returned to the kitchen, Valentine was scrubbing pots and pans from yesterday's dinner at the biggest sink—a small mercy, as it was the footman's pantry I needed for the Epsom salts. This time I made no effort to catch his attention but slipped past, counting on the general noise to cover my steps.

The pantry was narrow, with low drawers on all three sides. There were shelves all the way to the ceiling, packed full of lamp oil and spare glass globes, cast-iron pans, and copper pots. At the back, on the narrow wall directly opposite the doorway, was a set of fat but tall jars. The glass of them was clear, so their contents were visible. I grabbed the one full of white salts and carried it out under my arm to the long table in the center of the kitchens. The other maids were preparing food for the day, but there was free space on the end where I could pour.

Out of the corner of my eye, I saw Valentine turn from the sink and head in my direction. I was resolute in focusing on my task, but it seemed he wasn't going to let me; I felt him freeze behind me, felt his eyes burning the back of my neck.

"What are you doing?" he asked, as if speaking to me were a duty rather than a pleasure—as if he wanted me to know that.

I kept my head down. "Refilling the Epsom salts for Mrs. Bornholdt's baths."

"That's not Epsom salt," he said, with real alarm in his voice. "I've been using the Epsom salt to scrub pots. Here."

He slid another jar onto the table. I put mine down and looked between them. His was more familiar.

"See how gritty the Epsom salt is?" he asked, and then, as if I were a child: "Like pebbles?"

"Yes." The back of my neck was getting warm.

"What you took is oxalic acid." He pointed to the jar. "I know it by the long grains. It looks like rice. See?"

"Yes!" I hid my fists in my apron. "I admitted already that you're right."

For a moment he was silent, and I thought he might have been embarrassed for bullying me. But then: "It's not about my being right. Oxalic acid is for bleaching. If Mrs. Bornholdt had bathed with it—if you'd spilled some on this table and they cooked with it, if anybody drank it, thinking it was going to help them pass their food—"

"You've made your point." My whole face was red, I could feel it, and I hung my head to hide it.

He was silent for a moment. Then, softly, he said: "I thought you'd be sorry to wrong anyone."

His footsteps carried him away, but I stood still, waiting for my cheeks to cool.

◆ ◆ ◆

I didn't see Valentine for the rest of the day. Mrs. Bornholdt had some visiting that she wanted to do—looking in on a friend who had been unable to make the dinner party. If it were just that, she might have taken me with her, but she wanted to shop, too, which meant she ought to bring a male escort instead. This was a terrible relief to me. To be in her company, almost like a friend, after what had lately happened with Mr. Bornholdt, would have been torture.

I sorted out my mistress's clothes for the laundry in her absence, and ironed what pieces could be worn again. I thought about how I would have felt if I had not gotten myself entangled in such a filthy, unvirtuous mess. I should have been sad, frustrated even, to lose this first day to reacquaint myself with my childhood friend, had that friendship been pure. But no matter: now that my friend had gotten a glimpse of my situation such as it was, he wouldn't even speak to me.

When she returned, Mrs. Bornholdt took her dinner in her room, deeply exhausted by her excursion from the house but happy to have gone out. She'd picked out fabrics for me to fashion into gowns for her.

Every one was some shade of green.

She believed in me. But was I any better than the last lady's maid just because it was beneath me to put her in purple?

There was a knock at my bedroom door that night. I could have convinced myself I'd imagined it, except I could not relax enough to imagine things of late. I was sitting awake, replacing the old stays in Mrs. Bornholdt's corsets. It was late; I'd thought everyone else in the house asleep.

My hand hesitated on the handle. What if it was Mr. Bornholdt? I had avoided him the entire day; perhaps he had made it his business to seek me out. He hadn't followed me downstairs that time I'd kicked him, but this was different: it wasn't so filthy on the third floor as it was in the kitchens.

That I should pretend to be asleep was my first thought. I was already in a nightgown. I hadn't locked my door yet, however. If he chose to barge in, I'd be at a disadvantage.

"Who is it?" I whispered.

No one answered.

From a dresser in the corner, I took out a thin robe, putting my arm in the wrong sleeve once before managing to get it on. I knotted the ribbon at the waist and approached the door.

Another knock. The taps were furtive, uneven and far apart enough to have been accidental—like a tree branch touching and dragging against a window, except there were no trees out in the hallway.

"Who's there?" I asked again.

Nothing.

Taking a deep breath, I drew the door open wide enough to peek through. The first thing I saw was burnished gold, and it *was* Bornholdt—wild-haired and mad, come to finish what he'd started. Then the person at the door shifted, so I could see an eye in the gap I'd made—a sober, brick-brown eye.

"Valentine?" The part of me that liked him pulled the door open, before the rest of me could stop her.

He shushed me, and looked fast in each direction down the hall. Understanding, I stepped aside. He slipped lithely through the door, and took his time shutting it again—so softly it made no sound. Then he pressed his palms flat, to either side of him against the door, and said: "Please forgive me."

"Forgive you?" I blinked. Was he—was he sorry after all these years, for not saying goodbye?

He couldn't seem to speak. He only looked pained.

Perhaps it was bigger than just that. Perhaps he regretted the game entirely, knew what we had done was wrong, that I had been awakened. Perhaps he blamed himself for what he'd seen between Mr. Bornholdt and me, and it weighed on him. I took a step closer, but he held out an arm.

"Stay back—back there. It's not proper that I'm here, but it's for your good that I come. I promise, I'll not do you any harm."

I backed off, and he didn't stop gesturing me away until my bottom touched the far window. Behind me, the wind whipped up into a mournful moan, and the chill draft raised goose bumps beneath my robe.

"All right," Valentine said. It came out as a ragged sigh. He put his hand through his hair.

"What's the matter?" I asked.

"I need to talk to you." He took a breath. "No. I want to talk to you, about this . . . this thing with Mr. Bornholdt. Because you've been a friend to me."

"Oh, Valentine," I breathed. I did not know how light I would feel at the mere prospect of talking about it—I'd been focused so much on ignoring it—but now I saw that he would understand. I could explain, and I wouldn't have to be alone with the fact of it. I only had to pick a place at which to begin.

"I've thought and thought about what to do," he was saying, speaking to the floor, his palms joined in front of his lips as if he were praying. "About my loyalties. Because I am Mr. Bornholdt's man. But simply aiding Mr. Bornholdt in achieving his ends—or standing aside, as the situation may be—that's a simplistic view of my role. My actual job is to serve the Bornholdt *family*; I must protect the whole over any one part, even if that part is the head."

He raised his chin, as if expecting a reaction—but I didn't see where I came in.

"I'm telling Mrs. Bornholdt," he said. "About you and her husband."

I clutched the windowsill. "Oh."

He regarded the ceiling, bracing his body. "He'll be angry in the moment, but he's not in his right mind. When his passion no longer prevails over his reason, he'll thank me for stopping the ruin of his family, for returning him to the moral path befitting him." He spoke as if he were reciting something he'd memorized.

I slid to the floor on weak knees. "Valentine, she'll put me on the street."

"That's not my fault," he replied, his voice remote. His eyes were unblinking, and here was the boy I remembered: the police officer. And it had not been me he loved, never me he wanted. It was justice he was interested in.

He had no idea of the part he'd played in my undoing. If I'd been awakened, it was an accident, my own evil flaring up at an innocent touch, and not his intention at all.

I clasped my hands. "I'll have no good reference. I'll never find work. I'll end up back in the workhouse—"

"You should've considered that." His fingers curled into fists, but still he did not look at me. "Before getting entangled with him."

Something was wrong with my throat, my chest—making them tight, as if I were choking. I barely said: "I'm not."

His gaze dropped like an axe. "Don't lie."

And there—his eyes had something in them then. They were hard and cold, and his mouth twisted with disgust. "I came here to warn you, Marian, for the sake of the girl you used to be, the one who told me that people don't lie if they—" His mouth spasmed; his whole face softened, stricken, but he dashed the air before him with his hand, and the expression was gone. He said, more quietly: "Who believed good people didn't lie. If you were ever that girl, the least you could do is be honest."

"Fine," I said, quaking, and with that one word the choking ceased, and more words came. "I *am* entangled, and I don't mean to lie to you. It's me I'm lying to. I'm in a nightmare and I can't escape." My breath hitched. I was crying.

"Escape?" Keeping his body against my door, he craned his neck forward. "You said you don't want to leave."

"Not here," I said. "Him."

Valentine stared. "But you were—"

"He paid for my mother's funeral." I wrung my hands in my lap. "I asked him to. I knew it would be terrible, but watching Mother go into an unmarked mass grave was worse. Wasn't it? Could you have lived with yourself?"

Only after I'd asked the question did I think about whom I was asking. I put my hand over my mouth.

"I must, for here I am," he said, speaking through his teeth. "I watched them dump her in."

"Valentine," I breathed. "I'm so—"

"But you make your point," he said, in a deadened voice. "If I'd only been older, if only I'd known a rich woman, yes—I could see seducing her for such a noble purpose."

"I didn't seduce him!"

"No?" he asked, his eyebrows rising like a challenge.

"No." I opened my hands to him. "I mean . . . if I did, I didn't mean to! I asked for a loan. I wanted him to stop my wages, so I could work to pay him back. But he has all the money in the world, Valentine."

He crossed his arms. "So you give him your body instead."

"No." I dropped my fist to the floor beside me. "That's what I'm saying! I avoid him, but he finds me. I fight him, but he fights back, and if you hadn't come last night—"

“You mean you don’t—” His hand jerked out, but he forced it back to his mouth in a fist and held it there. “You aren’t—”

I shook my head. “What?”

He ran a hand through his hair, his gaze darting all around, as if the words he wanted were set out somewhere. At last, he asked, “You aren’t trying to take the place of Mrs. Bornholdt?”

I laughed once, sharply. “There’s no sum of money I would take to trade places with her.”

Valentine tilted his head, studying me.

“On the morning I first met him, Mr. Bornholdt stuck his fingers down my throat—he threw me over a couch.” I looked down at my shaking hands and watched my tears hit them. I did not feel my mouth making words anymore, but I heard myself say: “I was only trying to light a fire in the grate.”

A cracking sound, so like the snap of the logs shifting in the study on that awful morning, made me jerk my head. But it must have been Valentine’s knuckles, only, which were white with the tightness of his fist.

Eyes resolutely shut, he asked: “Did he . . .”

“No.” The feeling in my lips was coming back—tingling.

Valentine let out his breath slowly, and for a long moment, this was the only sound.

I wiped my eyes. “I fought him off.”

“Good girl,” Valentine said, with quiet, vehement life.

I shut my eyes, to keep from meeting Valentine’s gaze, because he may not have remembered—but I did. My feet remembered running across the women’s work-yard at Parish Street; my eyes, the uniforms hung out to dry, snapping like white flags of surrender in the breeze; my wrist, the cruel surety of Valentine’s grip; my arm, the twisting dance it used to do.

Perhaps Valentine had never known that I fought him not to avoid my torture, but to prolong it. I opened my lips to enlighten him, but another part of me stayed my tongue—that same selfish part that kept me from being honest with Mrs. Bornholdt about her husband and me.

"Oh, Valentine," I sighed. I was not actively crying anymore, but I was worn down—like old pipes—and the water leaked out anyway. "I'm ruined."

"No you're not."

"You said it yourself." I smoothed the skirt of my nightgown. "I'm not a good person anymore. Maybe I never was."

"Wait." And finally he stepped away from the bedroom door. He crossed the room to me in quick strides, got down on one knee, and reached out his open hand. "I wasn't looking properly. Let me see your hand."

I limply gave it to him.

"Oh, it's a fine hand," he told me gently. "A good woman's hand. It needs a shine, that's all." With his free hand, he took a white cloth—a startlingly clean, crisp one—from his pocket, wrapped mine in it, and rubbed.

I made a noise I did not mean to make, which he must have taken for disbelief.

"Really," he said. "I would know. I'm an officer of the law. As you are aware, from your thieving days."

I gave a hollow hiccup of a laugh, for his benefit, when in truth the remark made me want to weep more.

"Look." He unveiled my hands with a flourish. "All clean."

"They're no different," I said.

He drew nearer. "Close your eyes."

I did, and felt a pair of tears fall, and then his thumbs, brushing them both at once away. Then the cloth returned, softly buffing my forehead from my hairline down, my eyelids, my cheeks, the tip of my nose, my mouth, my chin.

"All clean." This time it was almost a question.

I opened my eyes. Our noses were so close.

"I should go," he said, and I didn't stop him.

I watched him rise, and heard myself ask: "Are you going to tell her?"

"No, of course I'm not going to tell her—it's not your fault, you shouldn't be punished."

But I wasn't so sure. And his certainty was only guilt at making me weep. I could hear it in the frantic way he spoke.

After all, it seemed he didn't know what he had done, when we were young. Perhaps because he had been innocent. Of course he had. He was an officer of the law. I should have told him what I was, what I'd done, after he'd disappeared. It hadn't ended with throwing a tantrum at my mother.

That had been only the beginning.

15

It began in earnest on one morning when all the girls were to have baths.

"Line up!" the matron shouted, though we already had. I stood against the cold wall of the corridor outside the bathroom, as I had done on my first night at Parish Street. The moist air and the splashing sounds echoing from the next room were the same. The only thing missing was the little boy from Sultan Street, Camberwell, demanding to be brought home.

When I was fourth in line, I could peek around the corner to see the tub. A woman in a workhouse uniform hoisted one child out of the water as another put the next child in. They doused their victim—a girl of about five—with water that had long ago gone cold. Shaking, she tried to hold herself, but the ladies pulled her arms away from her. Together, the women scrubbed the girl until she was red and shiny. Then, as her feet scrabbled against the side of the tub, they lifted her out. One of the women set upon her with a towel, with all the gentleness of scrubbing stubborn grease stains.

I bit my lip.

The matron stood out of splashing range, overseeing all but saying nothing, rubbing the knuckles of one hand with the other and scowling.

I watched the little washed girl stumble away from the tub, in a fresh uniform, still shivering. Not one of the adults seemed to care where she went, now that they were finished with her.

I went toward the beckoning fingers of the woman nearest me, the one who was doing the undressing. She shucked my nightgown like the husk from corn—fast and rough, for she had a whole crop to divest. It had become my habit to daydream during this ritual, to escape the indignity and impersonality of it, but now I made myself feel the roughness of the woman's hands. I was airborne, then I was in the tub, and finally I was drenched. My lips quivered.

This was not what it felt like to be cared for.

I crouched, submerging my hands in the water around my knees, and splashed the face of the washing-woman who so mishandled me.

"Oi!" she cried, shielding her face with her arms. I could hear in her voice how she despised me. I scrunched my face against a surge of anger and swung my arms wide, to spray the room. Many more people shouted.

Mrs. Martin pulled me out of the bath by my underarms, and my toes whacked against the splintering rim of the tub. She threw a musty towel over my head and dried me herself, rough and heedless of my crying. Then she thrust a scratchy uniform into my hands. "Dress," she said, whipping the towel aside.

Sniveling, I stuck my arms in the shirt and buttoned it, and I kicked my feet through the leg holes of the trousers.

"Are you pleased with yourself?" Mrs. Martin demanded.

"Aren't you?" I whirled to face her. "Aren't you happier now, having somebody to hurt?"

Her lips thinned. "You are hurting yourself. How are you ever to better your situation if you are always—"

"I'm not at my worst, you are!" I pointed into her face. "You can't bear anyone to have a scrap of happiness, so you snatch it away!"

Puffing out a breath, she led me farther from the watching crowd of children, out of the bathroom and down the hall. Once we no longer had an audience, she swung me around to face her again. "Marian," she hissed, "if you won't be good, I will put you out on the street."

I pulled my arm out of her grip. "But there's nothing left to be good for! This is a bad place! Bad food, bad air, bad bathwater! I'm bad as the rest of it; I don't care!"

She leaned in close, her eyebrows arched. "You'd better, child. The world doesn't owe you goodness, Marian; you owe your goodness to the world."

"I was good, Mrs. Martin!" My eyes filled with tears. "But I can never be good again now I'm here, and you know it. You make sure of it."

Her mouth fell flat. I waited, trembling, to be slapped or shouted at—but I did not drop my gaze.

"Come," she said. Her tone and face, both, were something less than calm—closed, like a finished book. "I have a solution for you."

The hard way she took my hand made me plant my feet. But she was stronger, and she dragged me until we were on the other side of the workhouse entirely—near the boys' ward and yard.

"Here," Mrs. Martin said, and I could read the words etched on the glass pane of the door before us: Tailoring Room. She turned the handle, the door swung forward, and she shoved me in.

Sewing machines ticked along all four walls, as if the room were full of clocks; at first they raced to pass the seconds, only to get tired, slow down, and need to hurry up again. At each machine, people pedaled their feet, pushing fabric with their fingers. The girls seemed old enough to be almost women, but the boys were all ages. I could see the stabbing sewing needles even where I stood, for they flashed at me, catching my eye.

I turned to Mrs. Martin, but she was looking over my head. She clapped her hands, and the clattering of sewing machines ceased. "To the exercise yards, all of you."

They were so tall and terrifying, all of them running my way at once—these poised and focused workers suddenly turned wild. I cowered low to the floor, afraid to be knocked over.

The mob thundered off, the sound of their feet softening with distance. The door to the tailoring room whined shut.

"What are we doing here?" I asked.

Instead of answering, Mrs. Martin led me to the nearest sewing machine. She bent and lifted me under my arms, sitting me firmly on the high stool.

I peeked at the sewing machine—studying the needle up close, then looking under the sewing table, at the pedal that would make the machine move.

"You'll need to grow a bit before you can use it," the matron said. "But anyone can mend by hand. There's more mending to be done than machines on which to do it, so I'm going to have you work at that awhile."

"Instead of picking oakum?" I looked again at the needle, and I felt in my fingertips the sting of the rope fibers. To be stabbed by this tiny silver sword would be worse. The calluses I'd built in my fingertips would be no protection; the needle would penetrate much deeper.

"In addition to oakum picking," Mrs. Martin corrected. "You've made it clear you've got plenty of excess energy. You'll come to the tailoring room in the mornings and stay awake in the evenings until you make up the other work you miss."

It was meant to be cruel punishment, and it was. But Mrs. Martin must have expected to crush my spirit with overwork. What she did in actuality was give Valentine back to me.

Sitting on a stool in the corner of the tailoring room, all the sewing machines whirring and clattering around me, I reveled in my misery. I imagined it was him who'd set me this punishment. I saw him in my mind, a sort of ghost, floating up by the ceiling, watching me. I bowed my head in an effort to look demure. I'd been given the simplest jobs—minor rips in shirts—and been taught to execute a simple patch. And with Valentine watching, I grew conscious of my movements. I made my stitches as similar to each other as I could, and I poked my finger with the needle only once.

And late that night, locked in the oakum-picking room by Mrs. Martin, I was alone but not lonely—for this was the room where Valentine had first arrested me. I imagined I was in a prison cell and he was on the other side—my jailer, observing my behavior. I picked at the rope until my fingertips were raw, then laid the strand across my lap so he could see it.

The rope looked friendly where it was clean. I ran my finger down the hard, smooth bumps of the braid. Arranging my pale, callused hands in my lap, I held the rope as a proper lady might hold a book. It covered the driest parts of my skin. I looped the rope around my hands, crossing it between my wrists. I put my palms together, laced my fingers, and admired the effect.

The braid framed my hands, drawing the eye. My thin, sharp-angled fingers might have belonged not to a starving child, but to someone powerful—a lady clever and wicked enough to need restraining.

Back to work, thief, Valentine said.

"Yes, Officer," I replied, and went pathetically on, picking at the fibers despite the pain. I showed him how I suffered in his absence, and I felt his pleasure as if it were mine—that I was learning my lesson, and justice was being served.

For the rest of the week, I never faltered at the work, no matter how much I bled or how tired I became. I did not even lift my head from my task until the matron came to get me.

"This is fine work," she'd said one day, inspecting a patch I had completed. "Did you bother one of the older children to help you?"

"No." I hid a yawn behind my hand, afraid to be thought impertinent.

"Hm." She set the garment down, and studied me instead. Absently, she rubbed one hand with the other. Her fingers had an odd curve to them. "You'll have to show me," she said.

So that night, Mrs. Martin made me come with her after supper, and unlocked the tailoring room. We sat on stools facing away from the sewing machines, both of us bent over the same cloth: a long skirt that needed to be taken in. Her fingers guided and rearranged mine when words were not enough to make me understand what she wanted. When we were finished, she held up the skirt and said, "Well, well, that's my uniform mended."

I blinked. "Your uniform?"

She indicated herself. "Did you not notice? It's my skirt. Like this one."

I furrowed my brow. "That's not a uniform, it's just clothes."

"All clothes are uniforms," she said. "They show what purpose we serve in society. Some people even think they show how good we are. People see finely dressed folks on the street and think, 'There's a good person,' judging by a hat. Judging by gloves." She showed me a smile, as if she were sharing a secret. I'd never seen her smile before. "It's silly."

"Maybe people misjudge paupers in the workhouse, too," I said, emboldened. "When they think we're bad. Maybe it's just our uniforms?"

The light in Mrs. Martin's eyes flickered, as if it were swept over by a strong wind. But the gale passed, and the light prevailed. "Perhaps, Marian," she said. "Perhaps with the right opportunity, a pauper could prove those people wrong."

I searched her face.

"A person needs a trade, if she's to better her position," she said at last. "Tailoring is a fine one. Dressmaking. I can teach you."

The swell of feeling I got then, at the idea of getting out, was so big in my throat I had to swallow it. "Would you?"

"You'd have to promise me it's the end of your old nonsense," she said, putting a heavy hand on both of mine. "No more sneaking around, no more screaming and fussing. You'd have to be intent on growing up."

I nodded.

She pinned me with her eyes. "Promise me."

"I promise." I put my hand to my heart. "I'll do as I'm told."

She smiled. "There's a good girl."

◆ ◆ ◆

But the heavy sleep I fell into that night was the one that brought a dream of Valentine.

He'd faced away from me, in a room so bright I could barely make him out—but I'd known it was him by the stiffness of his back, and by the way he clasped his fingers behind it. He wore a velvet waistcoat and a shirt with billowing sleeves. I reached out to grab him by the cuff. The fabric was slippery in my fingers.

He turned his head to glare at me, his eyes shining with malice. "Let go, Marian."

"No," I said, even as I shook.

One by one, he pried my fingers off his wrist. But his touch was thrilling, and there was that shameful, furtive feeling again, between my legs.

He bent and leveled his face with mine. "You'll go mad if you don't let go."

I had been afraid of that, because of how I'd felt when we were together. That he would say it terrified me—as if it were plainly true that I was losing my mind because of him.

His gaze dropped, suddenly. Mine followed, and I saw my sooty hand—with its raw, red fingertips—on his crisp white shirtsleeve.

"Come on." His voice was softer—deadlier. "Let go."

But when I slackened my grip, his free hand clapped down upon it, holding me there.

I looked into his face. His eyes were dark, and his jaw was set.

"Do as I say." Somewhere below, his fingers squeezed mine. The heat spread like water beneath me, and I trembled. My knees buckled, and I tumbled to the floor, holding on desperately to his hand. I expected this to make him angry, but Valentine stepped in toward me as I dropped, so my arms stretched toward him and we did not break apart.

His stare burned me, and he held me so tight I could not wriggle myself even an inch from him. His tongue struck against his teeth, like a match across the box. "Let go."

The sick, swooping sensation in my stomach came again, strong enough to knock me down. I was tearing apart, stretched in multiple directions. It was torturous and exhilarating, and yes—yes, it was mad, like obeying the urge to leap from some high place.

The dream had been upon me still, when I woke: a nervous tremor, coursing through my body, each wave a little weaker. *Let go,* I'd thought, opening my eyes. *Let go,* in his voice, my stomach turning, and turning again—a screw loosening by his hand.

But of course he hadn't been there. I was alone, in the workhouse attic, where the girls slept. I'd sat up. My thighs chafed where they met, and I'd remembered waking in my parents' cottage, as a much younger child, having relieved myself in bed. A wave of shame overtook me.

But when I'd lifted my hips to run a hand beneath them, the straw was stiff and dry. I touched my trousers. But they didn't stick to me anywhere.

I'd turned my head in the darkness, which was fading. The sleeping shapes of the other girls were black against the charcoal attic air, like blots of ink on an already-saturated page.

I turned onto my side and tried to sleep, but I couldn't. What was wrong with me? What was happening? And why did I have to suffer it alone? The only person who could have possibly understood was gone from me, had left without a word.

My face hot, I cast my bedsheet aside, and stormed between the other sleeping girls. I found myself following the path Valentine had taken, to the side door by the kitchens, still unlocked. *Let someone find me,* I thought; *let someone bring me to justice.*

The blue of the sky outside, the creak of the stable door, the feel of straw under my feet—all of it was the same. It made the fact of Valentine's absence absurd, infuriating, and I could feel a swelling scream trapped inside me, squeezed fast in my chest as if by a livid fist.

The horse was back in its stall. He woke with an affronted whinny at my entrance. I squinted toward the house, wondering whether the sound had been heard—whether it would be investigated. I counted to ninety, then decided I was safe.

In the dark, I found what I wanted on the table by touch: first the bottle of oil and then the brush. The latter I took in one hand, placing my other one flat, palm down, on the table. Slowly, slowly, I touched the bristles to my knuckles. At the first prick I froze, alert for every feeling that would come after.

But there was nothing.

I moved the brush back and forth. It was rough, and distinctly mundane. The hairs on my arm stayed asleep.

Of course. The brush was but a brush. The magic had been his.

I threw the brush down, and the clatter made the horse stamp in nervous protest. There was nothing the animal could do to be rid of me, though; he was a creature meant to follow orders, not give them.

This thought made me look up. I squinted, and I could make out the shape of a crop on the wall.

The table was too high for me to throw my leg onto. I pushed the bottles and other tack aside to make a space for myself, but I was too weak even to pull my body up. I turned, peering into the dark. Beside the horse's stall I found a still-bound bale of hay, which I dragged to where I needed it. Using this as a stool, I gained the tabletop on hands and knees, rising with one palm against the wall. My fingers brushed the crop handle before I'd fully straightened up.

There. A jolt coursed through me as if the handle had been a lightning rod, leaving me wobbly-kneed and vulnerable, every pore of my skin open to the slightest brush of the air. Uncertain of where the table ended, I clung to the wall and drew the crop down, holding it against my side. Then I lowered myself again, reversing my course from the table to the hay bale and finally the floor.

The crop was long and skinny, with a thick handle. At the opposite end was a loop of leather that hung in the air.

Before I could think better of it, I brought the leather tongue down hard on the open palm of my left hand, and had to stifle a yelp. Dropping the crop, I swung my stinging hand by its wrist.

The pain was already fading, but my body had only begun to respond to it. My blood rushed hot under my skin, making me sweat. I felt wide awake all of a sudden. I could see more of the stable around me, and I stood steadier—my toes firmly rooted in the dirt of the floor.

Throwing off a sudden chill, I bent to retrieve the crop. Less afraid, I let the leather tongue touch my bare ankle. It was smooth, soft, when it wasn't being swung. Just as a thinking person drums her fingers or bounces her foot, I gently tapped the crop against my calf—never drawing back my hand but changing by degrees the place I struck. It was almost a tickle, like the brush had been. The bones at the front of my leg were sensitive, however, and when I touched them, I could feel the blunt force of the crop in a way that felt wrong—inelegant. Moving away, to the soft side of my leg, the sensation was purer, as if the sting of it came from inside me.

Drawing my hand perhaps a foot away from my side, I tried a real swing against my calf. The sting was different than it had been in my palm: less immediate, yet it lingered longer. Again, I felt alert. And yes, the army of hairs on my arms was at attention, too.

"Back again, thief," I'd said, making my voice as deep as I could. "What did you think I'd do when I'd got you? Give you a kiss?"

After

6 February 1867

Dear Friend—

Georgiana is a lovely name, and it sounds to me like she'll learn to please you in no time. I know you don't mean all that disparaging nonsense about her. You don't have to pretend for me; I told you I would be happier knowing you were not alone, and I am.

If anything, I'm relieved you did not settle for Lucette. I know she was keen, but she's all wrong for you—petulant and scheming. But now I do sound like a jealous person, so I'll leave off saying anything more about her.

As to the rest of what you've written here—you mustn't blame yourself so much for misjudging me. I gave you good reason. I was so consumed with shame for who I was—what was happening, what had happened before—I'm sure I behaved like a furtive, scuttering criminal. What matters is that, when things got even darker at Valor Rise, you stepped in.

Marian

Before

16

I woke the next morning with the distinct feeling that I had escaped something terrible, and it was so. I had not just nearly lost my job—I had spoken aloud the secret I shared with Mr. Bornholdt. Not to just anybody, either, but to my dear friend. That he was still my dear friend afterward was a victory in itself.

But the feeling was more precious for how tenuous it was. Yesterday was settled because it was yesterday; today held all sorts of dangers. One of them was that, at any moment, Valentine might discover my inner evil, which had sparked the master's interest in the first place, and spurn me. I worried over this first danger as I passed through the dining room midday, when the second danger happened to emerge from the adjoining drawing room.

"Marian," Mr. Bornholdt said.

I leaped a little. "Good morning, sir—or good afternoon."

He inclined his head. "Good day, at any rate."

I swallowed, stepping back as he stepped closer. "Is Mrs. Bornholdt looking for me, sir?"

"No, but I have been meaning to set aside some time for you, myself. To see how you are, after our little chat. Will you accompany me to my study?"

I licked my lips. It was only out of politeness that he put it as a question; it was an order, and as he turned his back without an answer,

I felt myself begin to follow him as if I were on a string attached to his greatcoat.

"Oh, Mr. Bornholdt, what luck that you're here."

We both turned.

Valentine strode up alongside the dining table, a silver cup in one hand and a polishing rag in the other. "May I ask you something, sir?"

Mr. Bornholdt looked at me—making me shut my startled mouth—and then back to Valentine, who stood in place, polishing fastidiously, a polite smile on his face.

"If it is quick, Hobbs," the master said.

"Well, on her shopping trip, Mrs. Bornholdt was telling me she is planning a ball for a fortnight from now." He furrowed his brow. "What was the beautiful language she used? Something like: all her friends are surely blooming like flowers in new summer clothes, and she wants to pick them, and put them all around her dining table."

"Yes?" Mr. Bornholdt prompted. "And what is your concern?"

"Oh, well, she wants me to go around with the invitations, of course."

Mr. Bornholdt stared.

Valentine stared back, paused in his polishing, his expression vacant—except, for just one moment, his eyes flicked to me. Realization dawned. He was trying to give me a way out of the room.

"Hobbs?" Mr. Bornholdt said. He was glaring so hard at his footman that he seemed not to notice my mincing back from both of them.

"Oh!" Valentine said, jerking back into motion with the polishing rag. "You mean what was my question—I apologize, sir. The mistress has chosen pork for the ball."

"So?" Mr. Bornholdt said. His neck was turning red. I took a larger step, even as I grew less certain I should go. What if he took his ire out on Valentine, on my account? Valentine didn't know how terrible he could be.

"Well, sir," Valentine said, "I'm uncertain which way the rump should go on the table—to the left or to the right."

"I am surprised at you, Hobbs." The words were dismissive. "If you do not know something, ask the butler."

"Oh, I would, sir, if it were a matter of fact," Valentine replied. "But this is a matter of preference of the man who cuts, sir. That's you, of course."

"You have not forgotten, I trust, that I am right-handed."

"Certainly, not, sir. But pork is not like other roast meats. There is no strictly logical starting place, because—here, let me demonstrate, sir." Seemingly excited, he set down the silver and his rag to open the nearby sideboard. As they both were looking down, into the cabinet through which Valentine was rooting, Valentine waved once, hard, with his other hand.

I took the hint, and fled.

◆ ◆ ◆

Mr. Bornholdt summoned me to his study again the very next day. But we found Valentine there, in the middle of a project: he was drenching the marble of Mr. Bornholdt's mantel with some milky mixture.

"It's been too long since someone's got the smoke off, sir," he explained brightly, "and as it's getting warmer, I thought for sure you'd be out in the grounds rather than working."

Mr. Bornholdt took an audible deep breath, and I thought of Mrs. Martin telling me that servants were meant to be neither seen nor heard as much as possible. Yet the master said nothing, did nothing.

The next day, Valentine was washing the mantel with soap and water when we came—the required next step, at the required time after the first, he said.

It was soon apparent that Valentine had picked up lots of tricks from the footman at his last job, and Mr. Bornholdt's study was in particular need of a footman's care. He devoted one whole evening to rubbing the end tables down with washleather, and he seemed to find new ink stains on Mr. Bornholdt's French mahogany desk every other day. These he took out with a feather, some lemon juice, and a gentle touch.

Every time the master was thwarted, I cringed and cowered a bit lower in his wake, watching the color change on the back of his neck. Yet Mr. Bornholdt would only make-believe I'd followed him to his study and shoo me away. It couldn't last forever—someday soon he would outwit his footman—but I appreciated each day's reprieve for what it was, just the same.

For a few days, Valentine brought the invitations for the coming ball from the Bornholdts out to all the important area families, returning with prompt responses. He flew away and home, away and home, and I caught sight of him in both directions, for I peered often out the windows, anxious in his absence, wanting not to leave my mistress's quarters until I knew he had returned.

Once he glanced up, and I was so surprised to be caught that I laughed. He grinned and waved at me, and I drew back from the window, equal parts pleased and guilty. He was so good, and he risked so much for me, while I kept my darkest secret from him still—about what he'd been to me, once, what I'd wanted.

Two days before the ball was to take place, Mr. Bornholdt swooped out of his drawing room as usual to accost me, but this time was interrupted by his wife instead of Valentine.

"Oh, Marian," she said, "would you know anything about flies? As summer comes on, they are attracted to my mirror glass. I have to cover it up, and I go the season without being able to see myself."

I started to shake my head. But Mr. Bornholdt was still standing there, waiting for me. "I can certainly try to tackle the problem, Mrs. Bornholdt." I curtsied to the master. "Excuse me, sir."

"Why don't you ask Hobbs, instead?" Mr. Bornholdt said loudly. "He seems to know quite a bit about good housekeeping."

"Oh, wonderful," Mrs. Bornholdt replied. "Come along, Marian."

"I thought you were going to ask Hobbs." This time, he was not entirely successful at cloaking some impatience.

"I am, darling, but no young man of his virility is getting into my quarters alone. Marian will make a fine chaperone."

I curtsied again to the master, and positively chased my mistress from the room. I thought she might ask me to find Valentine, which would mean being vulnerable to the master again while I sought him, but we ran into Ledford on the way, who said he would send the footman up in a moment.

Safe in my mistress's apartment, I discreetly let out my breath.

Mrs. Bornholdt arranged herself in her blue winged armchair to wait. I peered at her face. The back of the armchair was high, and the blue hue behind her afforded me an opportunity to see her skin more as it really was—at a disadvantage—and I was dismayed to note that her health had not followed her better spirits of late. In fact, she looked worse than when I'd met her—not just green now, but gray about her eyes. Workhouse gray.

"How are you feeling?" I asked, as casually as I could.

"Tired," she replied. Then her face lit up. "But I never said! My corsets are comfortable, and they have not lost any of their form. You are wonderful."

"Oh," I said, flustered. I hadn't been fishing for such a compliment at all. "Thank you, ma'am. Please let me know when they feel loose, and I'll do what I can to stiffen them."

Mrs. Bornholdt favored me with a soft look, and for a moment she reminded me of someone else, in some other memory I could not immediately place. Then there was a knock at the door, and her features grew haughty again. "Yes?" she said.

A low voice came muffled through the door. "It's Hobbs, ma'am."

Mrs. Bornholdt sat up straighter. "Come in!"

Valentine entered and gave a bow, keeping one hand behind his back. This was a rare opportunity to look upon him when it would have been impertinent for him to look at me. I watched his face—his whole frame, in fact—as he listened to Mrs. Bornholdt try to make him understand the severity of the fly problem. Every line of his expression was earnest, and he bent forward—carefully divesting himself of any manliness that might have been intimidating to the lady without going so far as to belittle her.

When she had described the trouble with the mirror to her satisfaction, I was left with the impression that Valor Rise fell victim to a veritable plague of insects come summer, but Valentine's features were firmly set, confident.

"It sounds dreadful, ma'am, but I do think I can prevent it."

"I welcome you to try," Mrs. Bornholdt said, "but do not take it too hard if it does not work. You would not be the first tradesman to find my problems impossible to fix."

I'm not sure who looked at whom first, she or I, but our eyes did meet, my mistress's and mine.

"Excuse me, ma'am," Valentine said. "I'll be right back."

In just over a quarter of an hour, he returned, and pulled from behind his back a small covered pot. Mrs. Bornholdt led him through to her dressing room, and I followed after.

When he saw the vanity, Valentine strode to the mirror. He took a small brush from his pocket, dipped it in the pot, and commenced painting the gilded frame.

Mrs. Bornholdt crinkled her nose. "Why, that smells like onions."

"Leeks." Valentine's voice was soft, focused. "The water from boiled leeks."

"Are you trying to keep the flies away, or me?" she asked, but there was laughter underneath her incredulity.

Valentine never turned from his work, but as I stood to his side, I could see him smile. "The odor won't follow you from the room, Mrs. Bornholdt, I promise you solemnly."

He stretched to touch the topmost part of the mirror's frame with his brush, and I could see the coral sheen of his bottom lip—the smoothness of his jaw—up close in the reflection of the glass.

Creeping self-consciousness made me look left, and I found Mrs. Bornholdt's eyes on mine. Caught staring, I was overcome with a prickling in my cheeks. But my mistress's expression was not judgmental—it was knowing. As if she'd read a secret in my face, and she approved of it.

I shook my head and put my hand to my chest, to signal that—whatever she thought—she was mistaken. Valentine was my protector, a caretaker, a guard. He wanted to preserve my virtue, not claim it, and that was the right thing.

Wasn't that so?

Beneath my palm, my heart was racing. My hand crept up to my cheek.

Mrs. Bornholdt went on wisely smiling.

"The glass is streaked," Valentine remarked, beyond us. "Shall I clean that, too, ma'am? Seeing as I'm here already?"

17

That night, I sat up in the housekeeper's office long after Mrs. Davies herself had gone to sleep, putting the finishing touches on Mrs. Bornholdt's dress for the ball. I liked the quiet, and the glow of the hearth before me. The room was dark otherwise, and the kitchens beyond only dim, for the lamps had been turned down.

Soft footsteps passed. I just caught a glimpse of Valentine going by with a pile of shoes in his arms.

"Polishing now and not in the morning?" I asked, through a mouthful of pins.

In a moment, he reappeared in the doorway. "Absolutely everybody's shoes are muddy at once," he said mildly. "Figured I'd get a jump on it."

He started to move away again. I should have let him. I don't know what possessed me to say, instead: "If you'd like, you could shine them in here."

I pretended to be interested in the dress, so I didn't have to check his face, and the silence that followed was torture. But then he said, "All right," and lowered his shoe pile to the floor. He left the room and came back with a candle, plus a whole drawer he must have pulled out of a fixture in his pantry. Then he settled on the floor between me and the fire, knees bent and ankles crossed.

"You could sit in Mrs. Davies's chair," I offered.

"That's all right. At least I know if I dirty the floor, I can clean it." As he spoke, he set out each pair of dirty shoes in a circle around him, then pulled from the drawer two metal tins, two handled brushes, some stained rags, and a thin stick with a sponge on it.

With conscious effort I drew my gaze away from his careful fingers, unscrewing the lid of one of the jars. I had my own work to do. In another moment, however, the shushing of bristles made me look his way again.

He had a shoe heel in one hand, and a brush in the other. He buffed the toe, moving in quick, precise circles. It struck me how earnest he was—his motions practiced, his eyes and mouth set—as if the owner of the shoes were supervising him. Or as if the shoes were his own.

But his shoes, now that I looked, were filthy with mud.

I pointed at them. "Who does yours?"

"Hm?" he said, not looking up.

I turned a bit toward him in my chair. "You clean everybody else's shoes. Who does yours?"

He smiled, but still didn't pause in his work. "I do them, of course."

"But that's criminal," I said. "That's like—like cobbler's children going barefoot."

He tilted his head. "Is it?"

"You should let me shine them for you. Will you tell me how?"

"God no," he said, laughing. "It's filthy work, and you've got your own drudgery."

I glanced at the dress form. "This? It's nearly done. And anyway, my eyes are getting tired in this light. I can't pin straight."

"So go to sleep," he said.

"But I'm so guilty," I blurted, more heated than I meant to, and the words hung, too true, in the silence afterward. Softer, I added: "You've been sticking your neck out for me for weeks now, at great personal peril—"

"It's not nearly so dramatic as that—"

"Yes, it is. It is or you wouldn't have to do it at all."

He set the shoe down, his smile gone.

"Let me do something to thank you, even if it'll never be equal," I said. "Please?"

He held out his palms. "All right. But you don't owe me anything." He straightened one leg, and reached for the toe of his shoe.

"Wait," I said, sticking what pins I had left in a cushion from my sewing basket. "Wear them. I'll be a shoe shiner, and you will be a fine gentleman. Come on, get up, sit in Mrs. Davies's chair."

Valentine laughed and shook his head. But he got up. He did as I said.

I gathered his tins and brushes and rags in my arms, and when I drew before him, I brought my feet tight together, straightened my back, and bowed. "Shoeshine, sir?"

Looking more embarrassed than anything, he smiled and dipped his head. "Please."

I kneeled before him, and as I did it, I saw myself as if from above, bent like a subject before a king, and had to shake off a shiver. I made myself busy moving about the polish and brushes beside me.

"The coarse brushes are for getting dirt off," Valentine said, pointing, "and the fine are for spreading the blacking."

I nodded. On sudden inspiration, I got up to get my basket. Shutting its lid, I put it down on the floor before him. "Lift your feet, please, sir."

He did. I slid the basket under, propping his boots close to me. Then I brought the two coarser brushes to the level of his feet and began to work.

The thicker chips of mud came off at a touch. Bringing the bristles to the leather, I moved my hands in clumsy circles, afraid to jostle Valentine's foot, but this did nothing for the dust that the mud left behind.

"Faster," Valentine murmured—soft, but certain.

Oddly, with speed came greater fluidity. My circles grew neater. The sound of the brushes and the rhythm of my hands was soothing—hypnotic. I could feel the friction of the bristles against the leather, and I found myself imagining the warmth of it. Could Valentine feel that heat, barely there, behind the hard wall of the shoe? Did he strain his toes toward it?

I glanced upward. He was sitting forward, watching me.

I blushed, my hands losing their momentum. "Is something wrong?"

He straightened. "No. Keep going."

There was no hint of laughter in his face anymore.

I had already gotten most of the mud off both shoes. I scuffed the tops one hand at a time, where his toes were, getting the last stubborn bits there. Then I set the brushes down.

There was no sound in the whole great room but the twist of the blacking lid in my hand. The smell of it rose up—smoky with soot, but sweet from the beeswax it was trapped in, and together not unlike the last breath of a candle.

"Oh." He sounded like he was coming out of sleep: "The sponge—"

But I'd already stuck my finger through the wax.

"Your hands," he said, his eyebrows bending under a real weight of guilt.

"It's all right," I said, giggling. "I'm at your service, sir. You're not supposed to bother yourself about me or my hands."

I heard the soft click of his tongue, and for a moment I thought I could feel a question waiting to be asked, heavy on his breath. But the words never came, and I took up the finer brushes, sweeping the blacking in circles.

As the wax warmed, it spread easily—and it was a pleasure to see the dry leather take on a wet and glossy darkness. The cracks, which had held some dust even after the first brushing, disappeared.

With the torches low, and our candle close by, I felt like . . . like I was doing a spell. As if this were a holy place, and Valentine were a knight who had come in the dead of night, to have his armor imbued with some supernatural hardiness before the battle of his life. I thought, perhaps he would be safe so long as he stayed in my good graces, and had to close my eyes against a sudden stinging.

"There you are, sir," I said, sitting back.

His shoes shone, worthy of the smile he gave as I lifted my head—worthy of the proud way he held himself, sitting above me.

"Thank you," he said, looking at his shoes first, then at me. "I—I wish you hadn't given yourself another chore. Your life is full of chores."

"But this wasn't a chore." And then, speaking to his feet: "I found it a pleasure—to serve a good man for a change."

I peeked at Valentine. His hand had crept up to his throat, where the collar of his shirt was knotted. His eyes searched mine, but I dropped my gaze—and it caught on his sharp shoulders as it fell.

"I worry so," I whispered.

"About Bornholdt?"

I nodded.

"I try always to be near you, you know, Marian, and I—"

"But that's what I mean," I said, and bit my lip, hard. "Someday he's going to lose his patience, and take it out on you, Valentine. When he cannot take it out on me. And that will be worse, because I'll know it was my fault, me that put you in harm's way."

He considered this a moment. Then he said: "I want to show you something."

◆ ◆ ◆

He wanted to take me to the master's apartments. When my eyes went wide, he added, "Just his dressing room. And I'll make sure he's asleep before I let you in."

"How can you be certain?"

"Charitably, he snores. Loud enough to hear one room over."

I hesitated. It seemed a giant risk—but Valentine wanted to share something with me. "All right."

We walked in slow silence together down the hall. He clasped his hands behind his back, and I held the candle that lit our way. We were like mourners coming up a church aisle—or that was how it would have seemed to anyone who came upon us. Yet there was something at the corners of Valentine's eyes, something I saw only because I was looking for it: a crinkle that ruined the whole dour illusion.

Still, the closer we came to the master's chambers, the slower I stepped. The walls seemed to me to darken, and my footsteps to sound louder—ominous, and impossible to sleep through.

I opened my mouth to say I wanted to turn back just as Valentine stopped. He stood before the most imposing door on the second floor. He inclined his head toward the richly polished panels but made no move to reach for the knob. At first I was perplexed, but then I heard it: a long, deep snarl, followed by a pouty puff of breath. A pause, and the sounds came again.

Turning his head a fraction toward the door, Valentine raised his eyebrows and gave me a mystified smile. It was exactly as if he were saying, *Isn't that the most dignified thing you've ever heard?*

I thought, if he could find it in him to laugh—however silently—then I was only being silly to fear.

I followed him to the next door over, and bent close with the light so he could see to put the key in the lock. Inside, he motioned for me to wait and took the candle with him through an adjoining door, to Mr. Bornholdt's bedroom. I drew my shoulders tight, waiting for a shout from the master, my body thrumming with energy. I was ready at any moment to flee. But the shadow-shape that returned was Valentine's. He had a thick bundle under his arm. He closed the adjoining door behind him, and I breathed again.

He beckoned me closer. As I watched, he picked the clothes pile apart. First, he showed me a white shirt with yellowed sleeves and a rumpled set of trousers. Next, a silver brocade vest, this with a deep stain of burgundy wine. There was a thick greatcoat that I could smell even from where I stood, as if perhaps after Mr. Bornholdt dumped his ashes on the drawing-room carpet—which was the fashion—he rolled around in them like a dog.

With a melodramatic sigh, Valentine drew himself up tall. He unlatched a panel in the wall and unfolded a long wooden board that sat flat on its hinge, like a skinny table. From a nearby drawer, Valentine took two different brushes, and from a lower cabinet he drew out several solutions in jars.

"This is what I do for Mr. Bornholdt," he whispered to me. "Watch."

At first, he worked with exaggerated disgust, touching the dirty garments with only the tips of his pinched fingers. By and by, though, it was as if he had forgotten I was there; he went from performing for my benefit to performing for his. His eyes pinned each imperfection down, tending it until it was restored to its proper crispness or color. Over the course of cleaning his master's clothes—brushing, beating, pressing—Valentine became master of them himself, exercising a control that Mr. Bornholdt, who only wore them, would never know.

"He needs me, you see," Valentine said, startling me a little. "I turn him from pig to prince each day. Also, I'm the only servant he's ever had who could get ink stains out of French mahogany."

I put my hand to my cheek. "It's you who ought to wear that fine coat."

The edge of his mouth curled in the candle's light. "You think so?"

Without any hint of irony, Valentine picked up the coat and slipped his arms into the sleeves. He drew it close around him by the lapels and did the silver buttons, watching his fingers. Carefully, he checked the collar—making sure it was folded correctly over. Only when it was perfect did he look at me.

"Oh, sir." I meant it in jest. But when the words reached the air, they were heavy with respect. Valentine's stature changed, to bear the weight of them, and I—to hide my blush more than anything else—dropped a curtsy. "What can I do for you?"

"I suppose you may start by explaining what you are doing in my dressing room," Valentine replied, with as much pomp as could be used to inflate a whisper.

"Oh," I said, "well—you see, sir—sometimes I come in here to smell your coats."

He narrowed his eyes. "Smell my coats?"

"Yes, sir," I replied, as earnest as Valentine was suspicious. "I could never in my lifetime afford to take up smoking, but this works just as well."

Valentine sucked his lips into his mouth, looked down to gather himself, and met me with a sterner gaze than ever. "I do not find that funny at all, Marian."

I tilted my head. "Why not, sir?"

"Because I have absolutely no sense of humor."

Both of us had to turn away so we did not laugh aloud.

"Come now, Marian," Valentine murmured, straightening his face. "As master of this house, I demand transparency in all things from everyone but myself. Tell me: Do you come here with that new footman to listen to me snore?"

"Not particularly, sir," I said, "but it is true that when I come here to see the footman, you are usually snoring."

"Damn it, Marian," he hissed. "You could be corroding my marriage to a perfectly pleasant woman!"

"A man of your prodigious skill doesn't need my help with that, sir."

"Well," he blustered, tugging his vest down, "thank you, Marian, that touches me metaphorically."

I curtsied again. "You're welcome, sir."

"But I wish you would literally touch me, Marian."

"You have made that clear." I stepped back, but giggled into my hand as I did it.

He threw up his hands. "And yet you persist in having decency. I do not understand it."

I frowned. "I thought you demanded decency in all things from everyone but yourself."

"No, that is transparency." He held up a finger. "Decency is decided on more of a case-by-case basis, where the appropriate behavior is determined by what stands to most benefit me."

I nodded. "I see, sir."

Pointing at the floor, Valentine made as if to stamp his foot—but did not put his weight down, and so didn't make a sound. "I demand you kiss me of your own free will, Marian."

"Will it shut you up, sir?"

His forehead crinkled as he considered it. "For the duration of the kiss, I suppose."

I grabbed Valentine by the lapels of the greatcoat and pulled, so his lips came to mine as much as mine went to his.

When I let go, all the laughter had gone out of his eyes. "I can't believe you did that," he whispered, all on the rush of a breath.

I blinked, wide-eyed. "I'm sorry, I thought—"

Then his hands were on my face, and we were kissing again. I tipped my head back, surrendering to his grip, and he parted my lips with his. The heat of his palms, the boldness of his tongue—these were victories, proof that what I dreamed of, he'd dreamed, too. I was not sick, or bad—or if I was, I was not sick and bad alone. And yet, instead of being satisfied to know this truth, to have his mouth on mine, I was all the hungrier. I wanted his touch elsewhere, everywhere, and my body arched in offering toward him.

Valentine's hands clutched my back, sturdy, comforting—but something else intruded: a remembered feeling, of being pressed against the doorframe in Mr. Bornholdt's study. I stumbled, breaking the kiss and backing into something. The master's washstand. It tipped over, crashing to the ground, its dislodged basin rolling loudly across the floor.

Valentine pulled me by my forearms to the door. "Run."

I dared not apologize or ask what he would do, for the sound of my voice, if overheard, would only make things worse for him. The only way I could be of help was to be gone.

I resolved not to look back but to keep running unless I was stopped. Even when I gained the servants' staircase, I couldn't bear to pause but hurried up onto the third floor. I found my room but missed the lock with my key several times. Finally, using both hands together, I managed to get inside.

I shut the door. Pressing my back against it, I let out a long breath.

If Valentine had been caught, surely it was only a matter of time before I was implicated.

I sat up waiting, running my fingers through my hair. When a full hour had gone by, I wondered whether nothing would come of it. But if Valentine had truly been at liberty, I was certain he would have come by my room himself to tell me all was well.

18

I saw Valentine only once the next morning. He'd brought down the pieces of one of the bigger entryway lamps and deposited them in the sink. His face looked clear—save for the concentration that comes over one when working. Passing behind with Mrs. Bornholdt's breakfast tray, I slowed to say a word to him, blushing furiously before I'd even opened my mouth—but Valentine widened his eyes. So slightly that it made only his hair tremble, he shook his head.

My eyes darted away. Ledford stood at the door of his office. He was watching us. I smiled at him, said good morning, and hurried upstairs.

It troubled me.

But the day's preparations were so involved that I lost myself in the work. I hadn't lied to Valentine when I'd said Mrs. Bornholdt's dress was finished (green again, this one a shining satin), but for a ball, the dress was only the beginning. After breakfast and her morning bath, I applied a carefully layered toilette of scent and rouge, then—once her hair had dried—twisted and pinned her locks into pleasing, but complicated, braids.

The colors of the afternoon had pooled together into a sunset by the time I'd finished, and the guests would be arriving at any moment. I stood on the second-floor landing, at the top of the grand staircase, to watch my mistress descend. She had sat stiff and still for hours while

I'd made her up, which hadn't been easy on her; I was proud of her for taking such measured steps, her spine straight, her shoulders back.

As she turned a corner on the stairs, I peered over the top banister to see down to the first floor. The house had been overrun with extra footmen to help with the laying out of food abovestairs. One moment they were there, scurrying in all directions as if the hall were a train station, and the next moment—the doorbell having been rung—they all disappeared in the direction of the dining room, like roaches fleeing the light.

Valentine hadn't been among them, anyway. He was probably tending to the master, somewhere deeper in the house. I wouldn't see him until the party was finished.

I receded to the servants' stairs, uneasy in my stomach at the prospect of passing the entire evening not knowing what had transpired after I'd fled the dressing room. After that kiss.

I slowed midway down the steps.

But whyever Ledford was on the watch, it couldn't be about the kiss. I'd gotten away. No one had seen me, and Valentine wouldn't have told.

But Valentine had been afraid of something that morning.

Frowning, I pushed open the door to the kitchen stairs and made my way down.

"Marian," Mrs. Davies said, "come and have something to eat!"

The center table mostly used for food preparation was laden with finished dishes—cuts of beef and duck and pheasant, each over beds of green, and sweetmeats in marinades. The maids were all making up plates.

"What's this?" I asked.

"Well." She put her fists on her hips. "No sooner did the footmen deliver up the trays for the buffet than Mrs. Bornholdt sent a full quarter of them back."

I looked from her to the table. "Was something wrong with the food?"

"I asked the same! But according to Ledford, Mrs. Bornholdt was shouting about how her servants must enjoy themselves for once—can you imagine? Flushed and gay, he said she was."

She stepped aside, inviting me to serve myself with a sweep of her arm. Moving slowly, I made a plate. When there was no more space on the dish to fill, I blinked down at it. Pheasant. Spinach. I didn't even remember choosing them.

I gazed at the people gathered 'round the table. Ledford was talking to the scullery maid, laughing so heartily that flowers bloomed in his old cheeks. Lucette was singing to amuse the young hall boy, swinging his hands in hers as they danced in place. Everybody had someone to talk to.

And maybe I could have borne being alone, if I could have been easy in my mind—if the memory of the kiss wasn't tainted by the furtive feeling of having done something wrong. A feeling I did not entirely dislike, which added another layer to my nervousness.

I looked at my plate. It was a lovely gesture, from a kind mistress to faithful servants. I didn't deserve it.

Sighing, I rose from my chair. Leaving my plate, I took a table lantern by its iron ring and turned away. No one said anything to stop me as I slipped through the servants' entrance, into the night.

The air was warm and richly fragrant. To breathe it was almost to drink it—summer's own sensual punch: enchanting purple wisteria, wet and dark as the prelude to a thunderstorm, honey-thick with tuberose and garnished with the swollen-cherry smell of phlox.

I stepped out from under the arches of the servants' entrance, moving from the stone path onto the lawn. A breeze—like a hand at the small of my back—guided me onward.

There was a different sort of revel going on in the grass, all the crickets making merry, calling to each other. And because the house could not quite contain the sound of the musicians hired to play for the dance, a waltz followed me on the wind, pleasantly muted.

Valentine would be standing among those people who danced. Perhaps he watched them turn together across the ballroom floor. Those couples could look into each other's eyes all they wanted, and no one would mind.

Indeed, wasn't that half the point, or more, of tonight? A celebration of love—an indulgence of love. For, among them, attraction and romance were sanctioned.

Filling my lungs with air, I channeled my frustration to my legs, breaking into a jog. At once my temples cooled, the night air rushing by me. Dew wet my stockings, yet my feet seemed to grow lighter with each step away from the house.

The working of my legs felt good, so I sped up. I passed the dairy barn on my right, first. Beyond that, on the same side, I glimpsed the silhouette of the Bornholdts' stable, its high steeple pointing up between the stars.

I stopped short. *And what did you think I'd do when I'd got you? Give you a kiss?*

Smiling ruefully to myself, I cut across the yard toward that steeple, the grass whipping at my ankles—until I'd drawn up along the side of the building. I slowed to a trot, and my lantern swung before me, throwing its light back and forth across the outside wall. When at last it lit upon a rough old iron handle, I slowed and stopped.

I pressed myself against the wooden slats of the door to listen at it, taking a deep drink of air. The thought of the number of stable hands about for such a large party as tonight's gave me pause. It was a bit foolish of me to even think of going inside after what had happened the previous evening. But every servant belowstairs was being a bit foolish at the moment, and—as I was not forbidden to be in the stable—why shouldn't I have chosen to do my foolishness there instead?

I waited, still panting from the run, but I could hear no sound within—only the thumping of my heart in my ears.

I released the latch, peeked in, and—seeing no one—slipped beyond through the gently creaking door.

I caught the smell of hay at once and turned my face willingly into it. The stable was lit with lanterns hung from the ceiling, drifting in the wind that blew through the open windows on either sidewall. I cast my gaze left and right, looking for anyone who might be there, but the only faces looking back at me were long ones—curious horses come to the doors of their stalls.

I couldn't hear the party at Valor Rise anymore. I might have been at Parish Street.

I took small, timid steps, and the floor helped to keep me quiet. It was made of dirt, and all the straw had been swept to the edges of the aisle. I proceeded past the horses, feeling like a child again as I gazed around—all the while expecting to be spotted and stopped, but nobody jumped out of the dark.

I set my lantern down on a workbench at the end of the aisle and followed the chilly, imposing smell of leather to a length of rein that was curled up beside a horse brush. From this my gaze leaped up, to the wall. There, three riding crops hung in a neat row.

This time I did not need to stand on a hay bale to take one down.

I held the crop in my hands, the handle across one palm and the tongue end across the other, and the very air changed—charging. Or perhaps it was my body that was different, attuned to a subtle, secret, ever-present energy. A chill ran up my spine, and bumps rose on both my arms.

The feeling was so like fear—the way it energized my legs and made my heart beat harder. And yet, my muscles loosened—as if I waded not into danger but warm water. So which was it? Was I like a cat, wanting to bolt just because something fell off a high shelf? Or was I an unfortunate mouse, indulging in some delicious, poisoned thing?

I closed my fist around the crop handle and dropped my arm. It was disorienting, not to know. Kissing Valentine had been like this: as if I'd been thrown into the air, my stomach spinning as I fell back toward the earth. I tapped the tongue end of the crop against my calf, wondering. How could falling bring on such euphoria in a thinking person, when she knew collision would surely follow?

"Marian."

I whirled, concealing the crop behind my back. Valentine stood at the other end of the stable, directly under a lantern. He'd traded his rich brown coat for a black one, and his gloves were shinier—like moonlight. There was a quiet delight in his eyes that unnerved me. He was near enough that he might have seen my private musings spill hot across my face.

"What are you doing here?" I demanded.

His left eyebrow quirked. "Well, good evening to you, too, Miss Osley."

I edged backward until I bumped into the workbench, and I rolled the crop onto it. "Shouldn't you be at the ball?"

"Oh, there are about thirty footmen abovestairs." He gazed around at the horses before returning his gaze to me. "I was nipping down to the kitchen for a bite when I saw you leaving."

I touched my hair, my cap. "Won't you be missed?"

He laughed and shook his head. "I've mostly only served as a soft obstacle for inebriated partygoers to stumble into." He tilted his head, and the line of his mouth drew even. "Do you want me to go away?"

"No!" I said, so loudly I made myself jump. "It's just—if the butler's watching you—"

"He's watching the thirty other footmen. He's anxious—Mr. Bornholdt's father is here, and making comments about the food. The man looks mightily ill." Quicker, quieter, he added, "If there's any time I can sneak off, it's now, and I wanted to speak to you, given—given what happened last night."

"Oh." I swallowed. "Right. Are we in trouble? With the master?"

He stopped a few feet shy of where I stood and studied the tips of his shoes. Then, with measured calm: "No, I would say . . . I am in trouble with the master."

My eyes widened. "Did we wake him?"

"Yes." He held up a hand to forestall my reaction. "But he has no idea you were there. When he came in, I simply told him I'd been clumsy with the washstand."

I leaned forward. "And he believed you?"

Valentine lifted his head as if to begin a nod, but he didn't bring his chin back down again. "Marian, if I'm gone in the morning, I want—"

"Is that a possibility?" I took a step toward him. Then another. "Do you think he's going to dismiss you? Why? For what?"

Valentine looked away. "When he came into the dressing room, I was still wearing his coat."

"Oh, Valentine," I gasped. "I made you—"

He shook his head. "No, you absolutely did not."

"But he can't just—"

"He can." His words were calm—as if he were resigned to going already. "He's the master of the house. And I was being insubordinate."

I stared at him. "Tomorrow. Do you really think?"

"I don't know. He was . . ." He shut his eyes. "Very unhappy with me. He said he would 'deal' with me once the ball was over."

All I could do was stare at him: his fine face, his straight body. He was there, a fact, a fixture of my life again. We stood improbably together after all the intervening years—in a drafty stable in the middle of the night. But by morning he might be gone. Same as last time.

And I'd have no one to step between Mr. Bornholdt and me, again.

Something thumped behind me. I jumped, turning—but there was no one. Squinting, I dropped my gaze. The riding crop had rolled off the workbench. I rushed toward it, my face draining of blood, but Valentine got there first, and now he was bending, reaching—

"What's this doing here?" His hand wrapped around the handle and straightened up, his eyes going to the others on the wall—and the empty space, the naked hook.

I wanted to say nothing and shrug. But then—no, I didn't.

Not if he was going to be gone tomorrow.

I squared my shoulders. "I took it down."

"But you're not a coachman." His tone was casual, but he was intent upon the crop for too long—he was deliberately *not* looking at me. Did he understand already? Did he judge me?

"No." I raised my voice, to remind him I was there. "I'm not."

"Well." Still easy, soft. Still speaking only to the crop. "Are you a horse?"

In my mind's eye, I saw the statue on Mr. Bornholdt's mantel. I remembered the reins, the man pulling down on them. "No," I said, firmly.

"Then what were you doing with a whip?"

Each word had been carefully spaced, so they were polite altogether—but there was something underneath his question: the answer. If he only saw my face, he would know for certain. But still he wouldn't look.

I lifted my chin. "I was playing." But it was too fragile a sentence, out in the silence alone. Haughtier, I added: "Or that was my intention. But you interrupted me."

"Really?" he wondered, and I braced for teasing, or worse. But he turned his head, and his eyes were serious. Then, timidly: "Were you . . . under arrest?"

Surely this was a dream. But I dug my nails into my palms and felt pain. I did not wake up.

"Well, no," I said.

He took half a step back.

"But I was . . . to be punished."

For a moment he didn't move. Then he came closer—close enough that the tongue of the crop he carried could have engaged me in a kiss. "For what?"

I blinked. I hadn't thought of that. I'd thought of the dancing couples at the ball. Of him seeing them. Of how brazen they could be in their love, when I couldn't. And how uneasy I felt, when everyone else got to be gay, all because of—

"Knocking over the washstand," I said, eyes cast to the floor.

"Well, that's silly," he pronounced at once. "That was an accident. If I were your master, I would never punish you for such a thing."

My gaze jumped upward. He was studying the crop again—turning it in his hand, as if it were a gift he'd just received.

With forced calm, I asked, "What *would* you punish me for?"

"That kiss."

He had not had to think, and the foreboding in his voice made me shrink from him, sudden anxious energy thrilling up my back.

I licked my lips. "But . . . you told me to."

"Did I also tell you to yank me like a bellpull?"

I cringed. But when I dared look, there was a sparkle in his eyes.

He wasn't serious. He was playing the game.

I clasped my hands primly behind my back. "I was only trying to show enthusiasm, sir."

"Ah, she laughs." He shook his head and put his free hand to his cheek. "She is forever laughing. Is this funny?" And with sudden vehemence, he swung the crop in the empty space beside him—so hard I could hear it cut the air.

I didn't dare breathe.

"Turn around," he said, inarguable as death.

I couldn't make myself move at all at first. Clumsy, slow, I faced away.

"Lift your skirt."

My breath caught on stuffy air. I smelled black tea, tasted tobacco—but no. I was in the stables. I was with Valentine. And I wanted to be, whatever that said about me. Biting my lip for courage, I gathered folds of my skirt in my fists and pulled.

"Stop," he said, almost immediately, and my hem swung, brushing the back of my knee. Had I misunderstood what he wanted?

For a long moment, all was silent.

Then the crop connected, and I winced at the sound—but it was not me that it hit. Again and again it found some other mark, softly at first, then louder. Every few times, Valentine made a thoughtful noise.

After a particularly sharp crack, Valentine gasped—as if he'd shut his finger in a drawer. In the stall to my right, straw shifted and one of the horses sputtered anxious air.

"Are you all right?" I asked.

"Don't you worry about me." The crop's tongue touched my ankle. My whole body focused on its light tickle as it journeyed upward, over the cool fabric of my stocking, the swell of my calf. I sucked in my breath, holding still. Behind me, I heard Valentine's feet shift. Then, his breath touching my ear: "Worry about yourself."

The tongue drew away long enough for my stomach to turn, and then it flicked me. It couldn't have been more than a twist of Valentine's wrist, but the pain lingered, spreading away from its starting point, mellowing—sweetening.

I panted, once. But it was such an unseemly sound. I held my breath.

The leather tip drew away, only to return again, harder—not in the form of a tongue anymore, but more like teeth, biting.

"What does it feel like?" Valentine's voice was not so close anymore. He must have stood back.

I squirmed. "It . . . stings."

"No." The crop traveled up my leg again, to where I held the hem of my uniform. "Inside you. What happens?"

Planting my feet, I reached down into myself for the answer, into the rush of my blood, but even on my lips, the feeling would not be made into words. It ran through my teeth, back down my throat, into my belly.

He struck my calf, a bit harder. The sound it made was softer than a finger's snap, but the sting flared bright—showing in sharp relief those corners of myself into which I had only ever been able to squint before.

"I catch fire." Even the words burned. It was a relief to let them go, and in a sweet, dizzy stupor, I left my lips still parted, so that when Valentine struck again, nothing stopped my moaning right out loud.

The crop's tongue abandoned me, like a bird leaving a branch. My eyes shot wide awake. But I couldn't take it back.

His fingers gripped my shoulder and turned me toward him. I tried to look at the floor, but he bent himself low, his face turned up to mine. He had a judge's eyes. "Are you enjoying this?" he demanded.

In my mind: Bornholdt, drunk. *You got the slap you asked for. Did you like it?*

"Yes," I said, the word coming thin. "Yes, God help me."

Grinning, Valentine slid his hand up, into my hair. My cap slipped as he gathered strands in his grip. He pulled—and I was in the study, and I was choking on the taste of tobacco, and my scalp was burning, burning, and I couldn't breathe.

I rasped: "Stop."

The hand disappeared, but my scalp was still on fire.

The smirk that had flickered on Valentine's face now guttered and died. "Marian?" he said, and reached out.

I jerked back. "You shouldn't be here."

Valentine caught his fingers in a fist, his eyes darting across my face. "Marian, what did I do?"

I opened my mouth, but I had no air. On my tongue, the phantom taste of tobacco choked me. I couldn't take a new breath.

"Did I hurt you?" he wanted to know, and again he reached out—not to touch me, but so his hands were to either side of me, as if he thought I might faint.

"He pulled my hair," I got out.

Something tipped over behind Valentine's eyes, staining them a darker color, hardening his mouth. Then, as if with one deft swipe of a cloth, he cleared the mess of emotion from his face. "I'll never do it again."

"I'm sorry," I said, shaking.

"No." Tentatively, Valentine touched my shoulder. When I didn't flinch, when instead I began to melt in his direction, he pulled me close to him, wrapping his arms around me. "It's him that should be sorry."

"It's my fault; I fell right in with him, with what he wanted," I said. "He gave me a silly order, and for one foolish moment, I thought I was with—" I sucked in my breath. He would resent the comparison.

Sure enough, he drew back. "Did I make you think that way?"

Guilt washed anew over me at the wideness of his eyes. I didn't know what to say, about what the game had meant to me—meant to me still.

"Did I give you that idea?" he asked again. "In your room when I thought—when I didn't understand? Marian, what he did is not your fault."

I stared at him. He didn't mean the game?

"Do you hear me? It is not your fault."

The corners of my mouth drew sharply downward, tears welling in my eyes. I fought them, tried to constrict the swelling heat in my chest, but they came through. I shook, and Valentine drew me to him again—but he didn't squeeze.

By and by, the tears were slower to come, and I quieted, sniffing only occasionally.

His chin moved against my shoulder as he spoke: "We'll not play this silly game ever again."

I twisted to face him. “Don’t say that. Oh, please don’t say that. He’s taken so much of my peace from me, my comfort. He can’t have our game, too.”

“Marian.” He shook his head. “If it’s no fun for you, then—”

“It *is* fun for me.” I punched my fist into my thigh, and behind these words were other words, buried words, clamoring to escape. “I’m wicked, but what does it matter? The world is wicked. It’s ruthlessly mean. So I’m an awakened woman! What do they expect but for people to follow after what feels good to them once they’re lucky enough to figure it out? I never wanted to get tangled up with him, and now, because I did, I have to give up the thing I really want, with you?”

Valentine drew back, and dropped his hands. He stared at me—and to think, he saw the whole truth, plainly. Finally. It was torture to endure his knowing. And yet, with every second the revelation was older, easier to bear between us. I was glad it was out, even if it would mean an ending.

His brows drew together, and he looked past me. He seemed so suddenly troubled, I turned my head over my shoulder, afraid we were no longer alone. But the stable was empty still of people. Behind me there was only a single horse, and a support beam going from the floor to the roof.

“What is it?” I asked.

“I have an idea,” he said. “For our game.”

19

Perhaps ten minutes later, I waited where he'd told me to, standing at quiet attention in an empty horse stall, my legs tingling. I could see the crop; it hung with the others, where it belonged. My lips were dry. I licked them, and took a deep breath.

The stable door swung open and Valentine burst through, striding down the aisle between the stalls, the breeze from the open windows twitching his hair. He stopped as he drew level with my stall, brought his feet together, and with superb unconcern, said: "Osley."

I hurried from my hidden place, stopping at a respectful distance and curtsying. "Good evening, sir."

He did not look at me. "I have just come from the ball. Take my coat."

"Yes, sir." I darted behind him—but lost my nerve somewhat as I reached toward his neck. I pulled uncertainly at his collar, and he rolled his shoulders back, helping me.

"Hang that," he said.

I turned, unsure, and decided to drape the coat over the stall wall. Then I faced him.

"The gloves next," he said, and offered me his hands.

With my own trembling fingers, I tugged at the ends of each of his, afraid to pinch him. Finally the cotton came, revealing pale, neat hands. The gloves were warm. I draped these, too, over the stall wall, beside his coat.

"Good." He stood in his white shirt and trousers, tugging on his cuffs. When he was satisfied with his sleeves, he pointed at a hay bale along the back wall. "Get that chair. I am exhausted."

"Yes, sir. Where shall I—"

"Here." With a decisive finger he indicated a square post in the aisle, which held up part of the roof. I set the bale down against it, and he nodded. "Very good, Osley, thank you."

I curtsied again. "My pleasure, sir."

Valentine let out a sigh as he sat, stretching his legs out before him. "Now the boots, Osley."

I approached slowly, in the thick air of a dream. I sank to my knees, and my thoughts sank, too, into someplace warm and insular. I loosed the bow of his laces, the smell of leather wafting up to my nose, and pulled his foot free. The second shoe went more quickly, for I was confident.

Valentine rolled his head left and right, groaning low in his throat. "That feels so much better," he said. Then he opened his eyes, fixing them on me. They were dark, with mischief in them. "Do you know what I want to do now, Osley?"

I swallowed. "What's that, sir?"

He stretched his arms up toward the ceiling, so his shirt grew tight around his torso—showing how his body tapered slightly, from his chest to his stomach. "I want," he said, still looking straight at me, "to hold on to this post." And he clasped his hands high around the wooden beam behind him.

My brow furrowed.

"Perfect." He shut his eyes, apparently heedless of my confusion. "I may spend my whole night like this. Osley, unbutton my shirt, will you?"

I sucked in my breath.

He opened one eye, his brow cocking. "Osley? That was an order."

"Yes, sir." I jerked into motion. But closer to his prone shape—the lewd suggestion in his pose—I trembled to touch him.

"First you untie the knot at the collar." He opened his throat to me, eyes still shut.

"Yes, sir." I bent close to his neck. The fabric was warm with the heat of his skin, and it gave when I tugged. He smelled of linen, and salt, and ink-like lampblack. I could see him in my mind, straight-backed and focused, polishing silver at the dining-room sideboard—so careful and controlled. His composure so completely unraveled me. I wished I could unravel him. I let down the starch-crisp ends with shaking fingers, his chest rising and falling slowly.

"And now the buttons. Start at the top."

"Yes, sir." I bent farther, and his body shifted under my fingers.

I managed one, two, three buttons—my eyes flicking from one to the next, trying not to catch on the wedge of skin they revealed, the fine amber curls.

"Pink is a lovely color on you."

My fingers jumped, and I jerked, away from the tickle of his breath.

"Are you shy?" he asked, and though I couldn't bear to look, I heard him smiling. "Whyever for? It's my shirt, not yours."

I bit my lip and fiddled with the next button in silence, but it wouldn't cooperate. I couldn't steady my hands long enough to get it through the hole.

He sat forward. In my ear, he said, "Tear it."

"What?"

"Tear it open."

I shook my head infinitesimally, fiddling again. "No, your buttons will fly off."

There was a silence.

"No?"

Eyes wide and still holding the stubborn button, I raised my gaze. "I only meant—after the greatcoat, if you're seen—"

"I will say I got caught on some inebriated woman's ridiculous jewelry," he said, but without any humor in his tone. His eyes were dark and hard. "Do as I say."

"Yes, sir." It was hard to look away from him, but I made myself. I drew the fabric into my fists and tugged. But nothing happened.

"Harder." It was a whisper—excited, encouraging.

I held my breath and tugged again.

"Come now, Marian." His tone certain, even proud, he said: "You are much stronger than that."

I gathered up the fabric in my hands. Grunting aloud as I did it, I ripped the shirt halves apart. The buttons hit the dirt a foot or so off, but my eyes flew up to Valentine's face.

"Now." His eyes appraised me. More. They challenged me. "Where were we, last night?"

I drew myself up and kissed him, hard, taking his jaw in my hand. My fingers followed his neck, down to his chest, tangling the soft hairs I'd seen. He moaned under my mouth, and his back arched to bring him closer to me—his arms still taut above him.

When I broke the kiss, he panted beneath me. "The trousers, next," he said.

I dropped my chin. But as soon as I saw the two pairs of brassy buttons, I stumbled backward.

He sat up. "Do you not want—"

"No!" I ran my fingers, fast, through my hair. "I do. But I . . . I want . . ."

I couldn't finish. I gave him helpless, aching eyes.

He smiled, tilting his head. And then, mercifully: "You want me to . . . let go of this post?"

"Yes," I said, so the word was a sigh. "Sir."

"I've let you have your way up to now," he said, his tone low. "But if I let go of this post, I will have mine."

"Yes." My mouth was dry.

He swallowed. "I don't want to take from you anything you don't want me to have, Marian."

I stared, wondering at the warning edge in his voice. As if he worried that I hadn't had enough time to think this through. Finally—something I knew and he didn't.

I came forward and bent to whisper in his ear. "It's all yours."

He tilted his head back, shutting his eyes. "Not yet it isn't."

I put my lips close to his, trying to tempt him. But his eyes stayed closed.

"Greatcoat incident aside," he said, "I have no desire to be like him."

"I know that." I spoke against his mouth, as he had done to me.

"So." He pressed his head back against the post, away from me. "If the resemblance ever gets too close for comfort, you will say his name, and I will stop whatever I am doing. Is that understood?"

I shook my head. "Oh, Valentine, but—"

"Promise me."

I put out my palms. "All right."

But still he didn't open his eyes. "Let me hear you say it."

"But—"

"I need to know you can. If you need to."

I took a breath. "Bornholdt."

"Good girl."

Valentine lunged, and we went down together. His hair falling into his eyes, he rewarded me with his weight, his mouth—a kiss deep enough to drown in.

I sank willingly to its very bottom.

Afterward, I lay under Valentine's jacket, dressed only in my stockings. I kept my eyes closed, focused on his fingers, which stroked from my temple to my lips.

I had never in all my waking hours imagined something so sweet as the strain of my muscles to their limit, had not anticipated finding an ocean within myself that could be whipped into a tempest.

But I had dreamed of something like it, once.

Let go, he'd said to me in my sleep—and in the morning I'd feared madness, thinking I might lose myself utterly in the fall. And indeed I had: I was stripped of everything. But away with all my careful control went my shame as well, so I was both naked and invulnerable. There was nowhere to hide anymore, and it didn't matter because there was nothing to be hidden.

"If I'm to be dismissed, I suppose I can't marry you yet," Valentine muttered.

I sat forward, fast. "Marry me? You want to . . . to marry me?"

Valentine sat up, too. "Of course. Why else would I—I wouldn't have—"

"I thought it was like the workhouse stable," I said, the corners of my eyes burning. "I thought this was your way of saying goodbye."

"Oh, Marian." He pulled me against the solid warmth of his chest and spoke into my hair. "I never said goodbye."

I had expected him to speak some other way, with sorrow or guilt. But his words were solemn as an oath. They settled over me in the straw, like another layer of his clothing—pleasantly warm from all the years it had been clasped across his heart.

The pain of our childhood parting fell away, a dead husk that had been hanging on overlong, finally shaken off.

I held on tight to him.

"Can you avoid Bornholdt on your own?" he asked. "Not for long—a week or two, that's all I'd need."

I shuddered. "I'd rather come with you when you go."

He shook his head. "In that case, neither of us gets a good reference for other work. If you wait, you might come up with a reason to give Mrs. Bornholdt that you must leave and part amicably from her. I would still find ways to see you. I could come to the village on Sundays."

"But imagine, Valentine," I said, my chest tightening, "imagine if Bornholdt found out I was meeting you, when I've been resisting him. I think he'd be more furious than he is now, to think of you getting what he wanted from me. He might try to take what he wants in a rage, and I wouldn't be able to fight him off."

The silence that followed was grim.

"All right, no visits. I'll focus on finding work," Valentine said, finally. "No one who knows the Bornholdts will want me. I'll go to London—maybe Mrs. Martin can help. At the least, I have enough for a few nights at a doss-house. I can sleep on the rope. Someone will have need of a tailor. And as soon as I can, I'll send for you. But before we get too caught up in planning, there's something else that needs taking care of."

"What's that?" I asked, wrapping his jacket tighter around me.

He reached for my clothes, in a pile beside us. "Here. Get dressed. We'll be missed soon, if we haven't been already. I'll explain once we're back inside."

We brushed straw from one another, once we were decent. Valentine went back to the house first, and I counted out a hundred seconds before I followed. I met no one on the lawns. My great fear was that the kitchen had gone quiet—and, thus, my return would be conspicuous—but luck favored me. Only Lucette had retired, and someone must have spread wine around to those left awake; the laughter and chatter were even more boisterous than when we'd left.

"Here," Valentine hissed, from the direction of the footman's pantry, as soon as I was in the house. I found him pawing around in one of the lower cabinets.

"What are you doing?"

"I know a recipe," he said, backing out with jars in his arms, "for keeping off babies."

"Oh." I felt myself go cold. "Oh, goodness."

"I know." He pulled down a gravy boat, of all things, and poured some brownish oil into it. "I'd be a monster to hamper you now. What if we have to travel, or stay somewhere filthy? Or, heaven forbid, if we were stuck here and you started to show. Even apart from whatever the master might do, Mrs. Bornholdt would dismiss you."

It was true. No self-respecting woman would keep a pregnant lady's maid; it would be scandalous, my swollen belly protruding as I served my mistress and her guests in the parlor. "You're right," I said.

He threw an anxious look over his shoulder. "Then you'll drink it?"

I drifted deeper into the pantry, numb. "Yes. It's wise of you to think of it." I stopped, staring at his back, a new thought occurring to me. "How did you come to know such a recipe?"

"The same way I came to know how to get ink off French mahogany," he replied, not pausing in his business with the oil and the gravy boat. "I keep my eyes and ears open. It's only three ingredients—easy to remember."

I hesitated. "You've never had reason to make it before?"

"No." It seemed all the answer he meant to give, but then he looked my way again. I tried to clear my expression, for it felt ugly, but he had seen it. He turned and closed the short distance between us.

"Have you ever had cause to take such medicine?" he asked, holding my hands.

"No," I said at once.

"Then why should my temperance be unbelievable?"

"Because . . ." Breaking his hold, I gestured upward. "Look at men like Mr. Bornholdt. Look how he is."

He raised his eyebrows. "For an exemplar of manliness," he said, "you might as easily instruct him to look at me."

I blinked, digesting this idea. It settled my stomach.

He turned back to the counter. "I found the recipe on a torn-off sheet. I was fixing a drawer in Mr. Bornholdt's desk and it fell out. The way I heard some of the so-called ladies talking tonight, when the mistress wasn't around, well . . . Seems like he's gone after other girls than you, and has better success with them. He's probably got some of this stuff in a flask."

I shook my head. "Poor Mrs. Bornholdt."

Valentine handed me the gravy boat. It was perfectly absurd—to match the unreality of the last hour—good and bad. I turned the spout toward me, the better to drink from it, and raised the boat to my mouth.

I caught a whiff of the concoction mixed within. I froze.

"I know," he said. "But it's like the suet pudding. If you go quick—"

I lowered the gravy boat.

"What?" Valentine asked.

"This smells like . . ." My eyes found his. "This smells like Mrs. Bornholdt's medicine."

20

"Are you sure?" Valentine asked.

"Yes—the oil smell is the same." I scrunched my nose as I stared at it. I couldn't think, yet. I only felt the offense of the smell—of the very idea. "What is it?"

"Turpentine."

"Turpentine." I sniffed the gravy boat. "And aloe, is it?"

He nodded. He'd gone pale.

"Hers has aloe, too; I know it." I held my head. "Valentine, would it make her sick like she is?"

"I don't know." He shrugged helplessly. "I suppose—anything meant to stifle life, taken over and over again . . ." He watched me, wide-eyed.

I studied the gravy boat. "But Valentine, they're *trying* for children . . ."

His brow furrowed. "Or she thinks they are."

My hand flew to my chest. "God, I have to tell her."

"What?" He shook his head. "That's a bad idea."

I pointed abovestairs. "He's lying to her! You nearly had me thrown out of the house for the same!"

"I know." Though he made a quelling gesture, his brows were bowed with guilt. "I was wrong to do that."

"No, you weren't—not if you'd been right about me!" I put my fists on my hips. "Come on, Valentine; I *know* this doesn't sit right with you."

"Of course not. But what could you tell her that she would believe, about how you found out?"

"The truth."

His eyes widened. "About what we did in the stables?"

"About what we did after the stables," I said. "Even if she were to dismiss us, aren't we going anyway?"

"That's not what I'm worried about." He ran his hands through his hair, leaning his palm against his forehead. "Marian, if she believes you about Mr. Bornholdt, she's going to confront him, and he'll want to know how she came by her information. Imagine if he found out, you said. If you tell Mrs. Bornholdt, we won't have to imagine it."

I didn't want the idea to scare me, but it did.

"But—but if I tell her to say she found the recipe," I said, and rushed on even as Valentine shook his head: "I think she knows I like you—maybe she even approves. Maybe if I say we're going to leave and marry, and we'd prefer it were a secret until then, she'd keep it one for us."

"A secret from Bornholdt?" He raised his brows. "Why would her lady's maid want to keep a match quiet from the master even on the point of leaving his house? Because she doesn't want to make him jealous?"

I made a face. "She won't think—"

"Why not? It's the truth."

I cringed. "But—no—I don't want—"

Reaching out to touch me, he said, "I know, I know. You don't have to tell me. And you don't have to tell her, either. You don't owe her that. Not at your own personal risk. You've got enough to struggle with by yourself; she can handle this one thing."

I frowned. After a long moment, I dropped my shoulders.

"There." Valentine let go of his breath. "That's settled."

I sighed. Toasting him with grim sarcasm, I tipped the gravy boat to my lips.

The "medicine" was thick, oily, and I nearly spat it out on instinct. I made my tongue bail it backward, down my throat, and swallowed it even as I gagged. A bitter film lingered on my tongue afterward.

Valentine allowed a moment of silence for the trial. Then he said, "I don't want to linger. We shouldn't be found together."

I nodded. No amount of talking would change the fact that the morning might bring about his dismissal, anyway.

"I'm not beneath begging to stay," he said, reading my mind. "And if that doesn't work, I promise you I will move heaven and earth to make a place for us somewhere in London."

"Do we say goodbye, then?" I asked. "Just in case?"

"Never," he replied, and kissed me, emphatic despite the turpentine taste of my mouth. Then he slipped out of the pantry alone.

I stood in the quiet, grimacing at the bitter, oily film on my tongue and the anxious ache in my heart—for Valentine, but for Mrs. Bornholdt, too. What a terrible end to a beautiful night.

Merry pandemonium yet reigned in the kitchen, but I did not dare look around until I reached the housekeeper's office. Mrs. Davies had fallen asleep by the fire. I broke up the pile of burning wood so the flames would soon starve and die, and put the metal screen in front. There was nothing else to do but wait for my mistress's bedroom bell to ring.

I sat on a stool in the kitchen, where what remained of the food was still laid out. The sight of it stirred the contents of my stomach unpleasantly. I tried to tell myself it was the medicine, only, that upset me—but I'd seen Mrs. Bornholdt in my mind, sending down the trays, saying the servants should enjoy themselves.

I discreetly pressed my fingers against my stomach, wincing. Valentine was right. To try to help her now would hurt me. Surely there were other people in her life to intervene on her behalf, someday—or other paths to her happiness than perfect health or children. I had but this one chance. I'd wished for this opportunity. Had I learned from others to love myself so very little that, having been given the gift I'd asked for, I would throw it away?

The bell-board called to me. I rose at once, away to my mistress's bedroom.

Poor Mrs. Bornholdt seemed asleep on her feet. She noticed neither my troubled expression nor my surreptitious sniffing of her medicine; it took all her focus to get her jewelry pieces into their boxes. But she was not inebriated—only exhausted.

"Wythe's father is in even worse shape than I am," she said through a yawn.

I undressed her: jacket first, skirt next, and finally her corset. Wonderful, she'd called me. For sewing some jean stays into the linings. And that night I'd served at dinner, after my mother's funeral, how she'd smiled—as if she were glad to see me again.

"He is in no fit state to travel home yet, so he is staying over. I pity him; he has no man here to attend his weary bones—no you in his life, in short."

I worried my lip. What had won her to me? A flattering dress. Less. Her last maid had set the bar so low. All I had to do was not actively sabotage her in every way available to me.

But there had been other times when she'd been mean.

This is not a brothel.

I took the warming pan Lucette had left from between her sheets and helped my mistress into bed.

"Do you remember," she said, turning on her side to face me, "the night we met, you said you wanted to pay your mother's way out of the workhouse?"

How naive I'd been. But I suppressed my frown. "Yes, ma'am."

"To repay the woman who looked after you." She put her hands under her pillow, shutting her eyes. "And I said I would be looking after you now."

"Yes, ma'am."

"But it is you." She sighed—and it was not a tired sigh. It was a contented one, untroubled as a cloud, drifting. "You look after me."

She didn't see me do it—indeed, she might already have been asleep—but I set my jaw and nodded. "Yes, ma'am."

◆ ◆ ◆

I passed an uneasy night, holding my roiling stomach and sweating beneath my sheets. I'd never felt so sick before, and was glad when it was time to rise, for having something to do would take my mind off my body. I dressed quickly, so I had time to find Valentine and take him aside, to ask for the recipe. He argued under his breath, but so did I.

"It's dangerous—"

"It doesn't matter that it's dangerous; what matters is it's right."

"It might be for nothing; she may not even believe you."

"She will. She trusts me. She values me—"

"How can you be sure—"

"And because she values me, she won't confront Mr. Bornholdt without assuring my protection. If he's guilty, just my being the source of information would make him angry. She'll anticipate that."

Valentine gave me a long and troubled look, but he went away to his room and brought me the folded sheet. We parted without touching—he to his chores, me to the footman's pantry to make up a jar of the medicine.

I screwed on the lid, tucked the hateful stuff into my apron pocket, and made up her breakfast tray as usual. Outside Mrs. Bornholdt's bedroom, I took a deep breath, forcing my shoulders low, and entered.

I opened the windows as well as the curtains, while she ate. The air outside was sweet, dewy. It made me think of Valentine's mouth. Such pleasant reminiscing I should have done at those windows if I were at leisure to sit by them. But then I would have been Mrs. Bornholdt—and though she may have had the windows, she did not have much about which to reminisce.

I laid her fire next, taking my time. At the end of her meal, she said, "I'll have my medicine, Marian." She sounded puzzled. Usually I would have set a measure of it on her tray already. Usually I would have been gone by now.

"Yes, ma'am." I rose from the hearth and poured the dose into a cup as she watched, bringing it to her bedside table. "Only don't drink it yet. I—I wonder if you'd help me first."

She looked into my face, as if to ask what she could possibly do for me when she was still in bed in a nightgown.

I brought out the jar from my pocket. "You see, Mrs. Bornholdt, Mr. Hobbs—" But the words wouldn't come. I knew exactly which ones to use, as I had been rehearsing them all the night instead of sleeping, but they would change everything. The version of me reflected in Mrs. Bornholdt's eyes would be different. Hated, perhaps.

But it would be an honest image, at least. She would know me.

"Mr. Hobbs gave this to me. For a problem of mine. You know how he is at solving problems."

"Yes," Mrs. Bornholdt said. "Not a single fly on my mirror this summer, not one."

I set myself to unscrewing the jar lid. It gave me an excuse not to look at my mistress, but the hammering of my heart was making my fingers jump, as if it pumped too much blood to them with every pulse. "It's important, you know, for me to be well enough to work, to do what is expected of me, so it was nice of him to—" As the lid finally came loose, the first whiff of medicine made me shudder, and I spilled some on the floor. "Sorry, ma'am."

She waved her hands. "Never mind. You can clear that up in a moment. But what ails you, Marian?"

"Nothing now, ma'am." I tipped the jar's mouth toward her nose. "But doesn't it smell awful?"

Mrs. Bornholdt's face was changing before she'd even sniffed—and why not? That vile, oily odor soured every morning that might have otherwise been pleasant and simple. It took the sweet aftertaste of her tea and toast. It was a smell she literally lived with. I had known it at once, but Mrs. Bornholdt knew it better.

She glanced down into the bottle, and her eyes jumped back to mine. They were dark, but I could see the dawn was coming. "Marian, you are not in any position to bear a child," she breathed.

I made myself hold her gaze. "No, ma'am."

"You would not be able to stay on working here," she told me, as if I didn't know, reaching out to touch my hand. "A pregnant lady's maid? Waiting on me upstairs? I would have to let you go. And how would you care for the baby? You have no husband, Marian. Why, it would be to choose your own ruination, why—why, why?"

I inhaled. "I hesitate to tell you, ma'am—"

She reached out for my hand, and when she clutched it, her nails dug in. "Has he said he will marry you?" There were real, shuddering tears in her eyes.

"Yes," I said, exhaling it, relieved that she had understood so soon and was not angry with me.

"He is lying," she declared, suddenly vicious. "He may dote on you, Marian, but you are a servant. Do not be a fool. Even if you give him what he wants, he will not put you in my place. He will say the child is mine, and you will be on the streets, and it will serve you right!"

She was shaking—not with weakness, but rage.

I stepped back. "Mrs. Bornholdt—"

"I cannot believe—is that why he lashes out at you? So I will not suspect?"

I held up my hands. "No, it's—"

"I suppose you think I deserve this? Because I have nice things that you do not have? Dresses and dinners and you, waiting on me—*you*." She drew herself up in the bed. "You are not a nice thing, Marian. You are a snake, a rat, and I will throw you out, like I did the last rodent that tried to make its nest in my husband's bed."

I recoiled. "Oh, Mrs.—"

"Whore!" she said, and slapped me.

The sting was nothing to the sharp edge of my shame, but I felt Mrs. Bornholdt's bitter heartbreak most keenly of all. In the ringing silence that followed, it was easy to tell the truth, to spare her.

"I meant Mr. Hobbs," I said.

"I do not believe you." Her words had a hollow ache. "You admit no unmarried lady's maid should hope to have a baby."

"That's what I'm trying to tell you." I gazed dispassionately at the oil stain I'd made in the carpet. "I don't want a baby. That's what the medicine is really for."

She scoffed. "That is not true."

"Why would I tell you, otherwise?" I whispered.

"What?"

"Why would I warn you if I was going to bear Mr. Bornholdt's child?"

"Warn me? Threaten, you mean! Probably thought you could get something out of me!" Then, more softly and a bit begrudgingly: "And why would you admit to an affair with the footman?"

"To look after you," I said.

Her lips parted.

"Mr. Bornholdt is lying, ma'am."

She set her tray beside her on the bed. "Well, someone certainly is. And we will sort out who right now. Ring for the butler, Marian, and bring me my robe."

21

I rang for Ledford, knowing the butler would bring the master—and the master would bring new danger.

I held Mrs. Bornholdt's robe open for her to put her arms in, my blood beating in my burning ears. Valentine and I could have fled the night before, could have run, and my feet had never felt more up to that task. I could have left her a note. If she did not believe me, that wouldn't have been my fault. I would have known I'd tried, had a clear conscience, and been far, far out of my tormentor's reach.

But in my heart I preferred my terror to the awful guilt I would have carried—that I could have done more, and hadn't.

I made myself breathe deeply. My conscience was clear. I was good, I *was*, and I would show that to Mrs. Bornholdt. If only she would look.

"Go in there," she told me, pointing through the dressing room door. She looked mistrustful of me, and I lingered on the threshold, wanting to speak some comfort.

But there was a knock at the outer door, and she stalked away.

"Is my husband in or out?" I heard her demand.

"I believe he is still dressing in his apartment, madam." Ledford's voice. "I have just been in to check on his father in the parlor, who said the master had not visited yet this morning."

"Then Hobbs is with him. Summon both of them here at once."

"Yes, Mrs. Bornholdt."

I waited through some minutes, staring at the floor.

"Good morning, my darling," Mr. Bornholdt drawled in the next room, too soon.

"Quite the opposite thus far," she replied.

I heard Mr. Bornholdt's footsteps crossing the floor. Another set followed, made by softer, slower feet. Valentine had the gait of a man going to the gallows, I thought.

Like his father.

"What has upset you?" Mr. Bornholdt sounded weary. "You know the doctor says you are not to agitate yourself."

"Does he say that?" Mrs. Bornholdt asked. "I would not know. It is you who takes his instructions."

"Diana, what—"

"Hello, Hobbs," she said, over her husband.

"Ma'am," Valentine murmured. That was all the warning I got before Mrs. Bornholdt burst into the dressing room. She gestured the men forward and stepped to the side herself.

Valentine was too intimate a vision for me in the same room as these others—both of them having less than favorable opinions about my virtue. It didn't matter that Valentine was fully dressed for cleaning; there was skin and straining muscle beneath his vest, and a trail of soft hair I could follow beneath his trousers. That the body underneath his clothes had overtaken mine made me feel that we both stood naked. Even as I looked away, I felt his panting breath in my ear, and heard the low, longing sounds he'd made—as if the very pleasure he felt were torture to him.

Mrs. Bornholdt slammed the door.

"Diana," Mr. Bornholdt began again, jumping, but the sharpness of her glance cut him cleanly off.

"Wythe, be honest with me," she ordered. "What is your relationship with my lady's maid?"

It was the first opportunity he'd had to take me in. He surveyed me as his portrait did, in his study: looking down from on high, unimpressed and impartial. "Why, she is a stranger to me," he said, and it cut me. Not because I wished it weren't true, but because it was *my* morality that made him honest in saying it, not his.

"I do not believe you," Mrs. Bornholdt said, viciously, and I realized she had seen me glaring at her husband.

"Diana, come." He gestured toward me with a limp, dismissive hand. "She is incompetent—"

"No. The last one was incompetent, Wythe." She crossed her arms. "And in any case, you never seemed to mind."

"But this one I mind very much, as I think you have seen—"

"I have seen what you have shown me," she spat. "Do you know what the lady's maid told me this morning? About my medicine? She says she recognizes it."

"Oh?" Mr. Bornholdt's eyebrows rose with his voice. "I did not know she had training as a nurse."

"She would not need training to know." With significant weight, she added: "That she is a ripe woman is enough."

I reddened to be talked of so, uncomfortably aware of my proximity to Valentine, to whom my eyes were damningly drawn. Yet he maintained an unreadable, if not distant, expression, his eyes cast down in the polite habit of the waiting servant.

Mrs. Bornholdt whirled, left the room, and returned with her medicine glass in one hand and my jar in the other. "Look, Wythe."

Both sloshing oils were an identical shade of brothy brown.

"Well, my darling." Mr. Bornholdt smiled, patronizing. "The patent is not in the coloring of the thing. They may well look alike and be different."

The smugness of his tone made me open my mouth to shout. But I knew better.

"Too right," Mrs. Bornholdt said. She set both down on her vanity, then opened my jar. Without asking, she put them under his nose one after the other.

"They are the same," she said.

After a pause, he agreed: "They are."

Victory, fierce and hot, rushed my blood.

"Yet one comes from my lady's maid's pocket, mixed to the doctor's precise instructions, I am told."

Mr. Bornholdt tilted back his chin. "How curious."

"So," Mrs. Bornholdt began, with no hint of victory—for what had she confirmed but her own worst suspicion? "I am inclined to believe Marian is trying to conceive."

"As am I." Mr. Bornholdt's eyes roved dispassionately over me, as if he thought I were an imbecile.

I glared at him.

"But she would be insane, Wythe, insane!" Mrs. Bornholdt pointed at him with the hand holding the glass. "Unless it is from you she would get the child. And pity me and the state of the world that this is what I am to deduce if I *trust* you."

"What do you mean, darling?" He shook his head, smiling in a bemused way. "I hardly follow."

He wouldn't give her anything. It was he who'd been called out onto the carpet, yet she was made to answer his questions.

Mrs. Bornholdt slammed the bottles down on the vanity so they spilled. "She defends herself by saying the medicine is not for bringing on a baby. She says it prevents them."

"Does she?" A shadow passed over Mr. Bornholdt's face, his eyes cutting over to me. Then, to his wife: "And—forgive me, but you still have not said—how would she know that?"

"She says—"

"I made my medicine for that purpose." I pulled the recipe from my pocket. "Following these instructions."

Mr. Bornholdt took the sheet from me, and I was sure I saw a flash of recognition in his face before puzzlement creased his brow. Surely the only thing he wondered at was how I'd gotten it.

"Aha," Mr. Bornholdt said, with soft certainty. "So we are both caught, are we, Marian?"

"What?" Mrs. Bornholdt and I demanded together.

"Such a noble sacrifice you have made," he said, "at the expense of your reputation, your living—I am afraid it will hardly prove worthwhile."

Mrs. Bornholdt clenched her fists. "Wythe, you are torturing me."

He stepped closer to his wife. "I am sorry, darling. That has never been my intention. Your maid is convinced I am a monster, Diana. I do not know why—I have been nothing but gracious, giving her everything that was in my power to provide, not least of all the funds required to bury her own mother. This is, I should hope, the act of a good man at heart, no matter the light in which it is viewed."

I had to shut my eyes so that I did not roll them.

"It is the act of a partial man," Mrs. Bornholdt replied, her voice thin.

"Perhaps," he admitted. "I do not deny, Diana, that I am weak in the company of women. You have forgiven me for this failing—or you say you have."

This made me look again. Mrs. Bornholdt had high color in her face for once.

"I would more readily say I have forgiven past failures, Wythe, as there is nothing that may be done about them. The failing itself is yours to fix at will."

He acknowledged her point with a bow of his head. "As you say. We both have eyes, so I will not insult your intelligence and say that Marian is unlovely. Perhaps the warmth in my heart is not so pure as you wish. But I swear on my honor, if I am moved by her, I have only been moved to the kindness of which you are already aware. Her mother's funeral.

She certainly does not bear any child of mine—and could never hope to. I have kept my distance—is that not so, Marian?"

He turned to me, awaiting my response as if he were merely curious. As if we were attending a play, and he wondered what I thought of an actor's performance, which—incidentally—was exactly what his monologue had been. My heart beat furiously against my ribs, but I couldn't speak out and he knew it; to correct his image of himself would be to falsify my own.

I could do nothing but fixate on his mouth, which almost—I could have sworn it—almost smiled.

"I am only interested in what you have to say, Wythe," Mrs. Bornholdt said. "How are you caught? What is the medicine for?"

"My darling." He stepped again closer, reaching out an open hand to her. What deep agony there was in his voice, and just a tremor of anxiety. "The medicine is a loving husband's best attempt—a foolish attempt, perhaps—to force himself to face reality while letting his wife continue to dream. To protect her body and her mind. If it was a deception, Diana, it was done in kindness, in mercy, and I hope—"

"What is the medicine for?" Mrs. Bornholdt's eyes bulged.

He sighed, clasping his hands behind his back. "It is as Marian says. It is for the prevention of children."

I exhaled.

"But . . ." Mrs. Bornholdt trembled, and I thought of how her temper had flared when she'd shouted at me. There was no fire in her now. She was like brittle, used hearth wood that could burst into ash at a touch. "But we were *trying*," she said. "I was trying and trying, and why would you *lie*? I want to give you what you want; why do you not *let* me?"

"But *you* are what I want." He reached out to hold her shoulders. "You, first and foremost. And, good Lord, Diana, you cannot know how near you were to death that day when the baby came too soon.

Your eyes were closed, hot with fever—all your faculties were turned inward. But I was there."

I fidgeted against the wall, frightened by Mrs. Bornholdt's face. The ice in her glare was thawing.

"I nearly lost you, my darling, and I did not know how I would go on." Mr. Bornholdt tucked some of his wife's hair behind her ear. "I made up my mind that we would never risk such an endeavor again—that I would not gamble with your life. But when you woke, you were inconsolable. You spoke of disappointing me, of being an unacceptable wife . . ."

"I was," Mrs. Bornholdt murmured. "I am."

I shook my head.

So did Mr. Bornholdt. "No, my love. But, then as now, though I sang your praises, your mood would not lift. So I said that no one knows the future." He dropped his hands. "It was only that, the idea of trying again, that brought the light of life back to your eyes."

"Because I wanted to fulfill my duty to you," she said. "The only duty I have."

"And you do it." He took her hand, running his thumb over her knuckles. "Diana, you have dutifully gone on with a smile on your face, hope in your eyes, courage in your heart. You choose every day to pursue the path that devotion requires at your peril; you are brave and selfless. It is I who selfishly values your life, your wellness, above the womanly favor you might do me."

"If you had only told me what you wished . . ." Her voice was soft. Too soft.

"Would you have believed me?" He tipped up her chin, locking eyes with her. "Or would you have been convinced of it as mere gallantry? And if gallantry it must have been, would you not have gone on chastising yourself? I wanted you *happy*, Diana—feeling as if you were doing what was required of you, only without the risk of it. Happy, but safe."

"But . . ."

Mr. Bornholdt brought up his other hand, so he cradled his wife's face from both sides, and so—I noticed grimly—she could not disengage from him. "What? Let us have it all now that we are in it, darling."

"You mocked me," she muttered.

I raised my eyebrows.

"Did I?" he asked, all in a sharp breath, as if he'd cut himself.

"At dinner with the Malahides. The flower bowl. Barren—you called it barren."

"Yes," he breathed. "You are right. I forgot sometimes that you did not know what I knew: that I had sacrificed something, which I had wanted, for your sake. Sometimes, when you buck against my authority, I have felt you to be ungrateful for my care of you, and I have let bitter words pass my lips. You must have thought I was disappointed in you, my dear, but all I wanted was your acknowledgment that I was a good husband—your adherence to my rule, as evidence of your confidence in me, in return for the favor I was doing you. But of course you had no idea. I am sorry for being cruel, for expecting you to have knowledge I myself kept from you. I hope you can forgive me."

"Oh." Mrs. Bornholdt hiccuped. "No, I am sorry. Oh, Wythe, forgive me."

And she fell into his arms. He'd done it. He'd disarmed her. The room seemed to tilt. I looked to Valentine, to steady me in what was real, but he would not raise his head. I could not reach my rebel friend—the steadfast footman was in the way.

"Well," Mr. Bornholdt was saying, in a weak and watery voice. He wiped his eyes. "We have put on quite a show for our attendants. Shall we send them away, so we may talk more privately?"

Valentine's head jerked up. But it was only readiness to hear an order; his expression itself was clear of feeling.

Over Mr. Bornholdt's shoulder, my mistress looked at me. She blinked a few times, ushering a pair of tears down her face. "That will be all."

"You may go, Hobbs," Mr. Bornholdt said.

I couldn't believe it.

Valentine passed before me into the bedroom and held the door to let me through. In the hallway, he bent and shut the bedroom door soundlessly behind us. Then, as if a different spirit entirely possessed him, his hands flew to my shoulders. He drew me close, so our foreheads touched. "Did you tell her it was me?" His mouth hardly moved.

"Yes," I breathed, invigorated by his return to life.

He closed his eyes—not hard, as if he were shutting out the fact, but as if he needed to think. "So he'll know any moment."

"She won't tell on me—"

"It won't be telling on you. He's not her enemy, Marian."

"How can you say that?"

Valentine hastened me down the hall, for my voice had risen. He peered at every door we passed, checking that none were ajar.

In the stairwell, I shook off his arm. "Don't tell me you believed his story over mine."

"It doesn't matter what I believe," he said, stopping two steps above me. His expression was resigned.

"Valentine, he's—"

"Her husband," he said, decisively. "That's the man she married, the man she loves."

"But he's so false!"

"Only from where you stand."

"Then I should go back in there." I pointed the way we'd come. "I should request a word in private and tell her exactly what he's like with me, and she—"

"To tell the truth is a privilege, don't you see? It comes with the money, with the suits. Bornholdt's power—he points and says how things will be for his clothes and his family and his business and his leisure. But he also points and says how things *are*. He decides whether he is a good man or a bad one. Your opinion may contradict his, but it will be wrong. That's your inheritance as a woman of no means: to be wrong at the convenience of your betters."

I shook my head. "Valentine, that's not justice. This doesn't sound like you—"

"No, it sounds like you." He came back down the steps, gripped my shoulders, and shook me. "You taught me that. I was wrong when we were small; you were right. Well-off people aren't in any position of power because they're good; they got the power first, and decided what goodness was with it—chose the things they like, the things that separate them from us. And us trying to argue won't convince anyone otherwise."

For a moment I could only stare at him. "But she suspects," I said. "Mrs. Bornholdt does suspect—he *told* her that he's longed for me."

"And that he resists you."

"He lies!"

"But she doesn't want his lies." Valentine seemed to be forcing himself to say the words slowly, clearly. "He offered her his love instead, and of the two, his love is a much easier thing to accept."

The idea nauseated me. I leaned against the end of the banister. "It's all an act, his marriage to her."

"Yes." Valentine laid a hand on my shoulder, but spoke quicker: "But she scripts parts of it, too. She'll tell him about us to get the pleasure of seeing the news strike him. She can judge him by his performance, which will undoubtedly be perfect: responsibly concerned, ruffled, but definitely not jealous. Then she can say you're a good girl, just a product of your class—as if she is not threatened by you—and then, if he's wise, he will dismiss you. But I think he's not wise, Marian, which will be worse for you, and we have to *move*."

A chill wave doused me, extinguishing my anger. This time when he pulled my arm, I came along on quick feet.

"Go and get what money you have, and meet me below—no, outside. Come to the stable. I'll find the coachman. I'll tell him it's an emergency, get him to drop us down in the village. Because you're ill, or something."

I nodded. We burst together onto the third-floor corridor, and when I stopped to unlock my door, Valentine kept going to his. I passed through to my room, going straight for the drawer beside my bed.

There was only stationery inside. My coin purse was gone, and months of wages with it.

I turned new, suspicious eyes on my room. Nothing looked out of place. Everything was as it had been that morning when I'd risen. I riffled through my dresser anyway, dumping the entire contents of the top drawer out on my bed, knowing I had not moved the money and, if anyone else had, they would have left with it.

I knew of only one person with a key to my room.

I did not see Valentine in the corridor. He was likely well ahead of me. I hurried down every flight of stairs to the kitchen. Valentine was not there, either—only Lucette, at the center table, laying out cold meats on a platter, for luncheon. She smiled at me as I stalked by, which she'd never done before; it should have put me on my guard.

I stormed into the housekeeper's office, where a bespectacled Mrs. Davies sat writing in her ledger of household expenses. "Marian." She gave me a nod before returning to the line at which her finger pointed.

I shut the door behind me.

Taking her glasses off, she asked, "Is this about your wages?"

I took a stunned step toward her. "Did you take them?"

"On orders, yes, I did," she replied, without a bit of shame or hesitation.

"Whose orders?"

"Mr. Bornholdt's, of course." She raised her brows. "And there's no point locking yourself in with me, young lady; I don't have them anymore, and anyway, I'm not a man, as we've discussed. I'm not moved by your particular powers of persuasion."

"My powers of—" Head hot with rage, I let myself out, slamming the door so Lucette jumped. Still I did not see Valentine. He must have gone out already, to find the coachman.

But I couldn't go out to him empty-handed. Even with my wages, we would have had hardly any chance of keeping ourselves fed and sheltered. I couldn't leave. We couldn't leave. Or rather, we could, but it would be only choosing a different sort of agony than the one we suffered. We'd starve in the streets, be turned away from work. Perhaps we wouldn't even make it to the city to look. We'd have to walk to London, to save what money Valentine had, and we might lie down at the side of some road to sleep and be set on by thieves. Murderers. Wolves.

But I'd *earned* those wages. My eyes welled with angry, bitter tears.

I had been right, Valentine had said. I had been right—all these years, when I thought I was bad. When I thought Valentine was bad. Because of how we were judged, by judges who were supposed to know what goodness was. But it was they who were wrong.

I didn't deserve this. I stormed toward the stairs.

Valentine would have reminded me that my fury was no shield from Mr. Bornholdt's power, warned me that by lingering in the house, I was playing right into the master's hands.

But I wanted to be angry—and to stay angry. I wanted a fight, even if I was doomed to lose.

22

What a feeling, to pound on a door. It required a recklessness I hadn't felt since I was a child, when I'd found out Valentine had disappeared from Parish Street. I did not wait to be called. I turned the knob and barged into the master's study.

Mr. Bornholdt sat in his desk chair, a cloudy sky visible through the huge window behind him. His elbow was propped on the chair arm, his fingers curled into a fist under his chin. "Well, hello," he said.

This I was not prepared for. He should have been shouting at me for storming in, or lunging for me as he did when he got me alone.

"How improper this is," he said next, with something like delight. "In for a penny, in for a pound, I suppose?"

I swallowed. Mrs. Bornholdt had told him.

"To what do I owe the pleasure of your visit?" he prompted.

In a hollow voice, much different from the one I'd intended to use, I said: "You stole my wages."

His eyebrows perked, but he let my words go unchallenged, perhaps waiting to see what else I would say to argue my case.

I'd had other words, coming in. I could not remember them now. I could think only of Valentine, waiting outside for me. What was I doing here? What had I been thinking?

"I cannot steal my own money, Marian," the master said at last.

"But it's my money after you've paid it to me," I said, dismayed to hear a tremor in my voice.

He gave a heavy, self-indulgent sigh and shook his head at the floor. "In a simpler situation, you would be correct. But you had taken a sizable loan with me, Marian. I may collect on it when I choose. Indeed, I am generous for not demanding the sum all at once, from my perspective."

I took a step toward him. "You told me you didn't want my money."

"But I have been exceptionally clear about what I did want." His eyes found mine, and his gaze was significant.

I tried to swallow again, but my throat was dry.

"I have been patient," he said, almost brightly, as he stood up. "I thought it was ladylike of you to be reticent, and I did not hold it against you. No doubt I was taking my impression of your virtue from your pretty face. But again, you have corrected me on that score." He rounded the desk.

I stepped backward, my legs stiff and slow. "You speak of virtue, sir. I would've fallen in your regard if I had succumbed to you."

"Yes. But." He kept coming, and he reached for my cheek. I turned my head—but he laid hands on the locks of my hair. "Succumbing to your master in the course of your service to him—there is a pitiable inevitability about that. Whereas bedding down with the footman *smacks* of deviation from the path. Of deliberate choice."

"Heaven forbid I choose something for myself in my wretched life," I said, the words forcing their way through even as I knew I should not say them.

"Indeed." He curled my hair around his finger. "What made you think I would tolerate it?"

I jerked back my head, so the tendril sprang free. "Perhaps I didn't think of you."

"I happen to know you did."

My eyes jumped to his, and I felt the blood drain from my face.

"To stop him in his passion, to stay his hand—or whatever appendage he applies—you invoke my name." He sneered. "You did not spread your legs in preference for him. You did it in spite of me."

"You weren't there," I breathed, a prayer I had not meant to say aloud.

"No," he agreed. "I would have intervened—after he'd warmed you up for me."

My stomach dropped.

Mr. Bornholdt turned to gaze at his mantel—at his horse statuette. "After the business with the greatcoat, I asked the staff whether Hobbs was misbehaving in other ways—for immorality is like an infestation. If you see one mite, you may be sure there are many. Lo and behold, the housemaid told me that Hobbs has been talking to you constantly—had been talking to you at dinner, in fact, just before I caught him in my dressing room."

"Lucette?" I said.

"She said she can hear when you come to bed, and by her reckoning you did not go to your room until about the time I was awoken by the toppled washstand."

I could feel color rising to my cheeks and sweat collecting under my arms.

"It is the butler's job to mind his men, but of course Hobbs would be expecting that. So I also asked the housemaid to tail Hobbs if she should see him go away somewhere with you."

I shut my eyes. She had been missing, when we'd come back in from the stable. She must've gone right up to the master. Afterward. And the next morning, while I was belowstairs getting Mrs. Bornholdt's breakfast, Mrs. Davies went up to my room for my wages.

"I must say I did not expect anything to happen so soon," Mr. Bornholdt was saying. "But again, I was working from the assumption that you had strong moral fiber. I had no idea how loose you were. I can hardly imagine what you are like now that Hobbs has cut your strings entirely."

I recoiled. "You won't be finding out."

He rolled his eyes. "Have you been listening? I am not interested in your body any longer." As he spoke, he made his way to the bellpull beside the empty hearth and tugged it. "You took that off the table."

I narrowed my eyes. "Then what do you want from me?"

"Nothing. That was everything you had."

He said it without a hint of threat—and that was why it scared me. It was the naked truth he was speaking, his truth, and what Valentine had said about his privileges finally came home in my head. To be wanted by Mr. Bornholdt had been a nightmare. What would it mean to be worthless to him?

A knock at the door.

Mr. Bornholdt smiled. "Come in, Hobbs."

It couldn't be him. He wouldn't have heard the bell, because he was outside, waiting for—

But there was Valentine when I turned around, hangdog in the doorway.

I bit back a groan.

"Come, come." Mr. Bornholdt stepped past me, beckoning. "No sense prolonging the inevitable. Shut the door. We have matters to discuss."

Grimacing, Valentine came to the middle of the room, his feet tight together, eyes wary.

I hesitated over whether I dared stand by him, and I decided it was proper enough—servants together, for the ease of the master, who lectured both of us—if I kept my distance. I drew myself in line with him and faced Bornholdt.

"I shall tell you what I know, first, so we may dispense with any denials you may be preparing," Mr. Bornholdt began, leaning against his desk. "You, Hobbs, made the medicine that so upset my household this morning."

Valentine cringed as he bowed. "Upsetting the household was not my—"

"Oh, it was positively gallant, giving it to Marian," Mr. Bornholdt said, his tone warm. "Quite responsible of you. You know I understand the wisdom of it, for you have ears, and surely you were listening. It was Marian who accused me."

I bit the inside of my lip.

Mr. Bornholdt waved a hand, standing. "But no matter! My wife and I are stronger breathing the same, clear air than we ever were in our separate fogs. I should be thanking you."

I gazed at the floor.

He loped toward me. "Your master has condescended to you, Marian. Will you not bend even now?"

I dropped a clumsy curtsy. "I'm pleased you're pleased, sir."

He leaned down, his face filling my vision, and licked his smiling lips. "At long last, do I really please you? Though . . . not as Hobbs here pleases you, of course." He straightened up, turning back toward his desk. "And that brings us back to the business of the stable, which is what brought about the business of the medicine."

Valentine bowed his head.

Mr. Bornholdt sighed. "You must know what you have done is grounds for dismissal. We cannot have affairs between servants, lady's maids serving tea to guests over their swollen bellies. Even at my most sympathetic for your desires, Hobbs—and I am sympathetic, believe me—I am bound by my responsibilities to my household to do the right thing. No good man would keep you on."

My eyes darted to Valentine, whose head had jerked up, but he focused his gaze ahead of him.

"But the situation is more complicated than it first appears. Marian's in a bit of debt to me. Has she mentioned it?" The master leaned against his desk again, studying his nails. "I had devised an alternative arrangement than her repaying me with money, which I thought she understood well enough, until she went and gave the thing she owed me to you."

Valentine was going pale—like used wash-water, or a long-suffering uniform, or the neglected facade of a grand old house. He was falling back into disgrace before my eyes. Last time, it had been his parents who had dragged him down. Now, the fault was mine.

Mr. Bornholdt was moving again, this time going behind his desk. "Thus, this morning I have begun collecting on her debt in the traditional way. I am sorry to say that repayment is going to take some time." He pawed through a drawer and pulled out a sheet of paper, which he offered to Valentine.

Valentine hesitated, then stepped forward to take it.

"These are just my notes, you understand," the master said, watching Valentine read. "I have in my desk the original papers for Marian's mother's funeral, casket, et cetera. Oh, and her hotel bill and coach. But you will see there, it comes to thirty pounds and some remainder."

I could not take the next breath I needed. He'd never given me the number before. I could earn that in no less than two years of work if I didn't need to spend money on a single other thing.

Valentine's face was unreadable, but his Adam's apple bobbed.

"So you see, Hobbs, I cannot let her go. It would be too great a loss, and I would invite anyone who scoffed at my decision to study my receipts." Mr. Bornholdt took his notes from Valentine, returned them to their drawer, and shut it. He meandered around the desk, toward me, at his ease for all the awful tension in the room. "Marian owes me her time and labor, and I intend to see that she pays it—which means, of course, that I cannot let you near her again, lest you ruin her for service."

He put a heavy hand upon my shoulder, revolting as a spider. But he was both venomous and vindictive; I could not brush him off, only stay still and try not to panic.

"She is my property," he said, "and I must protect her."

Valentine shut his eyes. He was entirely still a moment, and when he looked around again, his expression was calm. With no trace of hope or rue, he said, "So you're dismissing me alone, then."

Mr. Bornholdt contemplated a corner of the ceiling. "I could. I could send you off and tell my friend Christopher—your former employer, that is, Mr. Malahide—how badly you behaved, effectively ruining your chances at another job." He dropped his gaze to Valentine. "But I do not think that is in Marian's best interest."

Startled, I glanced from him to Valentine, whose brow was furrowed. That he had a question on his lips was obvious, and Mr. Bornholdt waited for it with expectant eyes. But whatever the words would have been, Valentine swallowed them.

"Marian, build a fire," Mr. Bornholdt said, not looking at me.

It was stifling in that room, but I went to get the wood anyway, wiping my palms on my skirt before handling the wood. I pulled the matchbox from my apron and, hands shaking, spilled matches across the hearth. Bornholdt said nothing about it, but I felt him watching me.

"There is a good servant hiding inside you, Hobbs," Mr. Bornholdt said, as I finally managed to light a match. "You take great care of the house and my clothes, and I suspect you want to take great care of Marian, too—otherwise, so tidy a man would not have made such an awful mess. You recognize, as a good man would, that what you have taken from Marian cannot be given back—to me or to her. And given that the irreversible damage was done by you, you might feel honor bound to have a hand in rectifying the situation."

The kindling had taken the flame, and the larger logs had begun to smoke, but the surge of heat I felt came from within. Mr. Bornholdt spoke as if Valentine had broken into my house and burned it down, because—had Mr. Bornholdt gotten into that proverbial place—that's what he would have done, how he would have thought of it.

"How would I rectify it, sir?" Valentine asked.

"Why, I will allow you to put your wages toward her debt," Mr. Bornholdt said. "Between the two of you, living modestly, you might settle everything in a year."

I stood, for the fire had flared, but Mr. Bornholdt said, "Build it up further, Marian. Two logs more."

"Yes, sir," I murmured, kneeling again. Sweat rolled down my back.

"And?" Valentine prompted. Then, softer: "Sir?"

"And? And nothing," Mr. Bornholdt replied. Cutting the word loose precisely with his tongue, he repeated, "Nothing. You will not touch her, nor even look at her—and I will use other servants' eyes to see with, as you have discovered I am able to do. If I find that you have so much as noticed my property, I will treat it as an act of basest disrespect—and dock your wages for it."

There it was. And thus a year would turn to two, and more, in a cycle of longing and hope, torture and shame. Even when we made no transgressions, Bornholdt could invent them. In trying to pull me out of a trap, Valentine had gotten ensnared himself—all because of my debt.

My eyes widened.

"Might I be sent to debtors' prison?" I asked, rising. "Then it's my own concern rather than Mr. Hobbs's. You can dismiss him, and you need not keep an immoral woman in your employ, either."

Mr. Bornholdt blinked, as if stunned, and I struggled to keep a surge of victory confined only to my chest. He could come up with any reason to reject this proposition, but he would no longer be able to pretend it was about the money.

If only Valentine had seen the change in the master, too. Alas, he had been staring at me, and in plain terror he said, "To live in squalor? So I may not be inconvenienced—when you might fall deathly ill, or else be—" He put his fist in front of his mouth.

Mr. Bornholdt allowed a silence. Then, with an air of reluctance, he said to me: "Only if you fled the house did I intend to involve the authorities. I did not imagine you would prefer—"

"I'll pay my wages toward the debt," Valentine said, stepping forward.

I lurched, shoved by shame and fury both. "Valentine, you don't have to—"

"You're not going." He turned, and his eyes shone. "Not when it's in my power to prevent it."

There was anguish in his eyes—every bit as much as I felt.

"What I need to hear now," Mr. Bornholdt said, as gently as if someone were sleeping in the room, "is that you will obey me, Hobbs."

Valentine faced him. "I will, sir."

I sank to the floor and hung my head.

"Say it fully," Mr. Bornholdt instructed.

"I will obey you, sir."

"With no wages for a year. Correct?"

"Yes, sir," Valentine said, adding deliberately, "in contribution to Marian's debt."

"And you will be a model servant, will you not? Because I reserve the right to dismiss you for anything less than total obedience. Will you do exactly as I say in all things?"

He bowed. "Yes, sir."

"Excellent."

Returning to his desk drawer, Mr. Bornholdt drew out a book and turned to the last-used page. He showed us both lines on which he had tallied debits and credits in a heavy, sharp hand. "Now, look. I am a man of my word, so every week I will mark down in my ledger what you both have paid me, as if you had returned money I handed to you. You can come to check the figures whenever you like. Indeed, let us make a weekly habit of it, at which time you both initial the appropriate line.

It will be a good reminder of our healthy distrust of one another; you check up on me, and know that I check up on you."

"Yes, sir," Valentine said.

"Come. Initial this line. Both of you."

Valentine went, and signed. So did I. It was the work of a moment.

Mr. Bornholdt shut the book with a foreboding thump. "Let us say that the new era of proper conduct begins now—with the exception of your separation. I need you both here for this." He looked Valentine up and down. "Hobbs, lower your trousers."

Valentine's eyes immediately found mine.

Mr. Bornholdt snorted. "Oh, come—it will be no surprise to Marian, else we would not be here."

Still, Valentine stood frozen.

"You did agree to total obedience, Hobbs."

His shoulders rose as he took a deep breath. At the sound of Valentine's fingers fumbling with the button of his trousers, I turned my head away.

"No, no," Mr. Bornholdt said, snapping his fingers at me. "The time for demurring was in the stables, I am afraid."

I looked past the cotton of Valentine's drawers, focusing my attention on Mr. Bornholdt.

"Bend over my desk, Hobbs. Hands behind your back."

Valentine fell into a deep bow. Mr. Bornholdt averted his eyes to the ceiling, as if directing this scene were beneath his dignity.

He held out his hand. "Marian, your apron."

I hated him, and yet I could only turn pleading eyes upon him, for there was no time to fight for what was right or fair. "Please, Mr. Bornholdt—"

"Do as I say," he said. It was hard to hear him over the rushing in my ears, my worry rising like a tide. With trembling hands I untied the knot at my waist and lifted the loop that hung around my shirt collar over my head.

Mr. Bornholdt extended his hand, and I approached, inching around Valentine in his pathetic, prone position. In my mind, I swung my fist, striking the master in the face. In actual fact, I held out the apron, dreading the touch of Mr. Bornholdt's fingers against my own in the exchange—but they did touch. He made sure of that.

"You may step away," he told me, and I backed toward the hearth.

Mr. Bornholdt spread the apron across Valentine's back. Then he pressed Valentine's hands down, so they pinned the fabric in place, and used the apron strings to tie Valentine's wrists together.

"Mr. Bornholdt—" I said.

"Shh," he said, sharp.

I sucked my lip into my mouth, bit it, and did not let up.

Smiling to himself, the master teased the skirt end of the apron through the V of Valentine's arms, and dropped the flap over Valentine's head. What had been a serious pose now looked ridiculous.

Mr. Bornholdt reached for a third time into his desk. This time he sought the middle drawer—the widest and shallowest—and pulled from it something long, thin, and black. At once I smelled the dark tang of leather, the scent of the stables. I could almost taste it.

I couldn't pick a focus; there was my contempt for Bornholdt, my heartbreak for Valentine, and amid all that, there was a robbery taking place. It was as if Bornholdt had stormed into my secret heart to systematically stomp on what few, strange flowers grew there. If he whipped Valentine—I would faint in another moment at the mere thought.

But Mr. Bornholdt approached me, not Valentine. And I did not faint, because the thing in Mr. Bornholdt's hand was not a riding crop: it was a branding iron.

I lost my breath.

"After the housemaid's report, I went down to the stables myself." Mr. Bornholdt passed me, stepping up to the fire. He nudged a gap between two logs and stuck the iron rod between them. "I could have sent someone, I suppose, but I would rather it be our secret."

I stared at him as he stood there, my eyes darting from the iron to his face. He watched the brand end as it warmed, his face lax—untroubled.

"The grazing stock get loose sometimes from my tenants' farms," he said, as if I were a guest at a garden party. "Or, now and again, unscrupulous people will steal them. I have them branded so, sooner or later, my property is returned to me."

Beyond him, in the corner of my eye, Valentine lay still across the desk, the bump of his clenched fists visible under the apron.

I made a grab for the rod, but Mr. Bornholdt was ready for the attack. Hiking the handle higher in his fist, he drove it shortly, sharply, into the soft skin of my stomach. I fell backward, hitting the floor hard, and groaned.

"Marian?" Valentine called, his voice high.

"Shut up," Mr. Bornholdt hissed. "I owed her that."

I unclenched streaming eyes to see the master standing over me.

"You make one more noise, you take one step near me, and there will have been no point, and it will happen anyway. Do you hear me?"

I nodded, shaking where I lay.

"That goes for both of you," Mr. Bornholdt said, turning away. I sat up, still trembling, not wanting to know what would come next but having to know all the same. Mr. Bornholdt was midstride across the room, the iron in his hand, its end red hot.

Behind his desk once more, he said, "Open your mouth." He lowered the bunched end of the apron out of sight, in front of Valentine's face. "Bite down on this. You may scream, provided you do not spit it out, or move. You understand?"

Valentine's shoulders twitched as he nodded.

I was reaching up to tear at my hair when the iron began to hiss against Valentine's backside. Its anger was terrible, and my legs gave out in fear of it—in revolt of what I was seeing—as Mr. Bornholdt looked on, resolute. I landed on the carpet.

There was a sound—a constant, aching sound that Valentine made, just audible under a loud ringing in my ears. He might have been yelling himself hoarse, begging rescue from the beach of a deserted island. And I—miles offshore in a heaving, upset ship—could hardly hear him.

Mr. Bornholdt held out the branding iron. "Lean this against the mantel, Marian," he said. "Do not let it burn my carpet."

On numb feet I rose and obeyed. Meanwhile, Valentine sobbed around my apron with such energy and open, bitter grief.

I turned from the hearth.

Mr. Bornholdt leaned over Valentine now, almost fatherly. "You cannot see the mark, of course. I will describe it. It is a big letter *B*. A bit ornate as brands go—with a little curl at the top." He bent, and must have drawn the apron out, for Valentine coughed.

The master said: "Tell me what the big letter *B* stands for, Hobbs."

"Bornholdt," Valentine rasped, as if his lungs were full of smoke.

23

I stood in the hallway, my ear pressed painfully to the study door. I had been dismissed, but Valentine was still within.

The wood was thick, hard to hear through. I was convinced that Valentine was crying still—there was a soft sound, like tearing bits of paper, that might have been his gasp or sniffle. Or maybe it was the fire, crackling. And over it, Mr. Bornholdt's low tones—impossibly calm. I couldn't make out the words.

Not that knowing what he was saying would make any difference. There was nothing I could do to take away Valentine's suffering.

And if Mr. Bornholdt found me on this threshold, it would all be worse.

I unrolled my apron as I drew away, putting it on without looking. I did not want to see the evidence—Valentine's bite marks, or spots of drool. I didn't even dare to smooth the fabric lest I encounter wetness and begin to cry.

Belowstairs, I looked up anytime a servant descended into the kitchens, but it was never Valentine. The Bornholdts' suppertime approached, and I overheard Ledford say to Cook: "Hobbs won't be assisting with the service—he's taken ill." I imagined Mr. Bornholdt telling Ledford this lie with a straight face. And I pictured Valentine in bed, curled on his side. I heard again his wrenching sobs, muffled by my apron, and had to duck into the footman's pantry to hide my face.

Valentine did not come to the table for the servants' dinner, either. Toward the end of the meal, Ledford made up a tray of food for him—but it was only bread and broth, with none of the richer leftovers from abovestairs, as if Valentine suffered from a stomach disorder.

"I'll take his supper to him," Lucette said, leaping bright-eyed from her seat.

"You will not," Mrs. Davies replied.

I might have loved her for it—but it was she who'd stolen my wages. Lucette was not the only one responsible for Valentine's pain or our imprisonment.

◆ ◆ ◆

Mrs. Bornholdt's bell rang at bedtime, and I went up to her with dread gripping tight to my throat. Either she would know what her husband had done and condone it or, more likely, she wouldn't know at all. And whatever she said, I would have to hold my tongue.

I wasn't sure I could.

But in her dressing room, she seemed as disinclined as I to talk. She sat in silence at her vanity, with cold cream and washcloth, the air sweet with flowers. Withdrawn as I was, I could not help noticing a new addition to the table: a vase with a bouquet. There were marigolds, each bloom like a crumpled bit of yellow paper catching fire. Arranged around these were other flowers—bittersweet, its purple petals open wide, and gladiolus, with blooms like frilly horns.

The smell was at odds with my uneasy and embittered mood—and the dark circles under Mrs. Bornholdt's eyes, for that matter. But I determined not to care. She did not seem to notice that anything troubled me—or at least she didn't mind. I was just a maid, doing my job.

I couldn't think why I'd tried to be more than that.

Turning my back, I parsed her cast-off clothing, hanging up what would serve her for another day, setting anything else aside for the laundry.

"You did the right thing, you know," Mrs. Bornholdt said, every few words like a separate pat of a hand.

I paused in picking up a stocking, wondering what she knew—or thought she knew.

She twisted in her chair toward me. "You told me the truth, even though you knew you would be punished, because you thought I was in danger."

Ah, the medicine. A lifetime ago.

She stood up in her nightgown, her hands clasped at her waist. "I know how hard that must have been, and I appreciate your loyalty."

I took a breath, but no words came to me. Bending back to my work, I gathered the pile of clothes in my arms.

"Men, you know, they try to do the right thing. Often they get it wrong." Her tone was gentle, but bright—inviting reply. But I said nothing, and she added: "But by Mr. Bornholdt's mercy toward you and Mr. Hobbs, you can see that his heart is in the right place."

I bristled, drawing my shoulders toward my ears.

She reached out, touching me. "Much as Mr. Hobbs's heart is. I am sure he did not mean to stain your reputation. He did not know what he was doing, really. They never do."

I sucked in my cheek and bit it.

"Are you angry with him?" She squeezed my arm in an encouraging way. "A little anger is healthy."

I blinked. "Angry with—"

"Mr. Hobbs, of course." She drew her chin down, frowning. "I hope you are not angry with Wythe, Marian. He is being very understanding about this—very. Why, his father would be appalled at his kindness, if he knew. Being lenient with immoral servants is one of those punishable good deeds that people warn about. He keeps your secret from his father, though, because he thinks you both deserve a chance to make it right."

Lenient with immoral servants. She had no idea what he had done. And she wouldn't believe me if I told her.

But then she said: "It is difficult, to watch someone in pain. To feel somehow responsible, and yet at a loss for what to do." The wobble in her voice reached me, pulling me back into my body—pulling me toward her. She whispered, gazing past me: "'Cauterize,' that is the word I want. That is what he did, cauterize the wound, because it was all he could do."

I leaned forward. "Ma'am?"

"He had to stop the . . . the loss of life," she said, reaching for the words as if they were before her, among all her flowered pots of powder. "Even though it would hurt me. So that I did not suffer yet more."

My shoulders sagged. Of course. She was thinking of herself only, as I had been doing.

"And he did not tell me only because he thought then he could spare me some pain, if I did not know about the change he'd made. But he cannot change *me*."

Mrs. Bornholdt opened a drawer in the vanity in a sudden way that reminded me of when I'd struck my palm with a riding crop, as a child—acting at once, to outpace my anxiety. She scooped out a locket by its silver chain and cradled it in her palm. In keeping with the theme of all her trinkets, the silver front of the piece was worked into a single flower. She opened the tiny latch with shaking fingers. Inside was a curl of dark, downy hair. She said: "She was *here*. And so I am still a mother. I *am*."

Sucking in a breath, I turned my head away. I shouldn't have been there. Perhaps Mrs. Bornholdt had forgotten me behind her. Softly, I said, "If you have no more need of me, I—"

"Funny that all this came out today," she said. "On her birthday." In the mirror, she caught my eye and held the open locket up—not just inviting me to look, I thought, but imploring.

I drew closer. "I am sorry, Mrs. Bornholdt . . ."

If she were my friend, I should have reached for her. But she wasn't my friend. She had no idea who I was, what worries I had, how I suffered. And I couldn't tell her, couldn't trust her—Valentine had been right about that—because we had Mr. Bornholdt between us.

She closed the locket with her thumb, as if the metal could feel her gentleness. She sniffed.

No, she didn't know how I suffered. She didn't know how she suffered, herself—not the half of it.

But I did. We had Mr. Bornholdt between us.

I leaned down over her shoulder. "Did she have a name?"

"Only in my head." She sat straighter, took a short breath, and held it. Her eyes searched mine in the mirror, as if she weren't sure she wanted to tell me.

I said, "I didn't mean to—"

"Carolyn," she said, like the "amen" at the end of a prayer.

"Carolyn," I repeated—all other words having abandoned me—and I felt a fool. But Mrs. Bornholdt's reflection smiled.

She gestured with her free hand to her bouquet. "Marigolds are for grieving. The gladiolus means 'I remember.'" Her voice thinned on the last word. She swallowed. Then, in a sturdier tone: "Wythe picks them for me, every year."

I was lucky that she did not look in her mirror then, and see my mouth fall open.

"Bittersweet actually means 'truth,'" she said, touching one of the purple flowers. "He puts it in place of purple hyacinth."

This threw me. For a moment I forgot my shock at the master. My mother had said Valentine had purple hyacinths for me, in her dream. "What does the purple hyacinth mean?" I asked.

"It means 'I am sorry,'" she said.

I tilted my head, and shut my eyes when the corners began to burn.

"But it's out of season by summer," Mrs. Bornholdt was saying. "Every year Wythe laments that it is missing. I tell him he grows it in his heart."

"That's—" I drew a breath and focused on the flowers. "That's a very kind thing. A thoughtful thing. I'm glad to hear he does it."

"He has always been attentive," Mrs. Bornholdt said, touching the back of her hand under each of her eyes in turn. "My pregnancy was awful. And rougher as the months went on. I was forever sick to my stomach, and yet he was always there, with something near to hand to meet my every need, doing all the things a nurse would have done—a cloth for my poor forehead, toast and water to settle my stomach and, when that did not work, a drink of Epsom salts. Everything in his power, he did."

I nodded.

"I know you think yourself misjudged, Marian," she said, her voice tight. In the mirror, the line of her mouth trembled but did not bow under the weight of her emotion. "You are not the only one. You must remember that your mother's grave is marked. You may go to the cemetery and see her. That was in Mr. Bornholdt's power to do, so he did it for you."

Her gaze shifted to the vase, and I turned aside myself, digging my nails into the flesh of my palms. Of course I remembered. I would never be allowed to forget.

"That was in his power to do," she repeated. "Do you understand?"

Something about the deliberateness of the words—the way they ground against her tongue and teeth—made me look around again.

"I can see you do not." She shook her head and, with eyes closed, said: "Carolyn was early, Marian. She was not baptized. And the Church is not so understanding as my husband."

24

I left Mrs. Bornholdt's apartments hardly aware of what else she said to me. The air was so thick with my shame, for thinking ill of a husband who could be so kind as he had been to her—to me. But out in the hallway, I could breathe. The door clicked shut behind me, and I wondered: Did it redeem him?

Mrs. Bornholdt should have been angry, as I was angry. Maybe she wouldn't have batted an eye to know what the master had done to Valentine, given he was a servant. But Mrs. Bornholdt was no lowly creature in her own mind, and she knew well enough what he had done to her, how unfair it was—didn't she?

I held my hand up to knock, to talk to her again. But I couldn't make myself do it. To argue with her would only seem cruel when she was grieving.

I made my way down the dark purple hall, toward the servants' stairs, remembering a time I'd thought that, if I knew what secret the house was keeping, I would feel better. Now that I did know, however, I had only become another of the secret's keepers, a part of the place, and alike to it: bruised inside, and silent.

The kitchens below were quiet and dark. Valentine must still have been in his room. I sighed. He wouldn't be fit for fleeing now, even if we could scrounge the money, and we couldn't risk a conversation, but

I would've felt better just to know he could stand, and shift for himself a little.

The only light came from the open door of the housekeeper's office. I peered in and found Mrs. Davies sitting up at her desk, with her ledger for house goods open before her.

I tapped on the open door. "May I come in?"

"Fine," she replied, not looking up. Indeed, by expression or stature she gave not a hint that the last meaningful discussion we'd had ended in her challenging my virtue, or in my slamming a door. She reminded me forcibly of Mrs. Martin, balancing her own books the morning of my mother's death—not quite ignoring my feelings. Rather, by her complete absorption, she seemed to acknowledge the existence of my emotions, to anticipate that they were strong enough to derail her important business and, thus, refuse to engage with them.

Perhaps that was to my advantage, her deliberate avoidance of feeling. She was a stickler, too, for things being done in the right way, no matter what. It's what made her hand my wages over to the master. I couldn't risk telling her about the branding, for many of the same reasons I couldn't have told Mrs. Bornholdt, but maybe—

"What is it?" Mrs. Davies asked.

"I've found out something," I said. "About Mr. Bornholdt. Ever since, it's troubling me. I think—I think we must stop it somehow."

"Oh?" She licked her thumb, turned a page.

I took a step farther into the office. "Mrs. Bornholdt's medicine is not what it seems. It's—it's almost a sort of poison."

Mrs. Davies sat back, and fixed me with serious eyes. "And how did you discover this?"

"Mr. Bornholdt admitted it in front of me, when she confronted him with the recipe," I said, and hoped the volume of my voice went some distance to explaining my blush away as anger. "It's for keeping off children. But Mrs. Bornholdt, she—she knows now, and I think she means to keep taking it, Mrs. Davies. It turns her green with nausea, and yet I think she'll go on drinking it to please him."

Mrs. Davies crossed her arms over her chest. "Did you bring the recipe to her, Osley?" And then, before I could answer: "What in the world would you do that for, just to make her miserable? Do you dislike her that much?"

"Dislike her? Why should—" My brow furrowed. "Did you . . . did you know?"

"Of course I knew," she snapped. "Who d'you think clipped the remedy? D'you think the master makes a habit of reading ladies' journals?"

I stepped backward. "But how could you? You're a woman!"

"Aye, and I'm a housekeeper. My job is to obey my employer, and *his* job is to decide what's best for his wife. Do you know what your job in this house is, Marian?"

"For God's sake," I said, and fled the room. She called me back, but I did not come.

◆ ◆ ◆

I had to find Valentine—not just to learn how he fared anymore or to ask him what was next, but to look into the eyes of someone who had seen the same things I had. If I didn't, I felt it wouldn't matter if we did find the means to escape, because I might have gone mad enough to stay forever, and to believe that wrong was right.

I took the servants' stairs two at a time. Just as I came out on the third-floor hallway, I heard a distant slam, and the floor shook just slightly where I stood—as if a door had been swung angrily shut in the room below.

I stood still, listening. I couldn't tell if what I thought I heard—muffled shouting—was just the wind at the windows. Was it any of

Mrs. Bornholdt's rooms, down there? I thought of the dark circles under her eyes, and something she'd said came back to me.

Wythe is only frustrated, and not at me—not really . . . It is my body we are angry with, together.

Grimly, I padded toward the servants' staircase to make my way slowly down. I strained my ears as I descended, but the stairwell was closed too firmly off from the rest of the house to make anything out. I came through to the second floor and made my careful way along the carpet.

There. The voice, a little louder, but not in Mrs. Bornholdt's rooms, thank goodness. Farther down. But it was Mr. Bornholdt shouting—wasn't it? It sounded like him, and yet it was off somehow.

I stopped where the sound was clearest, at a door I'd never gone through, and pressed my ear to the wood. "You are quite upset for an innocent man, Wythe," the voice said.

It was the master's father.

"Innocence does not preclude anger, Father," Mr. Bornholdt replied, "and I do not appreciate being accused of such awful things, when I open my house to you in your convalescence—"

"Your house? Is it?"

A silence, and then, with deadly calm and almost too softly for me to hear, the master said: "You are provoking me deliberately."

"I am trying to get the truth out of you," the senior Bornholdt replied. "Why is Diana so pale?"

My heart leaped. There was a higher authority in the house, and he was onto the master.

"My wife's health is my concern, not yours."

"She is skinnier each time I come here."

"Perhaps that is by design, Father. Perhaps I like her skinny."

"Perhaps she is unwell."

"Perhaps she is," he agreed, "and perhaps this is all a side effect to some treatment of which you are ignorant. Perhaps while mildly unpleasant, her weakness is better than some other state of being that would be worse. Perhaps you are not a doctor, and it is not your business—"

"It is my business, Wythe, for you have your wife and I do not have mine. I do not forget whose fault that is. Are you going to end the way you began, Wythe? As a murderer?"

I gasped, and clasped my hand over my mouth too late. I stood frozen, listening, begging God—or my mother—that the conversation just continue, so I would know that I was safe. But there were footsteps, fast footsteps.

I bolted from the door as it opened, but the master's hand came down fast upon my shoulder. "Miss Osley," he said, in a voice that was nearly sweet, his breath tainted with liquor. "Good evening."

I thought I might faint. "Sir," I said.

"Come to check on my father?" he asked, and turned me bodily in the doorway, so that I faced into the room. The senior Bornholdt was on a cot that clearly did not belong here. Parlor chairs and a chessboard had been pushed up against the windows to make room for it. And as for the occupant of the bed, he, too, looked stuffed away—smaller in the sheets than he had been at the dinner table when last I'd seen him, and waterier at the eyes.

"That is quite kind of you," the master was saying. "But as you can see, my father is about ready to sleep now. I was just tucking him in. I will escort you back to your room."

"That won't be necessary, sir, I can—"

"I insist," he said, and he never let go of my shoulder while he shut and locked the parlor door. I knew where we would go next; it was inevitable. He marched me there: his study. He pushed me in first, and followed after.

Stumbling across the rug, I looked to the hearth in the hopes that, perhaps, the branding iron—but no, it was gone. The door clicked shut.

"What did you hear tonight, Marian?"

I whirled. "Nothing, sir."

"Aha," he said, a word that turned into an actual laugh. "I surmise the opposite. I think you heard my father call me a murderer."

I stepped back as he drew nearer, shaking my head. "I just want to go to bed, sir."

"You just want to run to my wife, you mean, tell her stories and start another fire for me to put out. You will go nowhere until I set you straight, Miss Osley—unless it is your wish that I fulfill my father's prophecy after all, and wring your neck."

I swallowed. "No, sir."

"Sit down," he commanded, and jabbed his finger at the floor as if I were a dog.

I did as I was told.

He stormed up and down the room, never taking his eyes off me. At length, he said: "He is paranoid in illness. He thinks I am poisoning everyone, himself included."

"Yes, sir," I said, mechanically.

"You do not believe it," the master snapped. "But I will convince you that I would be a fool to kill my father."

He slowed, and seemed to gather himself, swelling with his next deep breath. "He hesitates to give me the money, the land, of the family. Instead, he gives me an allowance, like a child, and I live in this house with his name still on the deed. His will does not name me as successor to his fortune, for I have not earned it yet, he says." He raised his eyebrows at me. "You may ask my wife about that, and she will affirm every word."

All this made sense, good sense—but I saw with perfect clarity, through the screeching panic in my head and the rushing of my blood—how this had nothing to do with what his father had actually said. How he had gone from speaking on poisoning "everyone" to just his father in a blink, and expected me not to notice.

"I should have earned my living just by being his son, if he were sane," the master said, crossing the floor in a more thoughtful way. He stopped before me. "But I am in debt still for the wife I stole from him. Murderer, he calls me—murderer, for nothing I could control. Because my mother's pregnancy was hard, because her labor was hard, because the months after I was born were hard. Because she killed herself at the end of those months, somehow I am a murderer."

He fixed me with a glare after this pronouncement. I did not even know what face I made. I searched for words to say, but found none. It was terrible, if it was true. I did not believe it was. I had seen him lie as thoroughly as this to his wife.

"Oh, look at you, wide-eyed little innocent," he snarled. "Even when I tell you exactly why I do as I've done, you only see me as a monster, and see yourself as the helpless victim, cowering, waiting to be gobbled up. You have no idea how fortunate you are."

"Sir?" I was dimly aware that my teeth chattered.

"Look," he said, and pointed.

I hesitated to turn my head too far, to lose sight of him in my periphery, but moved enough to see he indicated his portrait above the mantel.

"See how the hair is done in such detail, spun fine as thread? The eyes carved, the cheeks and jaw sculpted, the mouth draped and pinned, into a satisfied smile. Always smiling, this man, from his high place. He prospers perpetually, untroubled by any thought—for we have not learned to paint those. Is that me, Marian?"

"Yes, sir," I stammered.

"No, it is not!" he cried. "He is not a person; he is a painting! I am human, and I suffer—you know better than most how I have suffered." This time he gestured toward his oxblood armchair. On the table beside it was a bouquet in a vase, almost identical to the one on Mrs. Bornholdt's vanity. Another arrangement for Carolyn.

"Yet no amount of suffering could equal the prosperity with which fate seems to favor me," he said. "If I complain about my lot, I only embitter those below me and befuddle those beside, and there is no one above my station to pity me."

"Sir, I don't understand what—"

"What I want you to say?" he asked. He bore down, gripping my shoulders with both hands this time, and spoke in a soft hiss. "Why, nothing. I want you to say nothing, for once. Because if you try again to topple what little control I have over my life, I will do so much worse than ravage your body. I will deliver you to Mrs. Davies, and tell her that you seem unwell to me, and that I would like her to look after you until morning, when I can have you seen by a doctor—and you do not want a diagnosis from any doctor I pay, Marian, trust me."

I shook in his grip, stunned silent.

"What I would like you to think about, for your own good, is how blessed you are to be able to suffer—how blessed, that suffering is expected of you—and embrace your role, and you can keep what freedoms you have."

I peered into his eyes as one does into a well—wondering how deep the darkness was, mindful that to fall in would be fatal.

A knock at the door. "Mr. Bornholdt?"

"Come in, Hobbs," the master said, with shocking composure for a man who had just a second ago been spitting his consonants into my face. And as the door swung whining in, his hand darted upward, grasping my cheek.

I tried to wriggle free, anticipating an attack, but far from lunging for me, he let me go. I overbalanced onto my back. I looked at Bornholdt, who had left his hand hanging in the air at the level where my face had been. Then I looked at Valentine, who was pale.

He averted his gaze. In a small voice, he asked: "Shall I withdraw, sir, and return in a quarter of an hour?"

"No, Hobbs, you may turn the lamps down now." Mr. Bornholdt's mouth was flat, but I saw the corners twitch—as if he were trying not to smile. "I will retire presently."

"Yes, sir," Valentine said, entering with head bowed, one hand cupped around the candle he'd taken to travel the dark hallways with.

I tried as best I could to catch his eye, but he never again glanced my way. I tried to signal that I wanted to communicate with him with a twitch of my foot, which should have been in his peripheral view, but either he did not see the signal or he ignored it.

"You are not," Mr. Bornholdt said, offering me his hand, "interested in Mr. Hobbs, are you?"

I ignored his hand but caught his meaning, and hastened as I rose to turn my whole body entirely away from Valentine to him. "No, sir. I . . . just knew Mr. Hobbs to be ill, so I'm . . . surprised to see him about, that's all."

"Ah, well," the master replied, and bounced twice on his heels. "Ill or no, he is my man, and knows his place is wherever I need him. Is that not so, Hobbs?"

"Yes, sir," he said, and bowed, his back bent low before his master.

◆ ◆ ◆

I walked back to my room in a stupor. For the rest of that long night, I lay awake listening to the indignant rattle of my window. I imagined a prisoner there, on the other side of the glass, and felt less lonely. This other inmate did the things for which I had no more energy: raging at the way of the world, screaming for justice as if there were somebody listening—somebody who might help instead of hurt. When no one came, not even to tell the prisoner to be quiet, he or she dissolved into frustrated tears. The water hit the windowpanes like thrown pebbles, goading the jailer to come and see what the fuss was all about. But the only thing that came to look in on us was the morning sun, and by then the other prisoner had dropped down—either in a disconsolate sleep or dead.

◆ ◆ ◆

The next morning, the news in the kitchens was that the senior Bornholdt had gone home in a coach, deeming himself well enough to travel. Ledford had begged him to stay, he told us, for the man was still very pale—but the master's father had been adamant.

Valentine was about his business again. I was petrified to speak to him—or anyone else belowstairs, for that matter, lest a single word of mine get back to Mr. Bornholdt and incense him. But I watched Valentine carefully whenever his back was turned: scrubbing pots at the kitchen sink, polishing silver pieces, fiddling with the oil lamps abovestairs. His stance was the wrong sort of stiff. Whereas before he had moved deliberately, he was now made of something weaker—something brittle—and he seemed afraid that he might shatter. He took care not to bear too much of his own weight or to lean too far in any direction, and he winced when people passed behind him, as if afraid of the slightest touch. It hurt my heart to see him, but it hurt even more to look away.

At midday we made up trays of meat and fruit for the mistress and master, respectively, but the rest of the staff was also about, so we did it at opposite countertops, our backs to one another. I might have been cutting an onion instead of an apple; I kept having to wipe my eyes on my sleeve.

There was a ringing clatter.

I turned, but because of the table at the center of the room, I could not see what had fallen, only Valentine's dismay. By the way his chest moved, I could tell he considered crouching down, then abandoned the idea. Clasping his hands tight, he slowly bent his knee.

I ached to help him. But Bornholdt had told me not to talk to him anymore, had spat those threats in my face—

"I'll get that," Lucette said, from across the room.

I stared down at the apple I'd been cutting.

For a moment there was nothing but the general noise of cooking. Then: "Thank you." Warm. Humble. A little laugh at the end, as if he felt silly. The voice he had used after the shoeshine I gave him.

"Anytime," she said, as if she dearly meant it.

I waited for Lucette's footsteps to carry her away before I looked over my shoulder. But Valentine had turned his back again. With a kerchief from his pocket he was cleaning the thing he'd dropped. He held it up to a light, to check his work, and I could see it was a large serving spoon.

He took his time turning it, so the metal flashed. I stared at him, willing him to feel the heat of my eyes. But he never did—or, if he did, he didn't mind.

◆ ◆ ◆

It was with great trepidation that I brought Mrs. Bornholdt her breakfast; her grief and my ungratefulness stood invisible between us. All the while I arranged her room, we didn't speak.

Her face was lively, however, her eyes following me all around. She wanted to know whether I was reformed, I supposed. I would have sooner said I was unformed: my perspective and my judgment, which had been attacked and critically injured, could no longer be trusted to bear weight. Unsupported, my spirit had fallen, split open, and all my certainty had run out of me.

I set Mrs. Bornholdt's medicine beside her bed, as I was expected to do, and turned away to draw her Epsom-salt bath while she took it—just the same as ever. I spoke only to thank my mistress when she dismissed me, then slipped away from her apartment.

Lucette sought me out in the kitchens, where I was sitting in a stupor.

"You got somethin' goin' with the master," she said, watching me. "Or you did, before your old mate came along. Are you switchin' back again?"

I put my head in my hands, my shoulders tight. "I have nothing 'going' with the master," I said.

"If you say so." Then, slyly: "Only I notice you an' Valentine aren't talkin'. I wouldn't mind takin' up with him, if you've finished."

I didn't have to answer. I rose, and stomped up the stairs. After all, she didn't know I had naught to do at the moment. But her question followed me up. What sort of relationship would ours be, Valentine's and mine—two people who couldn't even look at one another for a year? It wasn't enough for friendship, let alone love.

But then again, Valentine had been singularly focused on his work all the time he'd been with the Malahides. Why else would so handsome a man—eligible for more than a year—not have formed any romantic attachment? There had been available women at the house, surely, and in the village on Sundays. Lucette was likely not the prettiest person who'd ever tried to tempt him, or the wittiest. And yet he had passed over them, in preference for his solitude. He did not seem to share Mr. Bornholdt's professed weakness for women. Maybe he would wait contentedly for me.

I passed from the kitchen to the upper stairwell, where all was quiet.

Or maybe I'd changed Valentine. Given him a taste for something that up to then he'd not considered—much as he had done for me years before. What if Mrs. Davies was wrong about longing coming naturally to boys? Perhaps both men and women lived in innocence until they received the epiphany of desire; perhaps everyone had the great power to awaken others, at any time—anyone except themselves, living in total ignorance of their own potency.

My body missed his body. Did he feel similarly? And if he did, would the longing be to lie with me—or anyone?

◆ ◆ ◆

A week of work and worry went by, of passing Valentine belowstairs without a glance. He spoke and laughed, though not with me; I only ever overheard him. Whenever I might have caught his eye, he concentrated solely on his chores; indeed, it seemed to me that he scrubbed pots harder in my presence. When we met in Mr. Bornholdt's study, to sign the ledger for the week, I went second—and Valentine was gone by the time I straightened up.

At dinner each night, Lucette sat directly beside Valentine, who seated himself at the opposite end of the table from me. I could never make out what the two of them were saying—Ledford didn't like us to do more than whisper at the table—but one of their mouths seemed always to be moving and aimed at the ear of the other. That Valentine had spirit enough to talk at dinner was a comfort to me; that Lucette should give him cause to smile so often as he did was not.

Was it with new eyes and new ideas that he saw her? Of course she would put her breath in touching distance of his cheek—she'd warned me what she wanted—but why did he not turn his face from hers? I did not want to hold on to dark doubts or jealousy, but when I tried to let the feelings go, they only gathered in the air around me, making it heavy.

And then one night, the sky tore open over Valor Rise, pouring water—not in drops or sheets but heaving, like blood spat in heartbeat rhythm from a wound. It was the beginning of another thunderstorm; it would bring more rain than the ground could drink, and a night of pain too deep to withstand—even for me.

After

14 February 1867

Dear Friend—

Yes, it is nearly too much to think about, when I look back. That a rich man, held high in the esteem of others, would seek out in his glorious halls the few, elusive piles of filth, just so he could roll in them—it seems an awful lot of work. If that rich man could commit himself to depravity, he could certainly have managed to be moral.

Oh, I shudder to speak of it. And yet, I need to speak of it, too. I think it would heal me somehow, to see you—knowing we have sinned the same way—and to read in your face that you don't resent me. I'm not as certain as I was, the more time passes.

I wish you would come to visit. You did say, before we parted, that it wouldn't be the end. We could make new memories, to replace those awful days at Valor Rise. It would ease the pain in my heart, I think.

Tell me when you could come. Bring Georgiana with you, even. If you don't like to, if it's too strange, I'll understand—only don't blame me for asking.

Marian

Before

25

"Clothes have come back from the laundry," Mrs. Davies remarked, her eyes passing over me as if I were but a piece of furniture someone else was supposed to have polished. We'd just finished our evening meal. "Sort out what belongs to the mistress; after you see her to bed, you can hang her things in their usual places."

I rose from my stool, and she pointed me to a wicker basket by the servants' entrance. I made a pile, but my mind was elsewhere—thinking of the way Valentine had laughed at the dinner table, at some joke of Lucette's—and I nearly took the master's drawers as well.

The bell rang for Mrs. Bornholdt's apartments, and I brought the laundry pile with me. I found all the pins in her hair, helped her out of her day clothes, and held her nightgown open over her head, all without a word.

"Marian?" she asked me, standing closely by as I turned down her bedcovers. "Are you all right?"

"Yes, ma'am," I said—the only safe words—and I did not check to see how she took them.

Out in the hall again, I gathered up the fresh laundry and let myself into her dressing room from the outer door. I lit a candle on her vanity, laid the clothes across the chair, and opened Mrs. Bornholdt's armoire. The ornamental gold curlicues on its doors caught the candlelight.

The rain rushed constant as a river down the window. The garments I hung whispered together as they brushed close on the rod, as if there were a different spirit in each satin or silk, roused by my fingers before it flew to its resting place.

As I reached for the next article to hang, I heard something else: arrhythmic tree-branch tapping on the outer door.

I spun around, my heart already hurting, for I was sure I had imagined it—tricked by the rain. But Valentine peeked in, damp strands of his hair tilting with the angle of his head. "Is she asleep?" he mouthed, pointing to Mrs. Bornholdt's bedroom door.

I nodded, stunned.

He slipped into the room. His vest and coat were soaked, and rain shone on his cheeks.

"What are you doing here?" I whispered, anxiety stifling my joy.

"It's all right, Bornholdt's gone out," he replied, his words running together. "Lucette's asleep; Ledford assumes I'm in bed as well."

I did and did not want to ask how he could be so certain about Lucette. Instead, I said, "Mr. Bornholdt is from home? In this storm?"

"I've just been to see him off," Valentine whispered, gesturing to his drenched jacket. "The laid-up footman's roof is leaking. His wife threatened to complain to Bornholdt's father if he didn't do something."

"And the master went?" I raised my brows. "I'm surprised he didn't send you; you're his man."

The last words seemed to touch Valentine's eyes, disturbing them like a pebble does a pond.

"Seems a low chore, I mean," I stammered, hastening to pile dull words over sharp.

Valentine closed his eyes, and when he opened them again, their color stood fast. "I think it's a show for his father. If he accepts responsibility at all, he'll write for someone in the morning."

I put my hands on my hips. "Then what's he gone down there for?"

In truth, I didn't care. I only wanted him to keep talking—just as if it were normal, and he liked me.

"To give the woman his attention, I think. To affect interest in her little life." After a pause he added, his words heavier: "Maybe he wants to sleep with her."

He gave me a loveless look then—a look like the one he'd had the night he meant to have me dismissed. So he hated me again? For what? I was suddenly so frustrated by the situation and what it had done to us, it made me hot. I turned away to hang the next dress from the pile.

The hangers squeaked in pain as I pushed them to make room, and the rain was like one long, disappointed sigh. Valentine himself was quiet, but I fancied I could feel him sharpening his tongue.

But when the words finally came, they were hollow and reluctant. "Why were you with him?"

I drew my shoulder blades tight. "Is that what you came to ask? When you find a moment to finally speak to me after a week of total silence, you ask about *my* behavior?"

"If you choose to fall in with him—"

"Choose?" I whirled, hissing up close. "He dragged me there, as he always does. I am not free to keep from talking with him as you are free to keep from talking with Lucette."

"I may talk to Lucette," he scoffed. "Lucette has not, like some, tortured anyone dear to me."

"Oh, are you not dear to yourself? She's the reason you've got his mark on you. She told on us!"

"I don't think she knows what Bornholdt did," he said, making hushing motions with one hand and pointing with the other to the door that joined with Mrs. Bornholdt's bedroom. "She seems to think she has some chance of turning my head."

I clenched my fists. "Perhaps it's all your laughter and smiling that encourages her."

Valentine's eyes went wide for a fleeting second, as if he had been caught at something, and then all his features fell into a deep scowl. "I am only warm on the chance she is still reporting to Bornholdt. Better to let him think I am moving on from you, as he expects me to do—to relax him, make him less vigilant. I'm here, aren't I? He didn't take me with him. And if I see her off to her bedroom at night, then I know I'm free to come to you, now, unwatched." He stopped, and the hard lines in his face faded, leaving him with troubled eyes. "I thought I should fool him, not you. For your sake, I let him . . . I have been literally branded by my—"

"Yes, yes, and you resent me!" Face flaming, I turned away to hang the next garment from the pile. Holding on to it still, but facing the armoire, I began to cry. "He hurt you, and you have no money, and you must hold your tongue, however he treats you, and it's all my fault, and when the debt is paid, you'll go right away, because I won't be your problem anymore." I shoved the hanger onto the rod, too hard, so garment and hanger both hit the floor with a thump. I bent to retrieve them.

"My problem?" He huffed out his breath behind me. "Of course you're not my problem. Marian, you're my family."

I caught my breath, my throat blocked, my chest swelling with impossible, overwhelming joy. It was too wonderful to be true. And yet the seconds stretched, and he did not take it back.

I got to my feet and turned. "Oh, Valentine—"

But he held up his hands, and with a frightened tightness in his voice, he said: "You turned the conversation to me, rather than deny you are drawn to Bornholdt."

I recoiled. "Of course I'm not drawn to him!"

"He says you are," Valentine said, and in that moment, I saw again the boy I had known: small, stung, and trying desperately to appear as if he were neither. "Or you will be, by and by."

I stared, astounded—not by Bornholdt's sentiments at all, but that they could have lodged themselves deep in a mind so well defended as Valentine's. "How did he convince you?"

"He said you love monsters like him." He dropped his gaze. "Monsters like me."

I stepped back. "You're not a monster."

"Aren't I?" He held out his hands. "From when we were children, I've chased you, pushed you about, made you do as I bid, all the time enjoying it—just as he does. And in the stable the other night . . . I whipped you. I hurt you."

"Valentine—" I hesitated. I'd thought he knew this, and that I'd never have to say it. But his stricken mouth told me otherwise. I made myself hold his gaze. "Valentine, I liked it."

"Yes," he said, surprising me. "I taught you to like it. I linked violence with friendship in your mind. I could not bring myself to touch you tenderly, as I ought, but I had to touch you somehow, so I yanked and thrust, cowardly child that I was, and I . . . I made you vulnerable to men like him."

For a moment I dared not speak over the echo of his words: *I had to touch you somehow.* To know I had not been alone in what I'd felt—not just lately, but at any time . . . He'd made a present of my own past, given it back to me under love's wrap and ribbon, and I wanted nothing more than to sift through every piece of it with him, to laugh and sigh together over all the things I hadn't known were as precious to him as they were to me.

But he searched my face as a man gauging not the success of a gift, but the severity of a wound. "You said you fell right in with him," he pressed. "Bornholdt meant you real harm, and you thought he was playing a game."

"That's not your fault," I said.

"How do you work that out?" Again it was like when we were children. Beneath his police officer's mask, which was determined to be above his own subjectivity, there was desperation for an answer that would rid him of all his awful, self-destructive doubt.

I blinked, groping backward in my mind. "You didn't . . . The game didn't create a new feeling. It . . . comforted me so because the feeling—the need I had—was already there, and crying to be met." I touched my own shoulder, and I could feel an officer, a real one, throwing me into the back of his police wagon, after my mother. The awful uncertainty about whether I was a good child came with it.

"That does not comfort me," Valentine said, dashing the words out of the air. "Even if it's not my fault, you'll still—"

"I *won't* go to him. I'm not drawn to him—not as I am to you. You're not the same at all."

"But you said—"

"They're different games entirely!" I cried, even as he gestured for me to be quiet again. "His is for his own amusement, and hang everybody else. But yours—ours—is for me to enjoy as well as you. Yours ends the moment I no longer wish to play it—when his is just beginning!"

Valentine stared at the carpet. He still didn't believe me.

I reached out to slide my fingers along his jaw, and I raised his face to mine. He blinked in some surprise, but he did not resist me.

"Do you know what I felt when we played our game as children?" I asked.

"Afraid," was his ready answer.

"No," I said. "I felt important."

This seemed to startle him. At least, he gave up frowning for a moment. Lightning flashed, and far-off thunder followed.

"You were forever looking for me," I said. "Wherever I went, you came after. And you brought to me all your questions, and my answers changed your face. You let me decide—by how I chose to act—where the game would go next. Everything you did was a reaction to me."

"But you were always the one running," he murmured.

"Yes," I said. "I led, and you followed."

His lips parted.

Slowly, I got down on my knees before him. "Let me right the wrong of being with him, sir—let me atone."

He drew one foot behind him. "Marian, for God's sake. I'm not playing now."

"Neither am I."

"Marian." He took my hands and tugged, trying to pull me to my feet. "Your fondness for me deludes you. It declaws and defangs me. But these mean parts of me do exist, trust me. I live in my body and I feel them."

I squeezed his hands in mine. "I like those parts, because you are careful with them. You are not a wild beast, Valentine Hobbs. Don't you remember? You are the law."

He dropped my hands. "The law?"

With sudden, desperate haste, he reached into the inner pocket of his jacket. Lightning flashed, showing me in sharp relief two pictures: first, a length of leather rein stretched between Valentine's hands and, second, a dark, daring hardness in his eyes. Then thunder, so close it shook the house, but I dared not flinch nor allow a trace of fear to cross my face.

I waited on my knees at his feet.

"When I saw you with him," he whispered, and the words made him breathless, as if he had to work hard to pry them free from deep in his chest, "I couldn't stand it, and I couldn't change it, and so I went away in my head, and I saw—I imagined stealing you away, bringing you to my room, and binding you to my bed."

I shut my eyes, and was alone with his words in my darkness, my breath coming deep and slow.

"I went down to the stables before I slept, to take this. I've had it in my pocket."

It flipped my stomach to think of him, his back turned in the kitchens, but thinking of me, touching the reins like a talisman every time I left the room. I imagined him in his bed, sleeping with the leather clutched in his fist. Deep within me, muscles that had known him—had drawn tight around him—clenched now, wanting.

Opening my eyes, I raised my trembling hands, pressed together at the wrists, until they touched the leather strips.

He drew his hands closer to him. "Marian—"

"I can't imagine it—how it would feel," I said.

He stood a moment, unmoved. Then, with a grunt of frustration, he obliged me, brusque and businesslike as he twisted the leather once, twice, around my wrists. Then he raised his fist, taking my arms with him.

I could feel the bite of leather in my skin, the pull of his will, holding me up. My knees went weak. Control—of my body, of the situation—was shifting from me to him, and the feeling was sweet, like falling to sleep in safety, watched over by someone quite awake. I bowed my head, offering him my neck, on which every hair had risen.

"And what happens then?" I whispered. "As you imagine it."

I heard him lick his lips. "He sends for you, but you don't come. So he sets Mrs. Davies looking all over, and I watch her come and go, minding my business, shining the silver but all the while thinking of you, prone on my sheets. My captive."

My exhale was slow, and shaky. "Yes. And?"

"When you're not found in your room or the common spaces, the grounds are searched. And in all the confusion, I boil water in a kettle for tea. I pile a plate with cherries. I whip cream for them, and carry it all on a tray to my room. I lock my door against interruption. I stir sugar into tea for you, and milk. I straddle you, and tip the tea to your mouth. I press cherries to your lips."

"Valentine—"

"Wait," he says, and the word is savage. "You have to hear it all. I take you, next. So slowly that the bed won't creak. And when you moan, I put my hand over your mouth, because there are people going up and down the corridor outside who would steal you from me, and I won't let them." He bent his head down, close to my ear, and over another roll of thunder, said: "If you are going to follow orders, I want them to be mine."

"Valentine—"

So seriously he shook the fist that bound me, as if I should tremble to hear him speak so—and I did tremble. But I did not fear him. He analyzed the appearance of his idea only, but I felt its substance: how soft his bed would be under my body; how sweet the tea on my tongue; how deliberate, how reverent, the slow rhythm of his hips. His vision did not degrade me. It exalted me—for it was the lot of no less than royalty to lounge about ignoring summons, being hand-fed.

What a rakish brute, this man who would master me only to turn around and be my servant.

He jerked the reins. "This idea—this dark idea—it comforts me. Does my mind seem lawful, still? Would my wish be just?"

"Yes," I whispered. Lightning flashed.

"What?" And for all his power—his hold on me, physical and otherwise—he was pleading. "What did you just say?"

I opened my mouth to tell him—and then Mrs. Bornholdt screamed.

26

Valentine only just ducked in time, shielding me with his body as a vase smashed against the vanity mirror. We both tumbled down in a shower of ceramic shards.

"Get off of her!" Mrs. Bornholdt cried. She stood in the bedroom doorway, clad in only a nightgown.

Valentine rolled away, and I struggled to my feet. My eyes went from the reins dropped on the floor to the damaged mirror; in it, I saw my face fractured and distorted.

"Monster!" Mrs. Bornholdt said, as Valentine stood, his palms held out and open. "Do not come near me!"

"Ma'am, I—"

"Shut up!" she hissed. "I might have known. This is what comes of leniency; this is what you make of a second chance. And Marian, moping. All along I thought it was us making her miserable when it was *you*!"

"Mrs. Bornholdt," I said, my teeth chattering.

She opened her arms to me. "Come here, Marian. Come, it is all right."

But I stood, stuck, on shaking knees. "Mrs. Bornholdt—"

She bounded forward, took my hand, and pulled. I went—my head and shoulders first, my feet stumbling after, useless as rocks.

She shunted me through the doorway. I had to stand on tiptoe to see past her.

"Mrs. Bornholdt," Valentine said again, "please—"

"Get out!" she cried. "I want you gone from here within the hour—the half hour!"

"But, Mrs. Bornholdt—"

"Go!" she shouted. "Drown in the rain, break your neck in a carriage—whatever you do, you will *never* harm a hair on this young lady's head, not ever, ever again!" She threw the nearest thing to her—a hard wooden hairbrush.

It struck Valentine in the face. He threw the hall door open and fled.

◆ ◆ ◆

Mrs. Bornholdt ushered me farther into her bedroom. "Sit down, Marian."

I drifted forward, and the door clicked shut somewhere far away. The rain rushed down the windows still, and the thunder grumbled as if awakened from a needed, longed-for rest. I had felt so safe but a moment before—as if it were really true.

But I was alone. And because we'd been together, there was fresh danger.

Mrs. Bornholdt touched my shoulder. I threw off her hand. "Ma'am," I said, "I need him; if he's not here—"

"Shhh." She pressed me down into her own winged armchair, and I let her, in the hope that—this much being settled—she might listen. But when I tried to speak again, she said: "You are safe right here. What do you need him for?"

I shook my head. "I can't explain, Mrs. Bornholdt, please—" But she was flattening my damp hair with one hand, patting my cheek with the other, holding my head against her bosom. In the posture of a child, my words could only come out childishly.

She tutted. "I am sure he would like you to think your whole world will come crashing down without him. You are afraid, but fret not. I know what I saw, and Mr. Bornholdt will hear how it was."

I sat up straight. "Oh, please don't tell Mr. Bornholdt."

"Marian," she chided, jostling me, "it is all right. I promise you, you will not be dismissed."

"Oh God." I dug my nails into my cheeks, eyes wide.

Mrs. Bornholdt crouched down and gently pulled my hands from my face, her eyes searching mine. "I wanted something lovely for you. I wanted it enough to believe in it. Even after that unfortunate night, I told myself Hobbs was a good man—conscientious, smart, handy. I was so sure he meant to marry you, dear, and I fear—I fear I pushed you closer to a fiend. I should have recognized him for what he was as soon as you told me. My hope made me blind, just as love did to you."

"He wasn't doing anything wrong. I asked him to; it was me."

"Now," she said, so sharply I fell silent, "men may rule this world, and they may come to rule our hearts and minds, but your body is yours. I will not stand by and let that man hurt you."

"But he doesn't, I—"

She held my shoulders. "You are confused. You have been taught to seek what is bad for you and to resist what is good. I am older, wiser, and I am going to help you." She leaned in so our foreheads touched. "You are not married to him. You may be free yet."

We locked eyes. I said: "But he's not like Mr. Bornholdt."

Mrs. Bornholdt's eyes widened, and her pupils shrank. But before she could speak, a great boom shook the house, immediately followed by the sound of shattering glass. Mrs. Bornholdt jumped to her feet, her eyes wide. "Was that Hobbs?"

For a moment she stood irresolute. Then she rang the service bell by her bed and hurried into her dressing room. She returned wearing a robe, which she tied clumsily before darting into the hall. I ran to follow.

I caught up to her at the top of the grand staircase, where she had paused to peer down at the entry. She glanced back at me. "Where is everyone?"

I looked. It was indeed odd: though she had rung her bell, no one moved on the floor below, and no one emerged from the servants' stairwells at either end of the corridor.

"Come," she said at length, and went in the direction of the shattering sound we'd heard. I hesitated. I could run outside now, find Valentine, and flee. Unless he was not outside. Had he caused the sound we'd heard?

I ran to catch up to Mrs. Bornholdt. As I passed Mr. Bornholdt's study door, the rain grew louder—and there was another sound, of paper flapping. I stopped short, then backtracked. Mrs. Bornholdt was beside me again by the time I got the key in the door.

"Oh!" she cried, both of us struck as the wind forced its way past. All the lamps in here were blown out; between the moist, lively air and the darkness, we might have been standing on the cliffside. I hesitated on the threshold, irrationally afraid I would fall to my death if I took even one step forward.

"A window must be broken," Mrs. Bornholdt murmured. "Why does no one come to help? Marian, go and ring my bell again—and get a candle."

The wind followed me down the hall to Mrs. Bornholdt's apartment, warm as panted breath on my neck. Otherwise, the house was as it had been: silent, still. No one seemed about at all but us, and I did not see what good ringing again would do. I did it anyway, as I had been told to, and lit a candle I found in Mrs. Bornholdt's bedroom before returning to the study.

"Mind your step," Mrs. Bornholdt said, as I made my creeping way into the room. It seemed she could not bear but to follow me, though she did stay a stride behind. The wind dropped off as we advanced, like an unruly child caught at mischief, frozen and wondering what might happen next.

I lifted the candle higher and held it out as far as my arm would stretch, illuminating something long, crooked as lightning, and dark as stone. I didn't understand what I was seeing until I recognized the soaked and dripping scraps of green, which seemed to hang from nowhere, not as leathery wings but as leaves.

A tree had fallen against the house, swung one of its arms through the big window, and slammed like God's fist on Mr. Bornholdt's blotter, crushing his desk entirely.

"All his work," Mrs. Bornholdt breathed beside me. "Ruined."

I could only nod in response. I was not sorry, as a lady's maid should have been. Because Mr. Bornholdt's ledger was under that tree. The receipts that proved my debt had been in those drawers. Surely all the ink had run, and the paper turned soft.

I could flee, and he could not send the law after me. Unless . . . unless the originals were elsewhere in the room.

"Marian," Mrs. Bornholdt said, startling me, "there is glass. Let us get away from the window. Be careful, and go to the right. Show me the rest of the room, and we will see what we can save. Goodness, why does no one come?"

We went slowly, staying together so we could see. I protected the candle flame with my free hand. There were pages on the floor, but they were sodden through; they tore like warm bread in Mrs. Bornholdt's hand.

The candlelight caught the corner of something gilded on the carpet, and Mrs. Bornholdt gasped. It was Mr. Bornholdt's great oil portrait, facedown on the floor. It must have jumped from the wall when the tree struck the house.

"Oh!" Mrs. Bornholdt cried, bending down to examine it. "His image is surely ruined!"

"Perhaps not," I said. "Here, ma'am—hold the candle, I will lift it." I stood the painting on its frame; it was heavy, but I sensed that this was the weight of the metal, and the canvas was light, as it should have been. I turned it on its side so I could manage with it under my arm, half dragging it out of the room.

I propped the frame against a wall in the corridor, and Mrs. Bornholdt hurried over, leaning close, drawing the candle over the canvas from corner to corner before finally pronouncing that she could find no fault.

I stifled a bitter sound. Of course Mr. Bornholdt had survived his fall from on high without a scratch. I'd seen him do it once before.

Leaving Mrs. Bornholdt by the painting, I edged back into the study, meaning to check the drawers of the end tables for anything that might incriminate me. I went right, waiting for the oxblood furniture to materialize in my path. Going around a chair, I saw a purple petal on the floor—and then a whole bloom of bittersweet.

"Oh, Carolyn, poor love." Looking about, I found the vase tipped off its table by the wind but not broken. I put my candle on the carpet, righted the vase, and found the flowers one by one. I had never arranged a bouquet before and did not try to make it pretty; it was the rescuing of the flowers only that felt important—picking them up from their fall.

When I lifted the candle again to make sure I hadn't missed any of the flowers, I saw how wet the tabletop was. There was a drawer below, which I pulled open to check for any paper.

Inside was one sheet, folded. It was damp, and when I opened it to see whether the words were legible, I spotted Mrs. Bornholdt's name—and the word "ill." Before I knew what I was doing, I was reading.

> Mr. Bornholdt—
> First, allow me to ease your mind. That Mrs. Bornholdt is a bit ill of temper and body at this stage is perfectly normal. She is surrendering much of herself to

meet the needs of another human being, after all. Her stomach may be unsettled, and she may be exhausted often—all quite usual.

It is quite natural as well, now that she is so heavy with child, that she does not perform her wifely duties. It is hardly a matter of will—she truly must not, never mind her inclination one way or the other. Men must make peace with this in these later months—indeed, for the first few years after the child is born, for Mother will be more concerned bodily with Baby than you. Once the child is born, there will be very little you can do.

Men who mean to be Fathers may help Mother bear her stomach troubles with comforts such as weak tea, and bread soaked in water. If you were to administer anything stronger—having Mother drink Epsom salts, for example—Mother herself would be perfectly safe, but you would very likely lose Baby.

I hope that I've given all the information you might require in this stressful time, sir.

Yours,

Dr. John Abelforth

I'd hardly finished before I began again, and went slower. Some phrases seemed bolder. *Men who mean to be Fathers . . . Mother herself would be perfectly safe* . . . Was it just the bleeding of the ink that made them stand out? Or—

Are you going to end the way you began, Wythe? As a murderer?

I trembled.

So he was capable of killing.

I needed to get out. Now. But I couldn't move.

"Marian," Mrs. Bornholdt said, and it was as if she called across a graveyard rather than her husband's study.

I raised my head, trembling, to find her silhouetted in the doorway.

"What are you doing?" she asked.

"Carolyn," I replied—for it was the only word on my lips.

"What?" she said, coming toward the candlelight. With a small cry, she came around and picked up the vase. She gazed at the flowers a moment, then stood the bouquet on the table. Stiffly, she said: "Come away, Marian."

At the touch of her hand, I stood, on feet I couldn't feel.

Out in the hall, Mrs. Bornholdt set the vase down on the nearest table and turned to me in the fuller light. Her eyes landed on the letter I still held in my hand. "What's this?" she asked, snatching it out of my hand.

I could have run while she read, but—oh, I couldn't let her learn this alone, and leave her. I watched with helplessness heavy in my stomach as her eyes roved back and forth over the page. After some time of this, they stopped, then slid out of focus, so she went on staring into the air between her fingers even when the letter had fallen like a feather from her hand.

I reached out, afraid she might fall forward. "Mrs. Bornholdt?"

But she didn't seem to hear or see me. Nothing seemed to exist around her. Or it was she who had gone away—leaving only her body, her long-neglected house, behind.

A tear leaked out of one eye. She blinked it away, and then a shudder ran like an earthquake over her face, setting every familiar feature askew. Crumpling to her feet, she reached for me. I knelt.

"Help me," she said, her mouth moving against my shoulder. "Oh, please help me."

I put my hands gingerly on her back. She shuddered against me. I pulled her closer.

"Yes, ma'am."

◆ ◆ ◆

The bang of a door came first, from the floor below us.

Then the sounds of rain and wind intensified, and men shouted to one another inside the house. The sense of the words didn't matter to me. I leaned back to study Mrs. Bornholdt. Her face was impassive—a doll's face, with no little girl to come and enliven it.

I helped her to her feet and led her down the hall. We went away from the commotion, to Mrs. Bornholdt's bedroom. I led her to her armchair, and she sat without prompting. But, propping her elbows on her lap, she clasped her hands as if in prayer, bowing her head so her lips were against her knuckles. I put my palm on her back. Even on her sickest days, I had never seen her spine curve so.

"Mrs. Bornholdt?" I said. "Shall I . . . get you back into bed?"

She didn't answer.

Downstairs, the raised voices were still rumbling, unintelligible from this distance. Making up my mind, I set about turning up the gas lamps again, in the bedroom first and then in the dressing room as well. Having gone that far, I went through to the bathroom and lit the lamps there as well, prolonging the moment when I would have to return to her, seeking direction, having solved nothing.

I let my gaze linger on the walls and the furniture, bringing both feet together before I separated them again. I remembered walking over the threshold of Parish Street Workhouse in a fog like this one, to come here. I'd been stunned, chasing a witch's glamour of selfish hope, not knowing how little time my mother had when I left her behind.

I'd promised to free her.

I reached the doorway of the bedroom again, lost as I'd been when I stepped away. Mrs. Bornholdt lifted her chin and looked at me.

"Yes, ma'am?" I said, nearly as one word. I did not want to lose her to her thoughts.

She opened her mouth; then her eyes darted to the door. By the approaching sound, it seemed several pairs of feet were marching down the hall. I thought the noise had scared her nerve away, but then her eyes found mine again and steadied there. "I cannot—not for one more day," was all she had time to say before the bedroom door burst open.

"So you *are* about," Mr. Bornholdt declared, blustering in, drenched and half-dipped in mud, bits of grass and pebbles clinging to his shoes and trouser legs. "I knew you could not have slept through the disorder downstairs, and I am correct: your apartment is all alight, and here are you, sitting sweetly." He smiled with menace, his teeth clenched together. "No concern at all for your husband? For what might be happening in your house—the realm over which you are supposed to preside?"

Mrs. Bornholdt licked her lips. Softly, she said, "I am sorry, darling—I think I have been dreaming awake."

Behind Mr. Bornholdt, Ledford scurried in. He bowed his sparsely haired head, ducking Mr. Bornholdt's gesticulating arms, trying to brush the filth from the master's coat into a dustpan. After him came Valentine, who took a single sheepish step over the threshold, his eyes trained resolutely on the carpet.

I looked from him to Mrs. Bornholdt, but she looked only at her husband—who combed his fingers through his dripping hair, stomping in a line from one end of the room to the other, while the butler followed with his coarse brush.

"I go out in this wretched rain, to see to a problem I did not cause—for, whatever may be said of me, my power is *not* God's power. I can*not* will miracles any more than I may will catastrophe"—I saw Mrs. Bornholdt's lips twist at this point, as if she tasted something sour, and then fall flat again—"and for my attempt to extend my hand, I am rewarded—for it must be a reward, I cannot imagine being met with anything else but a reward in a just world, and yet I cannot figure it out, Diana. Is this fair?"

She clasped her hands tightly. "Wythe, I cannot make sense of it until I know what happened."

"On the descent into the village," he said, his eyes gleaming madly, "lightning struck a tree, scaring the horses. The carriage rolled off the road, and had we not been so near the bottom of the cliff already, I might have died."

Here, he glanced at Mrs. Bornholdt, and only then did she put a hand to her mouth and gasp behind it.

He narrowed his eyes. "It was a long, punishing return journey—with no way to right the carriage and get it back onto the road, though the coachman did waste half an hour making attempts."

Mrs. Bornholdt nodded. "Wythe, it sounds perfectly—"

He bore down on her. "Did you never wonder, 'Where is my husband?' Did you not think, 'My, should he not be home by now?' If you had, why, you might have sent someone down after me, and I might have been helped. But no—no, I give and give and never receive. I am responsible for everyone, and no one is responsible for me; is that not so?"

"I am sorry, Wythe." Mrs. Bornholdt's voice was distant. "I did go thoughtlessly to bed. It was selfish. Forgive me."

"Forgiveness," Mr. Bornholdt snapped and, at Ledford's latest touch, jerked his sleeve out of the butler's grip, threw off the coat, and shoved the bundle into the butler's arms. "The gift we assume costs nothing simply because it is not bought."

Mrs. Bornholdt nodded, swallowed, touched her hair. "Are you hurt, Wythe?"

He whipped his head around. "Of course I am hurt! I was thrown across the carriage while the ceiling and the floor changed places!"

"Shall I send for the doctor, sir?" Ledford put in.

"No, no." Mr. Bornholdt straightened his vest. "There is nothing to stitch, nothing broken or twisted. It is my insides that are jostled. My heart is jumping like a frog at flies, and my stomach does not appreciate the motion at all."

Mrs. Bornholdt lifted a hand toward me. "Marian, go and mix a glass of water with some Epsom salts to settle Mr. Bornholdt's stomach."

"Yes, ma'am." I hurried through to the bathroom, to the pot of salts by the tub. I lifted the lid and peered in. It was too near empty. I tucked the flowery pot under my arm and returned to the bedroom. "I'll have to go and get more from downstairs, ma'am."

"Go, then," Mrs. Bornholdt said.

The hallway was alive with activity—Mrs. Davies exclaiming about the glass and the water in the study, Lucette answering back to each order as the housekeeper gave them. Decorum set aside, several male servants came straight up the grand stairs in their darker cleaning uniforms. The coachman, too, was with them. He had an axe.

Not wanting to leave Mrs. Bornholdt alone any longer than necessary, I rushed the other way, to the servants' staircase, which was so still and quiet I could hear my own breath.

The kitchens were empty, too, with onion halves and garlic abandoned all along the preparation table. I noticed a fire still burning unattended in the hearth of Mrs. Davies's office. Not willing to further tempt disaster, I darted in to put the grate across it before proceeding to the footman's pantry. I set Mrs. Bornholdt's pot on the counter and headed in.

Everything there was in a state of disarray, too. I had to walk my way through shoes and black-stained rags, careful not to step into open pots of blacking.

On the back shelf, the jar of Epsom salts stood sedate above all the chaos and disorder. I reached out with both hands and pulled it toward me.

But then my eyes jumped to the jar behind it, full up with something white as well—almost like Epsom salts, only the crystals were long and thin, like grains of rice.

27

"At long last," Mr. Bornholdt huffed, as I reentered the bedroom with a laden tray: the flowery pot, a pitcher of water, and a pair of drinking glasses.

The master was seated in Mrs. Bornholdt's armchair, while she had moved to the footstool; Mr. Bornholdt had allowed her a corner on which to precariously perch, while he stretched his stockinged feet across the rest of it.

"Just another moment, sir." I went to the table by Mrs. Bornholdt's window and laid out everything I needed. With a spoon I'd pocketed downstairs, I scooped twice from Mrs. Bornholdt's pot, dumping the contents into one of the glasses. Then I added the water and stirred.

"Hurry up," Mr. Bornholdt said.

Spilling some, I glanced back over my shoulder. Mrs. Bornholdt's eyes were half-closed, her mouth drooping like a dying flower. "Would you like some water, too, ma'am?"

It took a moment for her to react, but after a moment her head perked up. "Yes, Marian, please."

I nodded and poured again from the pitcher. Mr. Bornholdt's glass I took in my left hand, Mrs. Bornholdt's in my right, and when I turned from the table, I stopped and took stock again, thinking: *Mrs. Bornholdt is in the right.*

I gave hers over first.

"For goodness' sake, who has had the ordeal tonight?" Mr. Bornholdt demanded.

"I apologize, sir," I said. "It's my instinct, as the lady's—"

He snatched the glass from my hand. He tilted his head back to gulp the drink down, and I watched his Adam's apple jump with each swallow.

I turned away, crossed the room, and stood at attention by the door. It was done—I had done it. I leaned against the wall, light-headed. I would be hanged for this, surely. Or locked away in a madhouse.

Mr. Bornholdt scowled down at his glass. "How disgusting. Misery heaped upon misery."

He lifted his gaze, looking for my reaction—which I could not bring myself to give him.

"You know something, Marian," he said, considering me, "the lesson I tried to teach has stuck better with Hobbs than with you. From the moment I returned, he has been most attentive—Hobbs has already organized the retrieval of the carriage, and it was he who alerted Mrs. Davies of a broken window in my office. He has me in mind even before himself. Perhaps I should have been as hard with you as I was with him."

"Perhaps, sir." My eyes slid from his face to Mrs. Bornholdt's, dreading the moment she would inform him of Valentine's supposed villainy. But she only sipped her water. She knew Valentine was in the room—he stood at rest a few feet away—but for all the notice she took, he might have been a portrait on her wall.

When I looked back at Mr. Bornholdt, he was supernaturally still, his hand cupped across his throat, eyes wide. So soon. My hands crept toward my mouth, but I forced them down.

Ledford noticed first. "Is something wrong, sir?"

"Hot," Mr. Bornholdt managed, before his head wobbled forward. Then he retched, spitting a brownish-green glob of something onto the carpet, bringing Mrs. Bornholdt to her feet with a short, sharp scream.

Valentine moved at once from the wall, but he did not go to the master. He crossed well to the back of the room. No one seemed to notice but me.

"Sir!" Ledford cried, rushing forward to help Mr. Bornholdt lie back in his chair. His hand grazed the front of his master's vest. "You're sweating, sir!"

Mr. Bornholdt slapped the servant's hand away. "Of course I am sweating!" he yelled. "I am hot!"

The door flew open, and Mrs. Davies and Lucette burst into the room, no doubt drawn by Mrs. Bornholdt's scream. "What is it?" they cried together—but no one answered. I flattened myself against the wall behind them.

Ledford peered into Mr. Bornholdt's face. "Is it a reaction to the Epsom salts?"

"No," Valentine said, with his back to all. He was frozen, his head bent, his shoulders drawn tight together, as he looked down at the table where I had left the pitcher and pot. He did not turn his head to look at me—he did not have to: in discovering the truth, he also discovered me. I shivered—naked to him in a new way, across the room, in the entirely opposite direction of his gaze.

"How can you know that?" Ledford asked.

I swallowed. I could feel sweat under my arms.

"Hobbs knows so many things," Mrs. Bornholdt said, a fact suddenly recalled; she studied him desperately as she wrung her hands, as if she couldn't quite see him, or the room in general.

"It's not Epsom salt," Valentine murmured. As if time had slowed, and with a sick feeling in my own stomach, I watched him turn. "It's oxalic acid."

His grave eyes found mine.

"Oh—oh God," I whispered, shaking so hard I could barely make myself heard.

"Oxalic acid?" Mrs. Bornholdt cried. She was pale, her voice pitched high.

"They look similar," he said, speaking to Mrs. Bornholdt while he went on looking at me. Surely he could see my panic—did he think it was performance? He had to know he had my fate in his hands.

Mr. Bornholdt coughed and wheezed between us.

"Find the coachman," Mrs. Bornholdt said to the butler. "Have him go for a doctor. Quickly."

Ledford dashed off.

"Snake," Mr. Bornholdt sputtered, and with everyone watching, he pointed right at me. "Murderous wretch!"

I went cold.

Mrs. Bornholdt came closer to him. "Wythe, for goodness' sake." She seemed to flounder, looking between him and me. Finally, and weakly, she said: "Marian has no cause to harm you on purpose."

I shivered harder.

"Yes, she has," he murmured. Then he lost the strength to hold his head up, his eyes rolling independently of one another.

Mrs. Bornholdt dashed to her washstand and wet a cloth with water from the pitcher. "Here, Wythe," she said, patting his forehead. "This will cool you."

"She thinks she can escape me," Mr. Bornholdt breathed, his eyes vacant as an empty mirror. Then, through a fresh fit of coughing, he said, "But I will have her."

Mrs. Bornholdt's brow furrowed. "Wythe, what are you saying?"

"The frigid bitch," he seethed, sucking his saliva back and forth through his teeth as he breathed, just as the moon heaves and yanks the sea. "Always resisting me." He laughed, or coughed.

The cloth hovered, dripping water on Mr. Bornholdt's cheeks. My mistress raised her gaze to mine. It seemed indecent to look upon her naked pain, but I willed myself to do it—for if I could see her anguish, perhaps she could see mine.

"It's nonsense, ma'am," Mrs. Davies said bracingly. "He's raving; he knows not what he says."

Mrs. Bornholdt glanced at the housekeeper, then at Lucette beside her, who nodded decisively. But when she looked again upon me, I denied nothing, and her eyes welled with tears.

"Ma'am," Ledford said, barreling back into the room, "the coachman has gone, but the storm is worse again. He had to take madam's open coach, which is lighter, and will need to be careful so as not to pitch it over like the last. I cannot tell how long he will be. Perhaps an hour."

Mrs. Bornholdt looked around, as if lost.

"We don't have an hour," Valentine said.

Ledford nodded. "Ma'am, we must take matters into our own hands."

"We must prepare an emetic," Valentine declared.

Mrs. Davies and Ledford moved toward the door. Clearly Valentine had decided on his course. I wondered, light-headed and terrified, if it was the course of justice; I did not know the term he used.

But evidently Lucette did, for she cried out: "No! If you make 'im sick it up, it'll burn 'oles right through his throat!"

Was that true? If she was right, then surely Valentine knew it, too. Which meant—

"If we leave it be," he said, "it'll burn holes in his stomach!"

He was trying to help me. To see that what I had begun was finished. "Oh God," I said again, and stuffed my own hands in my mouth.

"We need chalk," Lucette insisted. "We need to mix chalk with water, an' then—"

"There's no time—don't you understand, he's dying!" Valentine cried, and for a moment he looked entirely lost. His eyes touched other faces in the room—Ledford's, Mrs. Davies's—but he could get no purchase on them, their wide-eyed expressions smooth as glass. He looked at Mr. Bornholdt, then at me. The seconds stretched, and he did not look away.

But what could I say or do? What could I give him but wide eyes, the eyes of a criminal, spawn of a—

I let myself fall to my knees, and in clasping my hands—to the rest, I might have been praying—I touched my wrists together before my belly, as if they were bound. I looked to Valentine. I saw the officer's mask go up.

He rounded on Lucette. "As it's a fool woman's poor judgment that got us into this mess," he snapped, "I'm disinclined to let a fool woman's judgment lead us out!"

"Hear, hear, Hobbs," Mr. Bornholdt whispered. He smiled then, self-satisfied through his pain—or past feeling it—as if he were being waited on by his man at dinner. "Hobbs knows—his job," he said.

Mrs. Bornholdt kneeled on the floor. She was staring at me, but tore her eyes away to ask: "What is the right thing to do, Hobbs?"

"Salt water," Valentine said.

Lucette shook her head. "It'll take too long. If we gave the chalk first—"

"Lucette!" Mrs. Davies snapped, and the housemaid stopped short, as if she'd been smacked. "Do as Hobbs says; go and mix the salt water!"

Lucette looked from the master to Valentine. Then, scowling, she left.

"Make a full pitcher!" Valentine called after her. "Warm!"

Mrs. Bornholdt sent Ledford and Mrs. Davies to wait for the doctor. It was suddenly far too quiet. Mr. Bornholdt's face was paler, his skin shining with sweat. Mrs. Bornholdt stared at him, transfixed.

"Shall I go, too?" I asked her.

"No." It was the sharpest sound she'd made since she'd screamed. "No, you must stay. I need you."

I came closer and, after a moment's hesitation, reached out for her hand.

She gave it to me. Her fingers were slick with sweat. I wrapped the flap of my apron around them, and held tight.

Valentine looked from her to me, frowning. Then he clasped his hands behind his back and paced. On his third pass by the chair, he looked down at the master, slowing to study his eyelids, under which only the whites could be seen. How similar his anxiety looked to that of a man trying to save a life—rather than thoroughly end it. He would be fine, I thought, when the authorities came—he and Mrs. Bornholdt both.

Lucette ran in with a crystal pitcher of cloudy water. Valentine grabbed Mrs. Bornholdt's drinking glass from the table where she'd left it, and dumped the remaining water unceremoniously on the carpet. Then he held the glass out to Lucette.

"This is the wrong thing," she said, tremulously.

"Pour," he told her, his voice low and smooth.

I saw the strength go out of her—the way her limbs went loose. She shrank from him even as she tipped the pitcher with her hand. He held her gaze until the glass was full, then turned his face away—cutting the connection between them so ruthlessly that even I felt the sudden drop.

She went, red-faced, from the room and slammed the door behind her.

Valentine knelt next to Mr. Bornholdt. "Sir." When this elicited no response, he slapped the master's cheek, sharp and quick.

Mr. Bornholdt's eyes found his.

I watched them together—a knight playing nurse and a man regressed to babyhood. Valentine said, in a sweet whisper, "You will be sick soon, and better afterward." He tipped the glass to his master's mouth. "Swallow. Just swallow."

Glass after glass of salt water, Mr. Bornholdt continued to grow paler, the rain still rushing down all around. The doctor did not come. Nothing seemed to be moving, in the house or in the world.

"Did you really do it on purpose?" Mrs. Bornholdt asked, and the question made Valentine look straight at me. His eyes were wide, terrified.

But Mrs. Bornholdt was talking to her husband.

"Wythe?" she pressed. "How could you?"

"Do what, Diana?" Mr. Bornholdt's breath was a whistle. "What did I do?"

Mrs. Bornholdt blinked down at him. "I found a letter. From the doctor. In your study. About Carolyn."

He flinched at the word—or at some pain. But he did not lose the thread of conversation. "The baby."

"Why would you keep such a letter for me to find, Wythe?" she asked, her voice trembling, and it struck me that she was more baffled by his sloppy secret-keeping than his committing an unspeakable evil.

"Diana . . ."

"Why do you keep it in that drawer?"

"I don't, always—"

"Why not burn it?" she asked, and her voice pitched lower and lower until she was growling at him. "It had served its purpose, had it not? What more could you take from it? What more could you want—"

"Her birthday," Mr. Bornholdt murmured. His eyes rolled out of sight again, and he slurred his words. "Every year . . . so saddens you, I dig it up . . ."

"Do you regret?" she demanded, shaking him, her voice raw, eyes searching, and I knew: if only he gave her the answer she wanted, she would wish with her whole heart that I had not poisoned him.

"Remind myself . . ." He drew a rattling breath. "What I would have lost."

She dropped his shoulders, and he banged his head on the back of the couch. The salt water finally came up then, and Mr. Bornholdt was violently sick.

Valentine rushed forward to assist him, but Mrs. Bornholdt planted her hand hard against his chest, holding him back.

Mr. Bornholdt choked and gasped, his fingers clawing at his throat. His bulging eyes found his wife, who only stared down at him.

28

Upon his return, Ledford was shocked to find the master of the house dead. He excused himself immediately, undoubtedly to spread the news among the other servants. The village doctor who had accompanied him was not as surprised.

"It's the fastest poison, oxalic acid," he said, a casual observation from the safe remove of business. Taking in the tears on my mistress's cheeks, he added, "I apologize, Mrs. Bornholdt, for your great loss."

"Thank you," she said, giving her hand to him. Then she shied away, taking a turn about the bedroom. She lingered by the window as the doctor bent to examine Mr. Bornholdt.

Glued to my place by the door, I was aware that my fingers interlocked with each other across my uniform, and yet the idea that they were choked around the master's throat seemed truer and plainer. Any moment, the doctor would look back at me and know, and that would be the beginning of the end of it: my journey to the madhouse.

Valentine stood beside me, but I did not dare to glance his way—nor he mine.

There was a pounding of feet coming closer to the door, then Mrs. Davies shouting something that sounded prohibitive. In a moment, Lucette came through. Pushing me aside, she said, "Was Valentine Hobbs murdered 'im, sir!"

I opened my mouth to speak, but Valentine at that moment cleared his throat—too pointedly to have been natural.

I turned my head, to see what he meant by it, but he wouldn't look at me.

"Pardon, miss?" This was the doctor, looking up from the master's body.

"The footman killed Mr. Bornholdt," she said, pointing at him. "Was on 'is orders what we give 'im!"

I braced for Valentine to argue—but he only raised his chin, as if he stood by what he'd done.

I sucked in my breath.

"The footman administered the acid?" the doctor asked, watching as the butler and housekeeper tried and failed to subdue Lucette. "The butler said it was the lady's maid's mistake."

I stepped forward. And, helpfully, Lucette said, "Well, yes, sir—but if you ask me, the lady's maid didn' make no mistake."

The doctor's eyebrows went up even as his mouth dragged down. "That is for the law to determine," he said, "and hardly the purview of a housemaid."

"Yes, sir." She curtsied. "But home remedy *is* my—my lookout, please, sir, and Hobbs's, too. He didn' do what he should have, nor let me."

"Oh?" The doctor twisted around to face Lucette. "And what did Hobbs do?"

"Gave him salt water, sir."

He furrowed his brow. "Well. Chalk would have been better, certainly, but that is for me to know, not a footman, and salt water has never killed anyone, I'm afraid."

"I said he should have chalk, an' he told me off!" Lucette clenched her hands into fists. "He *knew* he was doin' it wrong, sir. He's sharp as a mother's tongue, sir!"

Peering over his glasses, he said, "Miss, settle yourself!"

Lucette deflated under the doctor's gaze, but used the last of her wind to cry: "He can get ink up with a lemon!"

All was silent for a moment.

"Aha," the doctor replied. "Yes. Well, we'll not debate your high opinion of Mr. Hobbs. A lemon, you say? Bear in mind, my dear, that the scissor is sharp in the hands of a child but dull in the hands of the knife grinder."

"Excuse me, sir?" Lucette said.

"Forgive me, I do not mean to confuse you, only to be polite," the doctor said. "I meant, just because Mr. Hobbs knows more than you do about the world—"

"That's not what I—"

"—does not mean he is competent in all things, especially not medicine." He favored first Lucette, and then Valentine, with a wistful grin. "He may be like God to you, and I would not venture to change that—but for others he is, after all, only a footman."

Valentine humbly bowed his head.

"It's not like that, sir," Lucette mumbled. "He likes the lady's maid; that's what I'm tryin' to tell you."

He turned more fully toward her, crossing his arms. "Oh, is that what this is about? Dear, I pity your personal injury, truly, but do you perhaps think that Mrs. Bornholdt's has been greater? Might we get back to her troubles for the moment?"

"Yes, for God's sake," Mrs. Davies agreed, taking Lucette by the arm. She beckoned toward Valentine and me. "You two as well—this should be private, between the doctor and Mrs. Bornholdt."

"Ah, no," the doctor said, his voice deeper, heavier. "Regrettably, these two should stay here until such time as the investigator comes."

My stomach turned.

Not just me, then. It was to be both of us.

And I was not the only one the news struck. Mrs. Bornholdt lifted her head, like a person waking. Some horror dawned in her eyes, it seemed, but she did not speak.

◆ ◆ ◆

The investigator came at once, or at least he did not wait for daylight.

He brought an entourage that swarmed to the cliff to roost like crows, in black, lantern-lit wagons painted with POLICE. I saw them through the windows as two men in uniform led me and Valentine to the entryway, where a man in uniform was waiting. He watched us descend the grand staircase as if he were awaiting his partner at a ball, right down to the expectant smirk upon his whiskered face.

It was by then something like three or four in the morning. Perhaps for lack of sleep, I walked as if through warm water, slow and not, so far as I knew, touching my feet to the floor. The master was dead—dead—and no matter what else came next, that could not be reversed.

After introducing himself as Constable Briggs, the man led us through to the dining room, as if this were his house and we his visitors. The two officers accompanied us, stationing themselves at the room's two exits.

Around the dining table sat the doctor, Mrs. Davies, Ledford, and Lucette. It was absurd: servants, who had scrubbed every centerpiece and fixture in that room, resting their bottoms in the chairs of their betters. I had to suppress a bitter laugh.

"Have a seat, both of you," the constable said.

Valentine went to the left at once, to sit in the empty chair beside the butler. I wanted terribly to follow him, but the strength of this desire alone was enough to warn me away from it. I went around the opposite way and sat beside Lucette.

Of course, once there I found Valentine directly across from me. His face, however, was indifferent to mine, his eyes passing down the table to the constable, who had been waiting for me to be settled.

"There is to be no talking in here while I conduct my interviews," Constable Briggs said. "I know this has been an upsetting time—to your emotions and to your routines—but I ask that you keep yourselves composed and silent in the interest of moving the investigation along quickly. If you cannot do as you have been asked by me, you will do as you are forced by my associates at the doors here. Is that understood?"

"Yes, sir," Lucette said, but the rest of us only nodded with a church-service solemnity.

The constable drew out a journal and consulted it. "Miss Lucette Weekeley, is it?"

She nodded. "Yes, sir."

"I'd like to talk to you first." He opened the pocket doors opposite the fireplace, revealing Mr. Bornholdt's drawing room: walls stained like wine, a white-marble mantel, standing ashtrays beside velvet couches. "Come through."

Lucette rose, and despite myself, I looked up at her. She smiled at me, then walked primly around the table, her hands clasped in front, her head held high and proud.

The constable watched her pass. Then he brought the pocket doors together again behind them, like curtains falling on a stage, and we the audience were silent and still.

I strained to hear their conversation, but the rumble of the constable was impossible to make out, and Lucette's voice apparently too high to carry far. Across from me, Valentine had leaned back in his seat and closed his eyes. He was nearer to the doors—to listen, of course. I cursed myself for not sitting beside him as I'd wanted to. Why was my second instinct always to deny my first one?

I twisted my fingers in my lap. Lucette knew more than the doctor had given her credit for. Was that why Constable Briggs had called her first? The world had turned on its head that night; of course the lowliest servant stood on high to look down on me. She would be the one to determine my fate.

I watched the mantel clock's minute hand make a full revolution before the doors rolled open again. Lucette must have been sent through to another part of the house, because I could no longer see her. Constable Briggs called for the doctor next, and for a while there were two rumbling voices, one whose speech curled upward in question at the ends, and the other who answered always with an even certainty.

Then it was Mrs. Davies's turn. She stood as if she'd been called to go to battle and bustled through to the drawing room with deep conviction in her cause.

This interview was shorter. Only twenty minutes had gone by when Constable Briggs returned and called for the butler. Ledford's exit was the stateliest of all—though out of pride or exhaustion, I could not tell. In any case, he gave Valentine no sign of recognition as he passed.

Not fifteen minutes later, Constable Briggs came back. "Valentine Hobbs," he said.

There was a thud as Valentine drew out his chair, and his eyes screwed shut in pain. He must have struck his knee on the underside of the table.

I leaned forward, reaching out to touch him—but when he opened his eyes, I jerked back as if he'd slapped me. The disgust I saw there! After all he had done in Mrs. Bornholdt's bedroom, to cover me—

Perhaps, in the aftermath, he saw how he had sullied himself for my sake.

I stammered, "I'm so sorry, V—"

"Don't you talk to me," he hissed.

I stared.

"Shut up there, both of you," one of the guards warned. Guilty, I glanced at Constable Briggs, who only waved Valentine toward him.

The two left together, the doors rolled shut, and I sat staring at Valentine's empty chair. I had once promised myself I would never be in the position of my parents. And Valentine had joined the fight to keep me good. I thought of his dusting cloth, felt it touching my cheeks and forehead.

Of course he was angry. For what had all the work been done, all the time spent, when its undoing was so quick and simple?

Unless . . . he meant to see that it was not undone.

I put my hands over my mouth. Was he confessing? Taking the brunt of my fall—again?

Fifteen minutes passed, then twenty. I could hear Valentine speaking, but as with the constable, I could not make out the words.

A full hour passed. All that time, I sat as if I were already dead. Guilt and shame pressed upon my shoulders—not just for the killing, but for the great tumble I had taken in Valentine's glaring eyes, and for whatever distance I had dragged him down with me.

"You're the last, Miss Osley."

I looked up at the constable, blinking eyes that felt frozen. I rose on stiff legs to answer the summons.

Constable Briggs shut the pocket doors behind us and gestured to the couch. "Have a seat."

But I couldn't obey. I was choking on the smoke in the air, despite the fact that, by my reckoning, there could not have been a pipe lit in there for at least a day. It was as if so much smoking had been done, over the years, that the curtains and the cushions themselves puffed away on what ash had been embedded in them, whenever no one else was about.

"May I open a window, sir?" I asked.

"Certainly," he said, studying my face. "You do look red."

I went to one. There were no police wagons' lanterns to be seen from here—the darkness was complete. I freed the latch and pushed the window out. The rain had stopped. I took a deep breath; the air was dream-soft, yet its freshness woke me somewhat to where I was—gently, like a mother might do. A breeze came to curl my hair in its fingers.

Perhaps hanging would not be the worst thing. Perhaps Mother could make a case for me to God, and I could be with her in heaven.

I turned.

"Better?" Constable Briggs prompted.

"Yes," I said, and went to sit on the couch opposite him.

He adjusted himself in his chair, drawing out his book. "Good. Have you been to bed at all since Mr. Bornholdt has died?"

My brow furrowed. "No, sir."

"Are you tired?"

"I—I suppose I would be, sir, if not for everything that has happened. I feel wide awake."

"That's to be expected," he said. "Your body is responding to disaster."

I nodded.

He leaned back. "Were you abed before Mr. Bornholdt returned from his carriage ride?"

It already seemed a lifetime ago, and I had to think back. The letter. Carolyn. I shuddered.

"It's all right," Constable Briggs said. "I'm not here to judge your work ethic. You can say you were asleep if you were."

"But I wasn't," I said. "I had clothing back from the laundry that had to be returned to Mrs. Bornholdt's room."

"Did someone set you that job?"

"Yes, sir. Mrs. Davies, sir, the housekeeper."

"And did she see you off to do that work?" he wondered.

"Yes, sir."

"Right," he said, jotting in his book. "When do you rise to work every morning, Miss Osley?"

"Five, sir."

"So." He checked his watch. "You've been awake over twenty-four hours."

"Yes, I suppose so."

"And at the time of Mr. Bornholdt's arrival—which I have from the butler to be near one this morning—you had been awake about twenty."

I blinked. "Yes, sir."

"Fine. And when are you due to menstruate?"

"I—I—is that—"

"An approximation will do."

"This week, I suppose, sir, but—"

"Thank you," he said. "That's fine, then. Go along into the hallway there and wait."

I rose, then stopped. "Sir, don't you want to ask me about Mr. Bornholdt? About the oxalic acid?"

He waved the questions away. "No, no. That's already sorted. I'll get Mrs. Bornholdt settled in here, then bring you and Mr. Hobbs back in, to settle the matter altogether. You wait in the dining room." I stared at him, and his eyes softened. "That way you don't have to be near that footman while you wait."

I pursed my lips, confused.

"Your mistress told me all about him," he said, not unkindly, "and I understand your heartache, misguided as it may be. He sounds a brute and a fool, going about so certain in everything he does and says. I'm sure that seems paradoxical to you."

I didn't know how to answer.

He gave me a pitying smile. "He's full of bluster, miss, and you must try to recognize men like that in future. Bluster is just a coat lads put on, when they can't tailor the truth to suit 'em. You will find better than him."

Utterly lost, my mouth slack and open, I let the constable lead me to the dining room to wait.

29

When next I entered the drawing room, Mrs. Bornholdt sat stiffly on the couch I had recently occupied. Valentine stood between her and Mr. Briggs's vacated chair. He looked to me like he was on trial, and the room tilted a moment before I could catch myself on the edge of a pocket door.

"Come along," Mr. Briggs said. "It's late, which is to say early, and the sooner we have done with this, the sooner your mistress can have some well-deserved rest."

I went to stand where he pointed, across from Valentine. The constable shut the pocket doors, and sat.

"First, Mrs. Bornholdt," he said. "I am very sorry, again, for your loss."

She folded her hands in her lap. "Thank you."

We passed a moment of silence together. The sun must have been rising in the village, for the blueness of the night beyond the window had a glow about it, a deep inner life that promised to gather strength enough to permeate the room. Mrs. Bornholdt's tears fell in the same way the stomach falls when breathing—automatically, regularly, apparently without her conscious involvement.

"Now, Mrs. Bornholdt," the constable began, his voice gentle, "I speak frankly, not to distress you but to help you think clearly about what's happened here this morning. My first concern, as you know, has been to determine whether your husband's death was an accident or deliberate."

"Yes," she said, when he paused. I held my breath.

"It is my opinion that the mistake about the Epsom salts and oxalic acid is a genuine one, made by two undereducated unfortunates. I give my reasoning for your consideration: First, that an ordinary woman has not the mind for violence nor the natural inclination to do harm, turned as she is by God toward motherhood—you said that, ma'am, I have in my notes. Second, the maid's romantic energies have been spent lately on the footman also here implicated, as he admits himself. Third, lately your maid and the footman have had a falling-out—he pursuing Miss Weekeley, as she confirms herself. This is a consuming distraction for lovesick women. Fourth, the simple woman—as you deem her, again from my notes—had been awake nearly a full day at the time of the poisoning, which is long enough that even the wisest of men with the clearest of heads might err. And sixth, the woman was yet more clouded in the mind due to typical premenstrual tension, as she admits herself."

I stared. It was absurd, and offensive in its absurdity. I might have screamed or laughed—perhaps both—if it had not seemed to me so obviously unreal. And yet he really did seem to believe it. Across from me, Valentine's shoulders lowered, and he let his clasped hands fall gently open at his sides.

Bitterly, hurling the words in the constable's direction, Mrs. Bornholdt said: "All you say is true—she is too empty-headed to have planned this." She sniffed. "And the footman?"

The constable spread his hands. "I fear I am mostly repeating the doctor, based on his interview with me: that Hobbs did as he thought was best, betting wisdom he did not possess against the master's life. From testimony of the housemaid and you, yourself, it's clear the lad has an inflated sense of his own skill. I would not go so far as to say he has a criminal mind. The butler tells me the master once suspected the footman of theft, but nothing was ever taken—further, when I asked what had aroused suspicion, the butler wasn't sure. I suspect no malicious intent, only man's hubris."

"Yes," Mrs. Bornholdt said. "I have seen his undue confidence many times."

Valentine bowed his head, as if he could possibly expect her to say such things. I could only gape.

"If you disagree with my opinion in any way," the constable said to Mrs. Bornholdt, "I am happy to begin the process of an inquest."

She sat up straight. "An inquest?"

"In a case where cause of death is uncertain, there would be a trial to determine—"

"No, no," she said. "God, let me suffer less. If it is an accident, let it be an accident."

The constable wet his lips, and frowned. "In that case, Mrs. Bornholdt, I am afraid the offense falls from a criminal one to one of gross negligence."

"All right," Mrs. Bornholdt murmured, rubbing her red eyes.

"Unless," the constable ventured, "you would like to argue that it was intentional?"

"I have already told you, Constable—I agree it was an accident. Hobbs is incompetent, probably has less sense than Weekeley and Osley put together."

I raised my brows.

"Well, then I . . ." The constable shuffled his notes and shifted in his chair. "I am sorry to say that I cannot overlook that you asked your maid to provide Epsom salt to your husband to settle his stomach, which would have been the right thing in his state, and that your maid—far from knowingly committing an act that might cause harm—knew herself only to be committing an act that should have minimized that harm. So it is not strictly gross negligence. Regardless of its effect, the act itself was meant conscientiously. I would term it negligence only."

Mrs. Bornholdt rubbed her temples. "I see. The point?"

"Yes, well"—the constable cleared his throat—"if you look at the legal decisions made over the past ten years or so, you will find, in rulings concerning servant behavior, the liability for criminal activity falls consistently to the servants, but . . . well, negligence of the servant often falls at the foot of the master."

Mrs. Bornholdt blinked at him, her fingers still touching the side of her head. "What are you saying?"

He gestured with an open hand. "Forgive me, Mrs. Bornholdt—it is not my place to lay blame, and I would not do so at this time, when you are aggrieved, especially since your late husband might have overruled any good intuition you may have had about the matter. It is my duty, however, to tell you how it will look to an outside eye. You have yourself admitted that your maid was found to be immoral, and the footman concerned as well, and yet neither was dismissed from service. Mr. Bornholdt seemed to even suspect the footman of further wrongdoing, yet even then did not remove him from the house. It would seem there has been great negligence on Mr. Bornholdt's part—negligence to himself, his home, and you, his wife. One knows not why he might have chosen to keep such unsavory characters in his home, but I can say from experience that, in the course of a trial, we would find out. The revelation, whatever it is, is not usually a happy one."

"Oh, for heaven's sake." She warded the idea off with her hands. "May we forgo the trial? I know my husband's secrets, Constable Briggs, and I have no wish to share them with the world."

"It would be stressful," he agreed, "but in the pursuit of justice for your husband—"

"Man's justice can do nothing for Wythe anymore," Mrs. Bornholdt interrupted, this time without any vigor at all—only cold certainty.

"Wythe is dead. Justice, if he is to have any, must come when he goes to meet his God."

Constable Briggs hesitated. "I take your point, Mrs. Bornholdt; you are right, and I didn't mean to argue with you—only to assert your rights." He bowed his head. "I feel, as you seem to do, that to settle the matter out of court makes the most sense."

Without even a glance at either Valentine or me, Mrs. Bornholdt asked, "Will the servants go to prison?"

"Not at once," he replied, not looking at us, either. "They are not murderers—only imbeciles. In the short term, they will be fined. The exact sum will be determined when I submit my report, but it will be no small amount, especially considering the prominence of your husband. Once you dismiss them, you will ensure they do not work in service to anyone ever again, and they will go—by and by—to the debtors' prison. Worry not—their fate shall catch up with them in time, as fate so tends to do."

◆ ◆ ◆

I watched from a window beside the front door as the butler escorted the constable and his associates out, and the police wagons pulled away. I let the sill bear my weight, for I did not fully trust my legs to hold me.

The constable's words about debtors' prison rang in my ears, an echo of my past come back to haunt me, but it made the fact of standing in the house, breathing free air, the sweeter. I held to the present moment and managed a shaky smile.

"You think this is a laughing matter, do you?" Valentine murmured from his place at the window beside me, and he laced his fingers with mine. For one shining moment it was as if the awful events of that morning had not happened, but when I glanced his way, his eyes were sad.

I frowned. "Valentine, I—"

"Marian," Mrs. Bornholdt said, behind me, "have they gone?" The chill had left her voice.

Valentine took his hand back, stepping aside from me.

"Yes, ma'am," I said, and as I turned, she collided with me.

My first confused thought was that she was angry, but she embraced me. She held me hard against her as she broke into sudden sobs.

"Mrs. Bornholdt," I said, "I—I am so sorry—"

"No, I am sorry," she whispered, vehement. "I am."

Of course, there was only time for this much before I heard the sound of Ledford approaching the door, and she pulled away from me again, and turned her back.

◆ ◆ ◆

There was no point in sleeping; we all went, dazed, from the drama of the night into our morning routine.

Mrs. Davies and Ledford seemed to have organized to keep Valentine and me from being alone together. Instead of supervising the whole of the staff, Mrs. Davies tailed me as I went abovestairs to bring Mrs. Bornholdt a breakfast she couldn't bear to eat. I passed Valentine in the halls, at the oil lamps, but Ledford was with him, watching. All I wanted was to run into Valentine's arms, but I didn't dare even to turn my head in his direction.

I didn't know what more they could do to us, really. But the exhilaration of surviving the night had given way to exhaustion, and I was in no shape to meet a new challenge.

At last, in the evening, a man came to the door to deliver a message to Mrs. Bornholdt. The butler went abovestairs to let him in, and while Ledford was away, the grocer's carriage pulled up to the servants' entrance. Mrs. Davies almost sent me to take the order, but couldn't bring herself to let me because I didn't know what ingredients to check for.

The moment she'd gone out the door, Valentine bolted up the stairs. I followed him, out of the kitchen and into the upper stairwell. I shut the door behind us both, and good thing—he immediately pressed me up against it, kissing my mouth first and then both cheeks, my forehead, my mouth again.

"Marian," he groaned—not with longing, but gentle admonishment, "God, surely you knew I wouldn't let him hurt you."

"What?" I wrapped my arms around him.

"I'd already fought my way back to you. You had nothing to fear." He drew me closer against him. "And the risk—"

"Oh, Valentine," I said, and when he drew back to check my face, I set my jaw. "I was not afraid."

It all came tumbling out of my mouth—the hair in Mrs. Bornholdt's locket, Mr. Bornholdt's attentiveness through his wife's pregnancy, the early labor. The Epsom salts, the letter in the study.

Valentine's hand slid up the side of his head, his face blanching before my eyes. "In the eighth month, you said, the baby?"

"Carolyn," I said, gently.

I saw it wind him a little—her name, and there was rust rage flaring his eyes. He nodded, mouth set. "Carolyn."

The wind picked up, to be heard whirling around the house.

"So it was just," Valentine said. "Or as close as we may come to justice. I hoped it was."

I stared. "You hoped so? You did . . . all that, and you didn't know, in your own way?"

He bowed his head—a concession. "You led, and I followed."

The message the man had brought to Mrs. Bornholdt had been a court summons, at which Valentine and I were to be sentenced and hear our fine. We stayed at Valor Rise, awaiting the date. The days themselves seemed to hold their breath with us. Mrs. Bornholdt was mute in all her dealings with me, though she nodded and bowed her head when I gave her food or water, dressed or undressed her, and turned down her bedclothes. She had at some point taken out the locket from her vanity drawer, and she wore it constantly, even to sleep.

Forbidding as she often seemed, I knew she was not angry with me.

The servants were another matter. Mrs. Davies snubbed me, the butler snubbed Valentine, and the two talked together while staring in our direction after supper in the evenings. Lucette was the worst, however. Rather than rail at us, which I think I should have withstood better, she would every other waking hour burst into tears—betrayed, bitter tears—and storm off to slam some door behind her.

On the second day after Mr. Bornholdt's death, when only Valentine and I were belowstairs with Lucette, she dashed the tears from her eyes and said, "I never should have let you shout me down. I knew what ought to have been done."

I couldn't look at her, and my gaze slid guiltily to Valentine. He was his softer self again, of cool head and warm expression—had been from the moment the constable had gone from the house. He seemed on the point of going to Lucette, of making her some apology, or at least giving some excuse.

But he said only, "You were right."

"An' you were wrong." She heaved the words at him, as if she didn't want them anymore.

"Yes," Valentine said, quiet but firm.

"You're an idiot," she told him. "A dumb . . . steer, that's you."

His lips thinned. Then he bowed his head, taking the blow.

"And I listened to you. I knew better, and I listened to you. Because I—because you . . . you . . . You're a . . . cad," she said, and though at first she only tried the word, it seemed to dawn on her fully then as fact. Planting her feet, she declared, "You're a cad, Valentine Hobbs. A scoundrel! You an' that sorry, schemin' woman deserve each other."

Fists clenched at her sides, she seemed to dare him to answer insult for insult.

But he said, "And you deserve someone who treats you better than I have."

Her features softened.

"See that you get it, Lucette. Settle for nothing less." Then he excused himself, Lucette staring after.

◆ ◆ ◆

Mrs. Bornholdt moved the date with the judge out a week, citing a grief too great to leave her apartment, let alone the property. She broke her long silence with me to confide that, in fact, she did not want to dismiss me from my post as yet—for I would have had to walk down the cliff when the ground was still soft from the storm.

In the courthouse, under the eyes of the judge, Mrs. Bornholdt wrote down the figure of our fine with seemingly vehement pleasure—two hundred pounds, each—only to count out this exact sum at her vanity that evening, before my wondering eyes, and force the notes upon me.

"I can't take this," I told her.

"Well, you certainly cannot go to debtors' prison," she replied. "I will not allow it."

I frowned, hesitating. "Forgive me, ma'am . . . but I know about Mr. Bornholdt's father, about the withholding way he handles money—"

"That was with his son." She drew herself up in her seat. "He has no quarrel with me. More, he knows that if he treated me uncharitably, I would raise my voice about it. He does not want to be thought a monster by our neighbors, not after what I have already been through. He has given generously for Wythe's funeral, more than I care to spend on the man, and so I can pass a great deal of the money to you."

I shook my head, but she opened my apron pocket and put the pound notes in herself. "You can pay your debt bit by bit, so no one suspects," she said. "Stay out of trouble by an inch, as if you struggle. Let the collectors come, let them think they take the money just as fast as you can scrape it together."

"Ma'am—"

"Shhh—I have something to ask you." She stood, putting both hands to my cheeks and looking deeply into my eyes. "Lately, you have done something that no one but I may understand, and I in turn have said things that only you may understand, so I accept that Hobbs may do or say things that you understand and I do not. Maybe I did not see what I thought I saw, that night."

I made to speak, but she shook her head.

"I will not have you end up like me," she said. "You will take care of yourself first. That money is for you—for you alone. You may go and work in London, and it would be hard, but you would do fine. Do you hear me?"

I nodded.

"You are free." She pulled me into her arms, holding me tightly there as she spoke. "I have power enough to give you freedom at least. Understand: you do not *need* him."

I nodded once more, my cheek against hers.

"Now, you tell me." She drew back. "Is he a good man?"

A shy smile sneaked onto my face. "Yes. He's good."

She tapped her chin with her fingers, gazing past me. Then her eyes found mine again, as if she'd had a new thought. "Did you communicate to him somehow what Wythe had done, after we found the letter?"

I shook my head.

"So." She crossed her arms. "Either he is an imbecile, as the constable said, or he played a part that morning all for you."

I nodded.

Mrs. Bornholdt's face was serious a moment longer—then she smiled, just as sheepishly as me. She opened the drawer in her vanity again, and pulled out a second bundle of notes. "I set aside enough for the both of you."

As I watched, she untied the bundle and counted out the whole of Valentine's fine, and even then she'd not gone through the stack. All told, there was an extra thirty pounds.

"This is too much," I said. "To pay our fine is already more charity than we deserve—"

"Why should you get to decide what you deserve?" She raised her chin. "Anyway, it is not charity. It is an advance on your salary as my lady's maid, Marian, for the coming year. I cannot send it to you. Take it now."

"But I'm not to be your lady's maid."

"Oh, yes you are," she insisted, and for all the absurdity of it—for everyone in the house knew that Valentine and I would leave in the morning—her voice was grave. "You must be. You may not bring my breakfast or draw my bath or make my dresses, but I cannot let you out of my employ because I still need you to perform the most important service a maid can do for her lady."

"What's that, Mrs.—ma'am," I corrected, for her face darkened whenever I called her by his name now.

Her gaze dropped to the floor. "Keeping her secrets."

I stood still a moment, surprised.

Then I reached out to touch her hand. "Oh, ma'am, but you didn't do anything."

"Yes," she agreed. She raised her head, but looked past me. "I did nothing. Exactly."

"But no one will ever ask me about that," I said, and when she raised her brows, I added, "Of course, if anyone did, I would keep your confidence."

She smiled, as if she knew it already. "You have been good to me, Marian, only good to me—even when I was not watching, when others have hurt me over and over, right under my eyes. I want you to be mine always, no matter how far away you go, for I know that, wherever you are, you are the same person, just the same as if you stood before me."

She pulled me to her, and her embrace was warm—close, as if I were a precious thing.

"Go to London," she said, sniffing. "You take your footman with you if you like, but you open a dress shop. Be as good as you are, and make the city better, and sometime I will come myself and see you—I will buy a dress. A purple one. Now that I do not take that awful medicine, I think someday I will glow gold again." She pulled back to take me in. "You will tell me truthfully how I look when you see me, will you not?"

I smiled. "Yes, ma'am."

She drew her brows close together. "But it will be a long time, a long time for both of us before I can do that. So you must do well and keep the shop open. Work hard, prosper."

A dress shop, in London, with Valentine. The idea came to life in a rapid blur, as if I were flipping through illustrations in a book: Valentine hunched over a long table, measuring out cloth to cut, his hair hanging over his forehead; Valentine standing at a till, behind a counter, saying something charming to a customer, coins cupped in his fine-fingered hand; Valentine looking up from his sewing, across a cramped workroom, to smile at me; and Valentine, when I did not at once lift my head from my own work, opening his mouth to whisper my name, like he used to do at the workhouse. And in the next moment, I would go to him, just go to him, and no one would stop me.

"I will work hard," I promised, blinking tears out of my eyes. "I will pay you back for all of it."

"I do not want your money, Marian," she said, jostling me. "I only want you to be well, and happy. If I were to ask anything of you for myself, it would be . . ." But she waved the thought away.

"I'll do it, whatever it is." I took her hands. "What is it?"

She smiled.

"Write to me."

Acknowledgments

It is a lie that writing a book is a solitary endeavor. I think that goes double for a debut, as it's not just the work that's lifted to higher places, but the writer, too. First, thank you to my agent, Chris Bucci, for your enthusiasm and kindness through this process, and for keeping the faith when mine was flagging. Thank you to my editors Jessica Tribble Wells and Angela James, for seeing what I saw at the heart of this book, and for challenging me to bring it out. Thank you to Kellie, my copyeditor, for catching so much that I missed. Thanks, too, to Rachael Herbert, Jill K., Sarah Shaw, and everyone behind the scenes at Thomas & Mercer, for bringing a dream of mine into the material world so beautifully.

Thank you to my workshop peers in the Western Connecticut State University MFA Program, and to all my mentors—especially A. B. Westrick, Anthony D'Aries, and Matthew Quinn Martin. You all taught me vital things about the craft of writing; a lot of the words I say to myself at the desk these days are yours.

Thank you to Elizabeth Little, who mentored this book through Pitch Wars 2020, for giving so generously of your time and your insights. Thank you to all my fellow mentees for your encouragement, especially Lyz Mancini, S. A. Simon, and both lovely halves of M. K. Hardy.

Thank you to James DeMarco for sharing your perspectives as a loss parent, for your willingness to be vulnerable, and for your honest feedback.

Thank you to Stephanie Layne for sweeping in to take the most perfect picture when I was at a low point. You saved the day with grace and poise, per usual.

Thank you to Missy Haywood for a thousand late nights on AIM, and for a bookmark I see every single day. Thank you to Kristen Holmes for saying that reading this story gave you the same feeling as reading a certain other book, the title of which I cannot put in writing because I'll blush for the rest of my life. Even if the comparison is not objectively fair, you meant it.

Thank you to Joshua Lucius Ives for always thinking I'm cool. Thank you for being relentlessly kind. Thank you for caring about what it means to be good, and especially what it means to be a good man.

Thank you to Tony Palmieri for reading this story first (and many times after), and for waking up with Marian still on your mind. Thank you for getting mad at me for all the good lines. Thank you for every cup of coffee, every carb, every cry that you never interrupted by telling me you knew I could do it (even if you did).

Thank you to my mom, Christina Porcelli, for reading me everything when I was a child, from the Danielle Steel novel on your nightstand to the backs of shampoo bottles. Thank you, also, for calling me midway through reading this book to ask how I sleep at night; that reassured me.

Finally, for saying "It's about time" when I told him I was pursuing a degree in fiction writing, and for a thousand other reasons, I would like to thank my dad, Brian McGuckin. I dearly wish I could.

About the Author

Photo © 2021 Stephanie Layne

Briana Una McGuckin lives in a charmingly strange old house in Connecticut. She has an MFA in Creative Writing from Western Connecticut State University and an MLS from Long Island University. Among other places, her work appears in the Bram Stoker Award–nominated horror anthology *Not All Monsters*, the modern Gothic horror anthology *In Somnio*, and *The Lost Librarian's Grave* anthology. Briana has spastic diplegic cerebral palsy, a perhaps concerningly large collection of perfume oils, and a fascination with all things Victorian. For more information visit www.brianaunamcguckin.com.